I0676324

The Last Stand

Blood on the Stars XIV

Jay Allan

system 7 publishing

Books by Jay Allan

Flames of Rebellion Series
(Published by Harper Voyager)
Flames of Rebellion
Rebellion's Fury

The Crimson Worlds Series
Marines
The Cost of Victory
A Little Rebellion
The First Imperium
The Line Must Hold
To Hell's Heart
The Shadow Legions
Even Legends Die
The Fall

Crimson Worlds Refugees Series
Into the Darkness
Shadows of the Gods
Revenge of the Ancients
Winds of Vengeance
Storm of Vengeance

Crimson Worlds Successors Trilogy
MERCS
The Prisoner of Eldaron
The Black Flag

Crimson Worlds Prequels
Tombstone
Bitter Glory
The Gates of Hell

Red Team Alpha
(A New Crimson Worlds Novel)

Join my email list
at www.jayallanbooks.com

List members get publication announcements and special bonuses throughout the year (email addresses are never shared or used for any other purpose). Please feel free to email me with any questions at jayallanwrites@gmail.com. I answer all reader emails

For all things Sci-Fi,
join my interactive Reader Group here:

facebook.com/groups/JayAllanReaders

Follow me on Twitter @jayallanwrites

Follow my blog at www.jayallanwrites.com

www.jayallanbooks.com
www.crimsonworlds.com

Books by Jay Allan

Blood on the Stars Series
Duel in the Dark
Call to Arms
Ruins of Empire
Echoes of Glory
Cauldron of Fire
Dauntless
The White Fleet
Black Dawn
Invasion
Nightfall
The Grand Alliance
The Colossus
The Others
The Last Stand
Empire's Ashes – Coming Soon

Andromeda Chronicles
(Blood on the Stars Adventure Series)
Andromeda Rising
Wings of Pegasus

The Far Stars Series
Shadow of Empire
Enemy in the Dark
Funeral Games

Far Stars Legends Series
Blackhawk
The Wolf's Claw

Portal Wars Trilogy
Gehenna Dawn
The Ten Thousand
Homefront

Also by Jay Allan – The Dragon's Banner

Chapter One

Vigillius Nebula
8 Transits from Calpharon (Hegemonic Capital Planet)
Year 323 AC (After the Cataclysm)

"Keep those formations tight. We've got to get in and get out fast!" Jake Stockton hunched forward in his cockpit, his hands clenched tightly around his fighter's throttle. The feeling was slightly different, the leather covering the cool metal softer, smoother, the positioning just…off…a bit. It wasn't the kind of thing most people would have noticed, but Jake Stockton virtually became one with any fighter he was flying, and the ship's controls were almost extensions of his arms and hands.

The ship was a new one, fresh from the factory, the lead fighter from the first batch of Mark V's. The new fighters were upgrades on the old Lightnings, and if things panned out according to the specs, they would be a major leap forward. Stockton hadn't decided yet, but so far, so good. The upgraded ship class didn't have a new name, but the pilots were already calling the sleek, dark metal craft Black Lightnings.

Stockton pulled back on the throttle, still feeling some

surprise as his eyes glanced at the small display, and he noticed the acceleration rate. The new ships were *quick*, much faster than anything he'd flown before, anything he'd *seen* before, but that wasn't the part he found most disconcerting. It was the dampeners that seemed like some kind of magic.

The first ships he'd flown hadn't had dampeners at all, and he and his comrades had been forced to endure g forces straight, with nothing more than pressure suits and cushioned seats to help absorb the pressure. More than any other factor, that had placed a cap on the acceleration fighters could utilize, regardless of the power of their engines. The introduction of dampeners a decade before had revolutionized fighter combat, and the Mark III's that had first featured the miraculous new systems had boasted more than twice the thrust potential of their predecessors. That had been a game changer in combat.

Dampeners revolutionized spaceflight in many ways, but they had always been touchy and fragile beasts. Every time Stockton nudged up his thrust, he winced, expecting the slight delay before the system adjusted. But there was nothing at all in the new ship, no pain, no pressure slamming into him, even for an instant. The dampeners were perfectly aligned with the engines. He could have been sitting on Megara, at normal gravity, unmoving, even as his ship blasted forward at maximum thrust.

It remained to be seen how much of the old fragility was still there when the systems were truly stressed. Combat would answer that question soon enough.

Stockton swung his ship around, changing the thrust angle, adjusting his vector to bring him on line with his target. The enemy ship was a big one, larger than any encountered in the battles of the previous year. That was enough of a concern. Tonnage generally aligned with combat power, at least with all other things being equal.

The Highborn ships the Hegemony and Confederation fleets had engaged before hadn't been especially large, but they had been enormously powerful. He didn't suspect the larger ships would be any easier to face than their smaller counterparts.

The thing in front of him now was *big*. And that made his stomach shrivel to what felt like a quarter of its normal size.

His eyes moved back to the display, focusing for an instant on the wings lined up behind him. It was a substantial force, over three hundred ships, but barely a recon mission compared to the massive waves of fighters he'd commanded in the conflicts of the past decade.

It *was* a recon, he reminded himself, at least of a sort. He'd been leading similar forces for most of the past six months, all part of the campaign to harry the enemy and slow their advance, to buy more time for the fleet to prepare for the final battle to defend Calpharon.

At least that was the official purpose. Stockton had another, one with a more brutal side to it. The arrival of the main Confederation and Alliance fleets had brought hundreds of fresh squadrons to the fight, but not one of those thousands of pilots had ever fought against the Others. *The Highborn*, he reminded himself. He didn't understand the name, but that was what the Heggies called the enemy, and he figured they knew more about it all than he did.

And you need to stop calling them Heggies. They're your allies now, and that's a damned good thing if you want to stop the Highborn before they roll right into the Rim and crush everything in their path.

Heggies had been coined during the previous war, and while it didn't sound particularly nasty, it had in every way been intended as a derogatory term.

Stockton tried not to think too much about why he

had truly brought his pilots there. It was for training, yes, but something more. Something darker. He was going to need an experienced force when the decisive battle started. And there was only one way to make that happen. He had to cycle his people through, throw them against small Highborn forces and see who survived. He had to forge them in battle.

Blood them.

That strategy had cost him heavily over the past six months, but it had also helped to slow the Highborn advance, to buy time. Whether that mattered, whether those precious weeks and months were used to good effect or not, was Admiral Barron's problem, not his.

Yours is just to keep leading your men and women to the slaughter, and to turn those who don't die into something that can fight these…whatever they are.

He checked his own vector again, and then those of the units formed up behind him. The enemy force was only three ships, but each of them was massive, five or six times the size of those encountered before. Stockton considered breaking off and returning to the base ships to run back to Calpharon and report the new Highborn ship class.

But that report will be a hell of a lot more useful if you have some idea of actual combat capabilities…

And even if he led his entire strike force to its end, the base ships were positioned just inside the transit point. Whatever happened, Admiral Barron and the rest of the fleet's command staff would know about the larger enemy ships.

"Alright, we're going in…and you all know what that means. Keep those payloads until the last second, and plant them right in the guts of that monster right up front." He listened to the acknowledgements, nodding to himself as one squadron commander after another shouted out on the comm, sounding almost eager to throw themselves and their squadrons at the deadly enemy ships.

Stockton felt something different, a grim darkness lit by flashing recollections of the last battle, of the losses his people had suffered when they'd joined the fight to save their new Hegemony allies.

He understood the eagerness of his officers. He'd felt that way once himself.

You haven't fought this enemy. None of you have…

That wasn't *entirely* true. Stockton had about a dozen veterans of battles against the Highborn with him, mostly in command roles. Enough to help him throw the force against the enemy in a wild assault, but not enough to reduce the cost he knew his people would pay.

He stared straight ahead, and he felt his face tensing. It was time. Stockton had lost count of the battles he'd fought, of the hours he'd spent crunched in his fighter, battling for his life against one enemy or another. One day, he knew, he would climb into his cockpit for the last time, and fly off into his final fight.

Then he repeated his mantra, the thought with which he'd always countered thoughts of his death.

One day…but not today…

* * *

Gelak closed his eyes, watching the battle unfolding a few hundred thousand kilometers from his fighter's position. He twisted, reaching around, scratching at the small implant and the cable connected to it. The Kriegeri wing commander had finally become accustomed to the neural link, if not exactly comfortable with it yet. The abilities to 'see' the battlefield in his thoughts, and to send commands to his ship without speaking or moving, seemed ready to usher in a revolution in small ship combat tactics, save for one problem. The Hegemony had a very short history of such operations, and despite the hurried manufacturing and training programs that had put thousands of Kriegeri warriors into cockpits, Gelak knew he and his comrades were still woefully inferior to their Rim counterparts—now allies—despite the link and the generally higher technology level of their ships.

That was something that rankled at him, and at his Kriegeri pride. It was unbecoming, perhaps, something a Master might have handled differently. But Gelak was driven by a need to match the skill of his allies, to lead his own squadrons into the fight as competently and aggressively as any Rim commander. But the Confed officer Stockton was in command, by order of none other than Commander Chronos himself, along with the Rim admiral, Barron. Stockton was a legendary pilot, one not even his Kriegeri dignity could deny was the absolute best. Stockton had once again placed Gelak and his Kriegeri in reserve, and Gelak seethed silently.

Gelak had been born to serve, to obey his superiors without question…and he had done just that his entire career. But Stockton was a Confed, and the Rimdwellers still felt like enemies to him. He found resentment eroding his grim acceptance of orders, and deep inside him, there was something entirely unfamiliar, an urge to ignore the commands he'd been given, and to lead his people forward into the fight without authorization. It was suppressed, under control, but for a Kriegeri veteran, it was disconcerting nevertheless.

He watched as the Confeds, this time supplemented by a wing from the Alliance, the mysterious nation from even farther out on the Rim than the Confederation, moved forward toward the lead Highborn ship. His resentment began to give way to respect as he watched the squadrons bearing down, holding their formations even as the enemy defensive fired began to take a toll.

The Highborn ships were large, much larger than the ones previously encountered. Gelak knew that didn't bode well for the prospects of the war going forward, but he pushed such thoughts blithely aside. Concerns of that sort were not for him. The Masters would make strategic decisions, and he and his warriors would do as they were commanded to do. That was the way, the only way. Gelak had been born into his Kriegeri status, a subject of the Hegemony his entire life, but his father had told him of the days before the Masters had come, of starvation and disease and endless conflict, and slow, painful deaths from radiation. The Masters had made his people their servants, at least in a manner of speaking, but they had also brought them the comforts of civilization, food, medicine, order. The average lifespans of his people had doubled almost immediately, and internecine warfare became a distant memory. Gelak served because he had no choice, because he'd been trained to obey. But also because he wanted to, because he was loyal and believed in the Hegemony.

He watched as more of Stockton's fighters were destroyed, eighteen in total. That was a large number, especially since the attack force was still more than thirty thousand kilometers out. The new Confed fighters, the black ones, were more or less a match for those his own pilots flew, save for the links, of course. But only about ten percent of the Confed force had the faster, more maneuverable craft, and the Alliance ships were even slower than the old Confederation ones.

Give us the order…you need help against these ships…

Gelak sat, watching the growing carnage, and wanting above all things to plunge himself, and his pilots, right into the middle of the maelstrom.

But he remained on station, true to his orders. It was the way. Obedience.

It was the only way.

* * *

Stockton watched in horror as the wave of missiles—at least that's what he guessed they were—moved steadily toward his formations. The volley was unexpected, something he hadn't seen before, and he didn't like the look of it. There were close to a hundred of the weapons approaching his ships, and that barrage had been launched by the lead ship alone. He had no idea how effective their targeting was, but the things had accelerated at better than 130g, and that meant they were *fast*.

Too fast for his ships to evade.

"All squadrons, adjust course thirty degrees in the y plane. Let's see if we can go around those things." His instincts had already answered that question, and a few seconds later, his calculations confirmed his gut's conclusion. No, his squadrons were not going to get around the incoming attack. The best he could hope for was to lessen the impact. A hundred warheads that maneuverable constituted a massive threat, one he knew could very well gut his entire force. But he decided to press on, to run the gauntlet.

Then, a hundred became thousands.

Stockton was a hardened veteran, the legend of the fighter corps, and a warrior almost invulnerable to shock. But he stared at his screen, paralyzed by the horror of what he was seeing.

Every one of the incoming weapons had split into twenty separate contacts...and every one of those was still coming on, still accelerating at more than twice the highest thrust capacity of any of his ships.

He gritted his teeth, struggling for a stretch of seconds that felt like eternity to regain his composure. He wanted to complete the attack, to take his ships in and see what these enemy behemoths were really made of. But he knew that had become an impossibility. If he didn't break off immediately, not one of his ships would make it back.

He wasn't sure any of them would anyway, but he didn't give up. Not ever.

"All squadrons, break off. Maximum thrust back to the landing platforms. Full evasive maneuvers." He caught the acidy feeling of bile in the back of his throat, even as he gripped his ship's controls, and blasted his engines at full.

His mind was racing, the hope of saving at least some of his pilots struggling with the growing realization that there was no escape from the approaching wave of death.

"Repeat, abort the mission. Return to the base ships at maximum possible speed. Full evasive maneuvers."

But that was mostly for his pilots, for what remained of morale. In his own mind, he was rapidly losing hope, and a dark and desperate thought began to emerge from the deep shadows of his mind.

Perhaps he *had* made that last, fateful climb into his ship.

Chapter Two

CFS Dauntless
Orbiting Calpharon (Hegemonic Capital)
Sigma Nordlin IV
Year 323 AC (After the Cataclysm)

"I'll have another..." Tyler Barron angled his head, and he looked toward his companion at the table. "You?" Then, without waiting for an answer, he glanced back at the steward and said, "Admiral Winters will have another, too."

"Ty...I think we'd better take it easy. We've got a lot on our plates right now, and if the latest scouting reports are correct, we don't have much time before the enemy completes their reorganization and renews the offensive. We both know they'll be coming this way as soon as they're ready. And we'd better be prepared when they do."

"Does it really matter? We win, we lose, what difference does it make? If we win, there's just another fight, worse than the last one. Maybe if we lose, it will finally all end." Barron respected his friend's abilities, but Winters hadn't seen the enemy the way he had. He still harbored some belief victory was possible. That hope had largely abandoned Barron.

The admiral turned again, about to yell for the steward, but the spacer was already on his way back to the table, a small tray in his hand. Barron watched as the man put the two drinks down, and spun around, walking swiftly away from the table.

As quickly as he could manage. That's okay…I wouldn't want to be near me either.

Barron picked up the glass, knowing it had to be something close to the last of the quality brandy in *Dauntless*'s stores. He'd never been much of a drinker, but when he did partake, it was almost always the best, a fine wine, or a topnotch brandy.

This time, though, part of Barron was ready to work his way down that particular food chain as supplies ran low, all the way to whatever homemade rot gut the ship's cooks would invariably manage to concoct from the galley's leftovers after everything else was gone.

Dauntless's officer's club was nothing special to look at—though it was far plusher than the small compartment that had served the same purpose on the old *Dauntless*. Barron had rarely frequented such establishments, at least not after his ascending rank had mostly barred him from predator-like visits to the poker games that often popped up at one of the tables. He'd always considered it unseemly for a commander to win money from those he led…and if he played, he usually won. His gambling skills were still legendary in the fleet, though accounts had become mostly secondhand, as so many of those who'd experienced one of his fleecings had been lost in one battle or another, or had retired, half broken and hollowed out by endless war.

"Ty, I know it's hard on you. I knew it would be when Andi gave me the message for you. But you have to look at the good in it, too. When you get home, you will see them both, Andi and the baby. And you have a child, another Barron. There is joy in that."

"When I get home?" Barron's tone was brusque, almost caustic. "You think any of us is getting home?"

"Ty, I know it seems…"

"I've *seen* these things, Clint. Their ships, what they can do. I know I called for the fleet, and thanks to Andi, we've got more force here than I could have hoped. But it's still not enough. When the enemy finishes licking their wounds and masses their forces, they're going to come here, to Calpharon, and they're going to hit us like nothing you've ever seen before. We'll hurt them, but we're not going to stop them. They'll get through us here, and anywhere else we manage to put up a defense with whatever force we've got left. We'll fight, because there is no choice, but we'll die here, somewhere out in the Badlands, far from home. It will be a mercy of a sort. But Andi and my child…" Barron paused, clearly struggling to hold back the emotions struggling to take control. "…well, I don't know what these…Others…want, but we both know Andi's not the kind to surrender, to grovel for mercy, don't we?"

Winters was silent for a moment. Barron looked over at his friend and nodded. "I know…I wouldn't know what to say to me either. Don't worry, I'll pull it together and be ready for the fight, Clint. You know me well enough to be sure of that. But it's…hard. I wish I could see her, just one more time…and my daughter." Barron was in a dark place, and he knew he had to pull himself out of it, lie to himself if that's what it took. Duty was calling, as it always did, and he knew he'd have to answer.

As he always did.

But not just then. He still had some time to feel sorry for himself.

He could imagine the plaque on his memorial. 'Tyler

Barron—he sacrificed every chance at happiness, everything he'd ever desired, for the Confederation.' Barron had never been comfortable with the pomp and adoration that had followed him from his birth throughout his famous career, but he'd never questioned his path. Until now. He looked at his life and saw all he'd missed, all he was likely to miss in the future. *That's worth a statue or two, I guess.*

He put the glass to his lips, and he drained it.

Winters looked uncertain, but only for a few seconds. Then, he rallied, and he looked back at Barron. "We will find a way, my friend. You'll get back. You'll see Andi again…and you'll see your child, your children, no doubt, grow up in peace." Winters managed to sound convincing enough, but Barron knew his comrade too well to believe he was anything like confident of victory. And, if he was, it was only because he hadn't seen the Others yet.

He let out a sound, something very close to a snort. "We'll see how you feel when the enemy gets here, when you see those ships…"

He paused, and he stared right at Winters, his eyes locking with his friend's. "…and what those beams of theirs do to a ship's hull."

*   *   *

"Are you insane?" Chronos stared across the table at his comrade on the Hegemonic Council with an expression that suggested he was barely restraining himself from leaping across the polished granite slab and strangling the other Master. Chronos had always disliked Thantor, but that had grown into full blown hatred as the second highest rated member of the Council had continued his campaign to discredit and obstruct Akella. Chronos was Akella's ally, and he tried to tell himself that was the sole cause of his fury. He was the eighth most genetically perfect human in the Hegemony, but he realized, somewhere in the cold recesses of his mind, where brutal reason trumped all other things, that his intellect had proven insufficient to deter himself from occasional self-delusion.

Akella *was* his ally, but she was far more. Hegemonic society did not support—or even allow—permanent pair bonding. Sexual relationships existed for recreation, and to produce children with suitable genetic partners, and nothing more. The marriages and other customs common in many of the Rim cultures, and in the imperial histories as well, were considered beneath Hegemonic Masters, who were expected to act as individuals in all things, and make decisions devoid of animalistic emotional constraints.

Except Chronos and Akella *did have* a relationship, one that would create a major scandal if it was discovered. His rage toward Thantor was fueled by that fact, and by the affection he felt for his lover—he wasn't ready to call her more than that, even in secret. Love and the other terms used by the Rimdwellers were forbidden to him, by Hegemonic law and custom, and he hadn't come far enough to utterly disregard all he had believed his entire life.

His anger stemmed also, he realized, from petty jealousies. Number Two was the father of Akella's first child, as he was of the second. He knew that shouldn't bother him, that he should be above such things...but he wasn't. It gnawed at him every time he looked at Thantor, and the fact that he knew Akella had never had any feelings at all for her first pairing partner seemed illogically irrelevant to him. The sight of Thantor infuriated him.

But there was more at stake now than his secret

feelings and jealousies. Thantor was pushing for something very dangerous…and stupid as well.

"Chronos, I am aware that you have bonded with the Rim warriors, shared whatever camaraderie has developed between former enemies now fighting together as allies, but the facts remain clear. *Colossus* is an irreplaceable asset, the greatest and most powerful vestige of the old empire available to us. *We* found it, *we* poured the industrial output of a score of worlds into its repair and deployment. It is ours…and finally, we have the change to take it back."

"Take it back? You think it is that simple? Aside from the tactical risks—and *Colossus* opening fire on Calpharon once the Confeds realize what we are doing is only one of those—we *need* the Confeds, and the other Rimdwellers allied with them. Your recklessness would cost us an ally, and hundreds of warships in the coming fight, in a pointless effort to retake a vessel that will be fighting at our side anyway?"

Chronos was careful not to make an argument based on loyalty or honor. The Rimdwellers were still considered barbarians by many of the senior Masters, certainly Thantor, and as such, unworthy of such concepts. To Thantor, the Confeds were fit to be used as he saw fit, and discarded once their utility had passed. Chronos had come to respect his allies, and even to regret that he had fought so long against him. Much of that conflicted with his long-held beliefs, and he was still sorting it all out. But he was damned sure he wasn't about to stab Tyler Barron and his spacers in the back…and he wasn't going to let Thantor do it either.

Whatever it took to prevent it.

"Chronos, I commend you for your years of service, but I wonder if working so closely with the Rimdwellers has colored your analysis. The Confeds have seen the enemy, they have faced the Highborn in battle. They understand the threat now. What options do they have? They need us, more perhaps than we need them. Once we have retaken *Colossus*, we will offer them recompense, some reward or another to appease their primitive pride. They are savages, after all, are they not? We have much to offer them that is beyond their technology."

Chronos didn't answer the question directly. It was a trap, and as much as he was being driven by anger, his intellect was still in play as well. Thantor wanted to discredit him, to make it appear he was too closely aligned with the Confeds.

"Have you even glanced at the battle reports, either from this war or the last one? Have you scanned the casualty figures as you sat here in safety? Have you learned nothing of our former enemies, now our tenuous allies? Think what you will of the Rimdwellers, but there are many of them, and they possess considerable military strength. The Confeds, their military in particular, are driven by a sense of honor and loyalty. It was difficult to bring them to our side, to overcome the bitterness from the recent war. Do you really believe they will accept your petty gifts after we have seized *Colossus* and killed more of their people in the process? Are you really such a fool, Thantor?"

Chronos clenched his lips as he cursed himself for letting the last line to slip out. Thantor was more highly ranked than he was, and in the Hegemony, that was the most important source of authority. Chronos knew Number Two was driven by wild ambition, to the point he'd begun to question his rival's sanity. But without any proof, his options were limited. And he knew Thantor had support on the Council. Perhaps even enough.

Enough to turn hard fought allies back into enemies. Enough to throw away any chance to hold off the Highborn. To save the

Hegemony. You can't let that happen.

"Your outburst is unbecoming, Chronos. You are a member of this Council, and we all expect you to behave as such. You are too close to the Rimdwellers, perhaps, to craft a clear visualization. This is forgivable, perhaps even understandable…but it cannot be the basis of Council decisions." A short pause. "I move that we vote on the measure to launch a surprise raid to retake control of *Colossus* and then to repair relations with the Rimdwellers in some yet to be specified manner."

Chronos leaned back in his chair, still angry at his loss of control. His eyes scanned the table, as unobtrusively as he could manage. He considered himself adept at reading expressions, and what he saw was unnerving. It was impossible to be sure, of course, but his gut told him the vote was going to be close.

Too close.

"Wait…" He stood up, raising his hand in front of him. "I would say one more thing. I will not participate in the Hegemony's act of suicide. If you would ignore the deadly threat approaching, risk losing the allies we have struggled so hard to attain…you will do so without me. I give my proxy to Akella for this vote, and I leave you all with this promise. Vote to try to retake *Colossus* from the Confeds, and you will also have to vote for a new supreme military commander…for you will have my resignation, along with my utter contempt."

He turned abruptly, with all the military posture and sharpness he could muster, and he walked out of the room, ignoring the cries for him to remain.

He walked through the door and out into the corridor, wondering if his dramatic display would be enough to prevent his colleagues from making a tragic mistake. He'd done all he could. Now, it would be up to Akella.

Chapter Three

Vigillius Nebula
8 Transits from Calpharon (Hegemonic Capital Planet)
Year 323 AC (After the Cataclysm)

Stockton stared down at the small panel under the ship's main controls. It was a little different in the new Mark V's, slightly lower and farther to the starboard side of the cockpit. But he knew just what it was. Stockton was notorious for his aggressive, and often reckless, tactics, and overpowering his ship's reactors and engines had long stood front and center in that arsenal of unofficial weapons of war. He'd done it so often, he'd heard it referred to more than once as the 'Raptor Maneuver,' named after his famous call sign. The tactic had saved the lives of many pilots, himself included...and it had cost no small number as well. Now, he found himself wondering how much extra power he could squeeze out of the new ship's reactor.

He hadn't expected to resort to his old tactics in the new ship, at least not so soon. But the new enemy ships, and the mysterious wave of approaching missiles, were forcing his hand.

He paused, holding his fingers near the panel before pulling back. No, he wouldn't overload the reactor. He couldn't. Only thirty of his ships were the new Black Lightnings, and there was no way Jake Stockton was going to break and run and leave ninety percent of his people behind.

No damned way.

But his people weren't going to escape either, not simply by running. The math on that was stark and unavoidable. That only left one option.

"All ships, cut thrust and come about one eighty. We're going to open up on those things, blast them all to atoms before they can reach us." His people would never get all the incoming weapons, he knew that…just as he knew he was trying to deceive his people into believing they could. Hopelessness wouldn't serve them, and if a lie squeezed a bit more effort from them, saved even a single life, he was okay with that.

He stared at the screen, even as his hands moved over the controls, adjusting the settings. An instant later, long thin lines stretched out behind each of the missiles, their approach trails for the last two minutes. The warheads were coming in fast, but also straight, with almost none of the kind of evasive maneuvers he'd trained his pilots to execute for so many years. Even with their massive acceleration rates, the incoming missiles would be relatively easy to target. The more his squadrons could destroy, the fewer would remain to kill his pilots.

"I want full AI targeting protocols. All ships, open up with lasers at maximum range, and maintain continuous fire." His ships still had their bombs, but they were next to useless against the incoming missiles. He considered ordering his people to dump the heavy nukes, but he held back. Dropping the bombs would increase maneuverability, but there wasn't time. The incoming missiles were less than half a minute from entering firing range, and his people needed every second they could get.

He flipped the arming switch for his own lasers, and he stared at the targeting screen, lining up his first shot. He wished there was more time, that he'd had the chance to develop a cohesive combat plan. As it was, his people would be firing wildly, wasting innumerable shots as multiple ships targeted the same missiles.

Even as he completed his own targeting, he faced the cold truth deep in his mind. His wings simply didn't have the firepower they needed, even if they managed to distribute their shots effectively. But there was no other way, nothing else he could do.

Or was there?

The Kriegeri. He'd kept the Hegemony squadrons in reserve, as he had on previous missions. He told himself, and anyone else who asked, that he was concerned about their inexperience, worried about meshing operational flying styles...anything but the truth.

The Kriegeri still gave him the creeps. Their heavy conditioning and rigid obedience to the Masters ran counter to every impulse that made Stockton who he was. And despite his greatest efforts, and the many lectures he'd given his pilots on the subject, Stockton still harbored some resentment and ill-feeling toward his old enemies. His wings had bled themselves dry in the war against the Hegemony. There had been such intense suffering, so much death...more than he could forget. He knew there had been no choice but to side with the former enemy, that the Highborn could very likely defeat the combined forces of the Rim and the Hegemony, much less either of them alone, but he still struggled to consider the Kriegeri as real allies.

But just then, he needed everything he could get. Every fighter, every pilot...every shot. He looked down at the comm for a few seconds, and then he slapped his fingers down on the controls. He sucked in a deep breath, holding it for an instant before he spoke.

"Kiloron Gelak…you are to bring your wings forward immediately. We have to target and destroy the incoming missiles, and we need every gun we can get on the line."

Stockton shook his head slowly, even as he listened to the Kriegeri's crisp and formal reply a few seconds later. The idea of the Hegemony fighters saving his squadrons, even his life, didn't sit well with him. But as he stared at the wall of approaching warheads, and he calculated the number of shots his people would get off, he knew that was just what he was about to see…his force saved by those he still thought of as enemies.

If they were saved at all. Kriegeri or no, he knew that was still at best a coin toss.

* * *

"All squadrons, full thrust. Rear units move forward. We are advancing in a single line." Gelak snapped out the orders in the same controlled and dispassionate voice he'd always used, but inside, he was on fire. It was widely believed that Kriegeri didn't experience fear or desire, that they were essentially automatons, following orders without question, with almost no regard for personal survival. Gelak had always known that was a myth, of course, and the tightness in his body put rest to any thought that he couldn't feel fear.

He *did* follow orders, though, even when they came from a Rimdwelling Confed who'd been placed in command of his forces. And he welcomed the chance to show what his pilots could do, despite their lack of extensive combat experience.

He looked down at the flight controls in front of him,

but he left them untouched. He fired up his ship's engines with little more than a thought, and he set his course with another.

No, not thoughts, he realized, not exactly. There was a very specific skill to connecting with the neural link, one that took considerable practice to master. The thing monitored specific brainwave activity, it didn't read his mind. But with the proper skills, it could reduce reaction times, and that could mean the difference between victory and death for a pilot.

His people hadn't seen the combat hours most of Stockton's Confeds had, but they'd spent enormous time in their ships learning their craft regardless. And they were Kriegeri, chosen for their aptitude, both for war, and specifically for fighter operations. And Gelak would put a Hegemony Kriegeri up against a wild and undisciplined Rimdweller any day.

Kriegeri were not immune to pride any more than fear.

His ship lurched forward, moving toward the Confed and Alliance fighters, and beyond them, the vast cluster of approaching missiles. He watched as Stockton's people opened fire, blasting one after another of the incoming warheads. In a matter of seconds, several dozen had been intercepted, and in the first minute, the number reached into the hundreds. But even amid the devastating defensive fire, the mathematics of the situation became ever clearer. The ships on the forward line were too few, their fire too light to clear away the entire enemy volley.

But if Gelak's ships could get up there on time…

He reran the calculations, checked the time until his lead ships entered firing range. Three minutes, fifteen seconds. That would get his people up to the line before the enemy warheads could close…just before. His ships would open fire, blast as many of the missiles as they could. But they would pay for that shortly thereafter, as the surviving weapons likely targeted them as well as Stockton's ships.

He pushed the thought aside. Death in battle was a possibility all Kriegeri prepared themselves to face. He wanted to live, as he knew all his pilots did, but there were worse fates than death in combat. And, while he generally avoided too much consideration of strategic matters that were beyond his purview, Gelak knew the Hegemony was fighting for its very survival. He was not only doing his duty, carrying out his obligation to the Masters…he was battling for the future, for the very survival, of his family, and all those he knew on his home world. For untold billions like them throughout the Hegemony.

He adjusted his thrust vector with another thought, a realignment his AI automatically transmitted to the rest of his ships. The wing's formation was crisp, as neat as the Confeds had been, or nearly so. His ships raced across space, zooming in on the beleaguered Rim fighter line, even as the approaching missiles closed. He waited, counting to himself, even as the ship's AI fed the countdown trough the neural link directly into his mind.

Ten seconds. He fired a thought through the link, activating his lasers. The weapons were fully charged and ready to fire.

Five seconds. His eyes scanned the small screen in front of him, even as the same data was projected into his mind. He picked out the closest missile, even as he directed the AI to order all of his people to do the same. His ships were at least a hundred kilometers from their nearest squadron mate, and that meant picking out the nearest target would minimize double targeting. His people were only going to get off a few shots, perhaps half a dozen. They couldn't afford to waste any of them.

He could almost hear the last bits of the countdown

inside his mind…three, two, one…

He stared right at his chosen target on the screen as he directed the lasers to fire.

His shot went wide, missing by perhaps two kilometers.

He could perceive the rate of his weapon's recharge, sixty percent, seventy, even as he watched the rest of his ships open fire. His one hundred fighters all discharged their lasers, and when they were done, he guessed they had taken out thirty of the missiles.

Thirty-two, the AI confirmed with a quick pulse into his mind an instant later.

His laser was almost ready to fire again, and he redoubled his efforts to lock onto his chosen target. His training had been heavy with evasive maneuver, both how to execute it, and how to target vessels engaging in it. But the enemy missiles were coming on with more or less straight vectors. There was no way he should have missed, no way almost seventy percent of his ships should have.

Using the neural link to fire was more difficult than employing it to navigate the ship, at least at the current training and experience level of his pilots. He suspected it would become easier, that eventually, it too would be a great superiority of the Hegemony fighter craft.

But that day is not today.

"All squadrons, switch to manual fire control." His hand gripped the controls, and he stared down at the targeting screen. Manual, he knew, was far from an accurate term. The AI was still crunching the numbers, and the computer system would input the selected firing vector. Gelak would simple pull the trigger, choose the instant to fire.

He did just that, closing his finger around the firing mechanism…and he watched as the pulse ripped across space, and obliterated one of the approaching missiles.

He took a deep breath, even as he 'heard' the recharge gauge in his head, the power flowing into his laser's capacitors, building a charge for the next shot…forty percent, fifty…

*   *   *

"Evasive maneuvers, now! All power to the engines." Stockton pulled his own throttle hard back and to the side, even as he shouted the command into the comm. His people had fired hard, blasted a huge gap in the approaching missile barrage, and they'd been aided massively in that effort by Gelak's squadrons. Stockton still resented the Kriegeri, but he had to admit, the relatively inexperienced Hegemony flyers had done an impressive job, and whatever chance his people had, any of them, to escape, they owed to their enemies turned allies.

Stockton had taken down ten of the enemy missiles, the most of anyone in the attack force. But all of his people had done well, and fewer than twenty percent of the warheads the enemy had launched remained out there.

But those were close now, coming in on their final attack runs. And they were still numerous enough to gut his force, if not to wipe it out entirely. His people didn't have the time to run, or to continue their defensive fire. They had to bet on their evasion tactics, and hope they were enough to counter whatever was driving the approaching warheads.

Stockton angled his ship hard, repositioning his thrusters to work his vector around. His ship was weaving, his positioning jets whipping the small craft in all directions, re-angling his main thruster for short bursts in seemingly random directions. The enemy missiles were the fastest things Stockton had ever seen, but now he was trying to turn that strength into a weakness. The warheads could counter his moves faster than any ship or weapon he'd ever encountered, but they were coming in screaming hot, their velocities well over two percent of lightspeed. Even at 130g thrust, it took some time to meaningfully change an approach vector at such velocities. If his people could sidestep the initial attacks, they might buy some time. Maybe even enough to get away, to race back to the waiting motherships, and return to Calpharon to report that the Highborn had much more massive ships than any that had been seen before...and another unknown weapon.

To report that the already unbeatable enemy had just become even more dominant and invincible.

Chapter Four

Grand Palais Hotel
Troyus City
Megara, Olyus III
Year 322 AC (After the Cataclysm)

Andi Lafarge sat quietly, looking at the child sleeping in the small bed, just across the room. Her child. Hers and Tyler's. It still seemed somehow unreal, an unlikely place and situation for one who'd come from where she'd been born, lived the life she had. She suspected the percentage chance of her surviving all she had would be shockingly low, if it could even be calculated. For her to end up on Megara, vastly wealthy and married to one of the greatest heroes in the Confederation seemed mathematically impossible. But there she was.

Still, the joy she might have expected to feel had given way to sadness.

Tyler is at war again, farther away than he has ever been...and he hasn't even seen his daughter.

Andi was somber, the vaguest hint of a smile on her lips hinting at the love she felt for her child, even as sorrow and loneliness pervaded the rest of her soul, challenging her as a legion of deadly enemies had never done. She was loathe to admit she needed anyone—even Tyler. But the idea that her lover—no, her husband, she reminded herself—might die in battle, hundreds of lightyears away from her, without ever seeing or holding their child…it was more even than a veteran warrior like she could endure, far worse than Sector Nine torture chambers and the pain of wounds in battle.

Andi didn't want for anything material, and that was something one who'd come from the deprivation of her early years was incapable of taking for granted. Her adventures had made her one of the richest women in the Confederation, and as the Barron family patriarch, Tyler controlled a fortune even vaster than her own. She could have a hundred servants if she wanted them. A thousand. But the only person she truly wanted near her was out of her reach.

She'd have followed Tyler, joined him at the front, faced any danger at his side. But she couldn't. Not this time. She would risk her wealth, her ship, her life, to see Tyler again, even for a short time. Nothing was more important to her, not wealth, not her life…nothing except Cassiopeia.

She shook her head as she glanced over again toward her sleeping daughter. She was a hypocrite, she knew, if only in a harmless way. She'd long chafed at the name her mother had given her, wondered how something like 'Andromeda' had come to be the name of a street rat from the Gut, why her mother had saddled her with such a moniker. Now, she'd done very much the very same thing to her own child.

Cassiopeia had been born into circumstances almost opposite to those Andi had endured. She was barely six months old, and she was enormously wealthy, loved and already adored by a Confederation population that almost venerated her father. A population that had never even seen her. Tyler Barron had always been uncomfortable with the public side of his life, but Andi was almost pathological in her distrust of those she didn't know *very* well...and that iridium-hard caution was on overdrive where Cassiopeia was concerned. She'd turned down every request by the media for photos or video of the child, sometimes politely, others less so.

The child's name *was* a mouthful, Andi acknowledged that...but it wasn't meaningless. She'd taken it from the same book from which she'd pulled the name of her ship. *Pegasus* had taken her from one end of the Rim to the other and beyond, and the trusty vessel had always brought her back. Andi wasn't superstitious by nature, but if that wasn't good luck, she didn't know what was. Besides, the book had once belonged to the Marine, the broken old warrior who'd saved her from almost certain death alone on the streets of the Gut. It seemed right to her to put that tiny bit of him into her child's name. She didn't know where life would take Cassiopeia, but if she traveled half as far from where she'd started as Andi had, she would truly reach the farthest stars.

Andi turned back toward the small desk next to her. A stack of building progress reports sat there, untouched. She'd begun the reconstruction of the Barron townhouse in Troyus City, more out of a general feeling that her child shouldn't grow up in a hotel than from any real interest or desire on her part. Building a home to share with Tyler might have been a wonderful enterprise, if he'd been there to share it with her. As things were, it was just one more pointless task, and a constant reminder that the man she loved was far from her, risking his life once again in battle.

She hadn't been entirely idle, though, while she'd been ignoring the work reports. She'd been reading over a whole series of dispatches, all the reports of what Tyler and his spacers were facing so far beyond the Badlands. Much of it was highly classified, and she wasn't technically supposed to see any of it. But she had her ways. Tyler had sent her more information than he should have, though less than she wanted. Her husband still carried some of the stiffness in mannerism his naval training and career—and breeding—had instilled in him. That was an affliction Andi did not suffer, and she rarely troubled herself with justifying what she wanted. It was far more productive to focus on how to get it.

Gary Holsten, her friend, and the Confederation's spymaster, had fed her a rather heavier flow of data, and a woman of Andi's skills and resources had encountered little trouble in getting the rest of what she wanted…from a variety of sources and far more cheaply than she'd imagined at first.

None of it was good. Even the combined might of the Confederation and the Hegemony, now supplemented by Vian Tulus's Palatian fleets, seemed far too weak to face the vastly superior technology of the enemy. Andi had almost become used to seemingly hopeless situations and overpowering adversaries, but there was something different about it this time, something that sapped her normal resolve. She'd worried many times about Tyler, about the danger he faced in his wars, but she'd always believed deep down that he'd come back to her. Now, she wasn't so sure. She didn't know if it was because she was back home this time, relatively safe…or if this new enemy just seemed unbeatable.

But it wasn't enemy technology, nor weapons, nor the prospect of more and deadlier battles that troubled her just then. It was something else, something at the edge of her memory, a hazy, almost forgotten nugget that seemed suddenly relevant. Her mind reached back, to her days in the Badlands, and then she looked down at the report on her screen.

The Highborn.

The designation of the enemy seemed unimportant, even random…save for an old memory, almost forgotten.

Aquellus.

Her mind filled with images of a world covered by a single vast ocean…and then combat, struggle, a desperate fight to escape. She had lost friends there, but she had come away with something, a trinket really, an item of no great value.

Or was it?

She slammed her hand down on the desk, and then she turned suddenly to make sure she hadn't awakened Cassiopeia.

Of course…the folio.

It had been years ago, before she'd met Tyler. A mission like so many others.

No, not like so many others. Far worse…

The sudden remembrance tore at old wounds inside her, ripping them open, and the faces of those who'd stood beside her, who'd followed her into the Badlands, stared back at her from the shadows.

Friends and comrades who hadn't come back.

Andi brought something back from Aquellus…something she'd almost forgotten.

A folio full of data chips. She'd hoped it would prove interesting, if not valuable, but radiation from the damage *Pegasus* had taken in the fight to escape had damaged it beyond. She'd taken it to an expert…at least as close to one as she'd been able to find in Dannith's Spacer's District, and he'd told her he couldn't do anything.

Nothing beyond translating the imperial dialect stenciled on the cover.

Chronicle of the Highborn.

She'd found that vaguely interesting at the time, and

then she'd put the thing in storage, and never looked at it again, never even thought about it. Until the day before, when she'd read the name of the new enemy.

Andi's mind was racing. The thought of Tyler facing some deadly threat, a hostile first contact with an alien race, perhaps, was upsetting enough, almost more than she could bear. But if the 'Highborn' had been a threat to the empire as well, a danger to a far more powerful and advanced humanity?

Now, questions fired off in her mind, one after another. Was there information on those data chips that could be useful? Data that could help win the war? That might save Tyler's life?

She didn't know…and it wouldn't matter, not if she didn't find some way to access the badly damaged data on the chips. She'd never made any further efforts after that first abortive attempt, nor searched for anyone else could do what the District computer expert had failed to do.

Sy…

Sylene Merrick had been Andi's best friend back in her early prospecting days…until a particularly tough mission had prompted the programmer and hacker to retire. Sy was Vig's sister, but even with that connection added to her friendship, Andi had lost touch with Sy. She tried to tell herself circumstances had intervened, that it had been inevitable that her friend would drift away from her. But she knew that was nonsense. She'd let Sy slip away. She had failed to reach out, to make the effort to stay in contact…and the fact that Sylene had done no more to communicate with her meant exactly nothing in terms of lessening her self-condemnation. Sy had been a friend, and she had deserved better…and Andi knew it.

Sylene Merrick was also the most gifted programmer Andi had ever known, and more importantly, an expert at sneaking into systems and accessing difficult to reach data.

Could she pull something from the damaged chips? Andi didn't know...but she was sure it was the best chance. And if there was any possibility those chips contained information useful to the war effort, she had to try and access it.

She knew where the folio was, at least. She'd left a pile of things in a storage facility on Dannith. Somewhere there, amid old weapons and equipment, and probably enough contraband to violate a hundred Confederation laws, was a large leather folio with a dozen imperial data chips tucked neatly inside it.

And just maybe, a way to help from behind the lines, where she was stuck. To aid the war effort. To support the Confederation.

But mostly, to help Tyler.

She turned and looked over at Cassiopeia, even as she tried to remember exactly where she'd last heard Sylene was living. She stood up, and walked across the room, looking down at her child.

"I hadn't intended for you to see the things I did when I was younger...but I think maybe we have to go to Dannith, my sweet one, to the District."

To you mother's old stomping grounds.

"I wouldn't take you there for anything else...anything except to help your father."

To help him come back to us.

*   *   *

"Mr. Holsten, we find ourselves deeply involved in a conflict vaster than any we have endured before, and yet we know almost nothing of our enemy. What information we do possess has come almost entirely from our new allies, so recently our deadly enemy. I trust my concern, and my reluctance to provide the levels of funding and support Admiral Barron requests, are both understandable to you. Perhaps worst of all, Admiral Barron requests all that he does without a shred of oversight. His headquarters is three months away by the fastest ships we possess, and he is acting almost as a viceroy in the Badlands, even a monarch." A pause. "No, his forces are now even beyond what we have for so long labeled the 'Badlands,' are they not?"

Gary Holsten stared, his eyes boring right into the politician's. Emmit Flandry was a pompous fool, and the Speaker's Philophoran drawl was digging into Holsten's skull like a set of metal claws. But the Confederation's most powerful Senator *had* been an ally of sorts, most of the time, at least. Which only meant he'd been scared enough to put political interests aside when it had been absolutely necessary. Holsten wanted to get angry, but he could tell from Flandry's expression and his tone, the Speaker was truly worried about controlling the Senate.

"Mr. Speaker…" The use of the title was more respect than Holsten generally showed to the politician, but as much as he disliked Flandry, he was pretty sure anyone who took the Senator's place with the gavel would be worse. "…I don't have to remind you that we are very likely in a fight for our lives here, one unlike anything we have seen before. The Union is destabilized…I have reports now even suggesting that open civil war has erupted between two factions, but of greater concern, we now have an enemy that is almost a total mystery. We do not know what the Highborn are, or where they came from. We certainly have no idea of their total strength, but after six years of war with the Hegemony, the obvious fear the Masters show is sobering. At least in my estimation."

"And mine, Mr. Holsten. But I am not your problem. The Greens and the Reds have been at each other's throats since I first came to Megara as a Senatorial aide eons ago...but Cyn Avaria and Kettle Vaughn have never agreed with each other more than they have in the past several months. The constant requests for more funding, more resources, more ships...it has become difficult for many of our Senators to accept, especially when the grave threat we are meeting is still somewhat amorphous, at least to their views."

Holsten was about to speak, but Flandry continued before he started. "And, we cannot forget these troubles in the Union. Montmirail is a *proven* enemy, one we have fought against for a century. I have no idea what is happening there—and that is an area where I submit your own organization could be more effective—but this latest request from the admiral, for half the already thin forces that remain in home space to be detached immediately to the Hegemony front, makes that of considerable concern. We would be hard-pressed to meet any significant Union attack, even now. We can hope their internal struggles continue until we are able to recall more of our forces, but that seems a very tenuous strategy. Perhaps more importantly, it is one I—we—will have considerable difficulty presenting to the Senate."

Holsten shifted on his feet. He didn't like Flandry, but he couldn't argue against the logic of the Speaker's words. It *would* be difficult to convince the Senate to authorize so many remaining fleet units to depart Confederation space...and that *would* leave the home sectors almost entirely unprotected. Even his notorious Red files might not be sufficient to gain the votes needed.

"Perhaps we could enlist Andi Lafarge's aide again. She was quite successful at...persuading...the Senate to send the initial reinforcements to the war zone." Holsten didn't like the idea of dragging Andi back into the political swamp. He'd tried to leave her alone as much as possible, to protect her in Tyler's absence. At least as much as someone with Andi's skills and experience needed protection.

There wasn't the slightest doubt in his mind Andi would already have been at the front and in the thick of the fight at Tyler Barron's side, save only for Cassiopeia. But, even as his mind rattled off the various reasons not to involve her, he knew he would have to ask for her help again. And she would give it, if only because it was the one way she could support Tyler.

"Captain Lafarge is a...formidable...individual, Mr. Holsten, however, I am not sure she will be helpful in this instance. There is considerable resentment in some quarters regarding her...tactics...in pressuring the Senate to authorize the deployment of the main fleet to the warzone."

Holsten just nodded. He had already decided what he was going to do, and he didn't care to waste his time and effort arguing with Flandry.

Yes, Speaker, they resent her...but they are afraid of her, too, and I have found few things work as quickly and effectively as fear.

Chapter Five

Stockton ran the calculations in his head for the fourth time, and he got a different answer yet again. The first time, he'd thought his people just might make good their escape. Then, that hope faded in an instant, replaced by the grim realization they were all doomed. That change had been triggered not by doubts or fear, but by new data on the maneuverability and thrust capabilities of the approaching missiles...and the fact that they had just kicked up from 130g to over 160g. There was no way his people could evade anything with that kind of engine power.

Then, seconds later, some fragile bit of hope streamed back into his mind, this time courtesy of an ally whose abilities he doubted, one he still thought of as the enemy. Kiloron Gelak's ships were screaming forward, accelerating at full power even as they opened fire on the remaining missiles.

Most surprisingly to Stockton, they were hitting a

number of them.

He'd ordered the Hegemony reserves forward, but they'd surprised him with the rapidity of their approach, and now they were shocking him yet again with the accuracy of their fire.

Stockton was impressed with the marksmanship he saw, and even as he realized it might save his life, he felt a bit of irrational resentment at seeing the Hegemony pilots come so close to the abilities of his own people. He'd long felt pride in the skill and training of his pilots, and watching the Heggies do so well dinged that conceit. The Hegemony was new to fighter ops, and whatever technological advantages they may have possessed seemed inadequate to bridge the gulf in abilities.

Now he wasn't so sure. He was still confident his people could win out in a dogfight against any force out there, but the Hegemony squadrons weren't the enemy anymore, and the Highborn didn't appear to have fighters of their own. That reduced the prospects for a massive scrum between squadrons almost to zero.

He should have been happy about that, he knew, but on some level he almost wished his people had enemy fighters to match in a good, old fashioned dogfight. Stockton had become an expert in bombing tactics over the past seven years, but at heart, he was a fighter jock of the old school, and somewhere inside him, he felt the only truly worthy battle for a pilot was to match up with his counterpart, one on one, jousting to determine who was the best.

He remembered those days well, the massive dogfights with the Union wings, and he knew, beneath all the false humility and disciplined caution, that he had been the best.

Stockton watched as more and more of the incoming missiles vanished, and his respect for his new allies grew—grudgingly—with each one that winked out on his screen. He stared for perhaps half a minute, distracted, lost, save only for the instinct driving his evasive maneuvers…and then his laser focus returned.

He pulled his throttle to the side, so hard, he felt a jarring all the way up his arm. The move re-oriented his thrusters yet again, even as he shouted into the comm. "All squadrons, come about and reengage." The Hegemony squadrons had turned the tide, but they weren't going to eradicate the incoming wave, not entirely.

Not unless his own ships joined in.

He tightened his fingers on the firing stud yet again, and another missile disappeared. His eyes scanned for the next target as his lasers recharged, and his mind dove into yet another analysis of his people's chances to escape. The odds had improved, but by every measure he could conceive, it was still a wild guess.

He saw the Hegemony ships, approaching from behind his own formation. The sleek vessels were faster even than his new Black Lightnings, and while he found that troubling on one level, just then he was ready to take any advantage he could get. He watched as another half dozen of the enemy warheads disappeared.

Then, the surviving weapons began to detonate.

* * *

Gelak blinked, watching in surprise as the enemy missiles made their final approaches and began to explode. The warheads were massive—almost certainly antimatter-armed. They couldn't take out more than one fighter each, despite their massive yields, not at the ranges between units in the Rim formations. But it took far less than a direct hit for one of the massive warheads to take out a fighter. An explosion within half a kilometer essentially vaporized the target, and one within a kilometer and a half, even two, destroyed a ship, or did something very close to that. Detonations as far out as five kilometers caused significant damage, often crippling one of the small vessels.

In the current fight, that kind of damage was effectively a death sentence.

Gelak had watched as almost sixty of Stockton's fighters went down in less than a minute, more than half of those blasted to atoms, and the rest badly battered, floating helplessly in their shattered vessels, beyond rescue, without hope. Those pilots were all dead, even as they sat in their cockpits gasping for whatever air damaged life support systems were still able to produce. Gelak had been trained and conditioned to approach war coolly, dispassionately, but that hadn't relieved him of his human emotions, neither the ones that fueled lingering hatred of the former enemies from the Rim, nor those that generated respect and empathy for fellow warriors facing their own death struggles.

He was still firing, still tracking any incoming contacts, until he suddenly realized the enemy missiles were gone. His people and the Confeds had destroyed all those that hadn't detonated on their own. Gelak's mind raced, his usual focus on orders and discipline weakened somewhat by his thoughts on the implications the enemy weapons held for future battles. His squadrons had been trained largely in imitation of the Rim wings, but those very forces, led by none other than the famous Jake Stockton, had been savaged by a single vessel's attack. The master of fighter combat had been roughly handled by an enemy that didn't even appear to possess fighters, and Gelak knew, before he even analyzed the situation more closely, that small ship tactics were going to have to change.

No one will realize that more quickly than Admiral Stockton…

Gelak still frowned as he thought of Stockton, of how many Kriegeri the Confed pilot's wings had killed in the war. But there was respect, too, and he realized he was already relying on Stockton's skill, depending on his former enemy to lead the fighter wings—all of the wings—toward a new way to face the enemy threat.

He was starting to look on Stockton as his leader.

It was a surprise of sorts, but amid his mixed and confused emotions, Gelak realized that he had confidence in Stockton, and for all it still stung, he was ready to follow the Confed into the desperate struggle that lay ahead.

Gelak checked his status monitors again, more of a habit than anything else. He hadn't been close enough to any of the warheads to suffer damage. But as he sat there, he realized he didn't know what to do next. The surviving ships in the attack wing still had their bombs. Would Stockton lead the battered force against the original target? That seemed wildly reckless to Gelak, but he'd come to expect the unexpected from Jake Stockton. And he would follow orders, whatever they were.

The question became moot a few seconds later, however, as Gelak checked his scanner and he saw another wave of the deadly weapons launching from the original vessel…and from the other two positioned behind it as well. The initial volley had almost obliterated the attack force, and now three times as many missiles were inbound. Gelak wasn't in overall command, and for an instant, he imagined himself following an attack order from Stockton, in spite of what he was seeing…leading his people forward to certain death.

That would be foolish, wasteful…a sacrifice without purpose. But if the order came, Gelak would obey. It was who he was, and he knew he didn't have it in him to refuse. Even one that meant certain death.

He would die, if necessary, as he had lived. As a creature of discipline, one of obedience.

* * *

"Get the hell out of here, all of you. Now! Back to the motherships." Stockton was already bringing his ship about, setting a course back to the landing platforms. His strike force had survived one volley—at least some of it had, courtesy of the Hegemony squadrons' intervention—but there was no way any of his pilots would escape a second assault, much less one three time the size of the first. There was only one choice. Run like hell.

He checked his reactor reading. He was at full thrust, and he could already see the thirty Black Lightnings moving ahead of the rest of the formation. The Hegemony ships were farther toward the rear than the rest of his forces, closer to their own mother ships. The rest of his forces were more or less together, about twenty thousand kilometers in front of Gelak's Kriegeri…and the pilots in the newer ships were going to make it back ahead of the rest of the Confeds and Alliance birds.

That was fine. He wasn't going to order his faster squadrons to wait for the slower units. But it wasn't fine for him to be with them.

He knew what Admiral Barron would have said, that his life, his skill and experience, were vital to the outcome of the war, that it was his duty to get back, regardless of what happened to the rest of his squadrons. But Stockton wasn't wired that way and, for that matter, neither was Barron. Stockton had revered the admiral since the days when he'd been a squadron commander under *Dauntless*'s then-new CO. But he knew for all the admiral's honor and courage, he'd be spewing outright hypocrisy if he urged his fighter commander to run for home ahead of his people. Tyler Barron had never left his warriors behind to save himself, and if there was one person truly vital to the war effort, it was the navy's supreme commander.

He tapped his throttle forward, easing slightly off on the thrust level to match the rest of his ships. A few seconds later, he eased off a bit more. The Alliance fighters were slower even than the old Lightnings, and Stockton was no more ready to leave them behind than he was his own pilots. There was time for everyone to get back, at least there was if the enemy missiles didn't have any more surprises in store for him.

He stared back at the screen, watching the oncoming volley, struggling to keep hard analysis in place over the fear and frenzy of combat. He was going to have to develop tactics to face the enemy weapons, and his mind was already working on it. To no avail, at least not as he sat there, staring at the missiles pursuing his fleeing force. He had no idea what to do, how to lead his wings in the next fight. And he doubted the enemy would give him long to think about it.

The difficultly in establishing scanner locks on the enemy ships required his squadrons to close to point blank range before launching their weapons. But that would now mean enduring multiple waves of the deadly cluster warheads. He tried to imagine a battle line of the larger enemy battleships, and the barrage of warheads they would unleash on his attacking wings. That would be devastating, a bloodbath.

And any ships that got past the missiles would have to endure the regular defensive fire from turrets on the ships themselves. He had no idea what the new, larger vessels carried, but the smaller ones had mounted substantial point defense arrays, and Stockton would have bet a sizable amount the heavy units were just as well armed with the small, rapid fire lasers.

He pulled himself from his analysis long enough to check and recheck the range calculations. His ships were still plotting ahead of the incoming missile barrages. There would be enough time to land all his survivors, and for the motherships to pull out of the system. There wasn't a large margin, but it would serve. Barely.

It wasn't enough, though, to stop the drumbeat sound of his heart echoing in his ears. Or the sweat pouring off of him. The flight suits were new, too, and they were slimmer and less bulky than the old ones. But they were hot, at least when the internal life support systems were off, as they were inside the cockpit.

He looked over to the edge of the display. His forward squadrons were approaching their landing platforms. His pilots were inexperienced facing the Highborn, but they were veterans in every other way. The motherships were undamaged, a pleasant change from the situation in many of his past battles. That mean his experienced squadrons would land quickly.

That couldn't be soon enough for him. He knew he'd be back, that he'd face the same dangers again, probably in vastly larger numbers. But just then, he was ready to take any respite, to gain any opportunity to pull back and think about the new problems his wings would face. They had suffered terribly in the war against the Hegemony, but now he wondered if any of them would survive the new conflict beginning all around them.

If any of them would see home again.

Or if there would even be a home left when the enemy was done.

He didn't have any answers. But he knew he had to get back to Calpharon and tell Admiral Barron about the enemy's massive battleships and their cluster missiles.

If there is anybody who can figure a way to fight this enemy, it's Tyler Barron.

But for all Stockton's faith in his longtime commander, the hard pit in his stomach told him he didn't believe his longtime commander would find a way. The Confederation had fought many battles, endured many challenges, and he had remained steadfast and resolute during each of them. But Jake Stockton realized he was losing what little hope remained to him.

He was becoming more and more certain that last battle he'd so long imagined, the final day he would step into his fighter, was rapidly approaching, that one day soon, he would take off and fly into his destiny.

Chapter Six

Warehouse District
Port Royal City
Planet Dannith, Ventica III
Year 323 AC (After the Cataclysm)

"It's good to see you, old friend, even if it's in this dusty old place. I know we left some trinkets in here, but honestly, with all we've made since, I can't imagine you need to sell off a bunch of old crap." The voice was immediately familiar, and a smile slipped onto Andi's face, despite the sad and somber shadow that had shrouded her for months.

"Vig! Thank you so much for coming." She spun almost one hundred eight degrees, and she threw her arms around her friend's neck. "I hoped you would be able to make it."

"Be able to? Andi, you have to know I'd have come from the galactic core if you beckoned. And so would the others. They're all back at the spaceport. The whole crew, together again."

Andi was usually stone cold, a block of granite immune to emotional appeals, but Vig's words, and the loyalty and devotion of her old comrades of which they spoke, almost had her blubbering like a child. She held the tears back, barely, but her eyes were moist as she struggled to force out her words. "Thank you, Vig...so much." She tightened her grip and hugged him even more firmly.

Vig was silent for a moment, and then he took half a step back, and he looked right at Andi. "So, tell me...what is this all about?"

"Do you remember Aquellus?"

Vig's faced seemed to go pale. "I'll never forget that place, Andi...no matter how hard I try."

The mission to the water world had been a difficult one, and she and Vig had lost friends there.

"I found something there, something I kept. I'm sure I showed it to you, but you might not remember." The trip to Aquellus had been a contract job, and the imperial artifacts her people had found had been delivered to their sponsor. All except for one item. "It was a folio with a dozen data chips in it. I thought it might be interesting...hell, I probably should have turned it over with the other stuff we found, but it was damaged in the battle. The data on the chips was scrambled by radiation. I had it checked out when we got back, but no luck. I almost tossed it all, but then I figured anything from imperial times was worth keeping, even if it was useless."

"I take it you feel it's not useless anymore?"

"I don't know, Vig. I always meant to have it checked by someone else. The District isn't exactly home to the Confederation's foremost data retrieval experts, is it? But I never did. Honestly, I forgot all about it."

"So, what reminded you...and sent you all the way back to this shithole to find it, no less at a time like the present?"

"I was never able to find out what the chips contained, but there was something written on the cover, something

I was able to get translated from old imperial. It didn't mean anything to me back then. Not until very recently." She paused, and she looked right into Vig's eyes. "How much have you heard about this new war, about the enemy we face?"

"Not too much, really. Just that we're now allied with the Hegemony. That was a lot to absorb."

Andi nodded. "Yes, it was. What else have you heard?"

"Just the name of the enemy...Highborn. I'm not sure what it means. Doesn't really make any sense to me."

"I'm not sure what it means either, old friend, but the words on the folio cover were, 'Chronicle of the Highborn.' Whoever these...people...are, they were known to the empire. They must have been a threat all the way back in imperial times."

Vig's expression changed, a look of surprise replacing one of curiosity. "You think the data chips carry information about the enemy? Information that might aid the war effort?"

Andi just returned her friend's gaze.

"But even if you find them, do you really think you can get someone who can retrieve the data?"

"That's where I need your help, Vig."

Merrick's look of confusion persisted, for a few seconds. Then: "Oh...you think Sylene might be able to do something."

"She's the best computer expert I've ever known, Vig." Andi paused and looked down at the floor. "I'm afraid I lost touch with her a few years ago, after she left Decarion." A pause. "I was hoping you knew where she was." Andi could feel tears welling up again, and she endured a wave of self-hatred as she thought about her friend. "If she'll even help me after all these years."

"Of course she'll help you, Andi...why would you

even doubt that?"

"She was my best friend, Vig, and I don't even know where she is. I had to ask you. I haven't seen her in years, haven't even exchanged letters with her."

"You've been busy, Andi, right at the center of all that has happened to the Confederation." It was Vig's turn to pause. "I'm sure Sy would have kept in better touch with you, but she's...struggled...in her own way since she left *Pegasus*."

"Struggled? She should have had more than enough money. If she needed more she could have come to me."

"Not money, Andi. Sy left the ship because...well, because it all got to her. The danger, the loss of friends. Captain Lorillard's death was difficult for her to accept. I don't think she could have endured losing you, too, and I think that is what drove her away. But, of course, by leaving she did just that. She had a place with you and the others, Andi. It was the closest thing either of us ever had to a real home. I think she left because she thought she couldn't handle the stress, that she might fail you at some crucial time, and my coming aboard helped her feel that she wasn't leaving you without someone you could count on. But she was lost after she left."

"That's why she moved around so many times?" Andi had made an effort to stay in touch with her friend at first, but Sylene hadn't remained in one place for more than a few months.

"Yes...she finally managed to adjust, to an extent. I think she probably wanted to reach out to you a hundred times, but she felt as though she'd let you down."

"Let me down? I let her down."

"No, Andi...neither of you are to blame, not in any real way. I wanted to tell you all of this years ago, but Sy insisted that I not say anything. She didn't want to be a burden."

"A burden? She was my best friend. How could she think I would..." Andi let her words trail off. Then: "Why didn't you tell me?"

"You're my best friend, Andi, and my captain. I owe you everything I have, everything I am. But Sy is my sister, and, well you know...I guess I figured she'd change her mind, reach out to you herself. Then, time slipped by, and..."

Andi just nodded as Vig in turn allowed his voice to fade to silence. Finally, she asked simply, "Do you know where she is now, Vig?"

He nodded. "She is on Sebastiani. She's been there a year, no more. I think she's been more comfortable there than anywhere else."

Andi leaded forward, reaching into a large trunk she'd opened. She pulled out a dusty rectangular object, a box of sorts with a leather cover. "Here it is." She looked back at Vig. "Now, let's get back to the spaceport. *Pegasus* is there, and ready to fly us to Sebastiani."

*   *   *

"Vig, Ross, Dolph, Rina, Lex...this is Cassiopeia." Andi felt strange introducing her daughter to her old crew— her friends. She couldn't imagine any of them had ever thought of her as a mother. But next to Tyler, they were the most important people in the galaxy to her, and it seemed somehow right.

"This just goes to show that none of us can predict the future, Andi." Vig smiled, and he leaned forward, extending his hand even as the child reached out and grabbed his finger.

Andi stood and smiled as her crew gathered around, making various sounds at Cassiopeia and congratulating her in one way or another. "This is Lita Mareth," she said softly, extending her hand to the older woman standing against the far wall. "She helps me take care of Cassiopeia. She did the same for Tyler, she's told me."

The woman smiled and nodded. "I did indeed. Young Tyler was somewhat of a terror, I can tell you that much." Mareth looked about seventy years old, her whitish-gray hair tipping off her age in a way her nearly wrinkle-free skin and upright bearing never would have. "It is a pleasure to meet all of you."

The crew exchanged pleasantries with Cassiopeia's nanny, and a few minutes later, Andi looked at them all and said, "I have to go to Sebastiani. I am going to see an old member of the crew, one who'd left before I met all of you. She is Vig's sister, which is why I contacted him. I didn't realize he'd round you all up, pull you from your lives. If Sylene is able to help get the information I am seeking, I may ask Vig, and any of you who are willing, to take a trip back into the Badlands, farther even. I would go myself, but I'm afraid my days of venturing into the depths of space are gone for quite some time."

"Andi, we all owe you, most of us our lives, all of us the prosperity we've enjoyed. But none of that matters. We're your friends. If you need us to do something, we'll do it. All it takes is you asking." Lex Righter looked at her, even as the others all nodded.

"I love all of you. You are the best friends anyone could ask for." Andi stood for a few seconds and looked at her crew. She could see other faces, too, floating in the background, those who'd been just as close to her, just as loyal, but who'd been lost out in the Badlands. Gregor and Jackal, and Captain Lorillard, the man who'd taken her in, who'd left *Pegasus* to her. Her life had been a hard one in many ways, but she'd met some extraordinary people, too. All in all, she rated herself pretty damned lucky.

Though the prospect of losing it all, everyone she cared about, loomed like a shadow over her. She was on Dannith because she wanted to help Tyler, because she thought the data on this chips might prove useful. But mostly, she was there because she truly believed it would take absolutely everything she could do, all that Tyler and his officers and spacers could give, the full effort of the Confederation, if there was to be any chance to defeat the enemy.

Any chance to save the Rim.

"Why don't we all settle in? It will take some time to get launch clearance." Andi hadn't always waited for formalities like permission to take off. But she was trying to keep her brief visit to Dannith as quiet as possible. She loved Tyler, with every fiber of her being, but she despised the fame that came with being his wife. She knew he didn't like it any more than she did, but he'd been born into it, an inescapable trap, and he'd become more adept at handling it than she had in such a shorter time. If he couldn't get away from it, she would share it with him, as she had shared danger and pain and war, but that didn't mean she wouldn't try to shake it when she could.

"I'm sure you all remember where your quarters are. I haven't changed a thing." She smiled and passed her eyes over them all, feeling a renewed burst of gratitude, along with guilt for dragging them all to Dannith. Then she turned and she went to her own cabin, and she sat on the bed, sucking in a deep breath as she felt the façade of strength she'd held in place crumble, and the tears begin to stream down her face.

Andi felt sadness, guilt for dragging her young daughter across space, for leaving her in the care of others, for bringing her to places like Dannith and its notorious Spacer's District. It helped a little that she'd enlisted the aid of the woman who'd cared for Tyler as a boy, but mostly, she railed inside against a universe that could make her breathtakingly wealthy, and yet deny her even the simple choice of protecting her child from such things.

But, of course, she also knew that was just what she was doing, protecting Cassiopeia. She wanted her daughter to know her father. She wanted Cassiopeia to grow up and live her life, and not die at the hands of a deadly enemy or to be carried off in chains by the conquerors. Andi had endured that particular vision far too many times in recent weeks. Tyler had tried to sound upbeat in his messages to her, but she knew him far too well for that to succeed. He was scared, not of physical danger, but of losing the war. She was sure of it. And if the fleet was defeated and destroyed, there was no doubt in her mind, the Confederation would fall soon after. Andi would die fighting to the end before she would yield, but that was not a choice her daughter could make, nor one she could either, not while Cassiopeia depended on her. She'd imagined taking off in *Pegasus*, fleeing to the farthest deeps of unknown space, anything to save Cassiopeia. But she'd pushed those thoughts away. She wasn't ready to accept defeat, not yet. Nor even to plan for it. The war wasn't over yet, and she was damned sure going to do all she could to make certain the enemy got the best possible fight.

It was all she'd ever really known how to do, the one thing she'd been truly good at. No one who knew Andi Lafarge would call her anything but a fighter, and one hell of a scrappy one at that.

And the Highborn, whatever the hell that name meant, were going to find out just what that truly meant.

Chapter Seven

CFS Dauntless
Orbiting Calpharon (Hegemonic Capital)
Sigma Nordlin IV
Year 323 AC (After the Cataclysm)

"I was surprised you wanted to come up to *Dauntless*, Commander. I would have shuttled down to the surface. Your command staff is all down there, after all, as well as the main tactical center." Tyler Barron sat across the table, trying to decipher the edge he could feel from Chronos. He'd come to know the Hegemony commander pretty well, and despite his lingering resentments, he'd also developed an admiration for the man, if not yet outright friendship. He was cautious about making wild assumptions on someone still fairly new to him, but he was sure *something* was wrong.

Something besides the deadly enemy approaching, and the desperate fight that loomed over all their heads.

"I wanted to speak to you privately, Admiral, and to be honest, I was not confident I would be able to guarantee that on Calpharon. It is sometimes difficult to ensure one is not being watched...or listened to."

Barron had suspected something was wrong. Now he was sure.

"You can be confident no one is listening to us here, Commander."

"We were enemies not long ago, Admiral. I do not believe we serve any useful purpose in denying that fact. Nor do I believe our alliance has a chance to succeed against our mutual enemy, unless you and I can come to trust each other." A pause. "Many will say I am foolish to tell you this, that there is no need, that I would be best to keep my mouth shut. I have not even discussed it with Akella, but you are a fighting man, as I am, and, unless I have badly misread you, an honorable one. I pledge to you now that you will get nothing but absolute honesty from me as we fight side by side, and I will back that promise with this." He hesitated again, but only for the briefest instant. "There was a vote on the Council several days ago. Some of my people, some of the senior Masters, wanted to launch a surprise raid and take control of *Colossus* back from your people."

Barron stared back, trying to hide his shock. He wasn't all that surprised that some of the Hegemony Council members would propose such a scheme, foolish as it was in light of the approaching enemy, but he was stunned that Chronos had freely admitted it to him.

"I am grateful for your honesty, Commander." He wasn't sure he'd kept all the edge he was feeling out of his tone. He'd come to accept Chronos and Illius, and those of their Kriegeri warriors with whom he'd dealt. They'd spent six years trying to kill each other, but in the end, they weren't all that different. But he still despised the Hegemony's system, and the conduct of the Council members of whom Chronos spoke only confirmed that dislike.

"I owe you nothing less, Tyler." Chronos's shift to

informality was accompanied by a vulnerability in his tone. "I know of your political leaders, and I have heard stories of your past difficulties in dealing with them. It is no different, I am afraid, for us. At least not in essence. I was able to stop the vote from even taking place, but if we are to be allies, you have a right to be aware of dangers from within as well as without."

"How did you stop the vote?"

"I threatened to resign my position."

"I thought your genetic rating dictated your status on the Council."

"It confers on me the right to sit as Eighth on the Council, and it carries a heavy responsibility to do so. But there is no law preventing a Council member from resigning, and no restraint at all from giving up ancillary roles...like supreme military commander."

"You threatened to do that? You would really have left your warriors without you in the face of what is coming?"

Chronos just stared back at Barron for a few seconds. Then he said, "I believe your people enjoy an old imperial game, one played with cards. Poker, I believe it is called. Sadly, my people have not retained the custom, though I daresay I know enough about it to co-opt some of its tenets. Bluffing, I believe it is called." Chronos managed something close to a smile. "Perhaps one day, if we both survive the war, you can teach me how to play."

Barron locked eyes with his Hegemony counterpart, and he smiled. "I think you know more of the game than you let on, Chronos." He was still angry, furious at the pompous fools on the Council who persisted in seeing his people as little more than animals to be toyed with. But Chronos and Ilius were living proof that the people of the Hegemony were different from each other, even as those on the Rim were.

Barron wanted to trust Chronos to keep the

Hegemony politicians in check, but that was more than he could manage. He wasn't even sure he could handle the Senate back on Megara. He would have to rely on blind faith, on the promise of warrior to warrior.

And Chronos would have to do the same.

*   *   *

"The minefields are in place, just as Admiral Barron specified. Our analyses, both human and AI generated, show a range of probabilities of the enemy's approach course. The most likely scenario, at seventy-nine percent, is a direct assault through tube number three, with an additional eleven point four percent that the attack will come from both tubes one and three. As such, we have placed the greatest emphasis on emplaced defenses against an incursion through tube three, with secondary priority assigned to tube one." Ilius stood along the far side of the room, in front of the massive wall display. He held a long pointer in his hand, and he was moving it toward each location as he spoke.

"I am inclined to agree, Ilius, and yet, I imagine the enemy can analyze the data as well as we. It would be the most extreme arrogance to assume either that they are unaware of the importance of this system to us, or that, knowing the state of our stellar geography, that they will not scout the space around Calpharon before their main fleets arrive. Perhaps they will react by choosing an axis of attack we are less likely to expect, and for which we are more poorly prepared."

Barron listened to Chronos's challenge, and the tactician inside him agreed. If he was directing the attack, he would come from transit point four, the most difficult for an invader to approach and the farthest from Calpharon. Despite those disadvantages, it would be worth the delay and the extra effort to sidestep fixed defenses, at least in his estimation.

But he wasn't planning the enemy attack. The Highborn were. And if he'd learned one thing about this new enemy, it was their arrogance. They clearly considered themselves vastly above the human forces, to an extent that made the Hegemony's initial superiority complex against the Rim nations seem almost innocuous by comparison.

"I agree with all you say, Chronos…but nevertheless, I believe the enemy *will* attack as Ilius suggests. They do not believe we can stop them, no matter how they attack, and I seriously doubt the damage we inflicted on them at Pharsalon was sufficient to change that view in any material way. My guess is, they will say they underestimated our strength, that the arrival of the Confederation forces interfered with their initial plans. There is no shortage of ways to explain away losses, nor lack of excuses for failure. I very much doubt our enemy, however technologically advanced they are, have outgrown such flaws. They will reinforce their attack force, almost certainly. No doubt, that is the primary reason we have enjoyed the respite we have, but I do not believe they will waste additional time seeking out weaker approaches. They will come as soon as they are ready, and when they do, they will hit us hard. And they very likely believe that is enough."

"You seem convinced of this, Tyler. May I ask why?"

"Because it very likely will be enough."

Barron twitched slightly in his chair. His response had to be an uncomfortable one, but there was no time just then for diplomacy. But he immediately wished he'd been a little less direct. He was facing a desperate battle, but his new allies were defending their home planet. And he knew just how that felt.

"Our longtime enemies, the Union," he continued, subtly changing the focus of his argument, "often allowed their numerical superiority to color their judgment, and…" He paused, almost stopping right there. "…and I believe my people would have lost the war against yours if the tactics employed had been more…" Barron's voice trailed off, and he looked at Chronos. He wasn't trying to offend his new comrade, but he was well aware they all needed everything they could get just then, every tactic, every insight into the enemy. And for all the heroism of his people, he *did* believe the Hegemony could have conquered the Rim if they'd shown more respect for the abilities of his own forces.

"If we hadn't been so arrogant." Chronos was staring back at Barron. The admiral wasn't sure how the Hegemony commander had taken his comment, and he could feel himself tensing a bit inside. Diplomacy wasn't his chosen profession, and he could almost hear some Confed ambassador scolding him for insulting an ally.

Then Chronos did the thing Barron expected least. He roared with laughter.

"This is no time for humor, I know," he said after the initial burst, "but you are indeed a worthy ally, Tyler Barron. Skill, courage, endurance…they are all important, but nothing equals a comrade who can look you in the eye and tell you just how you have been a damned fool. And you are correct, of course, absolutely correct. My people were so certain of our superiority, technical, moral, numerical, we had no doubt of victory. We viewed your people with little more respect that we had planets full of radiation-mutated Defek…people, and we paid the price for that, did we not?" Barron had noted Chronos's efforts on a number of occasions to curb the use of language that seemed harsh to Rim sensibilities, or that pointed out differences in Hegemony and Confederation ethical constraints. He wasn't sure the Hegemony as a whole was ready to stop calling its radiation-damaged subjects as Defekts, but he also knew change often started in scattered bits.

"There is another consideration, as well, Tyler…one that perhaps fits your own direct and cold view of reality. Our resources are finite. With luck, we can complete the fortifications we have begun, but it is unlikely the enemy will give us time to bolster the defenses at all the transit tubes in the system. Put as I imagine you might say it, there is no point worrying about what we cannot change. We have agreed on the most likely axes of attack, and there is little to be gained by engaging in endless 'what ifs.' If the enemy does surprise us, we can at least expect some warning from our scouts. That won't allow us to build fortifications, but we will be able to redeploy the fleets, at least.

"Admiral Barron…" The voice of the Kriegeri officer posted outside the room came through on the comm. The Hegemony personnel had been very stiff around him, even uncomfortable, but he was starting to notice that lessening. He wouldn't say his former enemies were comfortable serving alongside his people, but there had been movement, at least. "…Admiral Stockton is here to see you."

Barron instantly knew something was wrong. He'd gotten word that the task force had returned just before he'd gone into the meeting. But if Stockton was already outside, that meant he'd likely blasted his fighter back ahead of the fleet and landed at once, even that he'd come to find Barron without a moment's rest or a shower. Without even going to see Stara Sinclair on *Dauntless*. He clearly had something important to report, something he wanted to tell Barron in person and not over a comm connection.

And Barron had come to understand that 'important' usually meant something very close to disastrous.

"Send him in, please, Hectoron." Barron was still getting used to Hegemony ranks, just as he continued to lean heavily on politeness when giving a command to one of his allies. The alliance between the Rim nations and the Hegemony was still tenuous, and largely informal. Barron didn't doubt the Kriegeri had been told to accept his orders, but he was just as aware they weren't technically in his chain of command.

"Admiral—and Commander Chronos and Commander Ilius—I apologize for my attire." Stockton wore a rumpled flight suit, and his hair was a wild, twisted mess. It was an inappropriate state in which to report to three superior officers, but all Barron could think of was how oblivious to that fact the young squadron commander he'd met so many years before would have been to that fact. Age and rank, and the crushing weight of responsibility, had dragged Stockton from his brash ways, but while Barron respected and understood the incredible abilities of the older, more experienced officer standing in front of him, he also missed the wild and eminently likable young rogue who'd driven him crazy on so many occasions. He saw something to mourn in the grimness of the officer standing in the room, and he lamented the reality that had forged the change, even as he recognized that the older Stockton was indispensable to him.

"That is of no concern, Admiral Stockton. Your insight is always valuable, and I would brook no delay in receiving it for foolishness like changing clothes." Chronos had responded even before Barron could.

"Commander Chronos is right, Jake. Tell us what you found." Barron was trying to hold back from making wild guesses, but the first glance at Stockton's eyes told him the news was, indeed, bad.

"Sirs, as you know, I have been combining our scouting and delaying operations with an effort to expose our fighter squadrons to action against the enemy. We discovered something new on the mission to the Vigillius Nebula...actually, several new things. First, we engaged enemy ships of considerably greater tonnage than any encountered to date. The vessels were *large*, at least twice the size of a *Repulse*-class battleship like *Dauntless*." Stockton paused, and the silence in the room testified to the shock and alarm his news unleashed.

"Perhaps that should not surprise us, after all, we had no reason to believe the Highborn lacked larger vessels." Barron was trying to sound as confident as he could, but his mind was replaying his memories of the Highborn ships he *had* seen, that his people had fought. Those ships hadn't been massive, not by the standards of ships of the line of the Rim and the Hegemony, but their weapons and technology had far outmatched those of his forces.

What kind of power will a giant battleship possess?

"I presume the task force captured significant scanner records of these vessels?" Chronos again. Barron hadn't had the easiest time reading his ally at first, but he was getting better at it. And he was sure the Hegemony commander was thinking very much the same thing he was.

"Yes, Commander...though, as you know, the enemy ships are highly resistant to scanner beams. My people would have captured significantly better data had we been able to close, but we were...compelled...to withdraw before entering launch range."

Those last words struck Barron like a hammer. All the years he'd commanded Stockton, he'd worried about the officer being too reckless. If Jake Stockton had pulled his people out before even attempting a close in attack, and run for it in the face of a new enemy force…

It was the kind of thought that created nightmares.

"Was the point defense so severe you couldn't penetrate and close?"

Stockton shifted on his feet, looking uncomfortable. "In a manner of speaking, Admiral. The ships are not the only new item I have to report. They also possess a weapon, one that is highly effective against bomber attacks." Stockton hesitated before continuing. "They are cluster missiles, Admiral, launched in massive waves. And each of them is a multiple warhead vehicle, separating into twenty separate missiles as they close."

Barron was staring straight at Stockton. The Confederation had mostly stopped employing rockets and missiles half a century before. Point defense energy batteries had become too adept at picking off physical weapons approaching capital ships. But against fighters, devoid of a battleship's massive defensive arrays? Still, fighters were much more maneuverable than line ships.

"We might have been able to evade them, Admiral, but they are capable of massive rates of acceleration."

"Massive?"

"We tracked several units peaking at 167g."

Barron felt as though he'd been gut punched. The Confederation had never developed an engine and power source that could achieve such enormous levels of thrust, and six years of desperate fighting against the Hegemony told him his new allies hadn't either.

"Antimatter drives on missiles?"

"That can't be the whole story, though." Chronos had a thoughtful look on his face. "We, like you, stopped deploying missiles in most cases some time ago, but we had experimented with antimatter propulsion earlier. We were able to attain moderately higher rates of acceleration, but the primary benefit, as it is in our spaceships, was in range. A far smaller quantity of antimatter can power vastly longer than large quantities of conventional reaction mass. The problem with dramatically increasing thrust always came down to flow rates, and generating the needed force without vaporizing the engine, and even the entire vessel being propelled. We have been able to increase maximum acceleration rates marginally with antimatter propulsion, but nothing like what Admiral Stockton is reporting." Chronos had been looking straight ahead, more or less at the wall, but then he turned toward Barron.

"There is an added benefit in a missile or other projectile weapon, of course, in that any remaining fuel will effectively add to the payload of the weapon, as it annihilates along with the primary charge. That is a tactical consideration we should remember. If these are indeed antimatter-powered missiles, their yields will be significantly higher at short ranges. I would think that presents a considerable problem, when our primary tactic for bomber assaults involves closing to point blank range. However deadly these weapons were to Admiral Stockton's squadrons at long range, they will be even more so against wings that continue to close. Assuming the vessels can carry more than one barrage of the things."

"They can. The lead ship launched a second attack. That is why I ordered the retreat. Another attack would have been literal suicide. Not a single ship would have survived."

"You did the right thing, Jake." Barron walked over and put his hand on the pilot's shoulder. He'd been immersed in navy culture as long as he could remember, before even his days in military school and then at the Academy. He'd worshiped the Confederation's heroes, listened endlessly to his grandfather's tales of combat. But he wondered about the rationality of a mindset that made someone like Jake Stockton—not only not remotely a coward, but actually borderline insane in some of his exploits—to feel he had done something wrong pulling his survivors out. That choosing to save some of his people over pointlessly leading them to certain death was somehow a cowardly act.

Barron could see that Stockton was still struggling with himself. He understood…he'd been there, too. But he needed Stockton at his best.

"Jake, you have to know that…" That was as far as he got.

The comm unit buzzed, and a voice blared out. "Commander Chronos, central control is reporting that vessels from Scouting Command Nine have entered the system. They are transmitting their report even now. They encountered hostile contacts at Celestia, Commander. The enemy is at Celestia."

Barron stood and listened, even as cold reality set in. He was no expert at Hegemony stellar geography, but he knew where the Celestia system was located, closer even than the Vigillius Nebula.

Just three jumps from Calpharon.

Chapter Eight

Highborn Flagship S'Argevon
Imperial System GH9-27C1
Year of the Firstborn 385 (323 AC)

"I have just arrived, Grand Admiral. I would have requested an audience by the usual forms, but the messages I carry cannot wait." The Highborn's voice was arrogant, even as it was clear she was trying to control it in the presence of so powerful a figure as Tesserax. They were both of the Firstborn, of course, the title given to the first and original group of Highborn to come into being. She was almost four centuries of age, as were all of the Firstborn, Tesserax included. Their ranks were different, his perhaps the higher, save for the fact that she had been sent by the Supreme Leader himself, his holiness, Ellerax, and in a sense, she carried his words. And she had brought a stern warning for the commander of the forces in the old imperial sectors.

"I am at your disposal, Seliax. I await any words and counsel you have to offer." It seemed that perhaps Tesserax was hiding his own resentment, and doing so with some degree of success. Seliax knew the admiral far too well, however, to imagine he welcomed her advice, or the communications she bore.

She didn't care, either. If her communiques—and orders—upset the pompous admiral, then so be it.

"His holiness, Supreme Commander Ellerax is not pleased, Admiral. The return to imperial space, the long-awaited cleansing and reclamation of these ancient star systems, was instigated at your urging, and that of your allies at Supreme Command. The need for more thralls, and the benefit of integrating the extensive and varied DNA lines present in these sectors is clear, and yet, many on the Command Council wonder now, about the timing. It is said that you and your officers sought a chance to aggrandize yourselves with victory over the humans, that personal vanity rather than cold reason and strategy was behind the timing. Surely, the rim ward systems of the old empire would eventually have been integrated into the Domain of the Highborn, and the humans broken to our will and given the chance to worship those who are gods among them. But was the timing appropriate? The new source of Thralls is necessary, certainly, but could it not have waited? The Domains face a far deadlier enemy than the humans, as you well know. Was it the fact that you have not been granted a command on the primary front that urged you to agitate for the invasion of the old empire, to create a leadership position for yourself? Worse, perhaps, you executed the initial attack so poorly that you were compelled to request frontline reinforcements. An operation to bolster our war effort with fresh Thralls has instead become a drain, diverting main battle units from the primary front. Your operation has hardly been crowned with success, Tesserax, and the Supreme Leader is concerned."

She could see that Tesserax was seething, his arrogance and anger swirling into a toxic brew. But he was controlling himself, despite her best efforts to provoke him. That was good. Despite the harshness of her words, she was fond of Tesserax, and she possessed as much primitive affection for him as she did for anyone. But her instructions had been clear. She had come to test him. The Highborn were highly advanced, a new race born to rule. But arrogance was endemic among its members, and it had caused problems more than once. No one expected Tesserax to be humble, nor to understate his own considerable abilities. But it was essential that he conduct his command with a level of cold reason and control.

"I maintain my position, Seliax, that it is precisely because of the primary threat, and the vast war on the coreward front, that our return to old imperial space could no longer be delayed. It was a grave error allowing a century to pass after our initial reconnaissance before committing to this operation. The humans are ours, by right and succession. They are our followers, our worshippers. They exist to serve the Domains, and to aid us in their own limited ways to assert dominance over the galaxy."

"I am pleased to hear your words, Tesserax, as I am sure the Supreme Leader will be. He does not contest your belief that we need fresh Thralls to feed the true war effort, and there is little question that the cultivated specimens have underperformed and continue to decline in quality. The ranks must be replenished, and the survivors of rimward imperial space are likely to exhibit endurance and learning abilities well in excess of our farm-raised specimens." She paused. "But, and I cannot state this clearly enough, you must complete your conquest with the forces currently at your disposal. The Supreme Leader has sent you the vessels you requested, but any additional transfer of forces would severely jeopardize our position on the primary front, and is out of question. Is that understood?"

"It is understood, Seliax. You may assure the Supreme Leader that I will see it done. The rimward and Far Rim sectors will be pacified, and the billions of humans inhabiting these many hundreds of worlds will learn to serve and to worship us as their pantheon of gods."

"I am certain he will be relieved to hear that, Grand Admiral Tesserax, but I will have to send your words back by communique. My orders are to remain here, and assist you in any way possible."

"I do not need a minder!" Tesserax's control faltered for an instant, but he regained his composure almost immediately. "It is not necessary that you remain, Seliax."

"It is indeed necessary, Grand Admiral, if for no other reason than the Supreme Leader wills it. My instructions leave no room for latitude."

Tesserax still looked uncomfortable, but he bowed his head and said simply, "All hail Ellerax, First of the Firstborn, Supreme Leader of the Domains."

"All hail Ellerax, First of the Firstborn, Supreme Leader of the Domains." Seliax repeated Tesserax's words, obeying the forms, as the admiral had.

*   *   *

"All forces are to proceed to designated jump points, and assume their specified positions. The combined fleets will jump in precisely thirty-four hours, and launch simultaneous assaults on the Hegemony capital world." Tesserax sat in the middle of *S'Argevon*'s main control center, his elevated platform placing him above the main deck. He had initially planned to approach the Hegemony home system more slowly, allow additional time to scout and to plan his attack with more meticulous attention to detail. But Seliax's arrival placed pressure on him. He didn't dare show a lack of confidence in front of her, appear to be intimidated by an enemy his superiors on the Command Council considered weak and outmatched.

Still, he was nervous, uncertain, and it took considerable effort to hide it. He had been surprised by the ferocity with which the humans had fought, and he was anxious to force the decisive battle before Ellerax and the high command could change their minds and withdraw the heavy frontline units he'd been given.

The heavy battleships would be a surprise to the enemy, certainly, and Tesserax was sure they would give him sufficient strength to prevail. Perhaps more crucially, he was far from certain he could successfully complete the conquest without the reinforcements. At least not without suffering crippling losses.

He didn't know if the enemy would fight to the end, if the war, against the Hegemony at least, would end at Calpharon, or if the humans would give up their capital and pull back what surviving forces they could. But he knew he had to inflict as much damage as possible. He would lose the large battleships eventually, that was almost a certainty. The instant things heated up in the main theater, the heavy forces would be withdrawn…and he wanted to be facing a heavily degraded human force by then. He had considerable power under his command just then, and he was determined to make the best use of it while he could. One more reason to avoid any delay.

He stared out across the control center. The room was filled with Thralls, primitive humans. The Thralls had originally been much like those facing his forces, but generations of captivity and farm-breeding had allowed the quality of the stock to wither. The flagship's crew was atypical, drawn from the very best, but across the Domain's vast military establishment, the decline in quality had become problematic. That was one reason

Tesserax had been in the forefront of the movement to initiate the invasion and subjugation of the surviving free humans immediately.

There were other motives as well, of course. His victory would almost certainly lead to his desired appointment as sector governor, and then he could see to the harvesting of fresh humans to fill the ranks of the Thralls. He would not make the mistakes of the past, reducing the spirited, wild humans to passive and caged farm animals. The Domains needed soldiers to feed the war machine, and the Highborn needed worshippers who could serve, not useless and pathetic followers who were little more than pets. He would crush the civilizations present on the human worlds, of course, and reduce their populations to scattered, warring groups. But he would not cage them. Their constant infighting and struggles to survive on shattered worlds would maintain their abilities, and enhance the quality of the gene pool as only the strongest and most capable survived and bred.

Operations were running smoothly, on the flagship, and a check on his displays showed it was the same across the fleet. Most of the Thralls assigned to naval duty were well broken, trained to obey and to respect those who were as gods to them. But they all wore the Collars as well, the surgical implants that assured blind obedience. Many others showed signs of different enhancements, various mechanical and electronic devices protruding from their bodies, and aiding in the completion of their assigned tasks. *S'Argevon*'s Thralls, especially those posted to control room duty, were of the highest order of ability, though to Tesserax and his brethren, they were still little above mindless animals. They served a purpose, but the place they had once held in the universe during the apex of the old empire, had been taken by their betters.

"Great Tesserax, all scanner reports are clear. No sign

of any enemy forces, but…"

"But? Speak. I would hear your thoughts."

"Great Tesserax, there are extensive asteroid fields in this system, as well as a number of massive dust clouds. It is impossible to complete a thorough and reliable sensor sweep without launching a large array of probes and waiting until they can…"

"No." Tesserax's voice was loud, the single word he'd uttered definitive.

"Yes, Great Tesserax, as you command."

Tesserax showed no doubt in front of the Thralls, no hesitation. Such would be unthinkable. But he knew the human officer was correct. Under normal circumstances, he would never rush through the system and into battle in the next, not without scanning every cubic meter of space between his fleet and its destination. But he didn't have the time. It had taken far too long for his request for reinforcements to be approved by Ellerax, and for the additional ships to reach his theater of operations. There was simply no more room for delay. If he did not show he was making good use of the frontline units, he would certainly lose them that much sooner.

A thought passed through his mind, vague and transitory, a realization that the Thrall had given wise counsel. For an instant, he wondered if he should speak, should praise the human, even explain why he had rejected the officer's advice.

But only for an instant. His mind quickly scoffed at the thought of giving praise to a Thrall for offering nothing more than an obvious suggestion, and even more forcefully, at the insane notion that he would explain *anything* to a Thrall. The humans existed to serve and to worship. Their continued existence was sufficient sign of Highborn favor.

Still, Tesserax felt nervous, edgy. He was confident his

forces could take the enemy capital, but he was a little worried about the losses they might suffer. He usually didn't care about such trivialities, but it would be difficult to explain heavy casualties, particularly among the main battleline units. The humans had limited technology and ability, but he was rushing his own attack, sacrificing the meticulous care he usually put into everything he did.

There is no point to worry. There is no choice, nothing to be gained by excess concern. It is time to fight the climactic battle, the crush the humans.

The Hegemony was by far the strongest of the Rim and Near Rim polities. Once they were crushed, the others would surely fall in turn. Whether the entire enemy force was annihilated in the next several days, or some battered force limped away, the war would, for all intents and purposes, end at Calpharon.

And the Domains would enjoy a massive influx of Thralls, billions upon billions of fresh and energetic humans to fill the ranks.

*   *   *

Yes, come…come this way.

Jake Stockton watched the enemy ships approaching. He didn't have any detailed analysis, only the limited information his passive scanners could provide, but even that had twisted his guts into knots, and turned the inside of his survival suit into a sweat-soaked mess. He had come up with the idea, the plan now underway, and he had fought to sell it to Admiral Barron. The admiral understood as well as Stockton himself did, just how dangerous, how utterly insane an operation it was. The odds were long, and the likelihood of more than a token of the committed force escaping back to Calpharon's system seemed almost nil. But the overall situation was no less desperate than Stockton's wild scheme...and if the enemy continued on their current line of approach, and didn't pause to initiate a more detailed scanning operation, it was just possible those losses would not be in vain.

Stockton knew his wings faced a nightmare in the coming battle, no matter how they were deployed. They had no way to hurt the Highborn save to close to point blank range. The enemy's strange hulls, and their ships' use of Sigma-9 energy waves, made securing long-range firelocks almost impossible, at least for a vessel as small as a bomber. Some progress had been made on the heavier vessels, adjustments to their large and powerful scanner arrays to compensate and improve locking capabilities. But a bomber was too small to carry the equipment needed, and that left only one choice...coming in to knife-fighting range.

Right through volleys of the enemy's deadly new cluster missiles.

Stockton hadn't solved *that* problem, at least not on an ongoing basis. But he'd come up with a gamble, a way to launch at least one truly devastating attack on the Highborn fleet. If everything worked just right.

So far, it all seemed to be going just as he'd hoped. If the enemy continued on without pausing for intensive scans, if all his ships remained hidden in the asteroid fields, if no errant energy leak or a single pilot's carelessness gave them away...then just maybe, he'd give the Highborn invaders a surprise, and one hell of a rough handling. He still wasn't sure how many of his ships would escape after, but if they could offer up some damaged and battered enemy ships to their comrades waiting in Sigma Nordlin, it would be worth almost any sacrifice. All the more because his wings would be gutted wherever they fought. If his people were going to die—if he was going to die—he was determined that it would be for something.

He took a deep breath, holding it for a moment as his mind counted down. Twenty more minutes until the enemy closed to the attack point. It wasn't long by objective standards, but he could remember some similar time periods that dragged on interminably. He suspected those old memories were due for an upgrade, and he girded himself to endure a wait that looked to feel like an eternity.

Nineteen minutes, forty seconds…and each instant was passing almost like a lifetime, his stomach tightening a bit more every time the chronometer blinked off another second.

Chapter Nine

Alliante Parish
Planet Sebastiani, Alexara III
Year 323 AC (After the Cataclysm)

"Your home is beautiful, Sy, truly. I am very happy you ended up someplace so quiet and peaceful." Andi was being completely honest, at least about the beauty of Sy's surroundings. Alliante Parish was a magnificent display of nature's magnificence, gentle rolling hillsides covered with grapes and olives, with half a dozen small rivers winding through its forty thousand square kilometers. Sy's house was small, but it appeared more than comfortable for her needs, and the patch of nearly one hundred hectares of land surrounding it was nothing short of paradise.

Andi was relieved that her friend had found the peace and solitude she'd left to seek, though she knew the truth was far more complex. Calmness of surroundings were all well and good, but the fact that Vig knew of at least four places Sy had lived since leaving *Nightrunner* suggested that true inner peace had proven rather elusive. Nightmares came regardless of trees and streams and gentle breezes.

Andi understood that. She had everything, by almost

anyone's standards, at least she had before Tyler had been compelled to leave for a new war, but she'd never shaken the demons, the cold darkness from her past that still haunted her. She woke up some nights drenched in sweat, shouting out until she realized she wasn't in some ancient imperial ruin or Sector Nine torture cell. Some wounds simply never healed. Andi had finally accepted that, and in that realization she had found peace of a sort. But she found it more difficult to extend that same rational analysis to others she cared about.

"Thank you, Andi." Sylene stood about a meter away, and even as she spoke, she stepped forward and hugged Andi again. Her friend's affection both eased and inflamed her inner turmoil. She was happy to see Sy well, and grateful for the apparent lack of resentment toward her, but the guilt was still there, digging at her with the constant reminder that she hadn't even bothered to check to see where Sy was all these years.

"It is wonderful to see you. Those days on *Nightrunner* were some of the best of my life..." Sy stepped back, and her face darkened somewhat. "...and the worst. We lost some good friends back then. Sometimes, I still can't believe Captain Lorillard is gone. I wake up and for a few seconds, I think I'm back on the ship, that he's just down the corridor."

Andi felt the words slicing into her like a blade. Captain Lorillard had given her a chance when no one else would. For all the difficulty and struggle she'd faced in her life, she knew she'd been fortunate to encounter some extraordinary people. The captain had definitely been one of those.

"I miss the captain, too, Sy. He was an amazing person, and he died far too young." Andi looked down at the floor for a few seconds, but then she regrouped and remembered why she had come. "Sy, I wish I could say I was here for a long overdue visit with an old friend, but I can't. I need your help with something."

"Of course, Andi...I'll do anything I can. What is it?"

Andi reached into the small sack she'd carried slung over her back. She pulled the old folio out and set it down on a table half a meter from where she was standing. "I found this, Sy. On a mission. After you'd left the ship. It's a set of data chips...imperial data chips. I think they were well-preserved when I found them, but we had a bit of a scrap trying to get out of the system, and I'm afraid they got a heavy dose of radiation. I took them to someone I knew on Dannith, and he couldn't retrieve any of the data. But he wasn't you, Sy. Not even close."

"It's been a long time, Andi. I barely touch computers these days, and I haven't tried to hack my way into anything since...well, since I left *Nightrunner*." A pause. "But I'll try. Give me a couple days. You're welcome to stay if you'd like. The place isn't huge, but I do have a couple of spare bedrooms."

"I appreciate the invitation, Sy, but I've got to get back to the ship."

"That's right. Vig told me you were a mother now. Cassiopeia, right? Is she here, on Sebastiani?"

"Yes, she's on the ship. That's why I have to get back. But I'll leave all this with you."

"I'll get on this right away, Andi. I can't promise anything, but I'll see if I can extract at least something. Radiation damage can be tough, but imperial chips have sophisticated shielding. There's a good chance I'll be able to get some data. Call it 50-50."

"Thank you so much, Sy."

"My pleasure, Andi. My mind's been idle for too long. This will be good for me." A pause, and then she hugged

Andi for a third time. "And it *is* good to see you, old friend."

"It is good to see you, too." Andi tightened her own grip on her friend, even as a single tear escaped from her eye.

* * *

"She's beautiful, Andi. I can't believe you're a mother. No offense, but I doubt any of us who knew you back in the day would have predicted this."

Andi managed a thin smile. "I don't think anyone could have predicted the road I've traveled, both for good and ill. But here I am. And here is Cassiopeia."

"And you're married to Tyler Barron...*the* Tyler Barron. The hero of the Union War and the Hegemony War."

"Yes, I'm very fortunate in that. Something else I imagine was unpredictable, especially considering I thought he was an officious pain in the ass when I first met him. But none of us were too fond of navy types back then, were we?"

"No, that's for sure. Still, I imagine there's quite a difference between Admiral Barron and some career junior officer spending his time chasing Badlands prospectors and petty smugglers."

Andi just nodded. The talk of Barron just reminded her of the fact that he was hundreds of lightyears away...and that, despite her best efforts to be optimistic, she didn't really believe he would return to her this time. She told herself it was her mind playing tricks, punishing her for not being up at the front where she belonged. She felt motherly instincts to protect Cassiopeia, but the other side of her mind argued that the surest way to secure her daughter's future was to win the current war.

"*Pegasus*, eh? I like it. I mean, she'll always be *Nightrunner* to me, but it's her spirit that really matters, not her name. And she's a special old ship, isn't she?"

"Yes, she is." It had taken Andi some time to get used to the name change, but the years and the adventures that followed had branded *Pegasus* into her mind. *Nightrunner* had been Captain Lorillard's ship, and it was part of her past now, as he was, something that lived on in fond and beloved memories. "She's been through a lot since you left. She's *Pegasus* now, and that name has its own history, one I like to think would have made the captain proud."

"He was always proud of you, Andi."

Andi was silent for a moment, fighting back the burst of emotion and tears Sy's last statement threatened to unleash. "I hope so," she finally managed to mutter.

There was a moment of silence, and then Andi said, "So, were you able to decipher anything from the data chips?" The past was calling to her, images of people important to her, people who were no longer there. But there was nothing she could do for a time and for people who were gone, no way she could save Captain Lorillard or Gregor, or any of those close to her now long lost. She might be able to do something to help save the present, though. Especially if Sy was able to retrieve any data on the Highborn.

"It was very difficult, Andi. The damage is considerable. If these were Confederation chips, they'd be garbage. But old imperial data units are a lot more sophisticated. There *is* some remaining data on them, I'm sure of that, but I can't say how much. It is very time consuming to retrieve it and rebuild the sequences, especially since my old imperial is pretty damned creaky. But I have managed to pull out some information, and I think you will find it is extraordinary. It's a damned good thing you saved this stuff, Andi. If I keep working at it, I just might be able to come up with some useful data. Certainly some things that will change our view of imperial times."

Andi felt a wave of excitement. She'd hoped Sy would be able to do something, but she was always cautious about her expectations. "That's amazing, Sy. Thank you so much for all your efforts. What were you able to decode so far?"

"Well, Andi…it seems the Highborn were known in imperial times. It's all pretty incredible, really…"

Andros Estate
Planet Samara
Tirion Vega System
Year 11,687 IR (Imperial Reckoning)
Year 47 BC (Before the Cataclysm) by Confederation Calendar
370 Years Ago

"My grandfather was the first to truly recognize the rot, the decay, that has infected the empire…or at least, he was the first to do something about it. We all see it, we have long known the vitality that led our forefathers to achieve all they did has been bred out. Our people were once heroes, men and women who took to the stars, who fought and bled, and forged an empire. Today they are listless and unfocused, and untold billions look only to the imperial support that sustains their meager existences. But even that is in peril. A treasury once filled by expansion, conquest, and industry, is now dry and empty. And the descendants of those who built all we revere spend their time on pointless amusements and petty squabbles over superficial nonsense. With each passing generation, fewer and fewer of our people know how to do anything useful. They consume, but they do not produce, and the empire declines." The man standing in front of the small assemblage was tall, and he was clad in the shimmering silky material then in fashion among the empire's elites. His coat seemed to constantly change colors, as the slightest shift in angle to the light sources altered the reflective image.

"We all know of the empire's problems, Andros. Indeed, I struggle to keep my own estates running at even half of the productivity my grandfather was able to extract. The empire is clearly in decline, perhaps approaching a grave state of decay. But the problem is not to identify the crisis. It is to determine what is to be done about it."

"You are correct, Belthas, truly. And thus was the question my father asked himself more than three decades ago. Unlike so many among our once vibrant nobility, he was determined to do something to arrest the decline, no to reverse it. He even obtained imperial support for his efforts, and a classification order from the emperor himself to maintain secrecy and to avoid interference. Though, I daresay, the reports to the throne were…edited…somewhat, to avoid harmful political interference."

The men and women gathered in the room, fourteen of the highest-ranking nobles of the empire, stared right at Andros. He had captured their curiosity, if not yet their support, though more than a few seemed a bit on edge at his talk of withholding information from imperial oversight.

It was time, a moment he'd been preparing his entire life to face.

He waited a moment before continuing. It was a turning point, perhaps the most dangerous step since his late grandfather had first told him of the great effort, and set him on an unalterable course to save the empire…from itself.

He pressed a small button on the table, and a moment later, a figure stepped into the room. He appeared to be human at first, but then, as he stepped into the light, it became clear he was somehow…different. He was taller than any human being, certainly, over two and a half meters. He was bipedal, and the most obvious difference from human norms was his size. He was muscular, and his eyes almost glowed with a vibrant blue-gray color, utterly different in some seemingly unfathomable way from anything those present had ever seen.

Finally, the man who had spoken previously turned his eyes from the new arrival to his host. "Who is this, Andros? And, perhaps more importantly, *what* is he?"

Andros looked out over the assembled group of nobles, and he smiled.

"Allow me to introduce you to Ellerax, of the Highborn."

Chapter Ten

The Citadel
Planet Calpharon (Hegemonic Capital)
Sigma Nordlin IV
Year of Renewal 268 (323 AC)

"Thank you for coming, Tyler." Chronos stood just inside the door. The silo, and that was the best word Barron could come up with to describe the strange cylindrical structure, was impressive. But he suspected he was seeing only the smallest part of what Chronos was about to show him.

"Of course, Chronos. I am always available when you need me." There was still an air of discomfort between the two former enemies, but they'd been doing all they could to overcome it. The deliberate use of first names was part of that, but so far, at least as far as Barron was concerned, it just felt stilted and uncomfortable.

"Well, I do have a legitimate purpose for meeting with you, but it joins nicely with a chance to show you a place we call the Citadel. It is mostly underground, of course, built nearly a century ago, when the Hegemony seemed less secure than…it did until recently." Barron caught the hitch in Chronos' speech. There was no doubt the

Masters had become accustomed to feeling a sense of security in the vast interstellar polity they'd created, but the very fact that Barron was there with his forces, helping to prepare a last ditch effort to defend the capital, was definitive evidence that, whatever kind of golden age the Hegemony had experienced, it was over.

"I will be most curious to see it." Barron didn't really care that much. He'd seen the ratholes political leaders had built for themselves before, and he found the whole thing distasteful. If such a place truly became useful, it would probably mean that he, and all his spacers—and Chronos and Ilius, too, unless he'd badly misread them—would be already dead in the fighting. He was ready to die for what he believed in, to save his people, for those he loved…but not so much to buy time for political leaders to scramble to some refuge.

"No, you won't." Chronos looked concerned, as though he'd allowed less politic words escape from his lips, but Barron settled the Hegemony Master's concerns almost immediately.

He did that by laughing.

"I'm afraid you're right, Chronos. I'm less than fascinated by where those who don't fight will be hiding while the rest of us are dying."

Chronos laughed in his own turn. "We agree on that, Tyler…for the most part. Though, there are those I would see safe while we fight, and no doubt there are those back on the Rim you would not have exposed to danger." Barron didn't reply, he just nodded. He'd been miserable without Andi, without a chance to see his daughter, but there was cause there for gratitude, as well. As much as he wanted to see them both, he would rather have them home, as safe as they could be.

He'd spent an enormous amount of time and effort during past confrontations, trying—almost always unsuccessfully—to keep Andi out of danger. She was a challenging woman to love, but of course, if she'd been anything different, she wouldn't have affected him as she had.

"Still, Tyler...if it helps your morale to consider this, if we are defeated, the Council members and others who take refuge down here will likely be dragged out of their refuge by the invading enemy...or simply incinerated in place. The specifications of this structure boast that it can survive a surface attack even with antimatter weapons, but that won't be of any help if the planet has fallen and the victorious invaders are here sending burrowing bunker busters against the place."

"There is no safety for anyone, none save victory." Barron had spoken variations of the same thing many times before, and as much as any single sentence, it encapsulated his core view. He'd retreated at times to fight another day, of course, but he never fooled himself when there was an enemy or a danger that had to be faced.

"No, there is not. But I asked you here for more than simply to show off my people's finest—what do you call such things, rathole?"

"Yes, rathole. And my people are quite good at building them, as well." A few seconds later: "Something else?"

"Yes...I have a project underway, and I have placed the prime movers, along with their immense databases, in this facility. It serves all of us to keep them as safe as possible."

Barron's eyes widened. "You have piqued my interest."

"Then come with me, and we will satisfy your newfound curiosity." Chronos gestured for Barron to follow, and the two men, each accompanied by two guards, a pair of Bryan Rogan's veteran Marines in Barron's case, entered a large elevator. The escorts had been mandated by the respective governmental authorities, though Barron was sure Chronos didn't like it any more than he did. The Council could argue with Chronos with all the apparent gusto the Senate was capable of directing at Barron himself, but it was clear that both assemblages of political leaders were too scared at the threat of the Highborn to risk their top commanders…or to fire them.

What do they think, the two of us are going to fight it out on the way down if we don't have minders?

Barron stood quietly, even as the car continued to drop. The rolling in his stomach told him the elevator was far from slow, and the time the descent took suggested wherever they were headed was many kilometers below the surface. He was impressed. Whatever kind of refuge the Hegemony Council had built for itself, it had clearly spared no expense. Barron was no engineer, but he knew excavation got *very* expensive when it was tens of thousands of meters below the surface.

Finally, the car came to a stop, and the doors opened. The room beyond was large, much bigger than Barron had expected. It was plush, too, looking more like the entry to a luxury hotel or opulent office building than a glorified bomb shelter.

"Very nice."

"It is a grotesque display of misused resources, which is how you really feel. I am afraid my people are less different than I might have hoped in that regard. Those in charge, who sit in the halls of power, want not only personal safety, they want luxury. But, please, let us continue. I am anxious for you to meet Professor Ellia." The two moved swiftly down a wide corridor until Chronos stopped in front of a large double door. He tapped the panel next to the entry, and the hatch slid open.

"Professor, I trust you are well. I have brought someone to see you. This is Tyler Barron, the supreme commander of the Rim forces. I would like you to update him on your work, and its status. Please, tell him anything you would me."

Barron noted Chronos's words, and his initial cynical thought that such a statement could have been well staged gave way almost immediately to belief. Barron was far from sure he could tell if Chronos was lying, but he was ready to bet on his analysis just then, and on his comrade's sincerity.

"Admiral Barron, it is a great pleasure to meet you. I am Ellia. I am, was at least, before this project consumed by every waking moment—and more than a few of my dreams as well—the director of the Capital University."

The woman speaking, and who had turned toward Barron, looked very young to be so accomplished an academic. Then, after a few more seconds, he realized that she was older than he'd thought at first. She was simply very well-preserved. Barron disliked the Hegemony's system of genetic hierarchy, but he couldn't argue that, superficially at least, the Masters did tend to look stronger and healthier—and to age more slowly—than any population he'd seen elsewhere.

"Professor, the pleasure is mine."

'Please, call me Ellia. I can assure you, Admiral, I did not support the war against your people. I understand the Council's motivations, and certainly believe that almost anything could be justified to prevent a recurrence of the immense death and suffering that followed the empire's fall. But my life's work has taught me, more than anything, that we do not know as much as we think we do. About the nations on the Rim…and about our current enemy."

Barron's interest was inflamed by her last comment. "Please continue, Ellia. And, I am Tyler."

The woman nodded. "Thank you, Tyler. Well, where to begin…" She turned and glanced down at her workstation. "Number Eight—Master Chronos—assigned me with the task of implementing a comprehensive search of all Hegemonic records of the empire, and of imperial times, looking for any indications of encounters with our current, and heretofore mysterious, enemy."

Barron turned and looked over at Chronos. He cursed himself for not thinking of that very thing. He knew almost nothing about the Highborn, about what they were or where they had come from, but suddenly, checking to see if the empire had ever encountered them seemed like a glaringly obvious course of action. He would send back a request to the Senate to do just that as soon as he returned to *Dauntless*.

"Would I be skipping too far ahead to ask if you have discovered anything?"

"Certainly not, Adm…Tyler. What question could be more crucial right now? But my answer may seem elusive. Simply put, I *believe* we have indeed found mentions of them, but as yet, no real data, certainly not of their origin."

Barron looked at Chronos again, and then back to Ellia. "You mean the empire encountered the Highborn? Were they defeated by imperial forces? Was there conflict?" Barron could feel the questions forcing their way to his lips almost faster than he could utter them. "Did the imperial military have tactics for facing the threat?"

"I am sorry, Tyler. I know how desperately we need those answers, but as yet, I do not have them. The scarcity of references to the Highborn suggests that any data existing about them was highly classified. It was only last week that my team was able to decisively ascertain that there were, in fact, references that likely referred to our present enemy. Much of what we found was in an obscure dialect of Old Imperial. I'm afraid the translations are extremely slow, and perhaps not entirely accurate. But I believe I can say with some degree of confidence that the empire *was* aware of the threat. I am hopeful we will eventually find additional data, perhaps even regarding the defensive measures taken at the time."

"I understand the difficulty of your work, Ellia, but we probably have very little time. 'Eventually' may be far too late." Barron's mind was just where he knew Ellia's was, and Chronos's too. *Did the Highborn play a role in the final imperial decline?*

In the Cataclysm?

"I know, Tyler, I know. We are doing everything possible to accelerate our efforts. I wish I could tell you more, even give you an estimate on when we may have further information. All I can say right now is that the imperial name for the enemy was similar to our own. They were called the 'Highborn' then as well, and we have also found references to something slightly different, a term we have translated as meaning, 'Firstborn,' though we have no information regarding whether the two are the same, or what differences there may be between them."

"Were they an enemy? Did the empire fight them? Or were they at peace back in imperial times?" Barron knew Ellia didn't have the answers, but the questions came out again anyway.

"We will endeavor to find out. All we have been able to determine is that, while it appears there was some kind of strife related to the Highborn, it does not appear the empire was at full-scale war with some alien enemy. We have a fair quantity of preserved military records and communications, and there is no evidence of any significant external conflict, no real warfare at all until the beginnings of the Great Death. There was considerable unrest in the decades before the collapse accelerated, and the empire responded with increasingly harsh reprisals, but nothing more, at least not that we've been able to discern. We have almost nothing from the subsequent time, the final two or three decades of the empire, the period we call the Great Death, and you the Cataclysm."

Barron shook his head. He'd found it difficult enough to accept that the Hegemony had encountered some hostile and previously unknown alien race. It made more sense that the empire had encountered the enemy first, but then the question was, why had there been no war? The Highborn seemed inveterately hostile, ignoring all communications efforts. Was the empire simply too powerful to attack, even in its waning years? Or was there something he and his allies just didn't know?

"Ellia, I am going to issue orders to my staff to provide you with every bit of data we have on the old empire. Some of our people specialized in exploring the imperial ruins in the space between the Hegemony and the Rim, an area of space we call, the 'Badlands.'" Barron felt a wave of sadness. Andi had been one of the elite of that group, a legendary Badlands explorer, if one who'd bent the rules on more than a few occasions. He'd ached enough missing her, but now he realized she might be a major asset to the war effort, and for once without diving headlong into a half-suicidal battle of some kind. He couldn't imagine what Ellia could do with Andi's stories, and with whatever scraps of imperial artifacts she'd kept hidden over the years. He'd never really discussed it with her, but while he knew she'd sold most of what her people had found, he suspected she still had a stash or two hidden somewhere.

"That would be greatly appreciated, Tyler. We have a considerable database of imperial dialects, history, and scientific documentation. I mean no disrespect to your people on the Rim, but it is very likely we will be able to learn more from such artifacts and information."

"No offense taken, Ellia. Sadly, my people have only expressed interest in items that offered short term technological gain. I'm ashamed to say, there has been little interest on the Rim for uncovering imperial history and lore. It has always been surprising to me how little interest most people have in where they came from." Barron felt very much like the Rim barbarian many of those in the Hegemony no doubt still considered him. His life had been mostly occupied with training and conflict, but, though his spacers had fought for worlds and territory, there had been little enough effort to gather knowledge for its own sake.

"Perhaps, together we can unravel some of the mysteries…and discover exactly what our enemy is, and where they came from."

"Yes, perhaps. I will give the orders as soon as I leave here. And, please, if there is anything you need, any way to aid you in your work, you have only to ask."

Barron turned toward Chronos, and he nodded. He knew, as he was sure his counterpart did, the value of information in war. The more they knew about the enemy, the better chance they had to find a way to endure the onslaught, even to defeat the invader.

That was a crucial, because Barron knew, as things stood just then, his people and their Kriegeri allies would fight hard, battle with resolve and courage…but, in the end, they would lose. The enemy was just too powerful to defeat.

Unless Ellia and her people could come up with some answers, a weakness or a way to defeat the Highborn...before the enemy subjugated every system from Sigma Nordlin to the galaxy's edge.

Chapter Eleven

Asteroid Field
Vexa Torrent System (One Jump from Sigma Nordlin)
Year 323 AC (After the Cataclysm)

Jake Stockton watched the enemy fleet move steadily forward. It was vast, far larger than the force the Hegemony and Confederation fleets had engaged at Ettara-Mordlin. Stockton tried not to think too deeply about the fact that the smaller enemy fleet had won that battle, that the closest to success the combined Hegemony-Confederation force that fought there had come was escaping with heavy losses. Avoiding annihilation was unquestionably preferable to the alternative, but it was hardly the stuff of victory.

Now we're looking at twice as many ships, maybe more. And fifty of those monsters...

He'd had a hard time pulling his eyes away from the enemy battleships. He had no idea what weapons they mounted, how deadly their fire would be against the Hegemonic and Confed ships of the line, but he knew just what they could do to his bomber squadrons.

Be patient…wait for the battleships to get close…

He had to hit the giant battleships…he had to hit them as hard as he could. But waiting meant letting the lighter lead vessels get closer, even to pass the places his wings were hiding. Every second that went by risked detection.

But Stockton waited. He was twisted in knots, and his muscles ached. He could only imagine how badly he stank to anyone who hadn't been sitting for days in Jake Stockton's recycled sweat. The forward scouts had given some idea of when the enemy would arrive in the system, but he'd needed to have his people in place and hidden before a single enemy ship transited. That meant getting there days early.

But fighters weren't designed for extended periods of operation. Anya Fritz had worked up the ejectable life support pods, yet another miracle conjured by the fleet's legendary engineer. That had increased the time a fighter could keep a pilot alive, but the problem of maintaining his people's sanity as they sat for days in their cramped cockpits, fed intravenously and contorting themselves wildly to attend to bodily functions, had been Stockton's alone. He'd managed to use a few modified freighters as makeshift landing platforms, so that a few dozen of his pilots at a time could get out of their ships and walk around for an hour or two, but beyond that, he'd resorted to tranquilizers…and to very strong amphetamines ready to counter their effect, ready to go on a moment's notice to bring his people back to maximum alertness.

He'd given the injection order half an hour before. His pilots were wide awake now, in their ships and waiting. Hell, he suspected most of them were crawling the walls…or what passed for walls. He needed them as alert as possible, though he knew, as wired as they all were after the heavy doses they'd received, many would get themselves killed through recklessness.

He'd have tortured himself about that, save for the fact that he didn't believe more than a handful of them were going to get back anyway. All that mattered was hitting the enemy battleships hard before they transited. He had two thousand fighters with him, an immense force by any standards. But there were four thousand more waiting in Sigma Nordlin…and if he could wear down the enemy battleships, they just might be able to make a difference in the fight to come.

He saw the lead enemy vessels beginning to move past the asteroid field. They were avoiding the navigational hazard, of course, just as Stockton had hoped they would. But they were still close. He found himself holding his breath, as if that could have any effect on whether the Highborn scanners detected his ship or not.

He felt the urge to give the command, to blast out of the small concentration of asteroids with the reinforced wing positioned all around his ship. That would be the signal to the others, to more than one hundred squadrons hiding all around, across sixty thousand kilometers of rock and dust filled space.

But he held. He needed to hit those battleships. And they were still ten minutes out.

Ten minutes was a short time, almost nothing. But it passed by glacially, even as more and more enemy ships moved by, heading toward the transit point. Stockton knew what was happening on the other side, seven lightyears and yet only a few seconds distant. Transit point three was the likeliest one for the enemy attack, the most fortified and defended approach. There was relief in that, at least, that the enemy was coming the way Barron and the other commanders had guessed. But Stockton saw the other side, the strength of the enemy, and their obvious belief that they had no need to search for longer, less well-defended routes. They clearly believed they could smash their way through any defenses that awaited them, and Stockton suspected that arrogance was also nothing but the cold truth.

But maybe we can give them something they're not expecting...

He'd been worried the enemy would scout the system thoroughly. They were a single jump from the enemy capital, and the system was one almost perfectly laid out for an ambush. But time seemed more important to the Highborn than caution...and Stockton was less than three minutes from the chance to make them regret that choice.

He looked at his screen, at the roughly one hundred ships formed up just around his fighter. They were close, insanely close by normal standards, and he could see at least a dozen of them with his own eyes. They would spread out when he gave the word, move toward a more normal dispersion pattern. And when they emerged from the cover of the asteroid field, the rest of his force, most of it so well hidden that his passive scanners revealed nothing, would follow his lead. They would blast out from their cover and launch desperate attacks on the enemy battleships.

Stockton didn't know if the cluster missiles had an effective minimum range, but his people would be almost at point blank range from the start. They would close in just minutes, and what defensive response they endured largely depended on enemy response times.

One minute.

His hand moved to his controls, but he did nothing. He would be crash starting his reactor, as would all his people. It was a dangerous move, one that would cost him 3-4% of his force almost immediately, at least according to AI projections. But there was no choice. His ships would never have remained hidden for so long if their reactors had been powered up. And stealth was the only thing that had kept them alive so long.

He pressed his finger down slowly on a small button to the side of his panel. He heard a pinging sound in his cockpit, and he knew the signal he'd initiated had gone out. It was short range, designed to simulate a natural occurrence. But the hundred pilots clustered around him in their bombers were waiting for it. And they knew exactly what it meant.

Fire up their reactors.

His fingers moved over his own controls, entering the startup sequence, and flipping the main reactor switch. He held his breath for a few seconds, even as he heard the loud whining sound and felt the cockpit vibrating. If the reactor lost containment, he'd probably never even know it. He'd be vaporized with his ship in an instant. But five seconds later, he was still there…and his power readings were rising steadily.

He grabbed the controls, even as he checked on the other ships. He could see a pair of explosions, two of his less fortunate people obliterated in thermonuclear fury. Another five ships were flashing red on his screen, signifying various levels of malfunction and damage. It didn't really matter how badly hurt the fighters were. Just about any level of damage was a death sentence on the current mission.

He pulled back on the throttle, feeding the accumulating energy into his engines, and he could feel the thrust pushing back on him as the dampeners struggled to compensate for the heavy acceleration. He'd been prepared, though, and he was surprised by the relatively mild intensity of the g forces. The new Black Lightnings were an improvement in almost every area of operation, force maintenance included. He wished his force had more of the new ships in action, but only two hundred of them had so far arrived via the long and tenuous supply line from Confederation space. He'd left half of them back with the forces in Sigma Nordlin, and he had the rest with him in the ambush force. They were only five percent of the total deployed, but he was ready to take any edge he could get.

He angled his vector slightly, increasing the distance between his course and a small group of asteroids. The field had been good cover against scans. The asteroids were rich in heavy and radioactive metals, and his ships had stayed close to them. But now it was time.

Time to do what they'd come to do.

His ship was starting from a dead stop, and even at maximum thrust, his squadrons would be coming in at relatively lower velocities than normal. That was a double edged sword of sorts. It would take longer to close, and give their targets increased reaction time, but his people would benefit from quicker and easier vector changes, increasing the effectiveness of their evasive maneuvers considerably.

He reached down and flipped on the comm unit. By then, he knew, all two thousand of his pilots had fired up their reactors, and probably forty or more had died in thermonuclear explosions. His people had managed to remain hidden longer than he'd dared to hope they could, but that part of the mission was over. The enemy knew they were there…and radio silence no longer served any purpose. His people deserved to hear from him before they went in.

Perhaps for the last time.

"Strike Force Black, this is Admiral Stockton. We have had a long wait, but now our patience has paid off. The enemy is here, and we have caught them flatfooted. I'm not going to waste your time with pointless blather and foolishness. You all know what to do. Let's do the job we came here to do…and the drinks are on me when we get back."

Stockton shook his head as he uttered the last bit. He didn't really believe many of his people would make it back…and those who did would likely be rewarded not with a party in any officer's club, but with a hasty refit and relaunch into what promised to be a deadly struggle around Calpharon. He knew his pilots would do what they had to do, as they had always done, but they didn't need to deal with the cold reality all at once.

His hand was tight on the throttle as he continued to increase his thrust. His eyes were on the scanner, the screen constantly updating as his active scanners pinged away, sorting out the closest targets.

There it was. The one he wanted. One of the big new battleships, almost dead ahead. Less than thirty thousand kilometers from his ship.

He stared down, unmoving, teeth gritting tightly. He felt a moment of normalcy amid the hopelessness of the war. The cockpit, in many ways, was the closest thing to a home he'd ever known. It was where he belonged, and he was about to do what he'd been born to do. Lead his pilots…and kill his enemies.

His feral instincts flared brightly. His people had the edge, only for a fleeting few moments, perhaps, but surprise was definitely their ally.

For the next seconds, for a brief instant of time, his people were the hunters…and it was time to chase down their prey.

Time to kill.

* * *

Reg Griffin's hand was wrapped tightly around the

fighter's controls. She was coming in on one of the lead battleships, and her velocity was increasing with every passing second. Her wing had been on the end of the line, closest to the transit point. That had been bad luck that had seemed superficially good at first. Her people had started closest to escape, but they'd been compelled to accelerate almost directly in-system to attack the enemy. With their vectors almost opposite those of the approaching enemy ships, they were rapidly closing the distance to firing range...and increasing it from their escape route.

Once they had completed their attack, their momentum would take them deeper into the system, farther from the transit back to Sigma Nordlin. Her people would have to decelerate hard before they could even come about, and she wasn't the sort to fool herself about the chances any of them had.

But if they were all doomed, they were damned sure going to extract a price before they died.

"You all heard the admiral. We came here to do a job, and that's the only thing I want any of you thinking about."

And not that we'll all probably be dead in the next hour...

"We've got two targets. Odds are going in with me, against the ship to our starboard. Evens, against that big bastard up front to the port side. And nobody launches until they're damned sure they've got a hard lock...I don't care what these bastards throw at us." Her voice was hard, cold, dripping with venom for the enemy. She'd served under Stockton's command for years, faced Union aces and then led her pilots against the deadly Hegemony battleships. But she'd never been as sure as she was at that moment, that she was battling a foe that would kill or enslave everyone she cared about if they prevailed.

If they got past the fleet. And she was damned sure

going to do everything she could to make sure that didn't happen.

She watched the velocity of her approach increasing, and the range to the target decreasing. She was within twenty thousand kilometers, no, eighteen thousand, when the target ship's defenses opened up. She'd been waiting for—and dreading—the cluster missiles she'd read about in Stockton's reports, but as she watched, it was point defense turrets that opened up first. She felt some relief, though that was quickly diminished, as six of her ninety ships went down almost immediately under the deadly laser fire.

She cursed under her breath, sorrow and anger mixing in her thoughts. At least half of the lost pilots had been sloppy on their evasive maneuvers. They'd gotten careless, no doubt hoping surprise would prevent any enemy fire, at least on their way in. They had been wrong about that, at fault, and she damned sure would give the whole wing a good tongue lashing about it if any of them made it back. But, at fault or not, it cut deeply at her that her pilots had paid for their errors with their lives.

Maybe if I'd told them one more time...

Her eyes were fixed on the targeting screen, even as her hand moved to the side, flipping the arming switches for her payload. Her ship was double loaded with plasma torpedoes, as was every bomber in the strike force. She didn't know how many of them would make it in close enough to launch, but the total ambush force had started with four thousand of the warheads, and that was a *lot* of destructive power, even against a new and technologically advanced enemy.

The cockpit shook wildly as she enhanced her preset evasion routines with a number of random jerks on the controls. The enemy fire was getting thicker, and she was losing more ships as the force continued to close. But the range was down to ten thousand.

Time to do this…

She looked down at the enhanced scanner screen. The image of the enemy ship was dead center on her display, shaking around a bit as the strange radiation emitted by the Highborn vessels played havoc with her targeting systems. It was better than she remembered from the first fight. The adjustments made to counter the radiation were helping. But not enough.

She would still have to go in…all the way in. Down under five hundred kilometers. Any farther out, and she'd need wild luck to score a hit.

And Reg Griffin didn't depend on wild luck to kill her enemies. She was going to take it right to them, all the way in, and damned the risk.

"Full evasion routines," she snapped the command into the comm, even as she reached out and prepped the bomb bay launchers. Her firing stud was now active, and two quick flicks of her finger would release the bombs in rapid succession.

Five thousand kilometers.

She'd lost sixteen of her people. That was bad, but not as bad as it could have been, she told herself. She was going to get her wing in more or less intact. She could see the enemy battleships in her mind, exploding into miniature suns under the impact of dozens of plasma torpedoes.

Then she saw it. At first it seemed like a smudge on her screen, but then she realized what it was.

Cluster missiles. A full spread. Launching from the target vessel, and coming straight for her approaching bombers.

Chapter Twelve

Spaceport – Sebastiani City
Planet Sebastiani, Alexara III
Year 323 AC (After the Cataclysm)

"This is extraordinary, Sy. I didn't know what to expect, but *this* certainly wasn't it. I'd envisioned the Highborn as many things, but..." Andi's voice faded off as she continued to look at the screen, her face a mask of utter astonishment. She'd been surprised enough when Sy had announced she'd been able to retrieve and translate some additional data from the chips, but now Andi was staring at the display on *Pegasus*'s lower level, and she was struggling to keep her jaw from dropping.

"I rechecked my translations, Andi. Twice. This is not what I expected either. Though, to be honest, I didn't know much about the Highborn going in. But, still, this is hard to believe. And, I'm only partway through the first chip. The events covered in this folio have so far been set sixty years or so before the empire's destruction. I'm hesitant to make wild guesses, but I'm starting to think the Highborn had something to do with the Cataclysm." Sylene paused, and she looked right at Andi. "They might have destroyed the empire, Andi...or at least played some role in the final fall."

The words were shocking, or they would have been if the same thoughts had not run through Andi's own mind moments before. She'd hoped the data chips would provide useful information, but she hadn't imagined anything like what Sy had recovered so far. Admittedly, there had been nothing yet on how to fight the Highborn, to defeat them, but if Sy kept at it, just maybe she could find something of tactical utility. Something that might help save the Rim.

Save Tyler.

"Sy, I'm going to leave these chips with you…assuming you're willing to keep at it."

"Willing? You couldn't tear me away from these." Sy was wide-eyed, full of energy, very different from the melancholy that had clung to her when Andi had first arrived. "I don't know what I'll be able to find. I've concentrated on the least damaged sections first. A few of the chips look like they're total losses, and some of the others are pretty badly hit, too. But I'll get something more."

"I know you will. Meanwhile, we've got to get what you've found already to Tyler at the front. Vig is going to take *Pegasus* out there. I'll go as far as Dannith, and then I'll get some kind of liner or charter back here to…"

"No."

Andi was confused. "No?"

"No. I'm not staying here. I can work on this just as well on the ship. It's got to be a month's long journey out to the front, Andi. I'm sure I will be able to recover a significant amount of data in that time. We'll get it all to Admiral Barron that much quicker this way."

"Sy…I can't ask that of you. Besides pulling you away from your home for months, maybe the better part of a year, that's a war zone up there. It's dangerous."

"We've seen danger before, Andi. And my peaceful home won't remain that way for long if the fleet loses the fight out in Hegemony space. I know a lot of people like to think we're fighting the Hegemony's enemy, that if we simply pull back, the Highborn will leave us alone. But I don't buy that, and I seriously doubt you do. I'm ready to do this." A pause. "Besides, I've been bored out of my mind since I left the ship. Wasted years chasing some sort of peace that doesn't exist, at least not when you've seen what I have...what we have. It's time I did something useful again."

"Are you sure? Really sure?"

"Yes, Andi...I'm sure." Sy looked around the room for a moment. Then her eyes locked on Andi's again. "As long as I can have my old cabin back." She smiled, and then the two of them shared a short laugh.

"Of course. It got a little banged up with the rest of the ship in one of our tight escapes after you left, but I had it completely refurbished. I think you'll like the way I decorated it."

"I'm sure I will." Sy made a face that reinforced the slight hint of sarcasm in her voice. Andi didn't take offense. She'd gone straight from being a Gut rat on Parsephon to a knife wielding Badlands adventurer. Her tastes were notoriously plain, and her shipmates had given her no end of ribbing over the years about her lack of imagination in spending her share of their swag.

"I am going to go back to the house and pack a few things, but if you can arrange clearance, we can lift off by tonight."

"I will see to it."

"Perhaps on the way to Dannith, you can help me organize what I've managed to extract, put it in an easier to read format. I'm sure that will be helpful once we get it to Tyler and the other commanders."

"Yes, I will do that. You commit all your attention to the extraction…I'll make it readable."

Andros Estate
Planet Samara
Tirion Vega System
Year 11,687 IR (Imperial Reckoning)
Year 47 BC (Before the Cataclysm) by Confederation Calendar
370 Years Ago

There was a rumble around the table as those present looked over at the figure standing before them. Sounds of surprise, and some of alarm, rose up, and also talk between various individuals. Finally, one of those present stood up and said, "What is this, Andros? Where is this…individual…from?

Another spoke, her tone sharper, more accusatory. "We are not amused by whatever surgical tricks you have employed to alter this…specimen…but if this is how our funding has been employed, on cheap circus tricks, I can assure you, you will face a reckoning. Are we to believe this is an alien of some kind?" There was disapproval in the tone, even disgust, and the nods and grunts following her words suggested many of those present agreed with the statement.

Andros was calm, unconcerned. He allowed the speaker to finish, and then he simply smiled. "I can assure you most earnestly, Belthas, Aliana—indeed, all of you— that Ellerax is no trick, circus or otherwise. He is nothing less than the future of mankind."

There was more unrest around the table. Finally, Belthas spoke again. "And how, may I ask, will an inexplicably tall man serve to solve the many problems besetting our beloved empire?" There was doubt in his voice, and just enough curiosity to tell Andros he'd piqued some level of interest.

" Belthas, esteemed colleagues, Project Obsidian represents the first true scientific advancement the empire has seen in more than a millennium. Many of you believed you were funding general research initiatives and programs to store imperial knowledge, to rekindle advancement and study." A pause. "Indeed, many of you were…encouraged…to adopt these viewpoints, for fear your support would be withdrawn if you had known the true scope of the project, what peaks we have dared to ascend. I apologize for any obfuscation, but I believe you will soon understand why it was necessary."

The room was silent, all the previous restlessness gone. A dozen faces stared at Andros, focused, unmoving.

"I will explain, my lords and ladies, but first, I will allow Ellerax to speak, to introduce himself to all of you."

"Thank you, Andros." The tall, massively built man looked out over the table. "Greetings, all of you. It is my pleasure to make your acquaintance at last." His voice was deep, booming, similar to human norms, but somehow greater, more impressive. He was clad in a simple black and gray suit, woven from fine material, but free of the extensive decorations that dominated modern imperial fashion. He looked almost like a vestige of a distant and imagined past, when the heroes of imperial lore had built an empire. His voice, his demeanor, his very bearing, seemed a direct challenge to the foppish frivolity so common among the late imperial nobility. "I can assure you that all Lord Andros tells you is the truth. I exist to bring the empire forward, to see that mankind achieves its destiny, instead of decline and descent into oblivion and extinction."

Andros nodded to the tall man, and then he turned

back toward the others. "Ellerax, my fellow lords and ladies, is the first of the Highborn."

"The Highborn? What is that? Is he human? Or are we indeed in the presence of an alien of some kind?"

"He is neither…and both. He is human, and not. He is the past, and the future."

"This is no time for riddles, Andros. You have dragged us all this way, almost to the Rim itself, and now you show us this…gentlemen? What is the meaning of all this?"

"You are the inner circle, and I have invited each of you here to see the final results of the program's first stage, the…creations, for lack of a better word…that will save our empire, and our very species, from the extinction that must surely result if decadence is allowed to continue its unrestrained rot, and imperial culture fractures ever more decisively over increasingly trivial issues and disagreements. You have supported the program, all of you, financially and with your political influence. Now, I will show you what you have wrought."

"What have you done, Andros? What have you done with the support we have provided?" Belthas's tone had hardened.

Andros nodded. "I understand your concern, Belthas, my old friend. You see here the ultimate end result of an effort begun almost sixty years ago, something that started only with one man's dream. Project Obsidian, as it came to be called, was the result of my grandfather's tireless labors, his research, in both historical and societal analysis as well as the genetic sciences. He obtained imperial support and funding, assembled a team of the empire's greatest and most capable, searching tirelessly to find those truly capable, among the legions of mediocrity that have nearly overrun our once vibrant society. By sheer will and force of mind, he broke free of the stasis of imperial science and charted a new course forward, a daring path, one that offers the hope of shattering the lethargy that has afflicted our species, and leading humanity—a new humanity—into the future."

"Are you saying this individual…Ellerax…is the result of a program of genetic engineering?"

"Yes, in a manner of speaking. He is that, and he is so much more. He and all of his brethren."

"You mean there are more of these…Highborn? I must say, I do not care for the name. It suggests they are above all of us."

"The name is perfect, and the Highborn are, indeed, superior to everyone here…myself included. That is the heart of the project, the reason it will succeed where so many efforts have failed. The empire declines not because it is old and worn out, but because we—humankind—are. The natural selection that played so great a part in mankind's development has been prevented at every turn from achieving its purpose. Where we have prevented nature from achievement, Project Obsidian has filled the void." Andros paused for a few seconds, his eyes scanning the room briefly.

"Ellerax, at least to the extent of our technological abilities to maximize human genetics, is what we should be, what we would have become, if our kind had been allowed to continue to evolve. He is thousands of years, even hundreds of thousands, ahead of us. He is nothing less than a glimpse of our future, or what our future would be, had we not blocked the ability of humanity to grow, to improve. We have seen the results of that folly, an increasingly unproductive population and an empire declining to the verge of collapse. We must reassert nature's way, my fellow lords, with science and technology, if our culture will allow no other way."

"You *created* this person?"

"I am not a god, Belthas, able to conjure life from nothingness, nor was my grandfather. We created nothing. We began with human genetic material, DNA gathered from the shrinking elite of the empire. We adjusted it, worked tirelessly to eliminate weaknesses, to nurture into being not just more people, but what humanity should have become over so many passed millennia. No, we are not gods...but we have created gods. Gods who will lead the empire forward, to greater heights of prosperity and achievement."

The murmur around the room intensified with Andros's last remark. Half a dozen of those present were shouting out questions, adding to the indecipherable cacophony. Finally, Belthas stood up and raised his arms, silencing at least some of those present.

"Andros, you have gone far beyond any acceptable actions here. The audacity...how dare you presume to...redesign...humanity."

"I have not redesigned humanity, old friend. The project has simply taken what we are, what we have always been, to its logical conclusion. Does it change humanity to eliminate disease, weakness, intellectual weakness? Is it wrong to enhance strength, health, intelligence? But do not take my word for this, any of you. Please, Ellerax is quite capable of speaking for himself." He gestured again toward the hulking individual, who'd been silent since his initial statement.

"As Lord Andros told you all, my name is Ellerax. Please allow me to tell you about myself. I was released from the crèche, what many of you would call born, though with some inaccuracy in relation to my case, fourteen years ago. At that time, I was at a stage of development comparable to a conventionally-birthed boy of seven. My growth from that time was considerably accelerated compared to human norms, and I reached a level equivalent to what you understand as adulthood, approximately four years later." Ellerax spoke calmly, his voice soft but commanding, almost melodic in nature. "I was educated by the program, and in two years, I undertook a course of study similar to that upper class imperial citizens complete by age 22. As of now, I possess the highest levels of knowledge in a number of fields of study, including genetics, physics, mathematics, military tactics, and engineering. I, of course, have no basis to understand how others approach such efforts, but Andros's analysis indicate I learn at approximately thirty times the rate of a typical human child."

"The highest levels? In all those fields? And military tactics? Why military tactics?"

"I speak so that all of you can understand, hence my use of the phrase 'highest levels.' In fact, my understanding of the previously mentioned fields of endeavor exceeds that of any living human being, and that of any now deceased. The knowledge capacity of my brain exceeds that of any conventional humans by a factor of ten or more."

"Your creation is humble, too, Andros." There was more concern than mocking in Belthas's tone.

"I do not seek to offend, Lord Belthas, I assure you of that. There is simply no way to explain who I am—*what* I am, as you inquired—without honestly detailing my abilities."

"Ellerax is what you would be, Belthas, what I or anyone here would be, or our descendants at least, in fifty thousand years, assuming we lived in a society that challenged us, that allowed only the strongest among us to survive and reproduce. The empire is failing, my lords and ladies, for many reasons, but foremost among them is the decline in humanity itself. Human development has been arrested for millennia. We cannot prevent the fall

that is coming unless we address this fact. *That* is the
purpose of Project Obsidian. Of the Highborn."

"And just how many of...the Highborn...did your
project create, Andros?"

"Enough to lead the way forward, Belthas. Enough to
save the empire."

Chapter Thirteen

Asteroid Field
Vexa Torrent System (One Jump from Sigma Nordlin)
Year 323 AC (After the Cataclysm)

Stockton pressed his finger tightly, and his bomber shook two times in rapid succession. He felt the urge to watch the bombs go in, to focus on the accuracy of his shot and not his ship's flight path. But there wasn't time. He had barely enough to pull up, to avoid turning his bombing run into a suicide attack. Even after he averted a collision, he had to revector his course, and make a desperate run back through the enemy fleet, past whatever defensive fire the hundreds of ships put out, and somehow make it back to the point, and navigate a transit in his Lightning. Just think of the sequence shook his usual rock solid confidence.

He was no stranger to low probability missions, but confidence notwithstanding, he understood math, too. A lot had to go right for him, for any of his people, to escape. A small fraction times a small fraction times another small fraction added up to a somber conclusion. He had one hell of a small chance of getting away. And all two thousand of his pilots were in the same boat.

No, not all of them. Three hundred are dead already, and another hundred or more are floating out there in crippled ships, doing whatever men and women do while they're waiting for death to come.

He shook his head, trying to drive the thoughts back into the depths.

No time for that, not now…

A small chance was still a chance, and he was determined to do his best, for himself, and for every pilot he'd led into the Vexa Torrent system. Jake Stockton knew he wasn't invincible, that he could very well be facing the end he'd imagined for so long. If that was the case, so be it, but he'd be damned if he'd die without fighting like hell. He'd never given up, not in all his years in battle, and he wasn't about to start.

And the only way he could help his pilots, the men and women he'd led into the system, was to set an example, to show them it was possible.

His ship was blasting hard, his thrust angle slowly changing his vector, first to avoid the enemy ship, and then to set a course back toward the transit point. He had one hell of a gauntlet to run, but at least his starting vector was more or less lateral to his escape route. Some of his wings had gone after ships positioned farther back in the enemy formation, and they had to virtually decelerate to a virtual stop and then accelerate back the way they had come. He didn't even want to think about much more time that would take, or how many of those pilots would make it back.

Or if any did.

His stern discipline cracked slightly as soon as he'd cleared the target vessel, and he glanced quickly down at his targeting screen, checking on the results of his torpedo launch. Two solid hits, dead center amidships. It was the best he could have hoped for, and as he stared at the screen, he saw that the squadrons he'd led in had scored more than dozen hits all together.

That had *to hurt that ship.* Sixteen plasma torpedoes would have obliterated a *Repulse*-class ship with destructive force to spare, probably even one of the Hegemony heavies. But the Highborn vessel was still there, and between its strange hull material and the Sigma-9 radiation it emitted, Stockton could tell that the AI's damage assessment was the cybernetic equivalent of a wild guess.

The AI was reporting numerous hull breaches and some degree of internal explosions and damage. But it was all very unsatisfying to Stockton. He'd continually reminded himself to dampen his expectations, that the enemy ships were extremely powerful and that damaging them was a useful enterprise on its own. As he sat there, he realized how unsuccessful an effort that had been. He wanted to see ships *destroyed*, to watch the enemy battleships obliterated in the fury of matter-antimatter annihilation. He knew the damage his strikes had done was tactically valuable as well, and he tried to tell himself some of the vessels out there were badly hit, perhaps even reduced to tactical irrelevancy. But there was no way to *know*. Not when his scanners couldn't penetrate the enemy hulls.

You'll know in a minute, at least, whether this ship was hit hard enough to knock out the cluster missiles.

That was the most important consideration to his people as they made their escape. If the enemy battleships were able to launch massive volleys of the high-speed missiles, his strike force would almost certainly be annihilated.

He angled his ship hard, and then again, more or less in the opposite direction. He didn't know yet about the missiles, but it was clear the battleship still had operational point defense turrets. The fire was fairly light, perhaps a third of what it had been on the way in. That was a good sign, and it was a big break for his pilots attempting to escape—at least until they ventured into the defensive zones of other, less damaged ships. But he knew the real question was the status of the missile launchers. His people had a chance, at least, to evade missile volleys from the other enemy battleships, those that hadn't been targeted or had taken less damage. But if the ship his group had just attacked got off a barrage of those damned missiles as his people were making a run for it…

Stockton focused on the laser fire, and he jerked his arm back and forth, doing all he could to give the enemy targeting computers the digital equivalent of a headache. But mostly, he was blasting at full thrust, bringing his ship around to a vector toward the transit point and back to the fleet waiting at Calpharon.

And checking every few seconds for any sign of a missile launch behind him.

* * *

"Condor, I'm picking up signs of internal explosions. I think we really damag…"

The voice cut off suddenly, replaced by static, and then simply by silence. Reg "Condor" Griffin knew with cold certainty what had happened to the pilot who'd been reporting.

Lieutenant Garavant…that was her name. Darkhound.

She wasn't *sure* the pilot was dead, of course. Perhaps her ship had only been damaged or had lost comms. But, in a certain sense, she hoped not. Better to go quickly. She wasn't sure any of her people were going to make it out of the system, but anybody whose ship was less than one hundred percent was dead, even if they were still breathing.

She glanced down at the screen, looking for Garavant's ship. It was gone.

That was one more of her people lost, but at least not another voice to call to her on the comm if she managed to get closer to the point, voices crying out, gripped by the cold realization that they were being left behind.

More than half her people were dead already. The target ship had managed to launch a spread of cluster missiles just as her people were closing to attack range. She'd been sure in that instant that they were all dead. But her people hadn't been entirely abandoned by luck. That is, if losing almost sixty percent of their number in less than two minutes could somehow be twisted into a version of luck.

It had been a disaster by any conventional standard, save only the one that mattered. Losing half her people was better than losing them all. And the survivors had screamed in like avenging angels, taking their vengeance by planting torpedo after torpedo into the target ship. Hardly a bomber had missed, and even the immensely strong and powerful Highborn battleship had been hard hit.

She saw another plume as she stared at the scanner, a massive explosion and ejection of fluids and gasses into space. Her stomach was tight, her hands gripping the controls so hard her fingers ached. It didn't matter much, she knew, if the enemy ship was destroyed, or if it was simply crippled beyond combat effectiveness.

But it *did* matter. It mattered to her, and to her dead pilots…and to those that would die on the desperate trip back to the transit point. War wasn't all about tonnage and guns brought to bear. It wasn't pretty, it wasn't the kind of thing those who'd seen battle talked easily about. But as far as Reg was concerned, anybody who didn't like it could all go screw themselves. She wanted to see the Highborn ship destroyed.

She wanted to watch her enemies die.

She turned toward the small long-range scanner screen. She wasn't sure she really believed she had a chance, that any of her people did, but her attention was far better deployed making the best effort she could instead of staring vacantly, hoping to see the enemy ship explode.

She was still decelerating, which meant she and her people were moving even deeper into the system, and the enemy fleet. With a little luck, in about fifteen minutes they'd at least be heading back toward…

Toward what? Not home, certainly. Calpharon had been the capital of her enemy not long ago. Now, she and her people were fighting, and many of them dying, to save it. It didn't make sense to her…and it did. She understood the threat the Highborn posed, and she knew it would take all the strength the Hegemony and the Rim nations could muster to beat them back.

But that didn't mean she had to like it.

She looked down at the small cover over the ship's safety controls. She'd planned to order her people to overload their reactors as soon as they came to a stop and headed back toward the point. Her logic had seemed sound. The longer they pushed their hardware past its rated endurance levels, the more pilots she would lose to critical failures. But there was no time. They had to give it all they had, and they had to do it now. Not in fifteen minutes.

"All squadrons, listen up. I want you to break open your safeties now. Let's get those reactors up to one ten." The words almost felt as though they had slipped out of her mouth involuntarily. Amping up the reactors was one thing, but one ten was a *big* overload.

But there was no choice, no other way any of them had a chance.

The gloom was all around her, difficult to fight off…at least until her AI's alarm sounded, and her eyes darted to the screen. To where the enemy battleship was.

To where it had been.

She stared at the emptiness, at a section of space that now held nothing but a surging vortex of energy and radiation.

Her people had done it. They had destroyed one of the Highborn battleships!

Pilots who had done that deserved better than to die running from some cursed system. By God, whatever it took, she was going to get her people the hell out of there.

Some of them at least.

"You all heard me…all reactors up to one ten. No…to one fifteen. Now!"

* * *

Tesserax sat in his chair, looking out at the Thralls at their stations. He was furious, and the sight of so many of his newly arrived battleships ravaged by the enemy's small craft threatened to push him into a wild rage. He wanted to lash out at the captive humans manning his ship's stations, to punish them for the losses his fleet was suffering before it even completed the jump into the target system. It was his sense of pride and dignity held back the rage, not any realization that the Thralls were in no way responsible for what was happening. It was beneath him to appear anything less than fully in control in front of inferiors.

He knew his decision to race through the system without proper scanning and patrol operations had backfired. The enemy had once again shown unexpected initiative. For an instant, he was ready to blame himself, but his hurried efforts to push forward had been driven not by his own recklessness, but by the time constraints place on him by Ellerax and the Command Council. The damage the battleships had suffered—and it was significant, though, perhaps not devastating—was going to be hard to explain, especially since blaming one's superiors was likely not the politic way to present an argument to them.

If he took Calpharon, if he could make an argument that he'd brought the war to the brink of a victorious conclusion, perhaps the damage to the main battle units would be less…controversial.

Yes, if I give them Calpharon, if I break the Hegemony's back in one great battle, even losses among the heavy units will be an acceptable price.

He wasn't entirely sure he believed that, at least to the extent that a victory at Calpharon would all but end the war. A thought was growing somewhere deep in his immensely capable mind, one with upsetting implications. The humans were not supposed to be so difficult to defeat. They were faring far better than the mathematical models suggested was possible. They were technologically inferior, barely more than animals compared to the Highborn. But there was *something* about the way they fought, a savagery, a tenacity, an almost mindless courage he couldn't really explain. It shouldn't matter, shouldn't make a difference, not in the face of the Highborn's relentless superiority…but it did. And in the backwater of his brain that was constantly analyzing his enemy, judging their moves, concern was growing. It wasn't a primary thought, not yet, nor anything that would affect his plans.

His confidence, his belief in Highborn superiority, were still firmly in control. But the concerns were slowly growing, nevertheless, building in strength.

But just then, as he sat in the center of the flagship's control room, one thought was primary among all others. It was time to move forward. Time to attack the enemy, to seize the Hegemony capital.

Time to show the humans their rightful place in the scheme of things.

Chapter Fourteen

CFS Dauntless
Planet Calpharon (Hegemonic Capital)
Sigma Nordlin IV
Year 323 AC (After the Cataclysm)

Another group, maybe twenty more ships…

Tyler Barron sat on *Dauntless*'s bridge, staring at the huge main display, watching as bombers transited into the system from Vexa Torrent. It had taken every bit of cold resolve he could muster to authorize Stockton's wild plan to ambush the enemy fleet, to lead two thousand pilots on a mission that seemed nothing less than utter insanity. The idea *had* seemed crazy, reckless…a hopeless attempt that could only throw away thousands of lives.

That last part was still a possibility—only a few hundred of the two thousand ships sent into the adjacent system had so far returned, and none of those carried Jake Stockton—but there had been some good news as well, at least in the communications from the first squadrons to emerge. Those formations were battered, most of them at half strength or less, but they all reported versions of the same thing. The ambush had been a complete success, at least in terms of damage inflicted.

The enemy had hurried through the system, disregarded proper scanning and patrolling operations…and Stockton had punished them for it, unleashing his hidden fighters just as the heavy Highborn vessels were moving past the asteroid fields.

The wings had paid a heavy price for their success, that much seemed a certainty from where Barron sat. Still, they had drawn enemy blood, and the fleet needed every edge it could find. At least two dozen of the Highborn battleships had suffered at least some damage, according to the reports, and perhaps ten had been badly beaten up. Even factoring in the tendency of fighter pilots to exaggerate, that was good news, better than Barron had dared to hope.

At least one of the huge enemy ships, again, if the information coming in could be relied upon, had been utterly destroyed. That was welcome news. It helped Barron just knowing that the hulking monsters, which he'd still only seen on scanning records, *could* be destroyed. The smaller enemy ships had been tough enough in combat, and he'd nursed growing nightmares anticipating the coming battle against the ships he knew were the Highborn's equivalent of his battle line.

"We're up to three hundred fighters transited through, Admiral." Barron could hear the tone in Atara Travis's voice, the intense effort she was making to try to sound like reaching fifteen percent of the strike force returned was a good thing. He appreciated his longtime comrade's effort, but she sometimes forgot just how well he knew her. The pain and grief she was feeling, and the fact that, even as she spoke, she was guessing in her head what the final number of survivors would be, came through to him loud and clear.

"They're still coming." Barron's own response was even weaker. He doubted anyone on the bridge, and

Atara least of all, would believe the fleet's commander was anything but distraught over the vast losses the strike force had suffered.

The strike force *he* had sent into Vexa Torrent.

Still, he knew as he watched, he would do it again. There were no easy paths ahead, no low cost strategies to win the war. This was no less than a fight for survival, and almost any cost was acceptable if the Confederation itself survived.

Tyler Barron liked to think that he thought of all his people equally, that he worried for each and every spacer in his command as much as he did for the officers who'd served at his side for years. But it wasn't true. He was human, subject to emotions and loyalties...and there were some people under his command who were just more vital to the war effort, more indispensable to him.

Barron counted Jake Stockton among the tiny group he considered his real friends, but perhaps more importantly, the commander of his fighter corps was the best pilot he had ever known, perhaps the greatest in Confederation history. And Stockton had developed into an even better leader, commanding the waves of bombers in the Hegemony War, and now against the Highborn, with astonishing skill. He'd created new tactics, honed the squadrons into devastatingly effective offensive weapons. Barron would mourn for his friend, but the idea of fighting the war without Stockton, the leader, was terrifying.

"Another cluster, Admiral...it looks bigger than the others, about forty ships coming through.

Barron looked at the display, hoping to see Stockton's ship among the new arrivals, but not really expecting it. He knew Stockton well enough to realize the strike force's commander would be the last to transit...or damned close to the last. Barron had urged Stockton to stay back from the fighting, to remain close to the transit point, but even as he'd uttered the words, he knew his friend would ignore them. Barron had wanted to push harder, to give Stockton express orders to direct the assault from a safer position…but that treaded too close to outright hypocrisy. Barron himself had never been very good at sending others into the fire while he stayed behind, and he couldn't bring himself to insist Stockton do what he'd never been able to do.

Not that it would have mattered if he had ordered his fighter commander to return first. Jake Stockton had always been a virtuoso at twisting orders, and sometimes outright disobeying them. The only way Barron could have kept him out of the center of the fighting was to lock him in the brig and send the squadrons in without him…and he needed Stockton out there, making magic with his wings, as he had done so many times before.

"More reports coming in, Admiral. It definitely looks like the wings did some real damage over there."

Barron listened to Atara's words, but he heard her true meaning, unlike everyone else on the bridge. The attack had achieved much, more than they could have expected…but not enough. The enemy was still coming on, still too strong to stop, and the reports trickling in also suggested the Highborn invasion of Sigma Nordlin would begin in just a matter of hours. Perhaps even sooner.

Barron stared at the display for another minute, but then he turned abruptly. He had hundreds of ships, tens of thousands of spacers, and they were all waiting for his commands. The battle he'd anticipated, discussed endlessly with Chronos, for which his people had been preparing night and day, was almost there.

"Bring the fleet to yellow alert, Atara…and get me a line to Commander Chronos." The combined fleet didn't have an official commander in chief. That would have been impossible. It was miracle enough that so many ships from different nations, so recently enemies themselves, had gathered together. Barron understood all of that, but he was a bit edgy about it, too. His years of combat experience told him one thing…confusion wasn't going to help the defensive effort. He believed that so strongly, he'd fallen into an unofficial and informal willingness to follow Chronos as effective overall commander. His trust of the Hegemony leader had grown considerably, though it was still shaky and conditional. But throwing his people at an enemy like the Highborn without meticulous cooperation between the elements of the fleet would be suicide. He wasn't' sure they had a real chance of victory no matter what they did, but he was damned certain they didn't unless they fought together as a single unit.

"All units acknowledge yellow alert, Admiral." A few seconds later: "I have Commander Chronos on your line."

Barron put his hand to the side of his headset, tapping the small control. "Commander Chronos, the bombers returning have provided some locational details of the approaching Highborn forces. It doesn't look like we've got a lot of time before thing start heating up. I've brought the Confederation contingent to yellow alert, and I suggest you do the same with the Hegemony commands. I've transmitted the positional data to your flagship. It's only partial, but I think the implications are pretty clear."

"I'll review it all, Admiral, but your yellow alert is good enough for me to bring the Hegemony forces to stage two readiness." Barron could hear Chronos shouting out the orders for a few seconds, directing his staff to bring all units to the Hegemony's rough equivalent of yellow alert. Then, the Hegemony's Number Eight was back on the line, speaking to him once again. "It's not our way to get terribly emotional about impending combat, but I think it is safe to say that we're both on the verge of fighting the largest battle either of us has ever seen. I would say the most desperate, but of course, they all seem desperate at the time, do they not, Tyler?"

"They do indeed, Chronos." Barron nodded, finding himself feeling closer than ever to his former enemy. It was hard to even imagine how someone as reasonable, as like himself as Chronos often seemed, could also be a Hegemony Master, and the commander who'd led his forces through Confederation space, to Megara itself.

"They do indeed, my friend," Barron repeated. "I have never gone into battle without the same feeling." A half-truth. Barron had always respected the danger of combat, mourned the fallen. But he'd never felt as certain that failure would lead to utter disaster as he did sitting there, and for all the distance back to the Confederation, he felt as though he was standing in some pass, holding the enemy back, not from the Hegemony capital, but from Megara itself, and from those her cared most about. From Andi…and the daughter he had never met, but already loved with all his heart.

The child he might never see…because he knew one thing for sure. He would take any risk to prevail in the coming fight. And if he could save Andi and his child by laying down his own life, he would do just that without even a second thought.

* * *

"Let's go…redline those reactors. And keep those evasive maneuvers going. You can still get shot before you make it through." Jake Stockton was watching his pilots race for the transit point. He was trying, with very limited success, to ignore the tattered wreck his formations had become. There was nothing left now of his superbly-organized strike force but a mass of fighters racing madly toward the transit point.

It was a decent sized mass, at least. Stockton looked on with some gratification at the numbers of his people who had made it so far. The mission had still been a holocaust by any conventional standards, and even if the remaining squadrons mostly escaped intact—far from a certainty—the loss rates would still be over fifty percent. But his people had drawn blood, and getting anywhere close to a thousand of his ships back was a win any way he looked at it.

He angled his throttle hard to the side. He was close to the transit point, but the enemy's first line was coming on hard, and their point defense fire was becoming considerably more than just an annoyance. He had to get his people through the point as quickly as possible, before the enemy battleships could close and blanket the area around the point with their deadly missiles. A few barrages of those damned things would turn an already bloody fight into an outright massacre.

"Stay focused, everybody. Stick to your formations…follow your wing commanders' orders. We'll get everybody through, but we can't all go at once." He was far from sure everyone would get through, but transits points were only so large, and if too many of his ships tried to pass at once, things were going to get even uglier.

He'd gotten back to the point right around the middle of the pack, but he'd pulled up, and now he was more or less orbiting the transit point. He had no intention of leaving the system, not while hundreds of his pilots were still trying to escape. He could almost hear Admiral

Barron's voice, urging him, ordering him, probably, to make the jump. But he wasn't going to go, not while his people were still trying to escape.

He flipped his scanner display to the mass of fighters lining up, trying to get through the point with something remotely resembling order. Stockton had done all he could. The only option that remained was to hope for the best. His pilots' training and experience would get them through without turning the point into a disaster of collisions and intersecting drive exhaust lines...or it wouldn't. He just had to believe in them, to trust in their abilities.

He switched the scanner back toward the approaching enemy ships. There were dozens of the Highborn vessels coming on, and not far behind the forward line, at least six of the giant battleships were also moving up. He waited and watched, feeling as though any second, hundreds of the deadly missiles would appear on the screen. That would truly mark the beginning of the end, and it would set a hard deadline on how long his people had to escape. A volley of hundreds of the high-velocity warheads hitting his wings all bunched up at the point would inflict horrifying losses...and probably wipe out anyone who remained.

His eye caught movement on the very edge of the display, something else on the screen. One of his wings...or what was left of it.

Stockton knew groups of his bombers had been trapped deeper in the system, that their angles of thrust had virtually doomed them, made escape almost an impossibility. They'd all been pretty much wiped out by then, and the few stragglers who'd survived her caught up in the scrum of ships trying to get through the point.

All except one group.

He tapped at his controls, trying to bring up the ID of

the ships. They were still pretty far out for that, and he was about to give up when the designation suddenly appeared.

They're Reg Griffin's birds...

He was shocked, and he almost rechecked the AI's reporting. 'Condor' Griffin was one of his best pilots, and a star among his up and coming wing commanders. He'd seen her people as they'd begun their attack run, and he'd felt his stomach shrivel as he saw the vector of their assault. Of all of the forces he'd brought into the system, their approach angle had been the worst in terms of ultimate escape, almost directly away from the transit point.

He'd felt pain, sorrow—he genuinely liked Reg—but, despite his feelings, he'd written off the entire wing. There had simply been no chance they could possibly make it back, no conceivable way they could get through the gauntlet of enemy ships and defensive fire.

Only they had. At least, sixteen of them had.

As he watched, one of the tiny dots disappeared.

Fifteen.

He switched the scanners back, watching again as more of the fighters massed around the point slipped through, traveling lightyears in a few seconds, all the way back to the fleet. Those pilots would get back to where they had come from days before...but not to the rest they deserved. The main fight was on them all, the enemy likely to follow closely on the heels of the retreating squadrons. The pilots who'd endured the hell of sitting for days in their craft, waiting in increasing discomfort, and then fighting a vicious battle that had cost them half their number, could look forward only to a few moments of stretching their legs, and maybe the chance to wolf down a sandwich while their birds were refueled and rearmed. Then they would be back into the struggle. The fleet needed everything it had, every fighter, every pilot, every gunner or engineer somewhere in the bowels of *Dauntless* or one of the other battleships. The fight would be the greatest the Confederation navy had ever seen, the vastest by almost every measure...and very likely the bloodiest.

Barron switched the scanner again, back toward Griffin's wing. They were down to thirteen now, and they had half a dozen enemy ships closing on them, firing as they did. But at least they were close enough now for communications.

"Condor...Reg...you're close now, keep it coming." Stockton didn't know how much his words could do, but he figured the exhausted officer and her remaining pilots could use any support they could get just then. The difference between escape and death could be a razor's edge, an instant's focus...or loss of focus.

"Admiral...we're coming. We'll make it through. But you can't wait for us, sir. You can't wait for the others at the point. You have to go now."

"I'll decide what I have to do, Commander." Stockton could hear the courage in Griffin's voice, and his admiration for the officer grew. But he wasn't planning to leave, not until all his ships, hers included, were through.

"No, Admiral...you can't. These enemy ships are right behind us. You have to get back to the flagship, get your ship refit, and get the wings back in Sigma Nordlin ready to launch. You've got to get the rest of the squadrons into position...and hit these bastards as they come through the point. Maybe you can engage them before they can launch missile volleys. You've got to go, Admiral. Please..."

Stockton felt like Griffin had punched him in the gut. Every natural instinct in him cried out to stay where he was, to wait until his people had all transited. The veteran pilot, the romantic warrior that lived inside him, screamed to stay, to be the last one out.

But Griffin was right. He wasn't sure the strike forces waiting back in the fleet's bays could catch the enemy as they transited in—he wasn't even sure the enemy would come right through at their current velocities.

But it damn sure looked like that's what they were planning to do. And if they did, just maybe, if he got back in time, he could have a reception committee waiting for them.

"Condor...you're in command here now, over all the remaining squadrons. So that means you've got to make it back here, you hear me. There are too many pilots counting on you. Keep it together, and stay alive...and get our people back through, you hear me?"

"Yes, Admiral. You can count on me. Just go. Go now. Make these bastards pay for every meter of space on the other side."

Stockton moved his hand to the side, angling his thrust toward the point. At least he tried to do that. But his hand didn't move, didn't respond. He knew what he had to do, but there were still hundreds of his people trying to get through, and for an instant, he wasn't sure he had what it would take to leave them.

You have to go. Reg is right...with some luck, you can hit them hard as they come through. But only if you get back now...

It went against every instinct he had, but the weight of those stars Barron had placed on his shoulder gave him no choice. His duty was clear.

He stared down at his hand, and this time it moved slowly, angling his thrusters, and accelerating his ship directly toward the transit point. Back toward the fleet.

And to the real fight that still lay ahead.

Chapter Fifteen

Free Trader Pegasus
Docked to Refueling Station Three
Planet Dannith, Ventica III
Year 323 AC (After the Cataclysm)

"Andi, you can count on us, you know you can. We'll make sure this data gets to Tyler. *I'll* make sure it does."

Andi listened to Vig's words, and she appreciated the devoted friendship she knew lay behind them. But the idea of staying behind again, of sending others forward to aid in the effort to hold off the enemy, to save everyone on the Rim, it was more than she could bear.

She turned, looking back toward her cabin, as close as she could come to staring at Cassiopeia just then. The child was asleep—she had no idea how her daughter was able to sleep through the things she was—but she was ever-present in Andi's mind, the only thing in the universe with the pull to keep her back in Confederation space.

But it's not that simple...

Andi's mind was at war with itself, every conventional motherly instinct screaming at her to go back to Megara with her daughter, to entrust the precious data Sy had extracted to Vig and the others. But there was another side, one no less powerful, one heavy with hard experience telling her she had to go, that the best she could do for her daughter was to put all she had into the fight, the struggle that would determine if Cassiopeia—and billions like her—even *had* a future. Andi had grown up in the Gut, and her memories of her mother, few and fading that they had become, were of a wildcat of a woman, one who'd done everything possible to protect and care for her daughter, even though they both lived in the harsh streets of the Confederation's worst slum. Andi had never been overly protected, nor isolated from the horrors of life, and she'd come a long way, farther than anyone could have imagined. If she decided to go with *Pegasus*, to bring the information to Tyler herself, she could send Cassiopeia back to the capital with Lita Mareth. The child could find no better caretaker anywhere, and the first daughter of the Confederation would never want for love and support.

But Andi was still uncertain. She wanted to go because she knew she could help, because there were very few people out there—and none, she was sure, with such close ties to the navy—who had her knowledge of imperial artifacts and history. If the empire had tangled with the Highborn, if Sy was able to uncover more information from the damaged data chips, Andi was sure she could help interpret it, put it to good use.

There was more than that, though. She would get to see Tyler again, and for all she'd fought back against the dark thoughts, she was deathly afraid it would be the last time.

If you go and leave Cassiopeia behind, she may never meet her father…

The thought cut deeply into her. *She* had never known

her own father. From all she knew, he'd died before she was born. She hadn't thought much about him in her life, not until recently. But the thought of her daughter never meeting Tyler, never resting in her father's arms, weighed on her like a boulder. Tyler Barron deserved to meet his daughter, and even if she was too young to remember, Cassiopeia had a right to meet her father.

This may be your only chance...

"Andi?"

Vig's voice pulled her from her thoughts. She turned toward him abruptly, unsure just how long she'd been ignoring him. "I'm sorry, Vig. I was just...thinking."

"I don't mean to push, but the refueling is almost complete. Your liner to Megara leaves tonight, so you and Cassiopeia should probably..."

"We're not going."

Silence for a moment. Then: "What? What do you mean, you're not going?"

"I mean exactly what I said. We're not taking that liner. We're not going back to Megara. I'm going with you to Calpharon. No one has the experience I do dealing with old imperial artifacts, and if the empire knew of the Highborn, if there is something in all of this to help in the fight, I *need* to be here, working on it with Sy."

"But Andi...are you going to leave Cassiopeia behind without you?"

"No...she is coming, too." She felt guilty even as the words came out, like some kind of monster disregarding her daughter's safety. "She has a right to meet her father...and I don't know if that will ever happen if I don't bring her now. We'll stay back from any fighting, keep her safe. But I can't look her in the eye in ten years, or twenty, and tell her I sent her to Megara and kept her from meeting her father. I won't have him be nothing more than a legend to her, a name she hears everywhere she goes, and nothing else."

Vig looked like he was going to argue, but then he just nodded. "I understand, Andi. She does deserve to meet her father." A pause. "So, the whole crew is back together then, eh? Plus one. Maybe the ship's future captain."

Andi nodded and forced a smile, but inside there was one thought, beating on her like a hammer. *Please no, whatever you do, my little one, don't follow in my footsteps. That is too hard a journey for you, too much sadness and loss.*

* * *

"That child of yours is quite a distraction, Andi. She's smart as hell, I can tell already."

Andi smiled at Sy. Her friend had done almost nothing on the trip so far except work on the old data chips and play with Cassiopeia…and as far as she had seen, those two activities had precluded everything else, including eating and sleeping.

"I hope I'm doing the right thing." Andi had been sure of her decision to go with *Pegasus*, and to bring her daughter along. But she was starting to have doubts. Her place was to protect Cassiopeia. She didn't doubt her daughter would face her own dangers and trials one day, but she was still too young for all of that.

It isn't her decision…or yours. The Highborn don't care, and if they win this war, she will die, or become a slave. Still, she was uncertain, bouncing back and forth between resolution and doubt.

"You are, Andi. Protecting someone is one thing, but would she really be safer on Megara? You know what is at stake here. The more I manage to pull from these chips, the more and more certain I am we face an almost insurmountable struggle. It's not like *Pegasus* is heading to

Calpharon to jump into the fight. We'll stay back, keep the ship—and Cassiopeia—from the real fighting. But with your help, I'll be able to translate all of this much more quickly…and your daughter just may get a chance to meet her father. Stop beating up on yourself. You didn't create this situation. You're just doing the best you can."

Andi nodded. She tended to ignore most of what she regarded as bullshit, and as much as she loved Sy, she knew her friend would say just about anything to make her feel better.

But you made the decision already, and there is no point in going over it again and again. Cassiopeia is surrounded by people who would die to protect her. How much better would she be back on Megara, in the care of one faithful nanny and a thousand political carnivores anxious to be seen as the protector of Admiral Barron's child?

"How is it going? Any progress with that chip?" Andi desperately needed to change the subject, and the last she'd left Sylene, her friend had been banging her head against the bulkheads trying to retrieve data from the badly damaged second chip.

"No, I'm afraid not. I think there might be something on there we can get to, but I don't know how long it will take. The third chip is in somewhat better shape, and I figured it made sense to get started on that one before wasting weeks on the second."

Andi nodded. "I agree with that. So, are you having more luck with number three?"

"Now that you mention it, Andi, yes I am. I've only translated a small part of what I've been able to extract, but it is very interesting, and likely very useful once we recover more information. And, if you'd like, I've got a lot of raw old imperial that needs translating…"

Imperial Secret Police Headquarters
Planet Samara
Tirion Vega System
Year 11,690 IR (Imperial Reckoning)
Year 44 BC (Before the Cataclysm) by Confederation
Calendar
367 Years Ago

"Well, do you have anything to report?" Velan Tragonis sat behind a large desk of black marble, staring out at the man who'd just entered his office.

"Nothing as specific as you would like, I'm afraid, Colonel. A lot of suspicious odds and ends there, but nothing that would stand up in an imperial court, I'm afraid. Lord Andros has been quite adept at covering his tracks. He's up to something, I'd bet my pension on it. But what, I couldn't say."

"There are other ways to handle this matter outside the conventional legal system, Trellic. I have considerable authority direct from the crown to handle matters of imperial security." Tragonis didn't say any more. They both knew what 'other ways' meant. "But before we go that route, we need some degree of certainty, even if we can't *prove* it." The investigation of Andros had begun rather innocuously, as an examination of possible fraudulent use of imperial funds. Tragonis had expected to find just another example of an imperial noble lining his own pockets, and he'd imagined collecting some level of restitution if he could put the case together. He would have handled things differently if it had been up to him, but outside of offenses like treason, the crimes of the nobility had been winked at for centuries.

There probably wouldn't even have been an investigation at all, except the parlous state of the imperial treasury had placed an emphasis on pursuing financial crimes to bring in additional revenue.

As soon as Tragonis's people began looking into Andros's Project Obsidian, however, they found one troubling detail after another and, worse perhaps, apparent links to other...problematic...events in different sections of imperial space.

Lord Andros the thief was a minor affair for his office to pursue. Andros the traitor—and Tragonis would need real proof to make that claim, and to send a termination squad—was something entirely different.

"There are signs Andros had people on Bellastre, right before the financial collapse there. And on Mandolith, just months before the first rebellions. But again, no real proof of involvement."

"Forget proof, Trellic. Tell me what you think? Is Lord Andros deliberately inciting rebellions and economic disasters on different worlds?"

"Forgetting proof? Before this last trip, I would have said no. What would a noble of Andros's station have to gain by such activities. He lacks the military support to make a play for the scepter, and what else could he gain by destabilizing important imperial worlds? But the coincidence of it all is becoming a bit much to explain away."

Tragonis shook his head. "I don't know...but I can tell you this. We're damned sure going to find out what is going on."

"I agree, sir, but how? I've got people watching Andros and his top lieutenants, but we have no idea who else he may be allied with."

"Let's take a look and see if we can trace any involvement backwards. The empire has been...troubled...for some time now, but we've seen a two hundred percent increase in major incidents on imperial worlds over the last three years...sharp economic declines, terrorism, even open rebellion. That is a massive increase, and far too much to blame on bad luck. *Someone* is behind it, some of it, at least. I want the team on every individual case file to reexamine their evidence for anything—anything at all—that points toward Andros or his known associates." Tragonis paused. "If we've got an imperial lord of that level plotting something, we need to know about it…as quickly as possible.

"Yes, Colonel. I will see to it at once."

The operative got up and nodded sharply toward Tragonis. Then he turned and walked out of the office, leaving his superior to sit and think in the quiet of his office.

What are you up to, Andros?

Chapter Sixteen

148,000,000 Kilometers from CFS Dauntless
Sigma Nordlin System
Year 323 AC (After the Cataclysm)

The Battle of Calpharon – The Warbirds Return

"*Dauntless*, this is Admiral Stockton...put me through the Admiral Barron!" Stockton was still trying to shake the disorientation from his head. Small ships like Lightning fighters were not made for interstellar transits, and they lacked the shielding larger ships employed to minimize the effects of alternate space on their crews. Stockton had been a trailblazer of sorts in his younger days, one of the first pilots to take a fighter through a point, and he'd done in enough times to be considered the foremost veteran of the procedure. But that didn't mean it was easy on him.

The strange, largely unexplained space in the points, combined with the bizarre forms of radiation endemic to it, and a host of other seeming unnatural factors, had variable effects on human beings traveling through. Those on properly shielded ships usually suffered no more than mild dizziness, headaches, nausea, and perhaps short periods of mild confusion upon exiting. Pilots in poorly protected fighters endured more direct effects, hallucinations, irregular heartbeats, extreme disorientation. A small percentage even succumbed to permanent effects, and could suffer heart attacks, strokes, permanent insanity. It was just another notation on the spreadsheet for a mission of the sort Stockton had just led. A single pilot took his chances, endured a small risk, one the bravado of most fighter jocks could ignore. With thousands of fighters going through a point, the rare but deadly side effects were a mathematical certainty.

Stockton blasted his engines hard as he waited for Barron to come on the line, accelerating toward the flagship with everything his depleted fighter had left. Still, it was going to take too long to get back, for his bird to get refueled and re-launched. He needed to get the rest of his people into space. Now.

The enemy had been right behind his fleeing squadrons, and from the looks of their approach as they'd neared the point, they weren't planning to wait. Highborn ships were going to be coming through soon, perhaps any minute…and Stockton wanted his fighters, the rest of them at least, the four thousand Confed, Alliance, and Hegemony craft still fresh and ready to go, in space to meet the enemy. He wasn't sure how many of the missile arrays on the enemy battleships his people had managed to knock out, but he knew however many were left would tear apart his wings if they were able to execute a coordinated launch. The sooner his bombers got into space, and the closer to the point they met the invaders, the better they would be.

And the better the fleet would be if his pilots were able to launch their torpedoes before the enemy missiles tore their formations to shreds.

"Jake…Tyler here. I'm glad to see you made it back,

old friend." Barron sounded distracted, harried. *Of course, he's got the entire fleet to worry about…as well as dealing with the Heggies.* Stockton had enjoyed little success in trying to avoid the derogatory nickname for his former enemies, now his allies. He'd been in good company with that, at least in the fighter corps.

"I'm glad too, sir…but right now we need to launch everything, every bomber we've got. The Highborn first line is *right* behind my squadrons. If we can go against those bastards as they come through, maybe we can get a free shot in…before they hit us with those missiles."

"I'll issue an order to scramble all our squadrons…and I'll request the Alliance and Hegemony forces do the same."

Stockton frowned as he heard Barron's words, and the tension behind them. He knew Imperator Tulus would do whatever Barron asked, and he couldn't imagine Commander Chronos would hesitate to launch his own wings along with those of the other contingents. But he felt uneasy about the disorganized nature of the divided command structure. It wouldn't take more than one disagreement—or even just a delay—at the wrong time to cause a disaster. Not that Stockton knew how to fix the problem. He certainly wasn't ready to serve under Hegemony command, and he couldn't imagine the Confederation's larger, more powerful ally would accept a subordinate role…especially not when it was their capital planet being attacked.

"Very well, Admiral. I should be landing in thirty minutes or so. I'll send a comm to control and have my flight team ready to turn my ship around so I can get right back out." His mind was on the coming battle, mostly, but the communique he'd just mentioned would serve one other purpose. Stara Sinclair would be relieved to hear his voice, to know he had returned once again.

And a few seconds with her once he landed—all he could really spare—would remind him of just what he was fighting for.

"Are you sure you're okay to go right back out, Jake?" Barron's words sounded sincere, but Stockton was well aware both he and the admiral knew there was no choice. It was, more than anything, a friend expressing concern for another.

Besides, *all* the survivors from the fight in Vexa Torrent would be turning around and launching right back out into the fight…and Stockton's place was to set the example to his exhausted and haggard pilots.

"I'm always okay, Admiral…you know that." A pause, and then a slightly more useful reply. "I'll grab another hit of stims before I launch, sir. Doc will probably give me a lecture, but if we get through this and all I end up with is a case of the shakes and a few days in detox, I can live with that."

"Take care of yourself, Jake…we need you."

Stockton just nodded to himself. There was true affection in Barron's tone, the sound of a man who didn't want to lose a valued friend.

Another friend. How many have we all lost?

There had been more in Barron's voice as well, the desperation of a commander who needed every one of his key people to face what was coming.

Stockton adjusted his course, and punched up the acceleration slightly. The sooner he was back in the landing bay, the better. Every second counted.

* * *

The fighter kicked hard with every burst of power to the engines. Reg Griffin did her best to ease the controls, to gently feed fuel into the reactor, but the ship still bucked wildly as she did. There was no choice. She'd just have to put up with it, and hope she only had to contend with discomfort, that her ship didn't give up the ghost completely.

Look on the bright side...

It was the kind of thing that pissed her off when people said it, but it was actually applicable to her situation. She'd been almost certain she was going to die in Vexa Torrent, and she'd had no less than six of the enemy missiles on her tail—almost close enough to detonate—when her Lightning slipped into the transit point. She'd held her breath as she slipped into the alternate space, traveling seven lightyears in a few seconds, and as best she could concentrate through the disorientation, she wondered if the missiles were still chasing her, if she would emerge back in Sigma Nordlin only to be obliterated within sight of the fleet.

She'd been through now for almost four minutes, and there was no sign of the missiles. No sign of *any* enemy ordnance. The Highborn weapons were a deadly danger to the fighter wings, but at least the warheads themselves didn't seem to be transit-capable. She didn't know why, whether the warheads were too volatile, or their shielding too weak. Perhaps the AIs controlling them went down inside the points. Honestly, she didn't really care. All that mattered was, she had gained a reprieve, that all of the pilots who got through the point had. The Highborn advance line wasn't far behind, but the battleships were a bit farther back...and that promised enough time for all the returned ships to reach their landing platforms before they could be fired on again.

Of course, that didn't account for the troubles damaged ships—like hers—might face.

She slowed the acceleration even more, but she knew that wasn't going to work. She'd run for her life back in

Vexa Torrent, screaming toward the transit point with all her ship could manage. Now, she had to decelerate before she reached *Confederation*. She'd been fortunate to be posted on one of the newest battleships in the fleet, and the vessel's crew and equipment were among the very best in the navy.

Neither of which would help her if her ship went screaming past at uncontrollable velocity.

She looked down at her screen, running calculations in her head, as her AI crunched the numbers. It all came out the same, just as she'd expected. Everything depended on two absolute parameters.

First, the performance of her battered ship wasn't going to improve, at least not before she got into the bay and her flight crew did their magic. And second, she had to reach *Confederation* with her velocity down almost to zero.

She pushed up the thrust level, trying to ignore the increased turbulence. Her ship bounced all around, but the engines were still online. Her dampeners were out, so she felt the pressure slam into her as the deceleration increased…3g, 4g, 5g.

She struggled to breath, the force slamming down on her chest resisting her efforts to fill her lungs with air. The life support system seemed to be working, but there was a hint of something acidic, a caustic fume in the cockpit's air.

She punched a few buttons on her workstation, something that required considerable effort under 5g of constant force, and the screen shifted. There were half a dozen icons on the display, and one large one right in the middle.

Confederation.

She'd sent the survivors of her initial wing on ahead, all nine of them. She'd stayed back as the rest of the strike force transited, taking Stockton's place as the last to come through. Now, she was close. But close wasn't the same as being there.

She checked the range, recalculated her vector and deceleration. Everything looked good.

She was back, and on track to reach the ship in twenty-four minutes.

As long as her ship hung in there that long.

*   *   *

"I know you have much to do, my brother, but I could not allow this monumental struggle to begin without wishing you good fortune. We are with you, all of Palatia's warriors. We will make our mark this day, and claim our share of the glory. Our swords will taste the enemy's blood, and we will make them pay a grievous price."

Barron sat on *Dauntless*'s bridge, listening to Vian Tulus, hearing the enthusiasm in the Alliance Imperator's voice. He'd listened to such speeches before, and he considered Tulus one of his closest friends, indeed as the blood brother he'd become in a scared Palatian ritual years before. Tulus was everything a friend and brother could be, and he had never once failed to answer a call to come to Barron's aid.

But Tyler Barron was tired of war. He didn't care about glory. He had once, he had to admit that, but such youthful desires had been washed away with blood. Tulus's speech was more like something he'd have said in his younger years, but it would have been more than half a lie even then. He'd followed the only path he'd felt was open to him in life, but choice or not, he made the best of it. He *had* craved glory, he had looked forward to chances to make his mark, to lead his people against the enemy.

But the cost had been too great, too many of his spacers dead, too many friend gone. Glory and victory were heady experiences, he wouldn't deny that fact.

But the price was always too high.

Tulus was the product of Palatian culture, and Barron knew enough about the history of that tortured world, of the misery that had forged the Palatians into iron, and led them from slavery to conquest. Palatian morals and ideas didn't match up very well alongside those of the Confederation, but then Barron would be the first to acknowledge that hypocrisy and dishonesty were rampant in his homeland. It was too easy to discredit a rival culture, to apply morals and ethics blindly, and often without acknowledgement of the failures of one's own society. The Palatians had suffered terribly because they had been weak, because they had trusted their neighbors. And that had led ultimately to a culture that prized strength above all, and whose warriors had set out from their newly-freed world and subjugated those who had once ruled over them.

Barron understood, but he wanted only peace. He missed Andi, and he longed to see his daughter. He'd done his part, fought more than his share of battles. And yet still, he had no choice. Without victory, all he cared about in the universe would be lost to him forever. It wasn't glory he craved, not anymore. All he wanted was peace, and a chance to live his life, to hold his child in his arms and to walk through the woods as he had as a boy, listen to the wind, and the water in a nearby creek.

He didn't have that choice, though. He didn't have to chase glory anymore, now it pursued him. And as always, it presented him a stark choice. Victory, and the spoils of the triumphant warrior…or defeat and utter desolation. Billions depended on him, looked to him to protect them, and he doubted any of them could understand the weight of that load.

He held back a small laugh, a sarcastic realization that he and Tulus would do exactly the same things, that their paths were still tightly aligned…and it didn't matter at all that their motivations had so radically diverged.

"And to you, my brother. Your warriors have followed you here because it was their duty to do so, because they are Palatians, and because you are their Imperator. But they have come for another reason, too. They, as I, recognize a true warrior, a leader who inspires courage in all around him. They have come because they are proud to fight under you, my brother, just as I am proud to fight at your side."

Barron had responded as he knew Tulus expected, as his friend needed him to respond. It wasn't his place to argue about why they were there, or to lecture Tulus on perceived flaws in his culture. No, only one thing was important to Barron. Vian Tulus had always been at his side when he was needed…and Barron could do no less for his brother.

"Our bomber squadrons will be ready to launch in five minutes, Tyler. They will follow your orders, and Admiral Stockton's, as though they came from my own lips."

"As always, Vian my great friend, I thank you for your steadfast aid."

"I have told you many times, there is no need for thanks between blood brothers. Fight with me, my friend, stand by my side as the enemy comes. I will ask no more of you than this."

Barron paused for a moment. He might have intended to say something else, but suddenly, it was gone, out of his mind utterly. There was something on the monitor, something that had seized his attention.

"I must go, Vian. Fortune be with you." He cut the comm line, and he looked right at the main display.

At the column of Highborn ships transiting into the system.

He hesitated, for only a second or two, but in his mind, he stood frozen in place for almost an eternity. Then he turned toward Atara, the spirit inside that sustained him in battle taking firm control.

"Launch all squadrons," he said crisply, coldly. "All wings are to advance at full thrust toward the transit point."

Chapter Seventeen

Temporary Hall of the People
Liberte City
Planet Montmirail, Ghassara IV
Union Year 227 (323 AC)

"Admiral Denisov...it is a great pleasure to welcome you home. You have been gone far too long, and your people have missed you."

Denisov bowed his head slightly. Ciara knew it for what it was, a makeshift greeting, a way to show some respect without saluting or anything else that might signify acceptance of her authority. That was far from unexpected, but the disappointment she felt told her she'd allowed herself to imagine, if not expect, that Denisov would support her without hesitation or condition.

There are always conditions...

"The pleasure is mine..." There was a hitch, and it was obvious Denisov didn't know what to call her. He wasn't yet ready to recognize her as First Citizen, but he clearly didn't want to offend her by falling back to her old title of 'Minister.'

"Sandrine, Admiral. We have known each other for how long? Formality seems unnecessary." Technically, they had known each other for more than ten years, but that was somewhat misleading. They'd never been close, neither personally nor professionally. But shifting to first names offered a way to avoid any...difficulties. Denisov clearly wasn't ready to recognize her as First Citizen yet, and the last thing she needed was anyone else around her getting those kind of ideas in their heads.

"Thank you, Sandrine. And, of course, I am Andrei." Denisov's tone was cautious, but not hostile. She figured being Villieneuve's enemy put her halfway, at least, to securing the admiral's backing.

Ciara smiled sweetly. She was quite adept at manipulating people, especially men, but she had a pretty good idea that wasn't going to work with the Union's famous renegade admiral. The treatment Denisov had received from Gaston Villieneuve—including an attempted assassination that had come *very* close to succeeding—had hardly predisposed him to trust anyone who'd been part of Sector Nine.

But, of course, sharing an enemy had been the seed of many a productive partnership...and the former head of Sector Nine, the dictator who'd sent killers after the admiral, was not an enemy to be trifled with, even if he *had* been driven off Montmirail.

Ciara didn't expect Denisov to trust her any time soon, but she couldn't imagine he had many options other than throwing in with her. Unless he wanted to become a permanent exile, and inflict that fate on all his spacers as well.

Denisov could take his fleet back to Confederation space, certainly, even out to the Badlands to join Tyler Barron in the new fight that had drawn the Confeds so far out into the unknown, but that would be a temporary solution only, and it would leave him facing whichever side won the civil war. It made far more sense to pick a side, to gain influence and position, and to secure, to the extent possible, a future in the new regime. Give a choice between supporting her and Villieneuve, Ciara wasn't overly concerned about how Denisov would land.

Besides, she was willing to bet the admiral was too much of a patriot to ignore the desperate struggle that had engulfed the Union, to remain in the safety of Confederation space while his nation tore itself apart.

And even less likely, to watch as his hated enemy, Gaston Villieneuve prevailed and imposed an even more despotic and paranoid rule over the worlds of the Union.

"Andrei, I believe you are at least somewhat aware of recent events, and the situation the Union now faces."

The admiral looked around the room, and then back at Ciara. "Sandrine, I wonder if it is possible for us to speak alone."

She was surprised at the suggestion. She'd imagined Denisov would want to spend some time looking around, talking to some of the others. She'd been ready to allow that, to an extent at least. But if the admiral was ready to deal, as far as she was concerned, the sooner the better.

"Of course, Andrei. My office—at least what I'm using as an office at the moment—is this way. I'd suggest someplace more comfortable, but here I can at least assure you there are no surveillance devices. *None except the ones I had put in, at least...*

"That will be perfectly fine, Sandrine." The voice was unreadable, cold without being hostile. She considered herself adept at reading such things, but she was stumped at what Denisov was going to tell her.

"This way, please. Can I send for anything? Drinks? Some food?"

"No, thank you. Nothing for me. I have come a long

way, and I would like to get right to our business at hand."

"Certainly." She gestured down the hall and led him to her office, a large room, nicely furnished…but not too plush. She'd been trying to establish her authority while also distancing herself from some of Villieneuve's excesses.

She stepped aside and waved toward the doorway, waiting until Denisov was inside to follow. "Please, Andrei, have a seat."

Denisov sat down at one of the chairs facing a large desk. Ciara was about to walk around and sit behind the desk, but at the last instant, she stopped and flopped down in the other guest chair. It seemed less formal, a better way to speak with an officer who was crucial to the success of her coup, but not yet fully onboard.

"As you know, the forces committed to me are fighting the traitors supporting Gaston Villieneuve."

"I detest Villieneuve at least as much as you do, Sandrine, perhaps more. But let us dispense with labels like 'traitor,' shall we? It is not difficult to imagine an officer seeing him as the rightful head of state. Good men and women have followed many bad causes."

"Yes, certainly." Denisov's directness struck her abruptly, and she realized the only way to deal with the admiral was with her own unvarnished directness. And with a lot more honestly than she usually employed.

"Very well, Admiral, let us get to the point. If Gaston Villieneuve wins this fight, I am dead…or at least, I will have to flee into exile and spend my life trying to evade his assassins. You, as well, will be forever barred from returning home, and I have little doubt you will find you have not had your last encounter with Villieneuve's killers. You may have formed an alliance of sorts with the Confeds, but *this* is your home. You may not trust my ability or intentions regarding governing the Union if I prevail, but I hope, at least, you believe I would be preferable to the monster who has so long held the power."

"I think you know I would never support Gaston Villieneuve." A pause. His cold mask of emotionlessness failed for an instant. "If I may be blunt, Minister Ciara, my time in the Confederation has opened my eyes in many ways. You and I have never crossed paths, at least not in any confrontational way, but you *are* Sector Nine...and we all know what Sector Nine is."

"Admiral..." The reversion to formal titles was not a good sign, but she didn't think she had any choice except to follow Denisov's lead. "...Sector Nine is a large organization with many..."

"Please, Minster Ciara...I will not insult your intelligence. I will be appreciative if you return the favor. I know what Sector Nine is, and I know what you have been. Your government would probably be less brutal than Villieneuve's, I grant you that, but you will still rule as a dictator."

"Admiral, I can assure you..." She stopped. She wasn't going to convince Denisov by lying. "Yes, you are correct. The Union has known nothing but autocratic rule for two centuries. I appreciate your infatuation with your friends in the Confederation, and I cannot guess at what makes their chaotic mix of scattered would be autocrats and marginal democracy work, but I can assure you, replicating that in the Union, at least in the short term, is a recipe for disaster."

"I agree."

Ciara stared back, stunned. That was just about the last thing she'd expected to hear.

"I'm sorry?"

"I did not seek this meeting to convince you to

transform the Union into another version of the Confederation. I am as aware of our history as you, and I know very well, for whatever skills I possess, I attained my rank through the same corrupt system that powered your rise to the top. Even if I was so inclined, I do not have the strength alone to wage a battle to establish a democratic Union government. If I possessed such strength, and sought to bring democracy to the Union, the vestiges of Sector Nine would almost certainly seek to destabilize any nascent republic." A pause. "No, Sandrine, I did not come here to make a pointless effort to convince you to give the people freedom. My goals, and sadly, my ideals, fall well short of so lofty an achievement. I am prepared to bring my forces to your side, but I need certain guarantees from you."

Ciara struggled to hold back a smile. Trading in political promises and corruption was her specialty. If they were down to horse trading, she figured she had already won. "What do you want, Andrei?"

"First, while I do not believe the Union can emulate the Confederation's ways, at least not for a very long time. But I have made promises to their officers and political leaders. My fleet has been their ally for several years now, and I will not be a party to any bloc seeking to continue the cold war between our nations—much less, to begin any actual future conflicts."

"I can assure you, Andrei, I am not looking for more enemies. Indeed, I may even be able to put your mind more at ease in that regard than you probably imagine." She hesitated for a moment, unsure how much she should say. But she needed Denisov, and that meant she had to trust him. "First, I must have your sincere promise that nothing I am about to say will leave this room."

"You have my word."

"My effort to overthrow Gaston Villieneuve was

financed, in large part, by Confederation Intelligence." She hesitated, unsure if Denisov was going to respond. But he was just looking back at her with a stunned expression on his face. "Our century of conflict with the Confederation was both pointless and destructive, I agree with you fully on that. I can promise you, if Villieneuve is defeated, the pointless animosity between the Union and the Confederation is over."

Denisov finally nodded his head, still looking like he was processing her unexpected response. "Very well. Second, you will grant an immediate pardon for all of my officers and spacers. No doubt, Villieneuve has condemned them all in absentia, and branded them all as traitors."

"He has. If we strike a deal in this room, the pardon will be issued within the hour."

"Very well." A pause, a longer one this time. "One more thing, Sandrine. I have a pretty good idea that Villieneuve has managed to gain the edge in this conflict, notwithstanding the fact that you still hold Montmirail." He put his up hand to silence her just as she was about to argue. "Please, Sandrine…this is not the time for lies or propaganda. If we join forces, I will need to know every detail of the tactical and strategic situations. Every last bit."

"I will do better than that, Andrei. Join me, and I will place you in supreme command of our forces, all of them. I will look to your skill and experience to help find a way to rid ourselves of Villieneuve. Our adversary has managed to secure the support of roughly seventy percent of the fleet, not counting your forces." She shook her head. She'd been surprised and disappointed at the number of flag officers declaring for Villieneuve, but then she thought about her enemy's paranoia. She realized she shouldn't have been surprised that he had all sorts of influence over many of the officers, all sorts of well-placed blackmail, bribery, threats to their families, anything it took to win allegiance. She was confident of her own abilities, but she'd gotten a refresher course in just how good Gaston Villieneuve was at manipulating and intimidating people.

"So, with my forces in the mix, we're looking at what? Something like an even match?"

"Yes, I believe almost exactly even. So, you see, Andrei, I *need* your assistance…very badly. Will you help me? Will you side with me so we can prevent Gaston Villieneuve from returning to power?"

Denisov stood up, and he extended his hand.

Ciara followed suit, and she finally let out a smile, and a deep breath, as she clasped her new ally's hand. She'd been on the verge of outright desperation just days before, but the return of Denisov's forces changed the situation completely.

At least it was an even fight now.

Chapter Eighteen

CFS Dauntless
Sigma Nordlin System
Year 323 AC (After the Cataclysm)

The Battle of Calpharon – Invasion of the Highborn

"Admiral Stockton has landed. The flight teams are working on his ship."

Barron nodded at Atara. He'd almost ordered another ship be prepared, and transferred to Stockton, one that would be ready to launch the moment the pilot landed. But Stockton had been in his cockpit for days, and he'd just made a desperate run back to the fleet. An hour walking around the flight deck wasn't exactly shore leave, but with the main fight still ahead, Barron figured it was a lot better than nothing.

And, perhaps, so did Stockton. The usually aggressive officer hadn't raised the issue either. *If Stockton thinks he needs a few minutes, even subconsciously, he damned well needs a few minutes...*

Besides, the wings were all launched and on their way to meet the enemy fleet. Ideally, Stockton would have been there with them, but the fighter corps had deep leadership, and the tactics for the first assault were almost absurdly simple. Race to the point, and hit anything that emerges…focusing first and foremost on the massive battleships. For all his skill and experience, Stockton could do little to add to the equation from tens of thousands of kilometers behind, trying to catch up with a strike force that would be on its way back before he got there.

Barron turned and looked at *Dauntless*'s giant main display. The system was laid out in all its glory, and a wide swath of small dots was arranged in a semi-circular formation around the planet Calpharon. Over twelve hundred ships had been massed, and they were sitting and waiting for the enemy. Another four hundred hung outside the displayed area, he knew, in reserve and waiting within striking range of transit point one…just in case the enemy came in from two directions.

"Still only the smaller vessels coming through, Admiral."

"For now…but we know they're on the way." Barron knew just how powerful those 'small' ships were, and what they could do to his fleet, and to the forces of his allies deployed alongside. He knew the bombers could hit the advance line hard, but he was wary to give them the go ahead…not when he knew the enemy battle line was still coming.

Though you will have to move at some point if the battleships hang back…

It felt odd *hoping* that the enemy battle line would transit, that the behemoths would come at his forces. Launching the bomber attack before the battleships had transited had been a gamble, one that would pay off if the enemy heavies came through as expected. But if the Highborn sent only their smaller ships at first, the attacking wings would have no choice but to hit them.

Every enemy ship damaged or destroyed was a good thing, but Barron knew any chance of ultimate success depended on neutralizing the Highborn battleships.

"Admiral...we're going to have to put someone in command of the strike force until Admiral Stockton is able to get out there."

Barron nodded, but he didn't say anything. Atara was right, of course. Sending the wings in without an overall commander was only risking confusion...and a failed attack with heavy casualties. But Stockton was one of a kind, and Barron didn't know where to start trying replacing his friend, even for an hour or two.

He was still thinking when Atara turned back toward him. "Listen to this, Admiral..."

He tapped his headset, and he instantly recognized the voice in his ears.

"...just follow my instructions. I'll be there shortly, but until then, I've got you all on my screens. Your formations look great, and I expect you all to keep it that way. We've got one chance to hurt these things before they can hit us with their missile strikes. Don't sweat that you don't see them yet, they're coming—and we're not going to blow it by losing our shit."

Barron looked over at Atara's station.

"He's in flight control. He's directing the attacking wings from there."

Barron just returned Atara's glance, and then he looked back at the display. It hadn't even occurred to him to order Stockton to flight control to command his people remotely until his ship was ready to launch. He was surprised to hear Stockton on the comm...and then he wasn't surprised.

You should have known he wouldn't rest, not even for an hour on a bench on the flight deck. Not while his squadrons are out there...

Commanding the bombers from *Dauntless* was far from ideal. The distance from the flagship to the wings was already causing a six second delay in communications. Not an eternity by any measure, but far from ideal in battle—and it would only get worse. Still, Stockton's tactical skill and his voice on the comm by itself was worth another fifty squadrons by any measure.

Barron leaned back in his chair, taking a deep breath, and readying himself. He was no stranger to desperate battles, but he knew even he had a limit to his endurance. The fighting in the system hadn't even started yet, and despite his efforts to hide it from himself, he felt a level of fatigue beyond any that had plagued him before. He was tired—*used up is what they call it*—and he dug as deeply as he could for whatever strength remained to him.

He thought of Andi, and of his daughter. It was a cheap trick, one he'd used more than a few times in the past weeks to keep himself focused on the war…on the reason he was fighting it. But it was still working.

He closed his eyes, planning to give himself a minute to center himself.

As it turned out, he only got about half that.

* * *

"Your Supremacy…Confederation comm traffic confirms our scanner reports. The enemy battleships have begun to transit into the system. Four confirmed, and energy readings around the point suggest more are inbound."

Vian Tulus sat bolt upright in his chair. His duty in combat could take many forms, but at that moment, nothing was as important as setting the example for his people. He was the image of the noble warrior, a man unafraid of death, of defeat.

It is a pleasant fabrication, at least.

Tulus was a Palatian, through and through, but he was a man as well. He denied his fear, even to himself, but that didn't change the fact that it was there, inside him, chewing away at every thought, at everything he did.

"Put me on the main fighter channel, Tal." He had no real place in the coming fight between the bomber squadrons and the newly arrived enemy battleships. There were eight hundred of his warriors out there, the second largest national contingent, but that didn't give him a role. Not when Jake Stockton was with them.

A young, impetuous fighter allowed himself to be governed by pride, by arrogance. Tulus was the Alliance's Imperator, a role that was half military rank and half a designation of his status as head of state. There was no place in his life for youthful foolishness. A true warrior stood up to any enemy, fought with all the strength that remained to him.

He also recognized ability in a friend, an ally. And he stepped aside to allow a more skilled comrade take control when it was warranted.

The Palatian fighters were already technologically inferior to the Confederation craft, and the new Hegemony ships as well. He wasn't going to increase the intensity of that disadvantage by denying his people the very best overall commander available. Even if he was a foreigner.

He'd been a bit concerned his pilots would object to being placed under Stockton's command. Palatian culture was based on a nationalistic pride which sometimes made it difficult to work with allies. For sixty years, the Alliance had been built almost entirely on the notion that the only way to avoid falling to conquest and slavery was to be the strongest.

But they weren't the strongest. The Alliance, for all the

bluster and courage of its warriors, couldn't have defeated the Confederation *or* the Union in a straight up fight, and even less so the Hegemony. Now, they were facing an even more powerful enemy. Vian Tulus had done all he could to lead his people into the new reality, and he'd realized that meant his people had to serve as the junior partners to Tyler Barron and his Confederation.

At least Tyler is one of us…

The blood brother ceremony that had bound him to Barron years earlier held a sacred place in Palatian culture. For all intents and purposes, Tyler Barron of the Confederation was also Lord Barron of the Alliance, and in every way that mattered, a Palatian warrior.

And Jake Stockton has almost godlike status among the pilots…even yours…

He was grateful Stockton's mystique had proven effective with his own squadrons as well as those from the Confederation. Tulus wasn't above a touch of Palatian arrogance, but he understood all he had seen, and he knew there was no chance for victory, none at all, not unless all the allied powers fought together as one. Petty rivalries, mistrust, half-hearted commitments…any of those would doom the war effort. Doom them all.

And defeat was inconceivable to a Palatian warrior. If it came to a choice, Tulus knew what he would choose, what all his people would choose.

Death first. Before defeat. Before slavery.

* * *

Reg Griffin looked down at her fuel gauge. Her tanks were close to dry. She still had enough to get back to *Constitution* and to land with some margin of safety, but not much more.

The AI had directed the small maintenance bots on

her ship with considerable skill, and her damaged craft was mostly operational. She was going to make it back.

Or she could turn and join the attacking squadrons, help manage the attack. No one in the vast mass of bombers even then heading toward the point knew the enemy formation like she did. She might be able to help target damaged Highborn ships, to direct the thousands of attacking vessels to the places they could do the most damage. She could give the wing commanders valuable intel, and probably vastly increase the damage they inflicted.

She could help, she was sure of it. But the cost would be high, perhaps very high. She figured she had a chance, maybe ten percent, of getting her ship on a course back to the fleet after the assault wave went in. That, at least, would point her in roughly the right direction. But there was no way she could make it back *and* decelerate and maneuver into the landing bay. She'd be depending on the rescue ships to match course and velocity with her disabled ships and retrieve her, and that seemed like a longshot in the middle of what was likely to be the largest battle ever fought. Unless she could get well to the rear of the fighting, wherever that was by then.

If you're going to worry about odds, think about what chance you've got of making it through another attack run, even one where you're not launching anything.

The fight ahead would be a desperate one, and just maybe, she could do some real good. But it had to be immediately. The chance would pass if she went back to the ship, and it wouldn't return. The next time bombers headed for the enemy, they would fly right into the teeth of the terrible missile barrages.

She was still thinking about what to do when her hand, seemingly on its own, jerked the throttle hard to the side. The positioning jets rolled her ship around, and then the engines fired hard, decelerating along the vector back to *Constitution*.

She hesitated, but just for an instant, and she eased off on the thrust...but she knew there was no time to think, no time to do anything but *decide*. Every second that passed by took her farther toward the fleet, the opposite direction if she was going to join the attack. She shook her head, and she decided to go back, to land and then to relaunch to join the fight. It would be insane to turn around, to dive back into battle with a damaged ship and depleted fuel tanks. It was fear exerting control, self-preservation, and though it was only a rational response, she immediately felt shame about it.

Her ship tore through space toward the fleet for another ten seconds, perhaps fifteen, while Reg Griffin fought another war, one with herself. Then her hand moved abruptly, jerking the throttle hard to the side. She brought her ship around again, repositioned the main thrusters, and blasted at full thrust...away from the fleet, toward the strike force and the still-transiting enemy ships. It wasn't a decision, at least not a conscious one. Her hand seemed to move on its own, driven by some part of her brain she couldn't unlock. Some part that scoffed at fear.

She'd done the calculations...twice. She would complete the required deceleration and then re-accelerate to match the strike force's velocity, just about the time the first line passed her position.

That would also leave her with less than five percent of her fuel load remaining.

She wouldn't have to make an attack run, at least. For all her knowledge of the enemy formation, she didn't have any torpedoes left. She just needed to stay close enough to help the wing commanders direct their squadrons.

Assuming they listened to her. She was just one of them, a wing commander, and one who'd led back barely fifteen percent of her wing to boot. But she had to try.

It was a chance to make a difference, to help the fleet. To try one more time to help defeat the enemy, to turn back the deadly assault.

To avenge her lost people, the pilots who'd left the landing bays with her a few days before, and who were now mostly gone, nothing more than names to be spoken solemnly at some memorial service after the battle.

If anyone was still alive to mourn, that is.

Chapter Nineteen

Senate Committee Chamber
Troyus City
Megara, Olyus III
Year 322 AC (After the Cataclysm)

"I can assure you all, the Union is not an imminent threat, not at this time. Confederation Intelligence has operatives in key positions, and the two prime factions are faced off against each other. There appears to be no chance of reconciliation between them, and short of this extremely unlikely development, no possibility the Union will be able to conduct offensive operations against us, regardless of how weakened our border defenses have become." Gary Holsten stood at the front of the room, trying to hide the disgust in his expression as he looked out over the senior Senators assembled for his briefing.

Holsten has always been cynical, but his years of work in Confederation Intelligence, and his constant interactions with the foul and putrid swamp known as the Senate, had only hardened and sharpened that callous view. He liked to imagine that the Confederation's government had been less corrupt in the early days of the nation, that there had been at least *some* honesty, and some dedication to national service and to the good of the people. Something besides constant maneuvering for personal power and influence.

Something other than self-serving nonsense that could be packaged as 'good for the people' in order to secure what needed votes couldn't be outright bought.

"I appreciate your report, Mr. Holsten, but I believe this committee requires some degree of evidence to feel confident. After all, the safety of the Confederation and its billions remains our primary consideration and our sacred trust."

Holsten felt acidity in the back of his throat. He'd likely have lost what control he had and failed to hold back the contents of his stomach at that kind of self-serving prattle...save for one thing. The words came from Speaker Flandry's mouth, and the Senate's highest-ranking member was actually his ally at present.

It was a disturbing state of affairs, but a necessary one. Flandry was as corrupt and self-serving a politician as Holsten had ever met, one who would normally have evoked his utter contempt. But something had happened to Flandry, and the power and responsibility of holding the Speakership seemed to have forged some kind of sense of duty in the scoundrel. He'd risen at least to the point where his petty power games could be separated from the Confederation's future, even its survival.

He'd grown up, in a manner of speaking, and he'd become an adult of sorts, looking over a group of spoiled and pandered to children. Otherwise known as the Senate.

It still wasn't easy for Holsten, and even as he continued with the script the two had rehearsed, he found thoughts invading his concentration, things like how many votes Flandry had gathered in his career from graveyards and crematoria. And how many he'd simply invented, phantom men and women who'd existed, such as they had, only in their votes for the Honorable Emmit Flandry, Senator from Philophoria.

The fact that Holsten had himself run roughshod over more than one set of rules seemed a more distant thought, one that was in there somewhere, but also…different. The thought that he was a part of the same grotesquely corrupt machine was too difficult to face head on. Better to push it back, to reconsider it another day.

"I cannot disclose the names of operatives, save for code names. I am sure you will all understand this is a matter of personal security for those involved, and in full compliance with Confederation law." That was normally true, of course. Operatives could be placed in grave danger if their identities were leaked. But in the current case it was more Holsten's desire to avoid giving the Senators all they wanted. Alexander Kerevsky was the primary source of intel from the Union, and the only real secret there had been that the military liaison to Montmirail was also a Confederation agent. That was information of limited sensitivity, now however, since Sandrine Ciara was well aware of Kerevsky's true identity and, at the moment, she was the only one on the Union's capital planet that mattered.

But Holsten held back the name, as much as anything because he had lost a bit of his trust in Kerevsky. He wasn't concerned the agent was actually disloyal…but he was a bit worried about the relationship that seemed to have developed between Kerevsky and Ciara. He had no problem with his operative gaining information through access to Ciara's bedroom, but he had a feeling the emotions involved had gone somewhat beyond pure professional necessity. He'd made a note to keep an eye on the situation, but the last thing he wanted was input from the Senate.

"You expect us to simply believe when you tell us you have an unnamed agent close to Minister Ciara or First Citizen Villieneuve?" Cyn Avaria's tone was moderate, indicating some mistrust, but perhaps not resolute opposition. That was a good sign.

"With all due respect, Senator Avaria…" And, in truth, Holsten thought very little respect was actually due. "…would a name give you anything of greater substance? I can show you identity redacted reports, operational records…enough to prove that we indeed have operatives in the Union, and that we have received current data on the situation there."

Data Holsten had carefully edited before he'd provided it to the Senators. The civil war was an unexpected opportunity to keep the Union destabilized, possibly even to see Gaston Villieneuve defeated, and to establish a far better relationship with his successor. There was only one problem with that scenario. It was beginning to look like Villieneuve was going to defeat Ciara and retain control. And Gaston Villeneuve's hatred for the Confederation was pathological.

"Yet you provide no battle reports, no real evaluation of the conflict. I assume you have contingency plans in the event First Citizen Villieneuve retains his position, and especially if he does so with his forces intact enough to become a renewed threat?"

Holsten took a deep breath. Avaria was corrupt, a woman with an almost unquenchable thirst for power, but that didn't mean she was stupid. She was chasing him down like a bloodhound, and it was pissing him off.

"Senator, of course we have contingency plans in place." He didn't. He'd gone all in supporting Tyler Barron at the front. Other than a desperate attempt to arrange an assassination plot to get rid of Villieneuve—

something that had failed half a dozen time before—he had no idea how he'd respond if the First Citizen won the civil war with enough of his forces intact to take advantage of the weak Confederation border defenses.

But he had done something, at least, to forestall that victory, to give Ciara a chance to prevail. Andrei Denisov had been prepared to lead his Free Union forces to the front lines in Hegemony space, to support Admiral Barron and the other contingents deployed there.

Then, word had come of the outbreak of civil war in the Union. Denisov had raised the issue first, suggesting that perhaps he should lead his forces back to his homeland. He'd been tentative, feeling as though answering that call might let Barron down. But Holsten had encouraged him.

Barron needed all the forces he could get, no doubt, but anything that allowed Ciara to defeat Villieneuve, or at least prolong the conflict, kept the Confederation border safe.

And it gave Holsten a good chance to send Barron the reserves and support he needed from other sectors.

"But, quite apart from plans to counter any Union offensive, we have taken steps to ensure that no such threat can materialize. Even as we speak, Admiral Denisov and his Free Union forces are en route back to Montmirail to support Minister Ciara. Our intelligence on force distribution is still based somewhat on estimates, but it is very likely that the admiral's arrival will place Ciara's forces at least on parity with Villieneuve's. With luck, she will prevail, and we will have a leader on Montmirail with whom we can negotiate a long-term peace. Even in the worst case, the war there will last a number of years, giving us the time to fully support Admiral Barron at the front…and still recall enough forces to strengthen the Union border in the event

Gaston Villieneuve ultimately prevails."

It all sounded good, but Holsten could think of a hundred ways he'd attack the argument if he was on the other side. He didn't need everyone onboard, just enough for force a majority vote on the floor, and his argument just had to be good enough to secure that support.

Separating the Reds from the Greens might just be an added benefit if he managed things just right. The two parties controlled over seventy percent of the votes in the Senate, and Cyn Avaria and Kettle Vaughn, the respective leaders of the two blocs, long in perpetual opposition to each other, had shown a disturbing tendency recently toward cooperation.

But Avaria was more concerned with the prospect of Union aggression. Holsten was shooting for a place in the middle, where his arguments were persuasive enough to secure Vaughn and the Greens, but not Avaria and the Reds. That would accomplish two goals in one...and a divided Senate would be that much easier to manage if he needed anything else to support the fleet.

"I must congratulate you, Mr. Holsten, on your management of the Union situation. No doubt, Admiral Barron would have found Admiral Denisov's forces useful, but this allows us to more fully support his efforts with Confederation vessels and supplies. I am still uncomfortable with the weakened status of our borders, but considering the severity of the situation in Hegemony space, and the fact that the Alliance forces are all far out in the Badlands and the Union fleets are fighting each other, I believe I can support your requests." Vaughn spoke slowly—annoying slowly, as he always did. But it was worth listening this time. Holsten had done all he could to secure the support of the Greens, but he hadn't been sure he'd succeeded, not until he heard Kettle Vaughn trying to spit out the words.

Cyn Avaria slammed her hand down on the table, a rare instance of the seasoned politician losing control of her frustration. There were two other Greens at the table, and they were both nodding a sign that Vaughn had his entire bloc behind him. Holsten looked out and he held back the smile trying to break out on his lips. He had them. His combination of persuasion and the quasi-blackmail supported by his secret files, provided more than enough support to carry a majority with the Greens, even if Cyn Avaria kept every one of her Reds in line.

"Very well…thank you, Mr. Holsten. I believe we have enough information to send this matter to the Senate floor for vote." Flandry exchanged a quick glance with the spymaster. Holsten felt a little queasy at how closely he'd become allied with Flandry, but as he listened to the Speaker's thick drawl, he could see his new ally was staying faithfully on script. He didn't trust Flandry, he doubted such a thing was possible, even if some unforeseen situation made it wise. But there was no reason an alliance couldn't be uneasy *and* successful.

He nodded his head. "Mr. Speaker, Senators…" He turned and stepped back through the door. He had an instinctive impulse to remain, to keep an eye on Flandry. But he needed the Speaker, and he had no choice but to accord his co-conspirator something at least close to trust. For now.

He walked down the corridor outside, back toward the main quad of the Senate Compound, and he finally let the smile find its way out. He'd already seen that most of the fleet was sent to Barron, and this latest effort was predominantly about supplies…and the new Black Lightning fighters, which Cyn Avaria had wanted to deploy to the remaining squadrons and the second line garrison pilots defending the border.

And he'd gotten it done without Andi, something he'd

been far from sure he could manage. The thought of his friend wiped the smile from his face, though.

He had no idea where Andi was, but the fact that she, her baby, and *Pegasus* all seemed to be gone from Megara had him on edge. Tyler Barron hadn't charged him specifically with keeping an eye on his family, but Holsten felt responsible…and he had agents all over the Confederation looking for any signs of Andi…or *Pegasus*.

It was a sense of duty to Barron, and also to Andi. She had worked for him before, and she had suffered for it, and Holsten felt he owed a debt he was still repaying.

He liked her, too, considered her one of his closest friends. And one of the ones most likely to do something crazy.

That twisted his guts in knots, and the realization that Andi Lafarge could probably lose his people slipping through the crowds at a spaceport only made it worse.

Where are you…and what are you up to?

Chapter Twenty

CFS Dauntless
Sigma Nordlin System
Year 323 AC (After the Cataclysm)

The Battle of Calpharon – A Condor Rises

"What the hell is she doing?" Jake Stockton stared at the screen, his eyes focused on single tiny dot, one among a sea of thousands. It was one of the handful he could see moving in the opposite direction from the main strike force, back toward the fleet, the last of the returnees from Vexa Torrent still heading toward their landing platforms.

Except one was blasting its engines in the wrong direction. It seemed to be turning around.

Stara Sinclair had been working at the scanner, her attention focused on the newly-arrived enemy capital ships, and on the main attack, the most massive bomber assault ever mounted by Confederation forces. It was understandable she hadn't noticed the change in thrust on one ship. She looked up as soon as Stockton spoke, and a few seconds later, she let out a gasp. "Who is that?"

Stockton's hands moved over the workstation's

keyboard, bringing up an ID badge. "Reg Griffin."
Condor.

"What is she doing?"

"She's turning to link up with the strike force."
Stockton's voice was soft, grim. He knew exactly what
she was doing, if only because he very well might have
done precisely the same thing in her shoes.

"She can't possibly have enough fuel left, not to fight
and…make it back."

"She's not worried about making it back, Stara. She
has the best information on the approaching enemy
formations of anyone out there…and she's going to use
it."

"That's crazy, Jake. I'm going to order her back." Stara
reached for the comm controls, but Stockton put his
hand on hers.

"No, Stara…don't."

"Are you crazy? What chance is there we'll be able to
retrieve her in the middle of this battle? What she is
doing…it's suicide."

"She's right, Stara. We need every edge we can
get…and she can almost definitely lead the squadrons
toward the weakest targets. The enemy was right on her
tail as she transited. She's got the most current scanning
data."

"But she'll die, Jake…"

"No, not necessarily." Stockton didn't like writing off
his pilots, and certainly not one of his best like Reg
Griffin. It felt somehow disloyal, but more than that, he
knew people had done it to him more times than he could
count.

And he was still there.

"She's good, Stara. One of the best. She'll try to keep
her combat vectors reasonably aligned with the return
course. With some luck, she'll manage to keep enough

fuel to at least get on a vector back to the fleet. And I'll get a retrieval boat out there, if I have to fly the damned thing myself."

Stara was about to continue the argument, but Stockton put up his hand. "Please, Stara…don't make this more difficult." It was unfair, perhaps, to silence her like that. But there was another reason for leaving Reg alone, one Stara wouldn't fully understand.

What no one but one of his veteran pilots would truly comprehend.

Reg knew the situation, the challenge the fleet faced. And she knew she could help the strike force. If he ordered her to return, she would disobey. And that would only weigh on her mind, make it even less likely she could survive. If she was going to take the terrible risk anyway, he owed it to her to give him her his blessing, and to wish her well.

I can do more than that…

His hands moved down to the comm. He flipped a series of controls, opening a channel to the entire strike force. "Attention all pilots. Commander Reg Griffin, callsign Condor, is hereby promoted to Commodore Griffin, effective immediately, and placed in command of the entire strike force until I reach the combat zone."

He glanced down at the chronometer. His ship was supposed to be ready in twenty minutes, but he figured he might just shave a few off of that figure if he got down to the flight deck and haunted the crews.

He leapt up, turning toward Stara as he did. "Stara, I've got to…"

"I know, Jake…I know." He could hear her fighting to hold back her emotion, but all she did was stand up and walk the meter and a half toward him. She reached out and hugged him, and kissed him once, even as the comm unit behind her began buzzing again.

She stepped back and paused for a few seconds.

"That's probably Condor…just tell her I'm on my way…and she has my complete confidence." Stockton turned halfway around and then hesitated. "Stara…" He paused. Outpourings of emotion were difficult for him.

"I know, Jake…I've always known." She managed a thin smile, one that hid the fear on her face for a few seconds. "I love you, too." Then she turned and picked up the comm, even as Stockton slipped out the door.

"Yes, Reg…it's official. You're in command until Jake gets there…"

The door slid shut, and Stockton raced down the corridor. Reg Griffin's promotion *was* official enough that no one in the strike force would question it, but Stockton wasn't sure he actually had the authority to promote someone to flag rank. He'd have to check with Admiral Barron.

When he had time, which he most certainly didn't just then.

He didn't doubt Barron would approve what he'd done…but that would have to wait until he was back out.

Out into space, in his fighter. With his squadrons, facing the enemy.

Where he belonged.

* * *

"I don't understand…" Reg was still processing Admiral Barron's words, and those Commodore Sinclair had just added. Sinclair was the fleet's overall flight operations commander, the lord and master, in effect, of all the launch bays throughout the entire Confederation fleet. Next to Stockton, her word was paramount, and she'd basically repeated what the legendary admiral had just said.

Reg understood the words, but it was still taking time to sink in. She'd hoped to provide some information, some guidance, to help the wing commanders maximize their attack runs. Suddenly, she was in command...of the entire strike force. Four thousand bombers, every one of then heading directly toward the transit point.

Toward the Highborn fleet.

She looked down at her hands, trying as hard as she could to stop the trembling. It wasn't fear of death threatening to unravel her, though that was clearly there. It was the unexpected and crushing weight of responsibility. She was sure Jake Stockton would be coming to take over the command role as soon as he could get ship launched. But until then—and Stockton wouldn't get there until after the wings started their runs—the mission was hers to lead. She felt as though an avalanche of granite had fallen on her, the weight bearing down from every direction.

She tapped her comm unit, activating the forcewide channel. Her throat was suddenly dry, and her first efforts to speak were mostly unsuccessful. Finally, she managed to force enough spit into her mouth to get the words out.

"All squadrons, this is...Commodore...Griffin. We're going to hit these battleships as they enter the system, and we're going to do it as quickly as possible. We want to strike before they're able to get their systems fully back online and launch missile strikes." She felt a little guilty about her words, mostly because she knew the only difference hitting the enemy faster would make was the bombers would be ravaged by missiles strikes *after* they launched their own torpedoes. She would lose hundreds of pilots no matter what, but if they moved quickly enough that would happen as they pulled back and not as they attacked.

They will get a chance to knock out more enemy ships, though, cut down on the number and strength of the volleys...

There was truth to that, of course, but it fell well short of alleviating her anticipatory remorse. "All squadrons, increase thrust to maximum. We're going to hit those bastards just as quickly as possible. Wing commanders, I'll give each of you navigational instructions. We've got some damaged enemy ships coming through, and we're going to leave them alone. We want those first bombing runs targeted at the ones with functional missile arrays. Good hunting to all of you." She flipped the comm control, switching to the command frequency.

"Okay...wings fourteen and eighteen, you've got three battleships almost directly ahead. The two farthest back have significant damage." She'd only intended to provide information, but now she realized it was on her to issue orders. "Fourteen, concentrate on the forward ship, the undamaged one. Eighteen, split into two groups and hit both damaged ships. There aren't any other fresh vessels within your arc."

"Understood, Commodore."

"Acknowledged."

The responses were sharp, respectful, but she knew there *had* to be surprise out there at her sudden promotion...if not outright resentment. She'd had a distinguished career, made her mark, but she was far from the most senior of the wing commanders. Fifteen minutes before, she'd held the same rank as every other one of them out there, and now, she was in charge of the entire strike force.

She shook her head, putting it out of her mind. She had work to do. She looked back down at the small screen, and then she tapped the comm again. "Wing six, target the battleship at 320.114.209, thirty thousand kilometers from your position. Wing eleven..."

She had one hell of a lot of work to do...

*   *   *

"The fleet will advance at 10g." Tyler Barron sat where he had so many times, in the center of *Dauntless*'s massive bridge. He could 'see' the officers at their stations without even looking, some combination of memory and a 'feel' he couldn't quite explain. He felt at home on the battleship's command deck, disturbingly so. As much as he loved his ship, his years aboard her, and her predecessor, had been spent almost entirely at war. Friends, comrades, and subordinates had passed through, arriving fresh faced and excited, and as often as not, leaving in body bags. Or not leaving at all. Barron had never tried to count the number of his people who'd been incinerated at their posts or ejected into space…and he knew, if he was lucky, he'd go to his own grave before he ever did.

"Fleet order…advance at 10g." Atara had been repeating Barron's commands since the days when the old *Dauntless* had been his only responsibility. His first officer—and a friend he considered closer than a sister—still served much the same role she always had, but now as his chief of staff and senior aide. The scope of responsibility had grown exponentially, though, and had expanded to the entire fleet, tens of thousands of spacers…and even the future of the Confederation itself. Barron had always been amazed at how well Atara handled stress. He knew she *had* to feel it. He certainly did, and sometimes he felt as though it would crush him like 100g of undampened acceleration.

But she almost never showed it, certainly not in any way someone who knew her less well than Barron would notice.

"All units acknowledge, Admiral." A short pause.

"Imperator Tulus's command as well." Barron knew Vian Tulus would do whatever he asked, and while the Alliance ruler wasn't technically under his command, he might as well have been. "Commander Chronos advises his forces are also accelerating." The Hegemony leader was more of a question mark, though perhaps less than he might have been. Barron and Chronos had discussed the battle plan in great detail, and they'd agreed completely on how to proceed. The Confederation commander-in-chief had found his Hegemony counterpart to be somewhat of a kindred spirit, something he found useful...and difficult as well. He wasn't ready yet to fully accept so recent an enemy in such a role.

"All ships, full evasive maneuvers." Moving the fleet forward, hitting the enemy as close as possible to the transit point, had considerable advantages. His people just might manage to strike the Highborn before they had arrived in full strength. But that didn't mean they wouldn't have to run a gauntlet through enemy fire. The main guns on the smaller Highborn ships outranged even the Hegemony railguns...and Barron was still only guessing at what the Hegemony battleships mounted.

"All ships acknowledge, Admiral. Evasive maneuvers underway. Distance to the enemy forward line six hundred thousand kilometers.

Barron didn't imagine even the immense enemy battleships had anything that could shoot *that* far. But he wasn't taking any chances. The evasive routines would slow the advance slightly, and maybe send a few spacesick crew members to the sickbays, but that was a small price to pay, especially since the enemy's effective range remained largely a guess.

"Admiral, the lead bomber wings are beginning their final approaches."

Barron angled his head, looking toward the side of the

huge screen that displayed the bomber squadrons. Thousands of fighters...all under the command of Reg Griffin.

Barron had listened as Stockton issued the orders promoting the veteran officer—orders that technically exceeded his authority. He'd almost intervened, not to reverse Stockton, but to make it official. But he'd decided it wasn't necessary. Stockton was a god to his pilots, and he didn't see any gain in undermining his air of total authority. He'd just punched a quick notation in his log, ordering the promotion himself. Reg Griffin was officially a commodore as she led the four thousand small craft against the enemy.

Barron just hoped she would have more time to carry that rank, that she lived long enough to return and put the actual stars on her collars. He didn't like to guess at his people's chances, but he figured she'd be lucky to have a coin toss on that.

* * *

Reg angled her ship hard, and she felt her stomach flop for a few seconds before it settled down. She was a veteran pilot, experienced in combat in three different wars. She was likely, in normal circumstances, to poke mild fun at a rookie who got sick in the cockpit. But her gut was reminding her that wild evasive routines could occasionally be too much, even for the cast iron pot she called a stomach.

It wasn't the nausea that troubled her, but she was well aware that the crazy moves were eating through her limited fuel supply that much faster. She didn't have the reserves the rest of the strike force did to sustain that kind of continued thrust, but there didn't seem to be any point in saving fuel only so her ship could be blasted out of existence with a little more in the tank.

The defensive fire was heavy. That wasn't unexpected, but it was stressful, nevertheless. She'd reminded the wings three times about their evasive maneuvers, the last time emphasizing the point with the kind of exotic profanity only a veteran spacer could spew with abandon. But she'd still lost over two hundred ships so far, and none of her people were inside launch range yet.

And that's with no missiles…

Reg had seen the missiles in action, and she knew how deadly they were. Their thrust capacity was almost unimaginable, and their existence had turned fifty years of weapons doctrine on its head. Her entire career, and even back to her days in the academy, there had been one rule taken almost as established fact. Fighters could evade physical weapons such as missiles.

Time to scrap that adage…

She angled her thrust again, and she tapped the throttle. She almost looked at her fuel stats, but she decided there was no point. If she was lucky, she'd manage to get herself on a vector back to the fleet, with a chance to get somewhere the rescue ships could get her.

Otherwise, she'd just continue straight through the rest of the enemy fleet, and, if by some miracle, she made it through that unimaginable gauntlet, she would continue on past the transit point, right across the Sigma Nordlin system, and out into deep space. She'd get to watch the battle, some of it at least, before her life support was exhausted and she spent her last moments betting on whether she'd suffocate or freeze to death first. But she'd be frozen solid long before her ship began its endless voyage across interstellar space.

Her eyes darted back to her screen. Another fifty of her ships had been destroyed just in the last minute. But her lead squadrons were finally beginning their final attack runs. The forward formations were battered, some of the lead units at half strength or less. But she knew Confederation pilot culture well enough to be sure those flyers were more focused on revenge than fear. They wanted blood for their lost comrades, and she was confident they would get it.

She watched as the angular formations cut in, and then as the first ships let their torpedoes fly. She was pretty far out—without any torpedoes, there was no reason to advance farther—but she could see the squadrons were scoring hits.

She watched one after another of the weapons slam into the Hegemony ships, waiting for the AI to develop some kind of damage evaluation program from the incoming scanner data. One of the Highborn battleships took no fewer than sixteen hits...and it was still there. She'd never faced anything, seen *any* ship that could take that kind of damage and still keep coming.

She snapped out a series of orders, directing and redirecting incoming waves, trying to send her people in like packs of scavengers, to direct the smaller groups to take down the wounded and battered enemy ships, after the untouched ones within range had all been hit. She felt a quick rush as one of the Highborn ships disappeared, the attack's first outright kill...the second overall against the enemy's battleships, counting the one in Vexa Torrent.

Then her heart sank as, almost immediately after, she saw a cloud of small dots appear on the display, moving forward from roughly half of the enemy ships, mostly the ones that had remained out of her squadrons' range.

Missiles. Hundreds and hundreds of missiles heading toward the strike force.

Chapter Twenty-One

Free Trader Pegasus
Somewhere in the Badlands
Year 323 AC (After the Cataclysm)

Andi looked down at Cassiopeia, and she smiled. The child was looking back at her with Tyler's sparkling blue-gray eyes and laughing. Andi knew her daughter didn't know where she was, that she was as content on *Pegasus* as she would have been back on Megara, in the opulent hotel suite that had been home for the first months of her life. Andi had no intention of allowing her daughter to get close to any real danger, but she was just as determined to make sure that Tyler got a chance to meet his daughter. She hated the fact that her resolution was driven by a fear he wouldn't survive the latest conflict, but Andi rarely ran from difficult realizations. The pain of losing Tyler would be indescribable, but it would be even worse knowing he hadn't even had the chance to hold his child, *their* child.

Andi smiled as Cassiopeia looked up at her and giggled. She was a happy child, and Andi tried her best not to think that was only because she had no idea of the universe into which she'd been born. Did a life of strife and pain await her daughter, one with the losses and struggles she had endured, and the immense challenges?

Or is there any future at all? If the war is lost, perhaps not…

She extended her arm down and held out her finger, smiling again as Cassiopeia reached up and grabbed it with a level of strength that seemed almost impossible. Andi knew, intellectually at least, that some people had children and raised them in peace. They lived normal lives and watched their sons and daughters grow up in quiet surroundings. But, realization or no, she found it hard to believe, at least in a practical sense. Her own mother had given birth to her amid the worst destitution imaginable, and had fought and scraped to protect and feed her a decade, before the darkness and death of the Gut had finally claimed her. Had her mother had any moments, even as the one she was having now? Had there been even fleeting instants of joy? Or just constant fear and sadness. Had she only endured the unimaginable misery of listening to her child crying because she was cold and hungry?

She felt a tear slip out of her eye and it ran down her cheek. She hardly remembered her mother, but she loved her, nevertheless. Andi remembered her later days in the Gut, when all she'd had to do was take care of herself, and she couldn't imagine how it had worn her mother down, what it had taken from her. *She must have been a strong woman in her own way.* For all her own battles and hardships, Andi knew she was fortunate. She had survived, she had escaped from the deprivation…and she had found happiness with Tyler Barron. Born into grinding poverty, she'd become vastly wealthy. Had there been *any* bright moments in her mother's life, even short instances of peace? She liked to think so, but she didn't really believe it.

Andi shook her head, trying to pull her thoughts from such long past pain. She'd been thinking of her mother more and more, a natural enough thing, she suspected, now that she had her own child. She'd been ten when her mother died and, while she realized intellectually there had been nothing she could do to save the woman who bore her and protected her for that first decade of her life, she still felt guilty that she had gotten out of there…and her mother never had.

She looked back at Cassiopeia. "I'm going to see that you meet your father, little one…and then I'm going to get you out of here, far away from this fighting and danger. I hope you never have to endure those things yourself." She took a deep and ragged breath, and she leaned back, closing her eyes. She sat and rested…for all of thirty seconds. Then the comm buzzed.

"Andi, it's Sy. I'm sorry to disturb you, but if you have a few minutes, I've made some progress on the fourth chip. I'm only about five percent of the way through the translations, but I think you'll want to see this. I'm getting closer to a real idea of just what the Highborn are, and where they came from."

"I'm on my way." Andi stood up and took a last look at Cassiopeia. The child was still awake, barely. Her eyes were closing, even as she still fought off the sleep that seemed inevitable. "Don't fight it, little one. There will be enough times when you can't rest. Now, sleep…and know I will do whatever I have to do to protect you, and to make sure you have a real future."

She turned, and she slipped out into the short corridor, gesturing to Lita Mareth as she walked onto the main area of the lower deck. The nanny nodded and stood up, moving back toward Andi's cabin.

Andi watched her go for a few seconds, and then she turned toward Sylene Merrick. The computer expert was hunched over the center table, with two workstations and half a dozen tablets strewn out in front of her. There were three cups, all empty, with just the slightest residue of the Combalian tea Sylene favored. Andi had lost track of the last time Sy had slept, or even taken a break, but from the looks of things, it had been a while.

A long while.

"Sy…"

Sylene hadn't even noticed Andi coming into the room. "Oh…Andi. This is fascinating. The Highborn are definitely *not* aliens. They were some kind of imperial creation. I've never seen such detailed information about imperial affairs before. This folio is one of the greatest finds ever, at least in terms of studying late imperial history. I'm glad you kept it."

Andi nodded. "Well, I'll give it all to the Troyus Institute when we're done with it." *Assuming there is an institute, or anything else, left on Megara when all this is through.*

"If you can help me translate more of this, I think we might be on the verge of some useful information. If we can determine exactly what the Highborn really are, we might be able to figure out their weaknesses."

Andi nodded, in complete agreement with her friend, save for one nagging worry hovering among her thoughts.

If they have any weaknesses…

Imperial Secret Police Headquarters
Planet Samara
Tirion Vega System
Year 11,691 IR (Imperial Reckoning)
Year 43 BC (Before the Cataclysm) by Confederation Calendar
366 Years Ago

"The Highborn? We've encountered that term several times, in communications intercepts and the like. But we haven't been able to match it to any other data. What is it, some group of nobles?" Velan Tragonis tapped a small switch on the edge of his desk, and the door closed. An instant later, a sequence of small blue lights flashed in succession. "We're completely secure in here, Trellic. Please speak freely."

"I have been investigating Lord Andros for the better part of a year, Colonel. I became suspicious almost immediately, but then I began to hit a series of dead ends. He *is* up to something, I'd bet anything on that. But I couldn't find any solid evidence, not even a rough idea of the nature of his secret operation. Finally, I was able to gain some information from one of his aides."

"Do I want to know how you did that, Trellic?" A pause. "No, never mind, I'm sure I don't. But by all means, tell me what you were able to find out."

"The Highborn is a group of some kind, but not just of other nobles. They were *creations* of Andros's, or at least of those in his employ."

"Creations?" Tragonis stared back over the desk, an inquisitive look on his face. "What do you mean by that? Clones? Cyborgs?"

Trellic shook his head. "No…I don't think so, at least not entirely. Something *like* that, perhaps, but far more complex. My source suggested the program that resulted in the Highborn has been in operation for more than sixty years, that it was started by Andros's grandfather."

Tragonis leaned back and rubbed his forehead. "I remember the old Lord Andros. I was young, just starting out, but the Bureau was investigating him for some kind of financial chicanery. The Andros family didn't get as wealthy as it is running those vast megafarms they control. There's only so much profit in feed grains. A fair amount of what they have was stolen in one way or another." Tragonis spoke matter-of-factly. His statement was nothing overly of note. Half the noble families in the empire owed their fortunes to some ancestor's misdeeds.

Tragonis's expression hardened. "Perhaps this is something of greater concern than we anticipated. Is it possible Andros is…creating…some kind of army?"

Trellic looked at the sector chief with a blank look on his face. "I don't know. I checked as exhaustively as I could, but I didn't find any large bases, or for that matter, excessive purchases of weapons. Some, certainly, but nothing that could outfit an army capable of destabilizing the empire. You're thinking, of course, he might be planning some way to seize the throne?"

Tragonis glanced down at the screen in front of him. "That would make any links to the various disturbances make sense. Creating disorder and then coming in as the one with the solutions…it's a classic strategy. But if there is a plot of that magnitude, I find it hard to believe we have missed it so badly. Andros would need tens of millions of troops, and he would need ships, too. He'd have to have a fleet admiral at least on his side. And we've seen nothing disturbing in our surveillance activities on the military. So, we would have had to miss that, as well, if Andros *is* planning a rebellion."

"Perhaps he has some other kind of plan, something more elaborate than simply a military coup. What if these…whatever they are…are some kind of specialists, perhaps elite troops who have received some form of biomechanical enhancements?"

"I don't know. What would he do with a small number of soldiers, no matter how effective they are? He'd still have to get them to the capital, wouldn't he?" Tragonis paused, but he continued before Trellic could respond. "An assassination team, maybe? A coup might involve targeting the emperor and a number of the other top imperial officials."

Trellic nodded. "That is certainly a possibility. With

your permission, I will resume my efforts to gather information."

"Yes, do that." Tragonis reached down and scooped up a small tablet laying on the desk. His tapped at it for a few seconds, and then he handed it to Trellic. "Here, I'm upgrading this case to level one priority. That will increase the resources at your disposal. Requisition any personnel you require, any equipment you need...but get me more information on what is happening." A pause. "I don't need to remind you that success in a mission like this is the kind of thing that builds a career."

"You can count on me. I will find out what Andros is up to."

"I know you will. Meanwhile, I am going to send a recommendation to the capital to place the imperial court on increased alert. I still find it hard to believe Andros is going to move against the emperor, but far better to be cautious and prepared. Just in case."

Chapter Twenty-Two

CFS Dauntless
Sigma Nordlin System
Year 323 AC (After the Cataclysm)

The Battle of Calpharon – Forward to Engage!

"We need those primaries, Fritzie! You've got to get them back online somehow." Barron sat on *Dauntless*'s bridge, his head leaning forward, doing what he'd done almost as long as he could remember.

Urging Anya Fritz to keep his ship functioning and in the fight.

There was an absurdity to it, of course. Barron's days as a ship captain were well behind him, and Anya Fritz had long been a flag officer and commander of the fleet's entire engineering establishment, a position Barron had invented just for her. But Barron was still on *Dauntless*—and Admiral needed a flagship, after all—and since he'd bumped Atara up to admiral and chief of staff, he'd managed to open up a way for him to act as the battleship's commander once again. He could have named a flag captain, of course, but there was still part of Barron that couldn't give up the feeling of leading his own ship. He was an admiral, a successful and decorated one, but in his heart, he was a ship's captain.

And Fritz's role as fleet engineering commander ceased to have any real meaning once the fleet went into combat. Ships fought and were damaged as individual units, and there was precious little Commodore Fritz could do to help the hundreds of individual teams on the fleet's ships. So, she also fell into old routines, effectively bumping *Dauntless*'s official chief engineer, and immersing herself in her old job with the same deep satisfaction, Barron suspected, that he did.

Taking a hit at such long range had been a surprise, and a very unwelcome one. Barron hadn't been careless on the approach. He'd implemented full evasion routines, and done everything he could to protect his ship. It was a stark reminder that luck stood tall next to skill, experience, and courage on the list of things determining the outcome of a battle.

"I'm on it, Admiral. I'll have them back before we're in range." Barron knew Fritzie enough to pick up the doubt in her voice. She wouldn't lie to him, he was sure of that. But she was also less than her usual one hundred percent sure she could get things back online in time. And that was unsettling.

"I know you are, Fritzie. Keep me posted." Barron was frustrated. He wanted to shout, to insist that she get it done. But if he'd ever commanded anyone who didn't need to be driven or pushed, it was Anya Fritz. The engineer had performed her wizardry time and time again, and Barron had never seen anyone who drove herself— or her people—harder. He'd seen her engineers more than once, wandering the corridors with a distant, vacant look. Anya Fritz exhausted her people in a way Barron had never seen before.

He turned back toward the display. The bomber attack

was still underway. Reg Griffin had done a masterful job at directing the fight, leading the squadrons toward the most vulnerable enemy ships with staggering precision. But the squadrons had already paid a terrible price for their success, and the intensity of their losses was rapidly escalating. Missiles volleys were tearing into their ranks, and almost a quarter of the ships launched had been destroyed or disabled. That sounded bad enough on its face, but it only got worse when Barron reminded himself that added up to nearly a thousand ships. A thousand pilots.

The old *Dauntless*, his first large command, had carried sixty fighters. He'd just seen more than fifteen times that number taken down…and the losses were still mounting.

He felt the urge to get on the comm, to order Reg Griffin to pull her people out. But he couldn't. He needed them out there. He needed every hit they could score, every enemy ship they could take out. Even if they were wiped out in the process.

It was a cold view, one he'd struggled with in his earlier years of command. Combat presented a dark and unforgiving calculus, and any commander worth the stars on his collar agonized over the losses his forces suffered. But Barron's realization was a broad one. He cared deeply for the pilots, for all of the almost quarter of a million spacers in his fleet, but he also knew he would have traded every one of their lives—his own included—to save the hundred billion or more in the Confederation, all of whom faced death or slavery if the Highborn were allowed to prevail.

He winced slightly as he saw a flash on his screen, another of the enemy's long range beams coming too close. He suspected the accuracy of the Highborn fire at *Dauntless* was coincidental, but it was disconcerting, nevertheless. He knew he should pull back, that his ship was only one of hundreds in the fight, that he shouldn't risk the fleet command vessel in the front line. But Barron had never fought that way. He could make some concessions to tactics, to combat realities, but he couldn't make himself someone he wasn't. He had come to Calpharon to lead his people into the fight, and that's just what he was going to do.

And you can't lead from behind…

"All battle line ships are to charge up primaries. We're going to open fire as soon as we enter range."

"Yes, Admiral." Atara's steely resolve was, as always, an inspiration. And in some way, he found the barest hint of weakness and fear he picked up there, something he was sure only he could hear, strangely reassuring.

He turned back toward the display, and his eyes moved to a single, tiny dot…one moving at extreme velocity. He knew just what he was seeing, without even checking.

Jake…

What he didn't know, at least not until an instant later when the data came in, was just how insanely the fleet's strike force commander was redlining his reactor to get so far out so quickly. He was horrified at the thought of Stockton taking such insane chances.

Horrified…but not surprised. Not in the slightest.

And he wouldn't have stopped Stockton, even if he could have.

Go, Jake…we've got to find a way to beat the Highborn. Or we're going to lose everything that matters…

* * *

Yes! Nicely done, Reg…

Stockton was looking at his fighter's small screen, trying desperately to ignore the losses mounting among his squadrons and to focus on the damage they were doing to the enemy battle line. The Highborn ships were immense, and they vastly outclassed anything the defenders possessed. But they were not invulnerable. His pilots were proving that.

Any doubts he'd had about his impulsive promotion of Reg Griffin was gone. She'd exceeded his every hope, and she had directed the squadrons with skill that surpassed his wildest expectations. Now, she was leading the survivors on a desperate race back to the motherships.

Stockton winced as he saw the casualties, over twelve hundred and still counting. The Highborn missiles were a deadly threat to his fighters, one that had been mitigated so far only by the speed of the first strike, and the fact that his squadrons had mostly completed their attacks before the first waves of missiles had launched.

The bomber attack had disabled at least some of the battleships' missile systems, too. Twenty-eight battleships had transited so far, and two had been destroyed outright. Of the other twenty-six, fifteen had launched missiles, just over half the initial force.

His eyes darted to the side. More battleships were coming through, and these would be untouched when they moved into range. Admiral Barron had decided to move the battle line forward, to minimize the enemy's range advantage. That made sense, but it also virtually guaranteed his squadrons wouldn't be ready to launch until the fight was well underway.

If they were able to land at all. The battleships would be entering combat range just as the returning squadrons arrived. The recovery operation would be a mess at best, and an impossibility at worst.

He felt an almost irresistible urge to race forward, to try to catch up with the final waves attacking the enemy ships. But he knew he'd never get there, not until the final runs were complete. He'd trusted Reg to lead the wings in, and she'd repaid his confidence tenfold. There was nothing to be gained by moving toward the Highborn line. He could do more nursing his wounded squadrons back in, helping the tired pilots execute difficult landings while their launch platforms were engaged with the enemy.

He brought his ship around, angling his thrusters to full deceleration position. He'd been blasting hard toward the enemy lines, and now he was doing the same in the opposite direction. His eyes dropped to the status monitor for his reactor. He'd been torturing the thing, driving it at more than one hundred fifteen percent of its rated capacity. He'd intended to back off, to drop down to one hundred, or even ninety. But he wanted to get back toward the motherships in time to direct landing operations. He hated that he had missed the fight, and part of him still wanted to turn back, to race forward alone and launch his two torpedoes. But that was pure foolishness. He wasn't sure what made less sense...the notion that he could somehow make it alone through the missiles and other enemy point defense, or the idea that his two torpedoes would make a difference in the battle. Still, he knew he might have done it, out of raw drive and stubbornness...but concern for his people overrode his wild thoughts. He could save lives, he was sure, get pilots who would otherwise die back into the bays. That left him no choice.

He stared at the screen, picking out the lead formations heading back to the fleet. He still had a considerable amount of deceleration to do, but he realigned the thrust vector slightly, doing all he could to put himself on an intercept course with those squadrons.

Stockton had landed under every imaginable

condition, and now he had to use that experience to get his people back onto their ships...so the flight crews could turn them around and get them right back out.

Back out to throw themselves once more into the maw of death.

* * *

"All ships, open fire!" Barron's tone was harsh, as he barked out the command with enough force to hurt his throat. He was focused on the battle, angry, scared, nervous. But mostly, he was frustrated...frustrated that the battle line had entered firing range, and *Dauntless*'s guns were still out.

He'd harassed Fritz again. Twice. But he knew the engineer was doing all she could. And all Anya Fritz could do was all anyone could. If Barron's battles had taught him one thing, it was that Anya Fritz was the best engineer the Confederation had ever known.

"All ships, open fire." Atara repeated the order into the comm, and a few seconds later, the display lit up with bright lines darting across the empty space, three hundred Confederation primary beams lancing out, seeking targets along the enemy formation. The particle accelerators fired from the single turrets of the oldest battleships present and the more common double barreled weapons of the fleet's mainstays.

And the quad batteries of the newest battleships, the *Repulse*-class monsters that were the pride of the Confederation fleet.

But *Dauntless*'s four beams had remained silent, along with those of almost forty other damaged battleships. The advance to firing range had been a costly one, and even though the newer primaries were less prone to damage than the models Barron remembered from his earlier days, they were still complex mechanisms, subject to a dozen different problems that could silence them.

Barron watched as many of the beams whipped past their targets, coming within a few thousand meters of the enemy in many cases, but only hitting in half a dozen or so. That wasn't unexpected. The range was still long, the firing ships far too distant from their targets to effectively adjust for the Sigma-9 distortion wreaking havoc on fire locks.

But that would change, at least assuming a reasonable number of Barron's ships were able to close with their primaries still functional. The scanner enhancements the Hegemony had shared with Barron's people would enable greater targeting effectiveness, as least at shorter range.

How many battleships would manage to reach close range with their main guns intact was another question. The enemy fire was increasing in frequency and accuracy, and when one of those deadly blue beams struck, even a mighty Confederation battleship shook to its girders. The Highborn fleet was still disordered, from the transit and from the desperate and massive bomber attack. But its formation was tightening with each passing minute, and as it did, the volume and accuracy of its fire was increasing.

Barron caught a flash out of the corner of his eye, from the far end of the display. One of the Palatian heavies blinking out, destroyed as its reactor lost containment. His own fleet had lost nine battleships and almost two dozen lighter ships, and as he scanned Vian Tulus's section of the line, he saw that the Palatians had lost six of their largest ships, and a dozen lighter units...a far higher percentage of their total force.

He was about to turn toward the Hegemony part of the line, to check on Chronos's fleets and the losses they had suffered, but a voice erupted into his headphones, distracting him at once.

"The primaries are back online, Admiral. I rerouted two of the main trunk lines, and I think I can shave thirty seconds on charging time. Give me a minute, maybe seventy seconds, and you'll have guns ready to fire."

Barron felt a wave of relief, a pointless and misleading feeling, he realized. As anxious as he was to get *Dauntless* fully into the fight, one set of primaries wasn't going to make that big of a difference.

Except to him. He wanted to open fire on the Highborn so badly, he could taste it.

"Thank you, Fritzie. You're a magician, as always." He turned and looked over at the main gunnery station. "The primaries are back online, Commander Jones. You'll have a full charge in less than a minute, and I expect you to make good use of it." The pressure wasn't fair, and the range was still long for hitting a Highborn vessel. But Barron didn't care if he was being reasonable. He wanted *Dauntless* to draw blood, and he wanted it *now*. It wasn't a tactically valid attitude, perhaps, but then he was human, too.

"Yes, Admiral…we're working on a fire lock now."

Barron stared at the screen, nodding to himself as he saw a small red circle surround one of the Highborn ships. Jones and his people had chosen their target, and it was the very one Barron would have picked himself. It was one of the big new battleships, one positioned forward in the enemy formation…and one that had been badly battered by Reg Griffin's and Jake Stockton's bombers.

He stared at the small symbol, and even as he did, he could hear the echo of his heartbeat in his ears. A dozen emotions intertwined—fear, pain, sadness about being separated from Andi and his daughter, frustration, rage. It mingled together in a toxic brew, and as he sat there, all

Tyler Barron wanted was to kill Highborn. He didn't know anything about the enemy, not really. He had no idea where they were from or why they had come. He just knew they were the reason he'd had to leave his home, the cause of so many of his people's deaths, of so much pain. He knew revenge wouldn't change anything, wouldn't undo the losses he'd suffered. It was almost always an empty and useless pursuit.

But he didn't care. He wanted it. He wanted vengeance. He *needed* payback.

His eyes moved to the charging display, and he saw as the small bar of light reached the far end of the gauge.

The primaries were ready.

He looked across the bridge, and his eyes met Jones's. He exchanged a glance, a knowing look that told each man the other felt the same as he did, wanted the same thing. Barron's voice was like ice as he uttered a single word.

"Fire."

Chapter Twenty-Three

Union Battleship Tonnerre
Gavarouche System
Union Year 227 (323 AC)

"We are approaching the…opposing fleet. I can have you transferred to one of the light cruisers. There is still time for you to leave the system and return to Montmirail, First Citizen. Or even to await word in the adjacent system." Denisov clearly found it difficult to describe the forces even then racing toward his own ships. He'd avoided characterizing them as enemies, but Ciara was more direct in her thoughts, and she knew that was mostly playacting, Denisov warring with his idea of who he should be.

The ships coming at them would soon be trying to kill them all, and she couldn't think of a better definition of an enemy than that. But Denisov was that rarest of creatures, an honorable man, a true patriot, and calling other Union spacers 'enemies' came hard to him.

But he's going to have to start killing them soon, whatever he calls them, or they're going to kill him…

Sandrine Ciara stood where she was, trying with all her resolve to appear comfortable about the upcoming fight.

It wouldn't do for her people to see fear in her, or a lack of confidence...though both were present in full force.

"Thank you, Fleet Admiral, but no. This is my place. The Union fights for its future, and no true patriot could wish to be anywhere else." She was still amazed at her at ability to spew bullshit. She'd have vastly preferred weathering the storm in the next system, or even better, some armored bunker back on Montmirail. She'd even seriously considered it. But there really was no choice. She'd moved past the point of no return when she'd launched her coup, and she had to see it through.

She might have trusted Denisov to handle things in her absence, though she had so little experience with honest people, she would have struggled with it. But the other officers, the task force commanders and their subordinates, who had rallied to her side, who now reported to Denisov...she didn't trust them at all. They were on her side because she had bribed them, or because she'd scared them into believing she would emerge the victor at the end of the war, or because they hated Villieneuve. But there wasn't one of them, besides possibly Denisov himself, who wouldn't abandon her in an instant if a better offer came along. She *had* to be there, to keep an eye on them all, if nothing else.

"The bridge is in the center of the ship, then. This is probably the safest place, unless you would like me to dispatch a cruiser. You can transfer and take station close to the transit point, and still remain in the system and observe the battle."

Ciara pushed aside the impulse to take Denisov up on his offer. "No, Fleet Admiral, I thank you for your consideration, but I will remain here on the flagship. Where I belong."

"Please, First Citizen, if you are going to remain, take the command chair." The admiral stood up and stepped to the side of his seat.

Ciara waved toward him. "Again, thank you, Admiral, but the command position is yours. The Union looks to you to lead its loyal forces, and to crush the traitors. I will sit at one of the spare workstations, and do my best to stay out of the way." She continually referred to the forces loyal to Villieneuve as traitors. A strict definition of the term fit *her*, and the forces on her side, perhaps better than their enemies. Villieneuve *was* a tyrant, a brutal dictator, certainly, but he was also—or had been, at least—the legitimate leader of the government. But Ciara knew repeating something was the surest way to make people believe it, and she wanted those loyal to her thinking of their enemies not as one time comrades succumbing to poor judgment, but as filthy traitors. Vermin who had to be hunted down and exterminated.

She walked across the bridge, toward the bank of workstations along the outer perimeter. There were three auxiliary stations, and she sat at the far one. She keenly remembered Villieneuve's skillful maneuverings during the unrest that followed the disastrous end of the last Confederation war, the way he'd managed to position himself as a man of the people while the government was collapsing, even after a career spent as the head of Sector Nine and a member of the Presidium. She'd come to appreciate the power of feigned humility, and also the gullibility of most people. She was determined to put on a show for Denisov's spacers, the grim, courageous, duty-focused woman trying to save her nation from Gaston Villieneuve's insanity. The more they liked her, sympathized with her, the more firmly they would support her.

"Commander Sianelle, please get a survival suit for the First Citizen."

"Yes, Admiral."

Denisov turned toward Ciara. "You may use my office to change, First Citizen, but I urge you to wear the suit under your clothes...just in case we lose pressurization in the battle."

Ciara nodded, but inside she felt her stomach twist into knots. She'd decided to see the battle through, but Denisov's caution had inflamed her fear, and the realization that *Tonnerre* would soon be exchanging fire with Villieneuve's forces—that its hull could be breached, and its insides torn apart by the great energy lances ripping into it—was a sobering one. Still, she was determined. But she was scared, too.

"Certainly, Admiral. Thank you." She got up and walked back toward the admiral's office, to wait for the other officer to bring her the suit, but mostly to hide for a few moments while she struggled to keep her guts from convulsing.

* * *

Gaston Villieneuve looked at the display, and the rage inside him grew. He held his control, his stony resolve holding his face as a mask to hide his fury. He had rallied the larger part of the fleet to his cause, courtesy of years of preparing for such an eventuality. Blackmail had been a major component in his toolkit, as had bribery. He'd promised promotions, political offices, vast cash awards. He'd even showered prospective rewards on officers he knew were ambitious enough to turn on him after his victory was won. Defeating Sandrine Ciara and her allies was the urgent need, the only thing that mattered at that moment. There would be time later to prune his own ranks of the most...troublesome...followers after he'd regained undisputed control over the Union.

He detested Ciara, of course, and he'd imagined her

fate at his hands a hundred times. But that wasn't the thing driving his caustic anger, not just then.

Andrei Denisov.

The traitor, the turncoat…the man who led a large chunk of the Union fleet across the border and aided the hated Confeds. Aided them! Helped them stave off a defeat that would have left them vulnerable. The Confederation had been the Union's hated enemy for a century, and Denisov had used the navy's ships to hold off their fall.

Villieneuve had seethed at Denisov's treason, from the instant he'd heard of it, and he'd done all he could to bring down the treacherous dog. He'd come a hair's breadth from success, too, with a Sector Nine assassination attempt. But the renegade admiral escaped death, if only by the slimmest of margins.

Now, Denisov had appeared again. Villieneuve hadn't imagined the renegade admiral could cause more damage than he already had, but now he was allied with Sandrine Ciara, and the return of his fleet, battered and depleted as it was after years of fighting alongside the Confeds, undid all Villieneuve's preparation had done. The odds that had seemed so in his favor were almost exactly even now, and the prospect of possible defeat had emerged once again in his deepest thoughts.

He looked at the approaching forces, his eyes moving from symbol to symbol, analyzing, calculating, trying to find some advantage to his side, despite the constant assertions from his officers that the two fleets were almost exactly equally matched.

Villieneuve had to trust in his admirals, and that was something difficult for him to do. It had been bad enough during wars, when defeat meant retreat, perhaps, or even an undesirable peace. A loss in the battle about to begin could very well mean utter destruction for his cause…and death for himself.

And victory will mean the same for the other side.

The civil war, the disaster unleashed by Ciara's coup, had become a deadly threat. It could end with his victory, almost immediately if the battle went well enough. In a matter of hours, perhaps a few days, he could see the traitors crushed, and order restored to the Union. And he could have his vengeance. He would have Ciara thrown to a pack of starving hounds if he laid hands on her, but his rage was even stronger, more unfiltered toward the admiral who'd been a thorn in his side for far too long. If Denisov was foolish enough to survive defeat, to fall into Villieneuve's hands, he would suffer agony as no man ever had.

But Villieneuve knew his own defeat and utter destruction could come as quickly, that even as he imagined his revenge, the next hours and days could see his own death. He'd rarely spent a lot of time considering defeat. He'd always believed his skill and intellect could find a way to victory. He'd been written off by many during the chaos after the Confederation War, but though all his old comrades on the Presidium were all dead, he had emerged more powerful than ever.

No matter how hard he tried, he couldn't entirely banish the thought that his end might have found him. He detested Denisov, but he couldn't ignore the admiral's unquestioned skill. Ciara's newest ally was more capable than any of his own officers. Villieneuve held on to his confidence, mostly. But he also promised himself, if defeat came, if the end was near, he would never let his enemies take him alive.

Never.

* * *

"Division Three, course modification, 8g thrust at 320.140.080." Denisov snapped out the command, his voice loud, firm, the very sound of confidence. Ciara was sitting at her workstation, wiggling around, still trying to come to terms with how hot and uncomfortable the survival suit was.

She knew Denisov, for all his honor and dedication, was lying as much as she ever had. It was a tone, perhaps, and not words, but she was sure the admiral was hiding the fear he felt, the trepidation at the uncertain outcome of the battle. She was confident in his abilities, as much as she could be when her own fate was on the line along with those of the admiral and his spacers.

"Division Three acknowledges, Admiral." Ciara looked up at the display, trying to make sense of the clusters of small dots. Each of the two forces had about two hundred ships, divided between battleships, cruisers, destroyers, and smaller escorts. There were smaller dots now, too, fighters, she realized. She was no expert in naval tactics, but she knew enough to realize the duel between the battle lines would likely decide which side won. The fights going on already, destroyer squadrons exchanging fire as they zipped past each other, and cruisers fighting along the flanks of the main formation, were just opening festivities. The real dance was yet to begin. The fighter wings would battle for temporary supremacy, and the battleships would close and fight it out until one side gave way.

She tried to follow the fighting on the two flanks, to get a feel for which side was gaining an edge. Denisov was unreadable, but she thought she'd picked up concern from some of the other officers. Whether that was just understandable fear and tension, or whether the battle was going poorly, she had no idea.

She glanced over toward the command station. She

wanted to ask Denisov, but she knew her fleet commander was busy. Distracting him might make her feel better for a few fleeting seconds, but it could only hurt her chances of victory. She turned back toward the display, just as half a dozen small dots vanished almost at the same instant. They were on the extreme edge of the formation, but it was clear the battle was heating up.

"Fleet Captain Duquesne on your line, Admiral."

Duquesne...she remembered the officer, and even the particular bit of bribery she'd employed to bring him to her side, but she wasn't sure what group of ships he commanded. She scolded herself, and promised if she survived the battle, she would make more effort to understand her forces and their organization.

She felt a tightening inside as another three dots winked out, all from her force, and then, just a few seconds later, a fleeting taste of excitement as no fewer than six enemy ships disappeared less than a minute later. The battle line had remained in place, but the fighting on the flanks had grown in intensity. She wondered what Denisov was planning, and what his counterpart might do. It was difficult to sit and wait to see how her subordinate proceeded, but she was smart enough to realize she could only impede the progress of the battle with her interference...and reduce her chances of victory.

She watched the furious fighting for another few minutes, and then her head snapped around as Denisov uttered a new set of orders. She listened to his words, and she felt as though some phantom hand had closed tightly all around her.

"The battle line will advance, Commander. All ships forward at 6g."

Chapter Twenty-Four

CFS Dauntless
Sigma Nordlin System
Year 323 AC (After the Cataclysm)

The Battle of Calpharon – Open Fire!

Barron watched as the scanners updated the results of *Dauntless*'s opening shot. The malfunction in the battleship's main battery had delayed its participation in the Confederation fleet's broadside, and while the range had not exactly been close, it hadn't been extreme either. The chances of a hit would have been less than one percent without the new scanner mods, but even the latest in targeting technology only increased the chances to perhaps six or eight percent. But that didn't take into account the strange mystique that seemed to follow Confederation ships named *Dauntless* into battle.

The blast had scored a direct hit amidships, all four primary beams striking the target. It was as good a first shot as Barron could have hoped for, and he almost let out a loud scream when he saw the initial report. He held it in, barely clinging to his command dignity, but half a dozen officers on the bridge had shown rather less control. Barron didn't admonish them. There was a thin line between fueling the élan of an elite fighting force, and maintaining discipline in battle. It was a balancing act he'd mastered after nearly two decades in command positions.

Besides, he'd been a hair's breadth from his own unseemly display, and he wasn't *that* much of a hypocrite.

He watched as the AI updated the damage reports. He felt a touch of disappointment when it became clear the enemy ship was still there, that whatever damage the shot had inflicted, it hadn't ruptured the antimatter core or caused other critical, ship-destroying damage. But his excitement at the hit remained, and it even grew as the reports of secondary explosions and expulsions of internal materials made it increasingly clear that the Highborn vessel *had* suffered significant damaged, even if it hadn't been outright crippled or destroyed.

"Maintain a lock on that ship, Commander. Gunnery, you control navigation…bring us in and hit that thing again." Barron felt a touch of discomfort at the venom dripping from his voice. It was his battle persona, he knew, at least in part. But he felt angrier than he had in past conflicts, and he craved the blood of his enemies with a savagery that was new to him. Perhaps it was resentment over being dragged away from his family, or exhaustion after so many years of almost uninterrupted war.

Or, maybe he knew this would be his greatest test, the hardest fight he'd ever endured. For six years, he had faced the seemingly unbeatable ships of the Hegemony, struggling to find a way, any way, to defeat them. Now, he looked out at an enemy whose weapons tore into those great battleships that had so ravaged his own forces, slicing them open like used storage canisters. It had been difficult to accept an enemy with superior technology. That had been the Confederation's place on the Rim for many years, the most advanced power. But now, Barron felt as though his people had lost two steps on that scale, and he wondered if they could catch up, if they would ever be able to hold their own against the enemy. Or next to their new allies.

"Primaries fully charged, Admiral."

He stared at the enemy ship, and he felt his hands clench into fists. He didn't know if his people could catch their enemy's technology, or defeat them in the long run, but he knew what he was going to do just then.

"Very well, Commander. Fire."

*   *   *

Reg Griffin sat in her cockpit, staring out at the black nothingness surrounding her ship. Her body was soaked in sweat, the survival suit slick and uncomfortable as it rubbed against her bare skin below. The perspiration had been more from stress than heat, but now, she'd turned her life support systems to minimal power, and the slickness turned icy and cold as the temperature in her fighter plummeted. She'd managed to set a course more or less back toward the fleet with her last drops of fuel, but with the battle line moving into a close-range firefight, she doubted there would be time to send out rescue ships to gather strays. If she was going to have any chance to survive, she had to buy as much time as she could…and that meant conserving her air and enduring the tooth-chattering cold.

She hadn't activated her beacon yet, and that meant, even if Stockton and the rest of the strike force were looking for her, trying to get a location to send help, they probably wouldn't find her. That was a problem, but with her ship moving at barely five kilometers per second, she was still closer to the enemy than she was to any friendlies. She figured there was a good chance the Highborn would ignore a single ship as small as a fighter, especially when it was moving away, but she didn't think it would be a very good idea to ping away with her beacon and challenge that assumption.

She was scared, of course, as anyone would be, both for herself, and for the rest of the strike force. The pilots who managed to return, who reached their motherships and their landing bays, would only turn around and launch again...and this time they would come out in small groups, as their launch platforms were able to conduct launch ops in the heat of their own battle. The bombers would move forward again, but this time they would endure the brunt of the enemy missile barrages in far smaller waves. Hundreds would die, perhaps even more, before the survivors got close enough to launch a second round of attacks. It was a grim prospect, but as daunting as the future might appear to the pilots she'd so recently commanded, the shadows looming over her were far longer. Without fuel, her life support would only last a few hours, four or five at the most. That wasn't long, not in terms of space combat. The pilots who would soon be heading back toward the enemy faced grave danger, but they had a better chance than she did, a reality she tried to ignore, if without much success.

She glanced down at the screen. It was dim, set to minimum power. She'd have turned it off entirely to conserve energy, but she had to monitor her location, pick the right moment to activate the beacon. It was probably her only chance, and as much of a longshot as it seemed, if she could manage to time it when the ships of the second wave were launching, she just might be able to get someone's attention.

It was worth a try. She waited patiently, her eyes fixed

on the screen as she shivered from the cold working its way ever deeper into her.

But cold wasn't going to stop her any more than despair was. Reg Griffin had done many things in her career, but she'd never given up.

And she didn't intend to start now.

*   *   *

"I want that transmission line functional in fifteen minutes, Lieutenant, and I'm only giving you that long because of the kindness of my heart." Anya Fritz stood on a catwalk, about ten meters above *Dauntless*'s main engineering deck, shouting out commands one after the other at her sweating engineers. She'd felt a little foolish at first, crawling around the access tubes of *Dauntless*'s engineering section in her flag officer's uniform, but she'd quickly found a solution to that problem. She had practically torn the coat from her back and thrown it to the floor. It was still down there, in the middle of the main deck in a crumpled heap. She had no use for it, and no one else had the guts to touch it.

"Commodore, we've got to test the new cables before we can reroute the power flow back." The officer sounded the same as all her people did. Stressed, at their wit's end…and not because they were in battle, facing a deadly enemy. No, the Highborn forces faced off against the fleet were an ethereal threat inside the battleship's immense engineering section, at least next to the force of nature standing right there shouting at them.

"Then you'd better get on it, Lieutenant. You wasted twenty seconds already. You going to throw more of your time away bitching at me?" Her tone was harsh, some might say caustic, but Fritz was focused on the real enemy, and she knew, perhaps better than anyone on

Dauntless, just what the Highborn's deadly weapons could do to the Confederation flagship, and every other vessel in the fleet.

"Yes, Commodore." The engineer didn't elaborate. She hadn't expected him to. There weren't many out there who could stand up to her when she was driving forward at full speed. She'd had that reputation for years now, since her days as a lieutenant commander, and even earlier than that. Her ascension to flag rank had done nothing to blunt it.

There was an absurdity to a commodore running around directing repairs on a single ship, she knew that…but *Dauntless* was not just any vessel. It carried one of the best crews the navy had ever known, not to mention Admiral Barron, in her view, unquestionably the greatest commander the Confederation had ever seen, his illustrious grandfather included. Plus, it carried Admiral Travis, Jake Stockton…and, of course, herself. If *Dauntless* fell in battle, it would be little less than a decapitation blow to the Confederation war effort. And she knew well enough that Tyler Barron would never hang back, that the battleship would be in the thick of the fighting, as she'd always been before.

All that was only part of the battleship's importance, though. The vessel had become a symbol to the spacers of the fleet, and she'd slipped into the place her predecessor had occupied, even gone beyond it. The old *Dauntless* had died saving the fleet from destruction, and the next vessel to carry the name—and much of the same crew—had inherited that glory, and added more.

The first hit Dauntless suffered had been a fluke, she knew, a lucky shot by some Highborn gunner or AI. The damage to the primaries had also been a case of extreme misfortune, one she'd now managed to correct. Fritz didn't care for the superstition so prevalent among spacers, but she couldn't ignore the chatter around her, the concerns that the early damage to the ship had been an unlucky start to the battle.

Fritz didn't want to believe in luck, but she'd seen things she couldn't explain any other way. Jake Stockton was an example, certainly. She wondered what the odds of his surviving as long as he had, battle after battle, one desperate mission after another. She remembered Stockton's mentor, Kyle Jamison, himself an outstanding pilot. Dead. The original Blue squadron...twelve out of fifteen dead, and one of the three survivors was Stockton himself. She remembered dozens of pilots who'd served in the wars in which she'd fought, and none had endured as Stockton had.

He was skillful, the best by any measure. But was that enough? Did he have something else, something not really understood by humanity? Did *Dauntless*? The old ship had been destroyed, of course, but her crew had survived to transfer the flag to the next hunk of metal to carry the name.

The whole thing fought with her analytic mind, but she realized, somewhere along the line, she had begun to believe in luck, at least to an extent.

She wondered what it was, how it worked. And, most urgently, she wondered how long it lasted...and what happened when it ran out.

* * *

Jake Stockton stood next to his Lighting, waving his arm toward his flight chief. "Just top off the fuel, Chief. I'm going right back out. I want to be in space to direct the launches."

"Yes, sir...we'll have you ready in ten minutes, maybe less." The gruff flight deck team leader shouted out a series of commands, as Stockton turned and walked across the deck toward the water station. He'd thought about grabbing a quick bite before he launched, but his stomach was too twisted in knots for that. But he was thirsty, and he reached out and filled a cup with cool water.

The launch operation was going to be a nightmare, he knew that already, and as if to emphasize the difficulties of sending out squadrons while the mother ship was in combat, the bay shook hard, and half the water in his cup spilled onto his flight suit. For an instant, he'd been afraid *Dauntless* had taken a hit, but then he realized it had just been a particularly hard evasive maneuver.

He stood for a moment, watching his crew already climbing all over his Lightning. He felt an urge to go back to flight control, to see Stara, even for a minute. The two had been together for several years already, after a fairly long period of start and stop flirtation, but they'd known precious little peace in that time. A few weeks of shore leave was just about all they'd known of life as a couple outside the rigors and danger of war.

No, you don't have time now. You can see her when you get back…

Stara was his first thought, but his mind moved on to other desires, everyday things that seemed like unattainable luxuries. Sleep…hours and hours of it, uninterrupted. And a shower, the feeling of hot water stripping away days of recycled Jake Stockton…followed up with a fresh, clean flight suit. But all of it was out of his reach, at least at that moment. He'd just refilled his cup and sucked down about half the water, when the flight chief signaled to him his ship was ready.

Barely seven minutes…better than I expected…

He took a deep breath, gulped down the rest of the water, and looked around for a few seconds. Then he walked across the open deck and back to his ship. "Thanks, Chief…good job." He nodded toward the head of his flight team, and he reached up and grabbed a rung on the small ladder, climbing up the side of his ship and leaping back into the cockpit.

He shook his head once, his face twisted into a sour scowl at the reek of the small space. There hadn't been time to do a normal cleaning, not after the mission to Vexa Torrent, and certainly not just then. But it didn't matter. It would only take a few minutes to become accustomed again to his own stink. He reached to the side, and tapped the controls, closing the cockpit's cover. He heard the familiar sound, the locking bolts sliding into place, and a few seconds later, the hissing sound as his life support reengaged.

He looked down at his console, at the row of lights, four of them green, and one yellow. The last one was his flight control status…the okay to launch his otherwise ready ship. He was about to reach down and call Stara on the comm, but then the light flicked over to green.

All systems were a go. Jake Stockton had lost count of the times he'd launched his fighter into space, but he knew it had been many hundreds.

And now, plus one…

He grabbed the controls, looked quickly around the bay, and he pulled the throttle back, blasting his engines hard, and propelling his ship down the launch tube.

Back into battle.

Chapter Twenty-Five

Free Trader Pegasus
Somewhere in the Badlands
Year 323 AC (After the Cataclysm)

"We're still a long way from Calpharon, at least based on the charts we've got. But I think we need to talk about what we're going to do when we get closer. Do we just fly right up to the Hegemony capital and announce ourselves? Or do we hang back, try to get some word to Admiral Barron? And what if we run into Hegemony patrols?"

Andi looked up at Vig. She hadn't been ignoring him, not really, but she was deep into the translations she was working on. Sy had managed to extract more data from the third and fourth data chips, and it was nothing less than fascinating. Andi had scavenged the Badlands for years, scooping up bits and pieces of old tech, but now she was seeing imperial history unfold before her, the most detailed information she'd ever seen on the fall of the empire...or at least the years leading up to the Cataclysm. She'd lost track of how long she'd been up, how any hours, days, she'd been hunched over the table, working tirelessly, with only short breaks to eat something or run to the bathroom.

She looked up at Vig, and a quick sniff of her shirt told her she needed to make time for a shower, at least. "I'm sorry, Vig, what did you say?. I was pretty deep into these files."

"I asked, are we going right to Calpharon, or are we stopping somewhere short of there and trying to get a message through?"

Andi could see Vig was tense. He clearly didn't like the idea of entering Hegemony space, much less venturing to the enemy—no, that wasn't right, they weren't the enemy anymore—capital.

"We're not at war with them anymore, Vig. We're allies now."

He nodded, not looking entirely convinced.

"I don't know yet. We've still got a long way to go before we need to decide that." She knew the Hegemony and the Confederation *were* allies now, and she wouldn't have given a second thought about flying right to Calpharon...except for Cassiopeia. She felt bad enough taking her daughter through the Badlands, and she'd tried to avoid the thought that they were getting closer to the Hegemony border. Reliance on an old enemy turned friend was enough to satisfy her concerns for her own safety, perhaps even for that of her crew. But Cassiopeia was another matter entirely.

"The scanners are clear, at least. If the war with the Heggies accomplished one thing, it was clearing the vagabonds and scoundrels out of the Badlands. We haven't had a contact on the scanner since we left Dannith."

Andi smiled thinly. "*We* were some of those scoundrels, my friend. I don't imagine you've forgotten so quickly."

"We ran into worse types than ourselves, Andi...didn't

we? I'm glad some of them are gone, at least. Makes this trip a little easier, less nerve wracking. At least until we cross that border."

"The Hegemony isn't going to give us any problems, Vig, assuming they've even got any ships left on the Rimward border. I have to imagine they've got all their strength massed at Calpharon."

"No, I know they won't, I guess. I just...don't like it. A lot of people died fighting them, and now we're helping them."

"We're helping them to help ourselves, Vig. Don't forget that. If going through all these files with Sy has proven anything to me, it's that the Highborn *will* subjugate everyone on the Rim if they get past the Hegemony. This fight is for *us*, for our futures, as much as it is for theirs."

It's for Cassiopeia, too...

Andi took a deep breath. She really believed what she had just said. She'd suspected it before, understood why Barron had to go, but now any remaining doubt was gone. The fight against the Highborn was the deadliest and most serious the Confederation had ever faced. They *couldn't* lose. Whatever the cost, they had to find a way to prevail, or at least to beat back the enemy.

"Hey...enough distracting my assistant." Sylene stepped out into the main room, and she walked toward the table. She'd only been gone a few minutes. Like Andi, she'd found it almost impossible to drag herself away from her work.

"Your assistant is still the captain of this ship, sister dear. And I need a few minutes with her once in a while, no matter how determined you are to monopolize her time."

Andi smiled. The brother-sister jibes were a welcome touch of normalcy, a distraction from the dark realization of the magnitude of the threat they all faced, that all mankind faced. But she felt the pull of getting back to her work, almost like the gravitation from a large planet. The parts she had already translated only increased her trepidation, but she knew the road to victory would be paved with knowledge, with an understanding of the enemy.

An enemy that had played a major, but yet unknown part in the empire's fall.

"I'll leave you two to your sniping back and forth. I've got work to do." She turned back toward the workstation.

"I have work to do, too. How about you, brother? I have to imagine there is *something* on the bridge that needs your attention."

Vig looked back at his sister, and then at Andi. "Fine, fine…but you two are going to have to get some sleep eventually, you do know that, right?"

Neither of them answered. They were both already neck deep in the old imperial histories. "Andi, I've got another section here. I've only translated a small chunk, but it looks important to me…"

Andi hardly noticed as Vig waved his hands and turned to head back to the bridge ladder. Her mind was centuries in the past, back in the waning days of empire.

Planet Alisia, Venta Tabalus III
Year 11,695 IR (Imperial Reckoning)
Year 39 BC (Before the Cataclysm) by Confederation Calendar
362 Years Ago

Smoke hung over the city, and streams of people ran through the streets, smashing anything breakable they could reach, and setting fire to anything that would burn. Chaos had gripped the capital city, a strange sort of collective madness that engulfed the administrative center of not only the planet, but of the entire sector. The news reports had spoken of disturbances and violence in different areas of the empire, but now the darkness had come to Alisia. It was almost as though a world was trying to tear itself apart, to embrace its own destruction.

The planet, a major world of the empire, part of a vast polity that had not fallen to an outside enemy in ten millennia, was destroying itself, its people driven, it seemed, to sheer madness.

The troubles had begun with an economic downturn, one that had quickly escalated and ultimately turned into a near collapse of order on a planetary scale. The empire, already deep in decline from one end of its vast dominions to the other, had dispatched aid, first advisors and imperial representatives to calm the people and assure them of the emperor's support. When such efforts failed utterly to stem the tide of decline, words were followed up by emergency shipments, food, medical supplies, crucial replacement parts, and money…as much as overtaxed imperial systems could supply. But it was all far too little and too late. The aid provided temporary pauses in the rioting, but in the end, it failed utterly to halt the decline.

"It is magnificent, Ellerax, is it not? In a dozen sectors, worlds burn, the people take to the streets, rampaging, destroying. The malaise that has gripped the empire is not all-encompassing. Indeed, there is little productive to what is happening, save that the rioters are driven by *something*. Humanity's energy is not spent, and once the decrepit old system is dragged down, we will see to a reinvigoration. The empire will be reborn, from the ashes, if necessary."

Andros was next to his ally—his *creation*—as the two stood on a hill looking out over the dying city. "It was costly, more so even than I had anticipated, to set this decline into motion. We only accelerated its arrival, of course. There can be little doubt the empire was on an unstoppable course to utter destruction on its own. We are not damaging civilization, we are saving it. We are limiting the damage, using it as a tool, bringing the empire low, but not into the deepest pits of despair. Then, when enough worlds have descended into darkness, when the screams of the people can no longer be ignored, we will make our move. You and your brethren, Ellerax…you will lead mankind out of the darkness. You will revitalize the empire, and lead mankind into the future."

"It is unfortunate that so many need be killed to achieve a goal that is unquestionably desirable to all parties. A revitalized empire will pursue renewed research and technological advancement, it will herald in an era of vast economic expansion. People will be relieved of the need to support corrupt leaders, men and women who are no better than they are, who are driven only by lust for power. Humanity requires guidance, and we will provide that. It is a testament to mankind's folly that such destruction must occur before a golden age can begin. The…humans…are weak, but they are my charge, and I would see as few suffer death and misery as possible."

Andros looked up at the figure as he listened, two-thirds of a meter taller than he was and perfectly proportioned, a view in his eyes of human perfection. Ellerax and his brothers and sisters of the Highborn, were brilliant, physically large and powerful, free from disease. They could go days, even weeks without sleep, and he could only guess at their intellectual capacity. They were humanity's future, what people would be—should have been—if only the best and the strongest had survived to pass on their genes. The project had corrected the wrong path humanity had taken, it had restored ten thousand years of genetic progress…and added millennia more to that. Ellerax was what people would have one day become if they'd allowed themselves…but he was there, next to Andros, ready to shepherd humanity forward to a bright new day.

That was worth some death and suffering.

"We will, of course, inflict the least possible damage on the worlds of the empire, kill as few as possible. But we must weaken what remains of the old establishment. We have been able to secure some support from elements of the fleet, but not enough to mount an open challenge to the throne. Your abilities, and those of your brethren, are astonishing, Ellerax, but you are few in number. Even with the waves of additional crèche groups of your kind, for now, we have only the five hundred of you…the Firstborn. There is no doubt your intellect will guide our efforts with greater skill than mine, but yet, I fear we have little prospect of standing up to tens of thousands of imperial warships, and untold millions of the emperor's soldiers. The program is nearly three quarters of a century old, and I fear it will be another twenty-five years before the empire is weak enough for us to make our final move. I will be old then, Ellerax, near the end of my natural lifespan, but you will still be young, if your kind even age at all. When I die, I will do so knowing I have done what was necessary to save the empire, that I have left the future of mankind in the immensely capable hands of the Highborn.

Chapter Twenty-Six

Colossus
Behind Sigma Nordlin VI
Year 323 AC (After the Cataclysm)

The Battle of Calpharon – Into the Flame

"Maintain position...minimum possible thrust." Sonya Eaton sat in the center of *Colossus*'s immense—bridge somehow seemed an inadequate term to describe the sprawling control center—watching over one hundred of her people toiling away at their workstations. The massive bridge crew was far larger than those in any Confederation craft, and even then, more than half the available stations were unoccupied, their original purposes more a matter for conjecture than anything else. *Colossus* was a testament to the might and technology of the old empire, and she found it difficult to wander its corridors in anything except dumbstruck awe.

The fact that she was in command of the thing, that the almost unimaginable total of forty thousand spacers under her orders amounted to what was essentially a skeleton crew for the gargantuan vessel, wore on her like a lodestone. It was too much responsibility, far too quickly. She wasn't ready, but Tyler Barron had assured her of his trust, and that, more than anything, was keeping her going.

Perhaps hardest aspect of all was the fact that she knew she sat there in Sara's place. Her sister had been *Colossus*'s first Confederation commander, but now the elder Eaton was gone, lost in combat along with so many others. Sonya understood why she seemed a logical replacement…and yet she didn't understand.

How could Admiral Barron think I'm ready for this?

The answer was painfully clear. *None* of them were ready for what they now faced. She'd spent her career looking up to Tyler Barron, and she'd followed his orders with a sort of reverence that went beyond normal military discipline. But as she sat there, she wondered if Barron himself struggled to grasp with the immense responsibilities he carried. Sonya was young to command something as powerful as *Colossus*, certainly, but Tyler Barron was young, too, at least to completely control the Confederation's entire military establishment. His grandfather had been one of the greatest heroes in history, but the older Barron had been almost sixty when he'd fought his famous battles. His grandson was almost twenty years younger…and he was facing an even more deadly adversary.

Eaton tried to ignore the doubts, to focus on her duty, her job. But it was hard for yet another reason. Her orders were to stay put, to sit quietly while the fleet fought, while thousands perished in combat. The inaction had been nothing less than torture.

Wait until the right moment. Until the enemy fleet advanced over the red line. Those were her orders. Then, she would act. *Colossus* would emerge from its cover behind the massive gas giant, and it would hit the Highborn forces in the flank, a total surprise, both in its appearance and its power. If everything went just right, if the fleet was still holding on, if the squadrons of bombers were doing enough damage, if the enemy behaved as expected…just maybe *Colossus* could make a difference.

Eaton knew the ship she commanded was enormously powerful, but as she looked at the scanner displays of the enemy fleet—transmitted through satellite reflection from the ships of the line—she doubted if even a warship as powerful as the one she commanded would be enough to turn the tide.

"Commander, advise engineering I want all systems rechecked…and I want the reactors ready to increase output on my command." It was a waste of time, perhaps. She'd already had her people check every weapon, reactor, and transmission line on the gigantic vessel, at least the ones they could get to. *Colossus* was as ready as it was going to be, and as she sat there, she knew the more important question was, would her people truly be ready for what they had to do when the time came?

Would she?

*   *   *

"Stara, come on…you need to light a fire under your people in the bays. On *Dauntless*, and even more on the other ships." Stockton instantly regretted the severity of his tone. It wasn't Stara's fault the launch was proceeding so slowly. By the standards taught in the Academy, the kind of operation his people were attempting, putting bombers in space from ships involved in a close range firefight, was impossible. The incoming fire, the wild evasive maneuvers…it all made launching fighters a nightmare.

Stockton had heard all of that before, but he tended to ignore words like 'unfeasible,' and 'impractical'…and, most of all, 'impossible.' It could be done because he wanted it done, because the fleet needed it. That was enough for him, and it damned well better be enough for those around him.

"We're moving things as quickly as possible, Jake, and you damned well know that! The battleships are in the middle of level one evasive routines. We're getting the fighters out two or three at a time between flight deck shutdowns, and it's a miracle we're managing that. Now, sit tight and leave me the hell alone. Do you know how difficult it is to link launch operations with evasive maneuvers like these?"

He stared at the comm unit for a few seconds, his regret at yelling at her mixing with the tension driving him. He wanted to apologize, but even as his hand moved to the comm, he saw that she had cut the line. He almost called her again, but he realized she was far busier than he was. His challenge would come later, leading the attack, once he had enough ships in space. Getting that force out to him was Stara's job, and he knew he had to let her do it.

He looked down at his scanner, his eyes panning across the enemy fleet, one line of ships after another. They were *close* now. The battle lines were savaging each other, and Stockton watched as two of the Highborn battleships opened up with what he instantly knew were their main batteries. The weapons were similar to the blue-hued beams he'd seen before, but they were arranged in sets of nine, eight circling one in the center, and when they struck a target, they tore through any physical substance. Armor, heavy sections of hull plating, anything that lay in the path of those beams simply vaporized, and the deadly fire emerged from the other sides of their targets. Even battleships were ill-prepared to endure that kind of damage, and only luck saved those struck from utter destruction. If the beams tore through non-vital areas, a ship could survive, albeit with considerable damage and casualties. If the beams struck reactors or vital power lines, even the greatest ships of the line were obliterated in an instant.

He felt sick watching the devastation ravaging the fleet, and the only thing holding him back from despair was the realization that less than a third of the Highborn battleships appeared to be up in the line, battling the Confederation and Hegemony forces. Many of the others were only damaged, of course, and some, perhaps, would be quickly patched up and would join the fight. But he'd rarely had the opportunity to see so closely the good his people had achieved. He'd struggled with losing over a thousand pilots on one strike, but as he watched the Highborn battleships tearing into their opposing numbers, he knew without question his people had saved more lives than they'd lost. Tens of thousands more spacers would be dead, he knew, if the Highborn had managed to bring their entire line to the fight unscathed, and any chance of victory, however slight it might seem, would have been gone.

That helped him, on some level. Nothing would make so many deaths a good thing, but in Stockton's book, dying for something was a hell of a lot better than dying for nothing.

His eyes shot to the side. Something was flashing, on the far end of the tiny display. He reached out, and tapped at his controls. The AI responded by adding a small label to the contact.

He felt a burst of excitement as he stared at the screen, and he reached out and slapped his hand against the comm unit. He almost called Stara again, but he knew her plate was full. So, he connected directly to fleet rescue command on *Renown*.

"This is Admiral Stockton…I'm transmitting coordinates. I'm picking up Commodore Griffin's beacon. Dispatch a rescue mission at once." Stockton had almost written off his newly-promoted second-in-command. He'd scanned all across the combat zone, looking for any sign that her ship had survived. There had been nothing. Stockton had almost given up on her. But as he looked down at the screen, he understood immediately. She had waited, kept her beacon silent until she'd cleared enemy range. He nodded, and even allowed himself a thin smile. He couldn't imagine the self-discipline *that* had taken, the pressure she must have felt to send the signal out, even as she sat in her cockpit, watching her life support slowly dwindle.

He'd made the decision to promote her spontaneously, but now, as he stared at the faint contact on his screen, he was even more convinced he'd picked the right officer. The one he needed to help him manage the wings.

The one to lead them herself if he didn't return from a mission.

He sat for a few seconds, and then he angled his scanner display back toward the fleet deployment area. He'd done all he could do for Griffin, and he wished her the best. Now, he had to organize the squadrons fitfully launching from the fleet's battleships, and he had to turn them into some semblance of an effective strike force.

A quick view of the struggle between the two battle lines told him two things. First, Admiral Baron and Commander Chronos were directing their ships brilliantly, inflicting more damage on the enemy than had seemed possible.

And second, that is wasn't going to be enough. He *had* to get his bombers back out there, whatever the risk, whatever the cost.

Because the fleet was losing the battle.

* * *

Shafts of light lanced through space, the mysterious weapons of the Highborn, blue beams speckled with dark gray, visible along the entirety of tens of thousands of kilometers of space as they sliced their ways to their Confederation and Hegemony targets. The Confed primaries were mostly invisible, as were the lasers serving as the secondary weapons of Barron's battleships, and the main armaments of the Palatian vessels. Hegemony railguns were invisible as well, at least away from the projectile itself, but all the deadly fire was lit up on the display. The energies at play, the vast amounts of raw destructive power the two sides were hurling at each other, almost defied comprehension.

Vian Tulus had faced danger before. As a Palatian noble, he had been raised since birth to be ready for his death. The concerns of a true Palatian were not to survive at all costs, but rather, to die well, with honor and courage. And he had watched the past hours as thousands of his warriors had done just that.

The Palatians considered themselves above the political distractions that plagued their neighbors. Tulus knew that wasn't entirely true, a nationalistic conceit that internal dissension and outright civil war had roundly disproven. But the best of Palatia was there, lined up next to their Confederation allies, fighting the enemy with every weapon they possessed, every watt of energy that remained in their ships' reactors…and the last breath of every man or woman sweating at their posts if need be.

It wouldn't be Tulus's decision whether the fleet was commanded to withdraw, or to stand and fight to the last. He only knew what he would do if he'd been the supreme commander and the world behind the fleet had been

Palatia. He understood the wisdom of thinking in terms of the war as a whole, of fighting for ultimate victory and not to defend a single world...but he was too much a Palatian to think he could make such a choice himself.

We are what we are, even if our ideals enslave us, drive us to defeat instead of victory.

Tulus was a capable tactician, and a good strategist, too. He understood the likelihood that the best possible chance of defeating the Highborn in the end might very well require abandoning Calpharon and pulling the fleet back while it still remained a force in being. Once, he would have scoffed at such notions, shouted loud cries of 'coward' to anyone proposing them. But he'd seen Tyler Barron abandon the Confederation capital of Megara and then return triumphant.

And if he knew one thing without any doubt at all, it was that Tyler Barron was no coward. It might not be something he could have brought himself to do if the world being abandoned had been Palatia, but he was able to understand and respect the decision if his allies made it.

Imperator Vennius shook hard, and Tulus's mind snapped from his thoughts back to the battle raging all around. He looked over at the main display, just one of the bits of advanced technology in the new *Imperator*-class battleships, courtesy of the Palatian treaty with the Confederation. Perhaps more, his mind focused on his status as Tyler Barron's blood-brother. *Imperator Vennius* mounted Confederation primaries, though not the newest models. It was the only ship in the Palatian fleet to carry such armament, though there were another six Imperator-class vessels under construction back in the Alliance.

Another advantage of retreating, of trading space for time. We, at least, will become stronger. We are still rebuilding, and so is the Confederation. If our losses are not too great, we will be stronger in a year, and much more powerful in three.

It was an alien way for a Palatian warrior to think, but just as Tulus had shown Barron the ways of the warrior, the Confed admiral had taught the Imperator a lesson or two. In victory. In winning, not just honor and glory, but the war itself.

Tulus felt the urge to issue orders, to micromanage his forces. But his people knew what to do. The computers were handling ninety percent of the targeting anyway, and his veteran gunners didn't need him shouting at them as they covered that last ten percent. His ships had shorter ranges than either the Hegemony or Confederation vessels, and he'd issued the orders to advance until all guns were in range, regardless of enemy fire. Regardless of the losses suffered.

Those losses had risen to about twelve percent of his ships in the fight so far, and he realized it could have been worse. Much worse. The enemy appeared to be targeting the Hegemony and Confederation ships with greater priority. They'd clearly—and correctly—assessed his ships as the lesser threat. That was mostly about technology, about the power and range of guns, but it was still a hard thing for a Palatian Imperator—for *any* true Palatian—to accept. And he felt an irresistible compulsion to ram it down the Highborn's throats.

"All ships, increase forward thrust to 5g. All gunnery stations, maintain full fire." It was all he could do to equalize the difference in equipment, to increase the effectiveness of his ships' fire against the Highborn vessels. Palatian targeting systems were less efficient than those of their allies, their guns weaker. The combination of those factors meant that Tulus and his warriors weren't carrying their share of the load. They weren't inflicting enough damage on the enemy ships.

"Overload reactors if necessary, but I don't want a gun

silent in this fleet, is that understood?"

"Yes, your Supremacy."

No, his ships weren't keeping up with those of his allies.

But he was going to change that, whatever it took.

Chapter Twenty-Seven

CFS Dauntless
Sigma Nordlin System
Year 323 AC (After the Cataclysm)

The Battle of Calpharon – The Battle Lines Meet

"*Hegemony's Glory* has taken another hit, Admiral. She's losing atmosphere."

Barron's head snapped around at Atara's words, and his eyes zeroed in on the Hegemony flagship. Barron still had a confused relationship with Chronos. There was a functional partnership there, and even something of a proto-friendship developing, but it all still lay under the shadow of the war the two had fought against each other. Deep in his mind, beyond the respect that had begun to grow, part of Barron still thought of the Hegemony commander as an enemy, He could almost hear the voices of thousands of dead spacers, like wind howling on a dark, storm-tossed night, calling to him to abandon the Hegemony forces, to leave them to their doom.

But friend or resented former adversary, Barron knew the war effort needed the Hegemony. It needed Chronos.

Akella was a brilliant leader, he'd decided that almost the instant he'd met the Hegemony's Number One. But the political opposition to her was too strong for her to defeat alone. Chronos was her most powerful ally, and his loss would not only deprive the allied forces of one of their best commanders, it would likely put the Hegemony on the road to domination under the megalomaniacal Number Two.

That would destroy the fragile alliance, and likely any chance the Hegemony had of surviving the war. The Rim forces would withdraw, and with some luck, perhaps, enjoy a short respite. But then, the reorganized Highborn forces would come to complete the conquest, and the Rim would have no chance on its own.

Chronos simply wasn't expendable...but he was a warrior at heart, even as Barron and Tulus were. There was no way he would agree to withdraw, to pull back while the rest of his forces, and his allies, were still in the thick of the fight. No matter how much damage hi flagship had taken.

Barron was frustrated at Chrono's stubbornness, but then he almost heard the sounds of laughter from all those who'd counseled, ordered and begged *him* to stay back from the front lines over the years.

He turned and looked back as the display, at the battle raging all around.

We've got to do more damage...we've got to hit them harder...

He tapped the side of his headset. "Fritzie, we need more power to the primaries. We've *got* to hit those ships with more punch." The statement seemed absurd to Barron, at least on one level. When he'd first seen the original primaries when he was still in the Academy, he'd been amazed that any weapon could be so powerful...and the newest models on his best ships were twice as strong as the old ones.

But he'd learned a harsh reality in his years of war. Someone always had something better.

"Admiral, we've taken considerable damage. If I increase power flow to the main batteries, the reactors could easily fail. We could lose a transmission line. Even the particle accelerators themselves could burn out. Or worse."

"I know all that, Fritzie, but we're losing the battle." Barron paused for an instant. He hadn't intended to say that out loud. "We need all we can get now, any way we can get it. Just do what I ask, Fritzie. Do your best…that's always gotten the job done."

There was a long pause, and then: "Yes, sir. I'll do what I can."

Barron turned toward Atara's station. "Same orders to all ships. I don't care if they overload every system they've got, we need more power going through the weapons, and we need it now. We've *got* to take down more of those Highborn ships, before they can get the rest of their fleet through the point and into position."

"Yes, Admiral." Atara's voice was grim, and Barron understood just what was going through her mind. It wasn't the aggressiveness of his command that troubled her, nor the danger. But *Dauntless* had Anya Fritz onboard, and none of the other ships did. Whatever chance there was of a catastrophic failure on the flagship, it was that much likelier on vessels with engineers who were mere mortals.

Barron watched as the ships of his battle line continued to fire. A battleship, *Columbia*, disappeared from the screen as he was looking. Another one of his heavies, and another eleven hundred of his spacers.

Eleven hundred fourteen, a voice from the back of his mind asserted.

The primaries were still lancing across the shrinking no

man's land between the two fleets, at least the ones that were still operational, but now, the distance had closed to secondary range, and the laser batteries of the ships without particle accelerators had opened up, adding what firepower they could to the mix. Barron wasn't sure how much damage a laser cannon could inflict on the advanced material of the Highborn hulls, but he needed everything he could get, and more…and he welcomed the batteries of his cruisers that were beginning to fire.

He looked over at the full system display, at the cluster of ships positioned facing transit point one. The enemy attack had come through point three, as expected, and with enough force to almost convince Barron the entire enemy fleet was coming through from there.

Almost convinced him, at least.

Clint Winters and his four hundred ships were deployed almost quarter light hour to the rear, positioned to intercept any enemy incursion from the point deemed second most likely to face an enemy attack. Point one was important for another reason. An attack from there could endanger the fleet's likeliest line of retreat, through point four. At least assuming Chronos and the other Hegemony commanders could be convinced to retreat.

Barron hadn't raised *that* issue yet. He wasn't even sure what he thought was best. He'd be in favor of retreating, of fighting another day if he believed it would be the likeliest way to eventually defeat the enemy. But it wasn't *his* capital that would be abandoned, nor billions of his people. And he knew how that felt, what it took from a man's soul to pull back, leaving billions of civilians at the mercy of the enemy.

He didn't know if he could convince Chronos. He had no idea, even, if the Hegemony fleet commander could order such an action himself, or if he would need Akella or the Council to issue a command of that magnitude.

He wasn't even sure he thought it was a good idea. He didn't believe they had a very good chance of success in the current battle, but he was far from sure it would get any better elsewhere. It was just as likely the matchup would be even more lopsided when the battle ravaged fleet reformed and stopped to face the enemy again.

His eyes were fixed on Winters' ships. He wanted to leave them in place. His gut told him the enemy *would* be coming through point one as well as point three. It was a perfect strategy. Perhaps most convincingly, it was what he would have done in the enemy's place. Timing and coordination would be difficult, but if a Highborn force came through when his people were heavily engaged, and Winters's ships *weren't* there to meet them, there could be a disastrous collapse of morale. His people were veterans, most of them at least, but there was a limit to what even an experienced warrior could withstand. The Kriegeri were bred for war, trained from childhood for combat, but Barron had come to understand not even the Hegemony soldier class was immune from hopelessness and fear. The Palatians were...well, Palatians, but he'd come to know that warrior culture well enough to realize that even they were not proof against normal human weakness. If the enemy came streaming through that transit point without Winters's ships there to meet them, the fleet could disintegrate, its spacers frozen at their controls, gripped by panic, units breaking down, ships making desperate attempts to flee.

But if he didn't call back Winters and his force, the main Highborn attack was going to break through. He'd calculated and analyzed every aspect of the battle. The bombers on their way in would hit hard. He had enough confidence in Stockton to be sure of that. But they would be gunned down in huge numbers as they attacked...and those that made it through would face another desperate challenge trying to land. It was difficult enough to launch a large strike force while the battle line was engaged in a firefight. It would be almost impossible to retrieve and rearm them. The battleships would be within point blank range of the enemy by then...and it was a fool's guess how many of the bays would even remain operational by then.

Stockton's people would hurt the enemy, badly perhaps. But it wasn't going to be enough. Barron needed more. They all needed more.

And there was only one place left to get help.

He reached down, flipped the comm channel. He took a deep breath, and then he started to speak. "Clint...I'm going to need you to bring your ships back here...at flank speed." A pause. Clint Winters didn't need explanations or encouragement, Barron knew that. But he gave them anyway, at least of a sort. "We're not going to make it alone, my friend, so do what you can to get here in time..."

* * *

"On me, all of you. Forget the wing organizations...individual squadrons, line up and lock on my coordinates. We're going in now." Stockton was staring at the screen as he spoke, his eyes locked on the center of the enemy line. He knew what he had in mind would be costly, deadly, that he was about to lead his pilots, at least those who had managed to launch at all, on a desperate mission. It was suicidal, he realized, to lead less than a thousand fighters forward, right into the mass of the enemy's fearsome battle line. But by the time the entire strike force had made it out, it would be too late. *Dauntless* and the other battleships would be gone, or floating wrecks, and the battle would be all but over. As they had against the Hegemony, the squadrons had proven to be one of the most effective weapons the fleet possessed against a stronger enemy, and he had to get them back into the fight while there was still time.

Regardless of the risk.

He pulled back on the throttle, firing up his engines, breaking away from the location he'd held near *Dauntless* for over an hour. Having a bunch of random squadrons—and, in some case, parts of squadrons— following not a battle plan, but simply the nav beacon he was broadcasting, seemed insane. No, it *was* insane. But staying put and waiting, watching as the battleships of the fleet were destroyed one by one, was even crazier. No fight would kill his pilots as effectively as being stranded in space by the destruction of their landing platforms.

He took a deep breath, pushing back against the fear he could feel creeping in from all around. There was darkness, hopelessness, lurking on the perimeters of his mind. Stockton had a strange relationship with fear. His reputation was of a man who simply didn't feel it, but he knew very well, that was a fiction. He'd been scared more times than he could count, but he'd always been able to push it aside, to turn it into something of a driving force. His confidence had always been immense, bordering often on arrogance, he knew, and crossing over that line no small number of times. But now, it was taking more conscious effort to stay the course, and he was beginning to realize that assurance, the ever-present belief he would somehow make it back from every fight, no matter how desperate the mission, was gone. He wondered if that was just the last vestige of his youth slipping away…or if there was something more sinister, more prescient, at work.

It didn't matter. Organized or not, afraid or not, Jake Stockton was going to take his people in. He was going to get back into the fight, and do everything he could to help the fleet achieve victory, or at least to survive the battle.

His eyes moved from contact to contact, picking out the strongest enemy vessels, the battleships that appeared to be the biggest threat to the fleet. They would be the deadliest to his people, as well, but that was functionally irrelevant. If his pilots couldn't help stave off defeat and save the fleet, they were all dead anyway. Deciding whether to die defiantly charging the enemy through a volley of missiles, or freezing to death in his stranded fighter after *Dauntless* was destroyed, was no choice at all, not for Stockton. And not for any of his people either, he suspected.

He watched as his velocity increased, and he continued checking each Highborn battleship, eventually picking out the eight strongest. They were massed together, positioned over forty thousand kilometers, dead center in the enemy line.

And they were blasting the hell out of the Confederation battleships, and the Hegemony monsters positioned to the port of Barron's fleet as well. The combined fleet had already lost over twenty of its heaviest warships outright, and most of the rest shad suffered varying degrees of damage. Stockton was amazed at the volume of fire the ships of the battered line had managed to return, but he knew that output would begin to drop rapidly unless his people got in there and hurt those Highborn ships. Now.

He upped his thrust, driving straight for the targeted vessels. A quick check showed him his people were following, just as he'd ordered. Their formations were disordered, but they were a damned sight better than he had any right to hope. The years of training, the examples set, not just by him but by the other heroes of the fighter corps, were paying off. He knew his people were scared out of their wits, but they had somehow managed to put that aside, even as he had, and focus on what they all knew they had to do.

The reduced size of the attack force would amplify the effects of the enemy defensive fire, he knew, but there was one saving grace. More ships would continue to launch as they were able and, with any luck, thousands more would come forward, perhaps in fragmented waves, but they would advance, nevertheless.

And just maybe, those things will run out of missiles. The Firstborn's conventional point defense fire was no joke, but if the enemy's supply of the deadly missiles gave out, his people would *really* make them pay.

"All ships currently with me, continue on course. All newly launched squadrons, form up around the battle line until more ships have assembled." He didn't want the rest of his birds coming forward in tiny, ineffectual packets. He would keep an eye on the deployment area, just to make sure none of his people got carried away. And he would determine who would lead the gathering ships forward.

His mind started racing, wondering who he could place in command of the subsequent waves. His first choice was Reg Griffin, but he wasn't even sure she was going to make it back…and he couldn't imagine, even if she did, that she'd be in any condition to launch again.

Officer's faces began to pass in front of him, but without knowing who would manage to launch and when, it was impossible to make any choices.

He turned his eyes back to the forward scanners, to the enemy. His attack force was about fifteen minutes from entering Highborn firing range, and about thirty-five from closing to their own launch range. That twenty minutes would be the test, the fiery gauntlet his pilots—and he—would have to survive before they could strike their next blow for the fleet.

Twenty minutes of hell...before they could release their own version of damnation on the enemy.

*   *   *

Tesserax sat still, stonily silent as he watched the battle continue to unfold. Losses had been heavy, considerably higher than his most pessimistic projections, but his forces were winning the battle, nevertheless. He would have to explain the casualties, answer uncomfortable questions about why the enemy had proven so much more difficult to subdue than he'd estimated. But at least he would have the victory, and the fact that *none* of the pre-campaign estimates had indicated the humans would be so effective in battle, nor that those from farther out on the Rim would so quickly and aggressively ally with the Masters and their minions.

He would have the Hegemony capital as well, and after that prize was taken, he was confident the Hegemony, and rest of the nations occupying the Rim sectors of the old empire, would quickly fall.

It is the small craft that have most upset the calculations. They have inflicted damage far in excess of any previous estimates, and they had blunted the strength of our main attack by taking so many ships temporarily out of the line.

His mind analyzed the tiny vessels—fighters, the enemy seemed to call them. They were small, maneuverable, difficult to target, at least in the vast numbers necessary to blunt their assaults.

The scouting reports on Hegemony space had not indicated any such weapon system. The attack craft were something new.

Or something from deeper on the Rim...

Tesserax had been in favor of more extensive scouting

operations, and he was on record as such. That, too, would aid him in making his case. It had long been clear there were provincial successor states to the empire farther out, and even that the more distant systems had escaped the worst of the empire's fall. The Hegemony had been built largely on the ruins of imperial worlds, but it now seemed likely the Rim nations had held onto at least a diminished version of imperial civilization and science, one that had never fully fallen. They had likely lost considerable technological knowledge and capability, but they had clearly retained significant power and capability.

The non-Hegemony ships are the weaker, the least sophisticated, perhaps the result of the deep Rim lacking its own high level technology base in imperial times. When contact with more central systems ceased, they settled into their own, lesser, technology level.

Yet, they are the ones with most of the small craft.

That was a fact he would have to consider. The Hegemony was the more advanced power in the alliance he was facing, but perhaps there was something else on the Rim, something the empire had lost, that the Highborn had been created to replace. The drive that had forged the old empire, the need to fight, strive, claw for advancement. The Pax Imperia had removed such pressures from human development, with ultimately disastrous consequences, but perhaps, those on the Rim, constantly fighting with each other, struggling to regain lost knowledge…perhaps they had regained what mankind had lost.

He would have to consider that at greater length when the battle was over.

The Hegemony railguns were a danger as well as the Rim fighters, but one he'd expected, planned for. The materials of his hulls, and the release of the Sigma-9 radiation waves to block targeting systems, reduced the danger from the enemy weapons. The Hegemony main guns hurt when they hit, even his ships, but they had trouble targeting the Highborn vessels. The small craft, on the other hand, pushed forward to insanely close ranges, ignoring losses as they did. At distances measured in hundreds of kilometers or less, something Tesserax had never seen or imagined in space combat, the tiny ships had little trouble locking their weapons onto the targets.

And with hundreds, even thousands of them coming in wave after wave, the damage they inflicted mounted up.

Worse, they had focused on his battleships, on the heavy units transferred from the primary front. He *couldn't* lose those ships, not many of them—though he'd already lost seven, all to the bombers, at least in part.

We have to match that ability. Somehow. He thought, his mind operating at many times the speed of a human brain. He analyzed, and he considered how best to proceed. He hadn't developed a finished plan yet, but he had the kernel of an idea.

"Scanning control…when the small craft attack again, I want a full analysis. Monitor their formations and communications. I want the command units identified and isolated. Is that understood?"

* * *

"Mother…I got in. The Academy accepted me. I'm going to be a pilot…" Reg Griffin's voice was weak, barely audible, but then, there was no one there to hear her delusional words anyway. It was years earlier, at least in her mind, twisted by lack of oxygen, struggling with the approach of death.

The remembrance of the day she'd found out the

naval academy had accepted her application had always
been a happy one, recalled just then perhaps by her
mind's own defense mechanism, to ward off the fear and
despair clarity would surely bring. But it had failed, and
the satisfaction drained away as other recollections forced
their way in, thoughts of her home as a child, of her
mother's face, tears streaming down them. Her mother
never knew Reg had been there standing outside the
room that day, watching the tears and the utter sadness of
a woman who'd tried valiantly to put on a brave face in
front of her daughter, and to support the dream that to
her was a nightmare.

*This is what she feared those years ago…her daughter, her only
child, gasping for her last breaths…dying alone, far from home…*

She tried to pull herself back from the hallucinations,
but then a single clear thought asked a simple, one word
question.

Why?

Why reach for clarity?

There was nothing she could do. She would never see
her mother again. Her death so far from home, in the
depths of foreign space, would not only be her failure to
be there for her comrades as they fought the rest of the
desperate battle, it would also be the ultimate realization
of Amanda Griffin's fears, the final blow, one last grief to
a woman who'd seen her daughter all of three times in the
last ten years.

*I'm sorry, Mother…sorry I have to leave you, sorry I didn't
come home more often…*

It was too late. There would be no time. No chance to
undo the hurt, even to say goodbye.

Death would be a relief in ways. She wasn't sure if that
was her mind's construct, a way to ward off the fear…but
she stopped resisting. It was over, and she would take any
comfort she could get in her final moments.

Then she heard something.

It was distant, hazy, and she ignored it. Just another delusion, the mind of a woman crossing death's threshold, flailing around in its final struggles.

She heard it again. Louder. And clearer.

"Commodore...do you read?"

She stumbled through the misty haze, trying to find the way back to the clarity she had so recently forsaken. Her oxygen deprived mind was lost, her perception distorted. Yet, something in her drove her forward.

Her hand slipped out from under her leg. She'd placed it there for what remained of warmth in the frigid cockpit. She was shivering, and she struggled to keep her hand steady enough to hit the comm controls. It took a few seconds, and three or four tries, but she finally managed it.

"Griffin...here..." The words echoed in her mind as some level of focus returned. But she wasn't sure how audible they were. She didn't even know anyone had heard her until the voice on the other end responded.

"We're three thousand kilometers behind you, Commodore. We've matched your vector, and we're coming in, decelerating to link up with you. Estimated time to dock, three minutes."

Griffin understood...and she didn't. The 'three minutes' floated in her mind, and somewhere, somehow, she understood. The rescue boat had come, they had found her, against all odds.

I don't have three minutes...

They had found her...but too late. Too late by the slimmest of margins. It was one last cruel blow, and she could feel the tears streaming down her face as she slipped into oblivion.

Chapter Twenty-Eight

Free Trader Pegasus
Somewhere in the Badlands
Year 323 AC (After the Cataclysm)

"This is incredible, Andi. I can't even believe what I am seeing. I've known about the Cataclysm my whole life, of course. But we're actually reading an account of what caused it...or at least one of the causes."

Andi was staring down at the screen in front of her. Sy's words pulled her attention away, slowly. "I'm sorry, Sy...what was that?"

"Exactly. It's hard to pull away from it, isn't it? We've always thought of the Cataclysm as this terrible event, as the end of the empire...but it was always vague, lacking in specifics. But now, we're actually reading accounts of how it came to be. We've got more information here on the empire's collapse than every scholarly study done in the last century...combined."

Andi nodded. "I think you're right. We spent a lot of time scavenging for imperial artifacts, but I'm surprised now how little I really thought about the events that brought about the Cataclysm. It's easy enough to say the empire declined and collapsed, and maybe that would have happened eventually anyway…but now we can see that much of it was deliberately instigated. It's hard to imagine a group of nobles and other imperials actually *trying* to hasten the empire's decline." She paused. "Though that's not entirely fair, is it? It's becoming clear they were trying to *save* the empire, not destroy it. We see enough pointless futility in our own society, unproductive lives, people as puppets, dancing on the strings of those pursuing political power. Imagine what it must have been like after ten thousand years of prosperity, of stability. People lost their ability and their drive, Sy. The empire was dying from the decay of its society, from its people sinking ever deeper into pointless irrelevancy…and then the one group that tried to save it, in their own misguided way, pushed it over the edge." Andi had gone a bit too far, she realized, or at least she'd inserted some of her anticipation and supposition on top of what they had translated.

"We have to keep going, Sy…we *need* these answers." She could feel the fatigue trying to close in on her, but she fought back against it. She knew Sylene had to be every bit as exhausted, but they were just beginning to learn about the Highborn…and Tyler would need everything she could give him if there was to be any chance of victory. The thought that Tyler and the fleet were battling those who very well may have brought down the empire itself—or at least contributed to that historical catastrophe—made it impossible for her to stop.

"I'm with you, Andi. You couldn't drag me away from these files." Sy looked over at her friend, and the two exchanged glances. Then, almost as one, they turned back to their screens without anther word, and they slipped back three centuries once again, to the last days of the old empire.

Andros Estate
Planet Samara
Tirion Vega System
Year 11,699 IR (Imperial Reckoning)
Year 35 BC (Before the Cataclysm) by Confederation
Calendar
358 Years Ago

"We have become closely watched, my friends. Our plan has proceeded as intended, but the costs have exceeded even my most extreme estimates. The empire is moving closer to the level of disorder and destabilization we require, but I fear that the secret police have learned at least some of what we intend. No doubt they suspect more typical methods of seizing power, and they lack the specifics of Project Obsidian, though even that is simply conjecture." Andros was downcast, his voice heavy with fatigue and concern. He had been the driving force of the project, ever since his grandfather's death. He considered it the ultimate act of patriotism, despite the realization that to the imperial authorities, it was nothing less than base treason. And now, he was beginning to worry his efforts would lead him not to ushering in a new age of empire, but rather to the scaffold.

"We   will   have   to   slow   down our…involvements…Andros, extend our schedule. We must review our operatives, and those involved in the project. If the emperor's police are on to us, if they even suspect, they have ways of obtaining information. We must fall back only to the most trustworthy of our associates." Lord Gratien sat next to Andros. The two were nobles of the first rank, the heads of prime houses, and they'd been friends since childhood. Andros trusted Gratien as much as he did anyone, and he agreed with his friend. Some of those he'd considered reliable might very well not be any longer. It was one thing to become involved in something like Obsidian, and quite another to remain strong in the face of scrutiny by the emperor's enforcers. The empire was weak, teetering, a shadow of its former self, and the emperor himself was an inbred fool…but that didn't mean the secret police still didn't know how to break people.

"We agree…" A pause. "My only concern is…well, the plan was conceived as a way to accelerate the already existing decline, to destabilize the empire and create an opening to introduce the Highborn. It is a carefully-calibrated operation, one requiring enough disorder to send the people into the arms of the Highborn, but not enough to trigger an unstoppable collapse. If we reduce the frequency of operations too much, we might very well fail to reach the controlled chain reaction we need. We would have served only to accelerate the final collapse by a few years, without creating the inflection point that allows the Highborn to step in and lead the empire back from the abyss."

Another voice echoed in the room.

"We must accelerate the pace of operations, Andros, not reduce it. The imperial police have a reputation, one that increases the fear they use as a tool, but in truth, they too have declined in effectiveness, even as all other branches of the empire's government. They may continue to make progress in identifying the plan and its attendant operations, but that will take them time. Their efforts are choked by bureaucracy and regulation. The danger is *increased* if they are given more time, far more so than by the pace and number of activities undertaken." Ellerax sat across the table, in a specially designed chair, one that comfortably supported his height and weight. His voice boomed off the walls, and he seemed in every way, somehow…greater…than his patrons. "My brethren and

I grow impatient. We tire of waiting to claim our destiny, our rightful place. We exist to lead the humans, to save them from the folly that threatens a dark age, and even extinction. The timeline *must* be accelerated."

Andros looked across the table at his creation…or at least an achievement attained by the vast team working under his direction. The Highborn had been sixty years in the making, and they were his pride and joy.

They were also becoming a concern. He was distressed by increasing signs of arrogance in the genetically-engineered specimens, and most recently in their tendency to refer to others, everyone but themselves, as *humans*. They, too, were humans, of a more advanced and genetically-developed form, perhaps, but humans, nevertheless. But it was becoming distressingly clear they considered themselves something else entirely.

"Funding is another issue." Andros tried to push aside his concerns about Ellerax and his brethren. The Highborn had been his life, Project Obsidian his obsession. It was inconceivable to give it up after so many years and so much sacrifice. "I have borrowed heavily to sustain the level of operations, and if we exclude our less trustworthy allies, we will also lose their money. If I draw any more deeply on family resources, I not only threaten my house with total collapse, I will almost certainly draw further suspicion. A certain amount of expense and borrowing can be explained away as mismanagement, gambling, even too many mistresses and the like. But past a certain point, such explanations will become inadequate. I have already parried several attempts to investigate my finances. Increasing the rate of expenditure can only instigate more of the same. If the police are successful in penetrating the web of shell companies I've set up, and they can identify any of a number of actual expenses, we will have more than agents to worry about. We'll have imperial battleships in orbit, and troops marching on these estates."

"All the more reason to move quickly, Andros. All you state, all you fear, will almost certainly come to pass…unless we bring things to a climax before they do. I have conceived some…alterations…to your original plan, a more aggressive approach, one that will bring the empire to the required inflection point in a matter of just a few years, rather than decades." Ellerax spoke calmly, but there was something else there, a sense of arrogance perhaps, in his tone. Andros had worked with the first of the Highborn closely for years, and he had begun to notice a difference in their conduct. Ellerax was expressing more opinions, and doing so more strongly. Now, Andros felt almost as though he was a child, listening to some kind of teacher grown impatient with a slow-to-learn pupil. He felt concern, wondered what was behind the change in his creation's attitude. But he again dismissed the concerns. Ellerax was smarter than he was, more capable of analyzing the situation. That was by design, of course, and it would be foolish to help develop so capable a being and then not listen to his counsel.

The troublesome part was that it was all beginning to sound more like orders than counsel.

Project Obsidian had been initiated to create the empire's new leaders. Andros had always known that, indeed, he'd reveled in the prospect of saving a civilization that teetered on the brink of disaster. But only recently had he begun to think in terms of his creations asserting themselves to *him*. The Highborn running the empire after his death had been his dream, his life's goal. But now, he had begun to imagine them ruling *him*, and the though formed in his mind that Ellerax expected *him*, the lead mover in the very existence of the Highborn, to serve *them*.

He felt a wave of panic, uncertainty. He tried to convince himself he was letting fear run wild, that his newfound concerns were excessive, born more of stress and fatigue that reasoned analysis.

He looked across the table at Ellerax. There was no time for doubts, nor for second-guessing. He was committed, and there was no turning back. Sooner or later, the imperial police would uncover what he had done. The plan would move forward, and it would succeed...or Andros would find himself staring at an executioner, his entire house utterly eradicated.

Ellerax had been the symbol of his dream, and now the Highborn leader was something else, two things. His only hope.

And his greatest fear.

Chapter Twenty-Nine

CFS Dauntless
Sigma Nordlin System
Year 323 AC (After the Cataclysm)

The Battle of Calpharon – Stockton's Assault

"Jake...what are you doing? You've got less than a third of your squadrons launched. It's suicide to go right at the center of the enemy line with so few ships." It felt strange to call over a thousand fighters 'so few ships,' but Barron and his people had come a long way in twenty years of almost constant war. The forces he would have considered awesome and immense in the early days of the Union War would have barely rated as task forces in the current fight. And the hundred or hundred fifty fighters or bombers he might have launched from three or four of what had passed then for heavy battleships, what would have constituted a major strike force, would now be at best, a reconnaissance in force. Real attacks now were made by hundreds of warships, and thousands of fighters.

It wasn't just the limited amount of offensive strength Stockton's strike would bring to bear on the enemy that troubled him. It was that the fewer ships in an attack, the heavier the enemy point defense would be on each of them.

"Admiral...you know there's no choice. No time. We've got to go in now, with whatever we've got. If I wait to get the whole strike force out, the fleet will be blasted to dust. The whole force will never even make it off the flight decks before their platforms are destroyed, with them still inside." A pause. "You know I'm right, sir."

Barron wanted to argue. He wanted to order Stockton to pull his forces back and wait until all his wings were ready. He wanted to call down to flight control and badger Stara Sinclair to get the bombers out faster...somehow. But there was no point in haranguing officers he knew were already the best.

And he knew Stockton was right.

"Jake, the fire will be..." Barron didn't finish. There was no point. He knew as well as Stockton what his strike force commander, and the disordered scattering of wings that had managed to launch, needed to do. A second or two passed—each moment that went by put more distance between Stockton and *Dauntless*.

"We'll manage it, Admiral. You know I'm right, sir. I've issued orders for the other waves to follow as soon as they're able to launch, however many are able." They both knew the battleships were taking heavy damage. More and more launch bays were going to be shut down, almost certainly before the entire strike force was re-launched.

Barron *did* know Stockton was right. But he also knew the odds of a pilot sent into that maelstrom returning, *any* pilot, even one as skilled as Jake Stockton. He searched for words, fought for a way to give his approval, to send his friend straight into the mouth of hell.

Stockton saved him from that nightmare.

"Tyler, please. You know I have to do this. Give me your blessing and wish me luck. Wish us all luck…and before I go, let me say that the greatest honor of my life has been serving under you."

Barron felt as though he'd been punched hard in the gut. He sat, knowing what he had to do, but entirely unsure he could do it.

Finally, he just said, "Good luck, Jake." He wanted to say more, so much more. But the words wouldn't come. Then, *Dauntless* shook again, another hit…and the bridge went dark.

*   *   *

The light was bright, harsh. She sat up, shouting, not sure where she was, or how she got there. She reached to her side, her hand flopping around, searching for her pistol. But it was gone.

Her flight suit was gone, too. All her gear. She lay in a bed, naked beneath a flimsy white gown.

"Commodore…please, calm down. You are safe. You're on *Constitution*, in sickbay."

The words didn't make sense, not at first. Then, understanding began to return.

"How?' She rasped out the word. Her throat was dry, but as she became more aware, she realized she wasn't hurt, at least not seriously.

"The retrieval boat, Commodore. They docked with your fighter, pulled you out of your cockpit."

She remembered. She'd been out of air. Out of time. The boat had contacted her, but it had been too late. "I…thought…I…was…dead."

"And, so you were, Commodore, for all of a minute, perhaps ninety seconds. The boat's medic revived you, and from what we've been able to determine, you have no serious injuries. You'll need some rest, and some fluids, but you'll be up and around in a couple days."

"Days?" She arched up and forward suddenly, tearing the sheet covering her to the side. "I don't have days. We're in a fight here." Suddenly, she was very aware of where she was…and what was happening. "I've got to get to the bay. Call down there, and tell them to find me a new fighter. Now!" She threw her legs over the side of the bed and dropped down to the floor. She felt the disorientation hit her as her feet touched the ground, and she reached out, instinctively grabbing onto the edge of the bed.

"Commodore…that is out of the question. You are in no condition to…"

"What did you call me…*Lieutenant?*"

The man looked confused. He was silent for a moment, and then he said, "Commodore…"

"That's right…and I just gave you an order. Is there something about the chain of command that is confusing to you? Last I remembered, a commodore outranked a lieutenant. Am I incorrect?" She stepped away from the bed as the dizziness faded.

"No, Commodore, but…"

"Well then, you comm the bay, tell them to have survival gear and a flight suit ready for me. Now!" She stepped toward the wall. "And get me something to wear down there… Whatever is easiest to find. Just something that will keep my ass from hanging out all the way down there." The man was still looking at her as though he didn't know what to do. "That's an order, Lieutenant!"

"Ah…yes, Commodore…but maybe you should wait and talk to the doctor."

She walked across the room, toward a pile of fresh scrubs stacked on a shelf. "Do you think that's going to change anything? Because unless that doctor's got a star on his shoulder...no, two stars...it's a waste of time. And we don't have a minute to waste right now." She reached over and grabbed the scrubs, pulling the gown off, and sending the flustered and embarrassed med tech scrambling out of the room.

"Now, Lieutenant, I saw to my own clothes, but I need them ready down on the flight deck when I get there. So get your ass over to the comm, and get it done!"

* * *

Stockton angled his ship around again, redirecting the thrust angle. The incoming fire was heavy...damned heavy. That wasn't a surprise, but it was still making him sweat a little. It would have been bad enough, even if he hadn't known the deadly missiles would be coming soon.

The enemy magazines could be empty, of course. Even Highborn ships were limited to the realities of space and tonnage. The missiles were large, and the enemy supply of them *had* to be finite. But reality painted a less optimistic picture.

First, the Highborn ships hadn't all been in battle for the same amount of time. There was some hope—a reasonable amount even—that the initial vessels through the point, the ones that had been hardest hit by his first assault, and by the subsequent exchanges between the battle lines, had exhausted their supplies of missiles, or seen their launchers put out of action. But there were fresher ships, new arrivals untouched by his earlier attack. He had no doubt at all that those vessels carried full loads of missiles.

"Stay on those evasive maneuvers, all of you." His voice was cold, harsh. He loved his pilots, and he respected them. But he knew he would lose many to carelessness, and he was going to keep that number to an absolute minimum, whatever it took.

Even if that was treating them like shit as they followed him into hell.

He ignored the acknowledgements, though the disordered nature of them concerned him. He didn't have a well-ordered force behind him. He had partial wings thrown together, in some cases, even bits and pieces of squadrons. *That* was going to increase the losses as well…and he reminded himself to stay aware that he was leading more a mob than a disciplined strike force. There would be no detailed tactics, no carefully designed plans. The best he could do was lead them forward, toward the enemy…and do what he could to pull as many through the withering fire they encountered along the way.

He felt a tightness inside as he saw the first missiles appear on his screen. Two ships had launched, almost simultaneously, and then a few seconds later, another one. The spreads looked menacing, but Stockton knew he was seeing only the smallest part of the apocalypse heading for his people. Those missiles would split when they got closer, and each of them would become twenty separate warheads, every one of them packed full of antimatter, powerful enough to take out any of his ships within half a kilometer or more.

He wanted to veer off, to order his pilots to change course and try to go around the missiles. But that wasn't an option. He had to hit the enemy center. His people *had* to do some damage to those enemy battleships before the Confederation line was gone, and the Hegemony and Palatian ships along with it.

Besides, there was no escape, no true solace in an effort to fly around the volleys. The missiles were too fast, too maneuverable. Even if he gave the order to go around, blunting the effectiveness of the attack in the process, it would be futile. The missiles would react, and their massive acceleration would allow them to catch his people, no matter where he led them.

There is only one way…straight ahead…

His faced tightened, and he gritted his teeth, pushing forward, jerking his ship around on a wild evasion course…straight for the center of the enemy line.

* * *

"Admiral Stockton is leading another attack, Commander. It appears he is moving forward with a portion of the total strike force."

Chronos sat in his chair, silent. He'd fought the Confeds for six years, cursed them, despised them for their tenacity, for their infuriating refusal to accept that they were defeated, that their superiors had beaten them. And he had hated none worse than the Confed fighter pilots, and most among them, their legendary commander. Now those squadrons that had plagued him were working for him, and Jake Stockton, a thousand times damned to hell in his mind, was his ally. It was strange, something he found difficult to fully comprehend.

There was no way else to put it. He was beginning to respect his former enemies, if not to outright like many of them. He'd become at least cordially friendly with Tyler Barron, but now he thought about Stockton, the Confederation's fighter master. Perhaps no one had caused him more harm in the recent war, nor was there anyone who could lay claim to greater credit for holding off the Hegemony invasion.

And now he is doing it to the Highborn…

Chronos didn't know much about the enemy, who they were or where they were from, but it was clear they didn't possess attack craft, much as the Hegemony hadn't. He understood, as few likely did, just how powerful a weapon the squadrons were.

I didn't have those missiles, though…

He was no expert on bomber tactics, but it wasn't hard to figure that leading the assaults in piecemeal was going to massively increase losses. But he also realized what Stockton himself no doubt had.

The fleet didn't have much time.

The battle was raging, and the forces of the Hegemony and its allies were making the enemy pay a high price. But they were losing. He'd analyzed the fight half a dozen ways, and he couldn't come up with a scenario that led to victory. At least not one with more than a one or two percent chance.

He'd been directing the battle, and trying to hold his own thoughts at bay. He was determined to fight, to the death if necessary, but the thought of seeing the enemy land on Calpharon, and knowing it was the end of the Hegemony, was more than he could endure.

The planet was his home, and the capital of his nation. He had served the Hegemony his entire life, and he had no desire to outlive it. But Akella was there, and Ajia. And his other children. Everyone he cared about in his life, at least those who weren't fighting along with him, was down on the planet.

And if the fleet withdrew, if the surviving ships retreated—soon—there would remain a force in being. Calpharon would fall, but the Hegemony and its allies would fight on. Hope would be tattered, tenuous…but it would still exist. And where there was time, there was a chance.

He knew he had to give the order, but he still held back. The very idea was anathema to him, and he was far from sure his directive would be accepted even if he issued it. He'd talked to Akella about the possibility before he'd departed the last time for the fleet, but they'd never reached a conclusion. She'd been as hesitant as he was to abandon Calpharon, but Chronos had argued, urging her to be ready to leave, reminding her she was the leader of the entire Hegemony, of hundreds of other worlds, all of which needed her. That was all true, and all the concerns he'd raised were valid, but he knew in his own mind it had all been manipulation. He'd simply wanted Akella and Ajia to leave Calpharon. He wanted then safe, no matter what happened to the fleet or to the capital...or to him.

Now, he wondered if he should comm Tyler Barron, if he dared to suggest the possibility of a withdrawal. Was it even possible? Could the fleet abandon Calpharon and still fight on?

Chronos had begun to consider just that possibility. His military intellect, the purely analytical part of his mind that understood tactics and combat realities, told him to withdraw. Victory was unlikely in the current fight, and however remote the possibility was, more time would allow for at least the chance of some change in the strategic situation.

The warrior part of him was firmly on the other side. Death before retreat! That side would have prevailed, if it was only his life at stake, or only the lives of his officers and Kriegeri. It was their duty to serve, to fight to the end if need be, and his honor would be better served by death in a heroic, if failed, defense than by an ignominious retreat.

But he knew it was neither of those sides that was prevailing. He was grasping with a cold reality. Akella wouldn't leave, not unless he and the fleet did. Even then, she would struggle and argue. She detested the job her genetics had mandated she accept, and she hated her role as head of state. But she'd always taken her duty seriously.

And Chronos wasn't sure he could convince her to leave, and to abandon Calpharon's billions.

But she wouldn't go unless he and the fleet did. And he wasn't ready. He couldn't bring himself to give up. Not yet.

And perhaps not ever.

*   *   *

Stockton's hands were moving almost on their own, his conscious mind barely aware of the decisions to angle and re-angle his thrusters. A lifetime of combat had honed his instincts, and they were firmly in control. The laser fire was heavy, but the worst danger was the cluster of missiles chasing his ship. There were three of the weapons on his tail, and they were accelerating with more than three times the power of his own engines.

But they weren't going to stop him. He'd done the calculations in his head twice, and the AI had confirmed the results. He—and the over one hundred bombers grouped right around him—were going to get to launch range before the missiles closed.

His people had run the gauntlet toward the targeted ships, endured the missiles fired by those vessels. They'd paid a terrible price, and over two hundred of their comrades had died in a brief few minutes. But all across the line, the survivors were coming on, and Stockton knew his people well enough to be sure there was only one thing on all their minds...the same thing that consumed his own thoughts.

Vengeance.

It was almost time. Time to make the enemy pay.

He stared at the main screen in front of him. His fingers moved over the controls, and the area view disappeared, replaced by the targeting display. Stockton knew his people would have to face the incoming missiles—and another trip back past the Highborn line—before they could return to their baseships.

Assuming any of the battleships that had launched them still had operational bays to land them. But that worry seemed distant and unimportant. Getting back past the enemy was enough to worry about.

Stockton stared at the targeting screen. He couldn't control the missiles pursuing his people, nor the damage the battleships were taking in the sustained firefight. He couldn't even do anything to help his own pilots. Each of them was on his or her own. They would hit or miss themselves. They would escape or fall as individuals.

All Stockton could do was make damned sure the two torpedoes he carried hit the enemy battleships in front of him. All he could do was kill some of the enemy.

And he was determined to see that done.

He watched as the range dropped rapidly. He was coming in fast and hard, like all his people. The return to the ships would start with an extensive period of deceleration, after which his people would have to come back, rebuilding their velocities as they moved back through the Highborn line.

He stared at the targeting scope. The ship in front of him was one of the least damaged in the enemy line. He'd targeted it for precisely that reason, but now he was paying for that choices. The ship's fire was withering, and Stockton expected another volley of missiles to launch any time. That wouldn't stop him from completing his attack run. The Highborn missiles seemed to have a minimum range before they could separate and arm themselves. Anything the ship managed to launch would just be that much more his people had to come through if they made it through the attack…and had any chance of getting back home.

He felt a twinge inside, a moment of harsh honesty with himself. He'd led his people in knowing few of them would return. He had believed from the moment he'd ordered the attack force to follow him that most of them, all of them perhaps, would die.

That he, too, would die.

The math supported that grim view. The way back would be difficult, nearly impossible, strewn with clusters of deadly missiles, and laser fire tearing across space all around. The only diversions that might aid his returning ships would be the disordered waves following them in, and Stockton couldn't hope that a loaded ship would be destroyed to save a spent one. The coldest calculus was in play, and he knew just how desperate the fight truly was.

But he didn't feel guilty, didn't bear the usual weight he did when he led his people into desperate danger. They were all dead anyway if the fleet was destroyed, and he couldn't imagine any of his pilots would choose a slow end from suffocation or freezing to a final desperate fight…and a chance to hurt the enemy one last time.

He saw the range tick down under one thousand kilometers. Once, that would have been the most extreme of short ranges for an attack, but against the hard to target Highborn ships, Stockton had trained his people to go in even closer. He'd led attacks down to five hundred kilometers, even four hundred or less. But now, he was going to go in even closer.

He breathed deeply, doing all he could to remain calm. Fear would not serve him, nor would tension. He had lived much of his adult life behind the cockpit, and he'd never felt so at home anywhere as he did there. It was where he belonged, where he could do his best. And if it was where he died, as he'd so long believed it would be, then so be it.

Three hundred kilometers.

He'd already armed his plasma torpedoes, and he'd set them to convert to energy the instant they left the bomb bay. He wasn't sure how that would affect his ship, if the transition to superhot plasma so close would damage his tiny vessel. As far as he knew, no bomber had every launched a torpedo set to convert the instant it was released.

That data set would soon include hundreds of samples, however. Every ship following him in had their torpedoes set the same way. He hadn't ordered it—there were certain things he just couldn't order someone to do—but he'd told them what he intended, fully aware of the effect it would have on his pilots.

Two hundred kilometers.

He was going down to one hundred kilometers before he launched. He wasn't even sure it was possible to pull up at that range, that there was enough time to react, to nudge his vector sufficiently to clear the ship he was attacking.

He wasn't even sure crashing in right after his torpedoes wouldn't be the merciful way to go, a chance to escape the nightmarish struggle to try, somehow, to get back to *Dauntless*.

Assuming *Dauntless* was even there by the time he made it back.

He sucked in another deep breath, and he held it, and, as his eyes registered the distance meter reading one hundred, he launched both of his torpedoes.

The instant they were away, he angled his thrusters as far to port as possible, and he blasted at full. In two seconds, he would know he'd cleared the enemy ship...or he'd be dead.

The time passed, somehow seeming glacial despite its being a brief instant. For a passing flash of time that seemed like a lifetime, he wondered if he had made it past. Then he knew.

He was still alive.

He checked the readings. He'd some less than a kilometer from the enemy hull. That wasn't just close. It was *close*…unheard of, beyond even the most insane things he'd attempted before. He wasn't going to calculate the margin of his escape, the fraction of a second in reaction time that had been the difference between life and death. There were some things it was better not to know.

He gripped his controls, decelerating his ship at maximum thrust. He didn't even check the targeting screen to confirm that he'd hit. At the range from which he'd launched, it would have been almost impossible to miss. Now, his concern was getting to *Dauntless*, and somehow leading as many of his people who made it through with him back to the fleet.

Chapter Thirty

Union Battleship Tonnerre
Gavarouche System
Union Year 227 (323 AC)

"Rebroadcast the communique continually." Denisov sat rigidly, like a statue staring coldly across the bridge. "And maintain full fire. Only vessels that have surrendered and powered down are to be spared…is that understood?" It had been difficult enough to go into battle against other units of the fleet, against officers with whom he'd served, men and women he'd fought beside, called friends. It absolutely sickened him to gun them down like sheep, even as they desperately tried to flee from the battlefield. But he was a creature of duty, and he understood his all too well.

He might have found it a bit easier if he'd believed the dying spacers were all like Villieneuve, that they were the same kind of human beasts, for whom extermination could only be considered a cleansing. But he knew that wasn't true. The fleet was far from free of power-grasping schemers, but he knew many of the officers out there were with Villieneuve out of blind obedience to what they saw as the legitimate government. Creatures of duty, even as he was.

More were there out of fear, or because Villieneuve and his henchmen had something one them. How many were fighting because families—spouses, parents, children, siblings—had been targeted by Villieneuve's operatives? How many had been given a choice, swear to Villieneuve or see their loved ones butchered in their homes? There was no limit to what Gaston Villieneuve would do to cling to his power, Denisov knew that all too well.

"Rebroadcasting, Admiral." A pause. "Admiral, *Villeroi* is requesting permission to fall back out of the line. She has reactor problems."

"Permission granted." Denisov could feel the exhaustion as he uttered the words, and he knew every spacer in the fleet felt the same.

No, not all of them. At least thirty thousand of them are dead...

The battle had been a fierce one, a brutal slugfest that had gone on for almost two days. He'd remained on the bridge, jacked up on stims as all his people were...and their enemies as well, no doubt. In the end, it had been skill, tactics, experience that had made the difference. Villieneuve had some of the fleet's top officers serving on his side, but none of them could match Denisov, especially not since the admiral had honed his skills for more than two years fighting against the Hegemony.

Alongside Tyler Barron.

The Confederation admiral was perhaps the one person in all known space that Gaston Villieneuve hated more than he did Denisov. He was also the most gifted naval tactician of his generation. Denisov felt that way, and he suspected almost every serving officer who had fought with Barron—alongside or against—shared that view.

"Admiral…we're receiving a communique from Cruiser Squadron Three. Commander Quillet is requesting we accept her surrender. They have ceased fire and powered down their engines as ordered."

Denisov nodded immediately, but his verbal response was delayed. He didn't know what changes Villieneuve had made in his forces, but if a commander was in charge of the cruiser squadron, that meant a lot of officers had been killed or incapacitated. He didn't know Quillet personally, but he was vaguely aware of her position in the fleet, at least before he'd left.

She couldn't have been more than eighth in line for command, if that…

He was still trying to come to terms with the bloodiness of the battle, though he knew on some level, he never would. His own fleet was badly damaged, but Villieneuve's had been hurt worse. Much worse. The former First Citizen had lost half his ships, at least when those surrendering, and the crippled vessels left behind by his retreating forces were counted. The battle had been a terrible one, a titanic clash that Denisov knew had cost him some part of himself.

But it had also been a victory. A complete victory.

Villieneuve had escaped, and that meant he was still dangerous. He retained a large force of ships as well, though how many of those were damaged and unable to keep up with his retreat—and how many would slip away and desert as soon as they could—Denisov didn't know. It wasn't enough strength for the deposed dictator to meet Denisov again in an all-out fight, but control of something like the Union was a more complex problem. If Villieneuve spread his forces, controlled as many systems as possible, it would take years to root them all out.

Denisov was grateful for the victory, though he feared

what a desperate Villieneuve might do, what kind of traps he might lay for his enemies. He was confident he could defeat the remaining enemy naval units, that he could crush Villieneuve's remaining military power…if he got the chance. He just wasn't sure it would be enough.

Even if Villieneuve was defeated, what would happen next. He would chase after the renegade First Citizen, hunt him down and destroy any forces remaining loyal to him, however long it took. That was his job. The rest he would leave to Sandrine Ciara. When Villieneuve was finally killed or captured, when the Union's tyrant had finally faced justice, he would discover his ally's true colors. Would Ciara become just a new Villieneuve, a brutal despot who kept the Unions billions under an iron boot? Or would she be something else, not a freedom fighter certainly, but perhaps a step in that direction. Would she rule with a lighter touch? Would she give the people at least some shreds of freedom?

And would she keep her word and end the century of animosity and war with the Confederation?

He was tentative on most of it, hopeful but far from convinced. But Ciara had been aided by the Confeds, and if the Confederation ambassador had indeed become, as all accounts suggested, her lover, it seemed likely at least that the two nations would enter a new era, of peace if not outright cooperation. He had reason to expect that she would honor at least that part of her pledge…and, if she did, they could build from there.

Don't get ahead of yourself. Gaston Villieneuve will be dangerous until he is dead on the ground in front of you. And you've got a year of repairs before this fleet will be ready to fight again. That's a lot of time for a man like Villieneuve to cause problems. To find a way to fight on.

He had won a battle, but he knew the war was far from over.

* * *

"Fools! Is there no one here who can match the traitor, Denisov? Are none of the vaunted Union admirals I have assembled a match for a single mongrel rogue?" Villieneuve stood in front of his high command, what was left of it at least, after the battle. Actually, that was most of it. His senior commanders had survived in far greater percentages than his spacers. Virtually every unit flagship had managed to escape, often leaving behind half or more of the original vessels in their commands. It was a pathetic display, and one for which Villieneuve would once have sent every one of them to the cells. But his position had changed, and he needed the officers standing in the room, perhaps even more than he had before. He was down, but he wasn't out yet, and he had to hang on to every ship he still had.

No one responded. The air was heavy with fear. *That* was something Villieneuve had cultivated all his professional life, but as he stood there, he wondered where he had failed. Clearly, his officers had been more afraid of Denisov and the rebel fleet than they were of him.

But that was going to change.

"I can only assume that you all lacked the motivation necessary to propel you to victory. For that, I accept blame...and I am ready to correct my error. I have dispatched orders, and teams of loyal Sector Nine operatives. They are even now en route to your home worlds..." *At least the ones I still control.* "They are charged with seeing to your families, my good officers, and ensuring that they are...safe." It was clear from the expressions in the room, everyone present completely understood his meaning. "When we again meet the traitors in battle, perhaps knowing that your loved ones are in…good hands…will help you focus on the matter at hand. Victory."

The officers shuffled around nervously, but none had the courage to speak. Finally, Admiral Fierra took a half step forward. "First Citizen, we are with you to the end. But we…cannot ignore that the traitors have gained a considerable advantage in terms of hulls and tonnage. The battle…should have gone differently, First Citizen…but it didn't, for whatever reason."

The officer was clearly nervous, but Villieneuve listened, and in his mind, a single thought developed. Only one of the men and women in the room seemed to have the courage to speak out. That might have angered him at one time or, more likely, tripped his paranoia over an admiral who might one day become a threat. But as he stood there, he knew he needed someone capable, an officer who could help him fight the war.

He needed his own Denisov.

"Admiral Fierra…" His tone was dark and menacing but, as he watched, he saw the officer stood his ground. *Very good.* "…you are entirely correct. We are not in a position to reengage the traitorous fleet, not immediately in any event. We must withdraw…to Aquitara. The system is heavily fortified, and both the planetary governor and the local military commander are loyal." *You hope they still are.* "We will be well defended while we reorganize, and both Aquitara and two nearby systems possess significant shipyards. With fortune, we will be able to replace at least some of our losses and repair our damaged units."

The assembled group of officers nodded their agreement, though Villieneuve suspected there was rather less sincerity in it all than he would have liked. After a moment, Fierra said, "Aquitara is also a long journey from here. That is a danger we must overcome, but it will be an advantage if we're able to reach there. Admiral Denisov will come after us, almost certainly, and the distance will strain his logistics. Any obstacles in his way will help buy us the time we need. Denisov may be against us, but that does not remove the fact that he is a highly-skilled admiral, the best in the service, in my opinion."

The other officers rustled nervously. It was always dangerous to push Gaston Villieneuve, and whatever the current situation, he retained the ability to lash out at those within his reach.

"You are correct, Admiral Fierra. Andrei Denisov is a traitor, a wild dog who needs to be put down...but it is at our own peril that we underestimate his abilities." He glared at the group of officers. "We have just had a reminder of that fact. Our situation has its dangers, and a successful pursuit by the traitors is only one of those hazards. And it is not one alleviated by further delay. We will set a course for Aquitara at once. All ships unable to keep up with the fleet are to be abandoned and scuttled to prevent their falling into enemy hands."

"Yes, First Citizen." The replies were shaky, uncertain. All save for one. In every way, Fierra was maintaining his discipline and courage, and Villieneuve made an immediate decision.

"Admiral Fierra...you are hereby promoted to fleet admiral and placed in overall command of all loyal forces." It was something that ran against Villieneuve's instincts. Fierra had a strong record, and he had sworn to serve against the traitors...but he was far from one of Villieneuve's creatures. He had less control and influence over Fierra than he liked, but he knew one thing above all others. He had to survive, and eventually, he had to win a military victory. And Fierra was the likeliest to achieve that goal. Throwing any of the others present against Denisov again would be like feeding children to starving wolves.

"First Citizen...I don't know what to say."

Villieneuve looked at Fierra, and then at the just-demoted officer standing against the far wall. Estaban La Ventrolle *was* one of Villieneuve's creatures, or at least he had been thirty seconds before. But he had also lost the crucial battle, turned an even match into a desperate fight for survival. Villieneuve didn't believe in allowing second mistakes, certainly not when the first was so egregious.

"Say 'thank you.' Or say nothing. I'm sure you have considerable work to do. Take whatever steps you deem necessary, Fleet Admiral, but get this fleet out of here and on the way to Aquitara at once."

"Yes, First Citizen. Thank you, First Citizen..."

"Dismissed...all of you." Villieneuve looked across the room, at La Ventrolle. The admiral had served him loyally for years, and he'd even turned in colleagues whose plotting had created too much suspicion. But Villieneuve had just humiliated La Ventrolle in front of the others, and he had stripped the officer of much of his power. Villieneuve understood very well how enemies and traitors were made. He had his doubts La Ventrolle had the stomach to truly oppose him, but he wasn't taking any chances.

"Estaban...please stay a moment." Villieneuve stood silently as the other officers left the room, leaving him alone with the admiral, and the two Sector Nine operatives standing quietly by the door.

"Estaban, I wanted to assure you that you possess my continued confidence. I just believe that a change right now will help to foster a recovery in morale. You will always remain in my confidence, and I will continue to look to you as one of my most trusted advisors." He stepped forward and embraced the admiral. But as he did, he looked across the room, his eyes meeting those of the senior agent present. The man looked back, and he nodded once, a communication whose meaning was clear. He had understood Villieneuve's command perfectly. Estaban La Ventrolle was too much of a danger.

The agent knew what he was expected to do.

Chapter Thirty-One

CFS Dauntless
Sigma Nordlin System
Year 323 AC (After the Cataclysm)

The Battle of Calpharon – Forward Colossus!

"We've restored full power to all areas of the ship, Admiral. It wasn't that bad of a hit, just in the wrong spot. My people have a temporary redirect in place, but give me twenty minutes or so, and I'll have fresh transmission lines installed."

Barron knew he owed the restoration of *Dauntless*'s power—on the bridge and elsewhere—to Anya Fritz's incredible skills, and no less to her unstoppable drive, but the first thought to come into his mind was a dark one.

If we have twenty minutes…

Dauntless had been hit twice so far, and each time the vessel had suffered power failures, first to the primary batteries and then to almost a third of the ship, including the bridge. He usually ridiculed such thoughts, but he couldn't help but wonder if some bill had come due for past good luck, for the close escapes that had marked his career. Had fortune abandoned him?

The battle was raging all around. Barron had watched as one ship after another signaled massive damage, only for most of them to vanish from the display or turn dark soon after. Those that disappeared had exploded, Barron knew, most likely because their reactors' containment had been breached before they could be shut down. The others, the small gray icons on the display, were dead hulks, vessels with no energy output at all, the ghostly remains of ships that had once been proud units in his fleet. The lack of energy output didn't necessarily mean their crews were all dead. Yet. Some of the contacts were even surrounded by escape pods and lifeboats, and others no doubt still had live spacers crawling around in survival suits. But they were living dead, men and women still struggling, but with almost no hope of survival.

Barron stared at the display, watching the rest of the battle. The Hegemony ships were taking even more fire than his. Clearly, the enemy understood those were the strongest and most powerful vessels present and, though the railguns were having trouble targeting the strange Highborn hulls, when they did hit, they inflicted considerable damage, more even than Barron's newest and heaviest primaries.

His gaze moved next to the Alliance forces, and he could feel his eyes moisten. Vian Tulus's Palatian ships had lower effective attack ranges, and the Imperator had responded by sending his ships right into the teeth of the enemy fire, closing to point blank range and blasting away. The lower range was aiding their targeting, and the less sophisticated Palatian guns were actually scoring a good number of hits. But the cost had been horrendous. Half of Tulus's ships were either gone, or strung out in a line of dead or almost dead hulks along the fleet's axis of advance. The human suffering that lay behind the almost antiseptic images on the screen was almost beyond calculation, and the Confederation's top admiral felt it wearing him down.

"Well done, Fritzie, as always." Barron realized he hadn't responded, that he'd just sat quietly as his mind wandered to his allies, and to the battered ships of his fleet. "Just stay on things. Keep us in the fight as long as you can." It was a vague command, pointless, but it was all he had. He didn't know what else to say. He knew *he* would be on the verge of issuing a withdrawal order if he'd been the combined fleet's sole commander. But he wasn't. If he pulled back, he imagined Tulus would follow, with however many of his ships were able to extricate themselves from the close-in firefight raging around them. But if the Hegemony fleet didn't retreat, too, he wasn't sure there was much point. The battered Confederation and Alliance fleets could never defeat the Highborn by themselves. That was clearer even than it had been before. They would need antimatter, for one thing, and the only remaining production source of that precious substance was a single world on the Rim side of the Hegemony.

He knew Chronos *should* retreat as well, that it was the right decision tactically. The war wouldn't be over, not if the combined allied forces maintained a significant force in the field. They'd hurt the Highborn in the battle, and the enemy would need time to regroup and repair their damage. Barron didn't overstate the likelihood of a delay changing the realities of the dark situation, but playing for more time was just about the only option he could see that offered even a hope of victory.

Retreat was always difficult for him to consider…and he knew it would be worse for Tulus. But Chronos was the real problem. Barron had to accept defeat, crawl away with what forces he could extricate and lick his wounds for the next fight. But Chronos had to abandon his capital. His home.

Barron knew how that felt, only too well. He'd given the orders to yield Megara, and he'd pulled his forces back from the Confederation's capital system. He could still feel the pain from that, the lingering wounds of leaving the planet's billions defenseless. Millions had died in the aftermath of his withdrawal, but his choice had been the right one. Remaining, fighting to the last, would have sated his warrior's honor…but if he had done so, the war would have been lost, and the Confederation subjugated by the Hegemony.

Chronos now faces that same choice. You need to make sure he understands, that he makes a decision based in fact, and not in pointless warrior's pride…

"Atara…" His voice was soft, and it was heavy with resignation. "…get Commander Chronos on my line."

She looked back, and their eyes met for an instant. Then she nodded and said, "Yes, Admiral."

She turned back toward her station, and Barron knew at least one other person on the bridge understood exactly was he was going to do.

The big question was, how would he respond if Chronos refused? What would he do? Would he stay, and condemn his people to almost certain death, the Confederation and the Rim to ruin?

Or would he abandon an ally, flee to fight another day in an effort that would almost certainly prove utterly futile.

He had no idea.

* * *

"*Lexiconia* has been destroyed, your Supremacy. And *Vexillania*." The aide's words echoed across *Imperator*

Vennius's bridge. Every officer present heard them clearly, and not one showed the slightest sign of emotion. The Palatians were likely to die, but if that was their fate, it was clear the flagship's bridge crew, at least, had decided as a group to die as they had lived. As Palatian warriors.

Tulus looked back, through the haze of smoke, ignoring the caustic assault the stinging chemicals launched on his eyes. His ship was dying. His fleet was dying. Half his ships were gone, and every hull that remained carried some degree of damage. It went against his Palatian creed to retreat, to even consider such a course, but he found himself wondering when the communique would come. When the word to withdraw would reach his battered vessel.

Tulus knew he could issue his own orders any time he chose. He was the Alliance's Imperator, and the sole and only commander of the Palatian fleet. But withdrawing from battle was almost anathema in any situation. The thought of leaving an ally—a *real* ally, like the Confeds—pushed the thought to the very edge of impossibility.

And the idea of abandoning his friend, his blood brother, of breaking off and pulling back—running—while Tyler Barron remained, fighting almost certainly to his own death, pushed it well over that chasm. Tulus would not leave, *could* not leave, until Barron did, and no number of losses, no butcher's bill would change that. And, while he fought, every Palatian would battle at his side.

"All ships, reengage engines, full thrust forward." His fleet had closed to short range, mostly to bring their own weapons to bear against an enemy whose reach greatly exceeded their own. That had been a costly exercise, but Tulus had some cause for pride in his people. They'd managed to do considerable damage to the difficult to target Highborn ships…and Tulus had a skill for keeping tactics simple. If something worked, then more of it might well work better.

If they weren't going to pull back, then he was going to lead them forward.

If we must die, let it be a death worthy, at least, of a song...

"All weapons, maintain full fire. Overload the reactors if necessary, but we're going in, and we're firing every meter of the way." His voice was hard, and venom dripped from his words. Tulus didn't want to die...but he had been prepared for death since the day he'd left his home to begin the Ordeal. That coming of age ritual had marked the beginning of his life as a Palatian warrior.

And every Palatian warrior was ready to die when his time came.

If Vian Tulus's time had come, he knew how he would face it. He was going to go down with his hands soaked in enemy blood.

* * *

The comm with Chronos had gone about as Barron had expected. His ally understood the situation, he was sure of that. But he'd remained indecisive. The Chronos he'd come to know, even to like against his initial impulses, was not one to prevaricate, but the decision to abandon Calpharon, to order whatever meager evacuation could be done quickly, and to leave almost all the planet's billions to the enemy's mercy, was too much for him. Barron had argued, urged his comrade, but so far to no avail. Chronos hadn't refused, but he hadn't agreed either. And they were running out of time.

The situation was bleak. The line wasn't going to hold much longer. If Chronos didn't make a decision, and soon, Barron knew he would have to make his own. And abandoning an ally would not come any easier to Barron than leaving Calpharon would to Chronos.

He looked around, grasping for anything, any way to stabilize the situation, to give the fleet a chance to hold. But he was rapidly running out of resources.

Winter's ships were still too far out. They weren't going to make it in time. The fleet would be destroyed before the reserves got into range. Barron felt hopelessness closing in on him, the final defeat he'd so long eluded hanging over him like a dense, black shadow.

But he had one last card up his sleeve.

"Atara…send a communique to Commodore Eaton. *Colossus* is to move forward."

"Yes, Admiral." Atara's words were calm, her voice stone cold. Barron knew she understood. It was time for the last effort, one final chance to try and stop the enemy assault.

Barron had kept the massive ship hidden, held it in reserve. He'd discussed the strategy with Chronos, and the two had debated the relative advantages and disadvantages. Keeping *Colossus* off the line cost a lot of firepower. But the enemy had moved deeper into the system, and now *Colossus* had a good chance of striking the Highborn flank.

Combined with Winters's forces…just maybe it will be enough…

It was a hopeful thought, for all of thirty seconds. But it died in an instant, crushed by a fresh wave of despair.

"Admiral…we have scanner reports coming from transit point one. Energy readings. It looks like…"

Atara didn't finish. She didn't have to. Barron could hear the words, almost as though she'd shouted them in his ear.

It looks like incoming vessels transiting.

Barron leaned back in his chair, feeling as though he'd been gut-punched, as if some spacer's god was toying with him, punishing him for his instant of hope. Clint Winters and his ships had served a dual purpose, as a general reserve, and as a force to guard against an enemy flank attack. Now, his ships would have to serve that last purpose, and that left the main fleet without any reserves, save for *Colossus* alone.

And the Highborn *still* had ships pouring into the system from their initial entry point as well.

"Send orders to Admiral Winters, Atara. He is to abort his movement toward the main line and bring his fleet about to defend point one." Barron had no idea what would be coming through that point so many millions of kilometers distant, but Winters's force was all he had left to face it. Four hundred vessels constituted a large force by any measure, even if it *was* light on capital ships and mostly made up of escorts and cruisers. Still, whatever the hardware, there wasn't a nastier wildcat he could throw at the enemy than Clint Winters. After all, it wasn't every day the enemy faced an admiral nicknamed, 'the Sledgehammer.' Barron didn't feel confidence, exactly, but if he *had* to depend on someone to defend the rear of his fleet—and his only escape route—there was no one he would have picked over Clint Winters.

"Yes, Admiral." Atara's usually emotionless voice betrayed her own exhaustion this time. Barron watched as she activated the comm, and sent the command to Winters. It would be almost a minute before it arrived, but that didn't matter. He knew Winters would do what he had to do, fight like a raging firestorm to hold back whatever came through the transit point. But it didn't matter. Whatever Winters managed to do, without his forces, the main line was as good as finished. His second-in-command would be fighting not to win the battle, but to hold open the line of retreat.

Assuming there even was a retreat.

* * *

"Full power to the engines. All weapons systems prepare to engage." Sonya Eaton stared straight forward, struggling with all her strength to ignore the fear, to fight back against the pressure pushing down on her from every direction. *Colossus* was like no other ship in the fleet, no other vessel that existed, at least as far as anyone on the Rim had ever known. Much of the vessel's awesome power came from mysterious imperial technology, almost as far beyond the Hegemony engineers who'd spent twenty years repairing it as it was any of her people. It felt at times, not so much like commanding a warship as petitioning for some supernatural favor. Anya Fritz had done everything imaginable to unlock the great ship's secrets and to train its engineering teams, but then she'd returned to *Dauntless* for the battle. It didn't make a lot of tactical sense—and Eaton resented slightly the loss of the engineering wizard—but she understood. War was about more than mathematics, and she knew exactly why Fritz had chosen to fight the battle on Tyler Barron's flagship.

"All engines engaged." The reply echoed in her headset. The speaker was on the bridge with her, just across and to the left. But *Colossus*'s control deck was so immensely huge, officers would have had to scream at each other to be heard. Far better to connect everyone via the comm system.

Eaton listened to the sounds of the ship, the strange, almost alien hum of the vast engines off in the distance, kilometers away, in the stern of the massive vessel. She had risen rapidly in the chain of command, too quickly, for her tastes. She had been ambitious once, driven to match, and even exceed, her older sister's accomplishments. But Sara was dead now, killed in action, and Sonya felt more lost than satisfied at the importance of her posting. Everywhere she looked in the endless corridors of the great battlewagon, she saw her sister looking back, a shadowy image watching over her…and perhaps judging her a bit as well.

Or was that last part her, judging herself, measuring her abilities against those of her now idolized version of the elder Eaton?

Whether she was ready or not, command of *Colossus was* important. The great vessel was a match for half the fleet, and she knew just how badly her comrades needed that strength. But as strong as the ancient ship was, as unimaginable as the energies roaring through her vast network of power lines, Sonya Eaton believed—knew, even—that it wasn't going to be enough. She'd spent the battle mostly cut off from the action. The gas giant that provided *Colossus*'s cover also blocked her scanner arrays. But Eaton had gotten enough data from satellite relays to draw some conclusions, and as she stared, as most of her people on the bridge did, at the continuing fight, and the massive losses the fleet had suffered, she realized just what *Colossus* would face when it entered the fray.

She'd been particularly horrified at the losses her comrades had endured, particularly the bomber squadrons. The fighter corps had always borne the burden of high casualty rates, but this was the second war in a row where they faced an enemy without their own small craft. That seemed at first glance, a good thing, one that should reduce losses. Dogfighting with enemy interceptors had long been the deadliest part of fighter-bomber operations. But the past seven years had shown just the opposite result. The squadrons had been compelled to make the most possible out of the fleet's sole tactical advantage, and that meant increasingly reckless attacks, through the worst point defense the enemy could throw at them. The loss rates had soared during the Hegemony War, but now it was evident that had merely been a precursor to the horrors of fighting the Highborn.

She glanced down at her screen, and she was startled by the thrust figures. She'd know intellectually, of course, what rate of acceleration *Colossus* could manage, but it still surprised her that something so large could generate such massive thrust—just over 70g—and that the dampeners were so effective, she felt as though she was sitting on a park bench on Megara.

She looked up at the main display, at the enemy fleet now appearing on *Colossus*'s own scanners. The ship had come out from behind the massive planet, and she knew, as she could see the enemy, they could see her. The Highborn had enjoyed a technological advantage during the entire battle...but *Colossus* was a match for anything they had, at least one on one. Even two or three on one.

But hundreds to one...

Eaton knew her duty, and her ship was on a vector toward the enemy flank. She would hit them hard, just as Admiral Barron needed. Her crew was still learning how to handle the great battleship, but she had faith in them all. Some of the very best spacers in the fleet had been assigned to her crew, veterans all.

"Main weapons systems...charge up and prepare to open fire as soon as we enter range."

She didn't believe a single ship, any ship, even *Colossus*, could make the difference and turn the battle around. But she was going to give it everything she had.

Everything *Colossus* had.

*   *   *

Stockton's wings were being torn to shreds. He'd lost a

third of his people going in, but now the survivors were launching their torpedoes. He knew the fleet was watching, Tyler Barron and the others likely stunned as they saw the aggressive tactics, the almost insanely close ranges to which Stockton had led his bombers before they released their weapons. Huge numbers of them had been destroyed as they came in, but then, almost as a mass, the survivors had sent their double loads of torpedoes forward...and all hell broke loose along the Highborn line.

Plasma torpedoes spat forth from his ragged squadrons, moving toward the enemy ships in great clouds of death. His pilots had run the gauntlet, they had taken their ships to the closest possible ranges. The torpedoes launched and converted to energy almost at once. At least a dozen of his bombers got caught up in the blasts of their own weapons and destroyed. Another twenty or more failed to pull up in time, and they slammed into the targeted Highborn ships, adding kinetic impact to the attack's effect, even as they perished.

The plasmas struck less than two seconds after launch. With no time for their targets to maneuver or evade, the superhot balls of energy slammed into the Highborn vessels. Not even the Sigma-9 emissions and the strange material of the enemy hulls could prevent more than ninety-five percent of the weapons from striking their targets.

Explosions burst out along the Highborn line, as hulls were melted and torn open. Compartments were blasted open by sudden decompression, and chunks of metal, fully or partially molten, flew away from the stricken ships.

But the Highborn vessels were tough, strong beyond anything possessed by the Rim nations or the Hegemony. For all the damage inflicted, the vast and cataclysmic forces unleashed by Stockton's desperate attack, the enemy line remained. It was battered, half a dozen ships destroyed outright, and scores of others damaged. Stockton's people had performed beyond even his expectations in valor and skill. But they hadn't made the difference.

The fleet was still losing the battle.

Stockton reached down and grabbed his ship's controls. He knew whatever disordered squadrons had managed to launch from the battered ships of the line weren't going to be strong enough either. But he couldn't give up. He wouldn't give up.

"Return to base, all wings," she snapped into his comm, as he blasted his own engines, decelerating hard. He could only hope his people could make it back to the fleet, past the enemy fire, and that they somehow managed to land on their beleaguered base ships. He knew many of those vessels had suffered devastating damage, that their bays were out of action, if not outright destroyed. But there was nothing he could do about that, so he pulled his mind away from such thoughts. All he could do was wish the returning squadrons luck. He wasn't going back with them. Not yet.

He stared at his long-range scanners, watching as a ragged line of bombers approached. There were three hundred of them, with maybe another two hundred strung out on a long line back to the fleet. All together, it was less than half the force he'd led on the last attack, but it was what he had, and he was going to take them in just as he had the others. He struggled to suck in a deep breath, just as the pressure of his ship's thrust exceeded the ability of the dampeners to absorb it. It would be about ten minutes before he could bring his ship to a halt, before he could begin the journey back to meet his approaching squadrons.

He twisted his head around on his neck, trying to stretch the best he could. He was exhausted, as tired as he could ever remember, but his gritty stubbornness was stronger than any fatigue. He closed his eyes once, for a few seconds, and then he opened them again. The enemy fire had slacked off once he'd flown past their line, but that didn't mean it had stopped. A pair of laser shots lanced past his ship, coming within two hundred meters or so. Then another shot, just as close.

He looked at the screen, trying to identify the source of the fire. There were four Highborn ships, all of the smaller class, and they were closing on his fighter. They were coming in from different directions, and he almost felt as though they were chasing *him*, herding him, cutting him off from any escape route.

He couldn't understand. Had they identified him as a commander, as a significant target among hundreds of other bombers? It seemed ridiculous to him at first, but then he began to think. His comm patterns, his position in the formation. Perhaps it *was* possible to pick him out as a likely commander.

Stockton knew one thing with cold certainty. He would be the first to go after enemy command figures if he could.

He jerked his hand hard, reacting to the incoming fire, increasing the intensity of his evasive maneuvers. His ship shook hard as he blasted his positioning jets in one direction after another. Four more laser blasts ripped by his ship, purging him of any doubt the enemy was targeting him specifically.

He could feel the sweat pouring down his neck, and his normally steely nerves began to fray. His hands were trembling as he gripped the throttle tightly, putting all his skill and experience into making himself as difficult a target as possible.

He brought his ship around, cutting the deceleration and reaccelerating along his current vector. He'd never make it back through the enemy line, not with four ships chasing him, targeting him the whole way. If he could clear the enemy line, break through to the space beyond, just maybe he could make his way back.

He was angry. Furious that the enemy was keeping him from linking up with his incoming squadrons. But he knew it would do no good for them, and certainly not their morale, to see him obliterated just as they were approaching the enemy.

If the Highborn were going to take him down, better it should happen behind their line, where it would be obscured from his pilots.

He swung his hand to port, then to starboard...and port again, and his ship shook wildly as it blasted deeper toward the edge of the Sigma Nordlin system. He checked his scanner, and he felt renewed waves of anger as he saw the enemy vessels still pursuing him. There was no longer any doubt—none at all—that the enemy knew he was a senior commander or some other priority target. Perhaps an AI deep inside one of the enemy ships had tagged him as an enhanced threat.

It didn't matter. All he knew was, he had to outlast them...or he would die.

He flew his ship hard, one wild maneuver after another, drawing on every bit of his training, every moment of combat experience in a lifetime. The shades of a hundred opponents flashed through his thoughts, pilots he'd fought, and every move he'd used to evade them, to turn the tables and destroy those who would destroy him. But opposing fighters he could fight...four Highborn cruisers were not enemy combatants he could engage. They were hunters...and he was the prey.

He lost track of his approaching squadrons. There was

nothing he could do for them now…save to wish them the best and spare them from witnessing his death.

He pushed his ship hard, flipping all the safety levers and overloading his systems. He could hear his heart pounding in his ears, feel the thumping in his chest. The whining of his ship's tortured reactor was almost earsplitting, but he ignored it. His mind was raw determination, but even as he continued his fight, as he put forth every bit of strength that remained to him, he knew he was cornered.

He jerked his ship hard to starboard again…but finally, he guessed wrong.

The fighter shook hard, and a shower of sparks flew over him from behind. He reached out, trying to grab the controls, but they were dead. The fighter spun end over end, even as spreading pain told him he was injured. His back was burned, and his survival suit was ripped to shreds along his right shoulder.

Then his eyes saw it. A crack in the cockpit, a big one…growing larger with each passing second. He looked down at his helmet, but he knew it was useless. His suit was beyond repair, at least any patch job he might try in the cockpit.

He looked up at the cracked canopy of his fighter, and at the cold death of space beyond…and as he watched the cracks spread, expanding into a growing web across the last protection between him and the vacuum beyond, he closed his eyes and whispered softly to himself.

"I love you, Stara…"

Chapters Thirty-Two

HWS Hegemony's Glory
Sigma Nordlin System
Year of Renewal 268 (323 AC)

The Battle of Calpharon – The Breaking Point

"Chronos, there is no other way, no choice. We are soldiers, warriors. If we can continue the fight, at least with any hope of victory, we must do it. But there is no hope of victory. None. If we stay here, we all die…and with us, any hope that remains to eventually defeat the enemy. A heroic last stand is appealing on one level, I'll admit that. Surviving defeat is perhaps a warrior's greatest challenge." Barron's last statement seemed poetic perhaps, but he knew it was nothing but the truth. Dying in one magnificent moment, fighting with one's last breath…Chronos realized, in many ways, Barron preferred that option to continuing the increasingly hopeless war against the Highborn. What could lay ahead save more death, more suffering, more struggle? And for what, a minimal chance of success, a frayed and dying hope for some miracle that saved everything? But it was clear the Confederation admiral knew it was his duty to keep the fight going, to hold off the enemy for as long as he could. To chase even that remote chance of success.

It was Chronos's duty, too, and Barron was clearly determined to make that clear. Chronos knew it, too, though it was still distant, ephemeral. Nothing he could quite grasp...not yet.

"That is easier for you to say, Tyler...Calpharon is not your home." Chronos stopped abruptly, and considerably more than the six second delay the distance imposed passed silently. Chronos realized his words had gone too far, that he knew what Barron was going to say.

"I *do* understand, perhaps better than you yet know. I stood where you stand, as you well know. Will you do as I did? Will you place the needs of the war, the fight to preserve the Hegemony, and not just its capital, but all its people, above all? Will you accept the pain, the difficulty, the sheer exhaustion of fighting on, or will you take the easy road, a quick and glorious death here? That would be a breach of your duty, Chronos. You are intelligent and a veteran commander. You *know* we can't win here, not now, with more enemy ships coming in almost behind us."

Chronos looked down at the comm unit, and inside his head a war raged. The tactician, the intellect that drove his thought, agreed with Barron. Completely. There was no chance to hold Calpharon. The enemy was *still* bringing ships through the initial transit tube, feeding fresh reserves into the fight on a constant basis. They would take the Hegemony capital whether or not he died there.

The hoped for reinforcements from Admiral Winters's command were lost, compelled to face the newly arrived Highborn force. That meant there were no reserves, no help left to come. The fighter wings would launch more attacks, at least as long as battleships remained with functional bays, but Stockton's people had expended themselves. They'd done more than anyone had a right to hope they could, but they were a spent force. Groups of a few hundred bombers launched intermittently from a dozen ships weren't going to turn the tide.

Chronos felt an almost overwhelming urge to defend Calpharon, to continue the fight, no matter what the cost. But he knew Barron was right. He could stand and battle the enemy to the end. Perhaps his new Confed and Palatian allies would remain with him, and die alongside his forces. It wouldn't matter. They were going to lose anyway. Staying would only serve the enemy, help them by allowing them to destroy all their opposition in one climactic fight.

Calpharon had ten billion inhabitants, but they were less than four percent of the total population of the Hegemony. There were hundreds of inhabited worlds, many with vast metropolises of their own, and populations also in the billions. He was the military commander of the entire Hegemony, Number Eight among its hundreds of billions, and his duty was not just to those on the capital. If he lost the entire fleet at Calpharon, he was condemning the rest to certain defeat and enslavement. He wasn't optimistic the war could be won given more time, but it was his duty to try.

"I will do what I can, Tyler. It is not my decision…not solely my decision." He would have to convince Akella. He might just manage to order a retreat if she was coming, and his daughter with her. If pulling back also meant leaving the two of them—and his other children— behind, he knew that would be too much for him. He didn't like the idea of taking advantage of his status, of getting those close to him off the planet, when billons would be left behind. But he would do it. He wasn't proud of it, but he knew he would. The evacuation, if such a small enterprise could be so labeled, would be centered on the very highest of the elite. Only the Council, and the highest ranked Masters could even know the fleet was withdrawing.

He nursed a thought, considered for a moment if it might be possible to exclude the more troublesome members of the Council. Chronos knew abandoning the capital would be a weight around his neck, a pain in his soul from which he would never recover. But he wouldn't shed a tear about leaving Thantor behind. Number Two was trouble…and he would continue to be just that if he survived.

Akella wouldn't consider it, though. He was sure of that. The Hegemony's highest-ranked Master was honest to a fault, and she possessed a seeming naivety that clashed with her unquestionable intellectual ability. He was far from sure he could get her to leave at all, but he was dead certain she wouldn't even consider it unless the rest of the Council withdrew as well, those who opposed her no less than those on her side.

Chronos admired that way of thinking, in a theoretical sense…but he also pitied it as divorced from reality. Still, however he felt, he couldn't deny that was Akella's mindset. If he was going to get her to leave, he would have to ensure the entire Council escaped.

He turned toward the communications station and stared silently for a moment. Then he took a single deep breath.

"I need a direct line to Number One. Now."

* * *

"Bring the children down to the spaceport. Our ship is waiting there. I've got to attend to some business before I go, but I'll meet you." Akella's voice wavered as she spoke. It was no surprise, at least not to her. She was consumed with self-loathing. She was Number One, the Hegemony's leader, the most genetically-perfect human being known…and she was about to abandon her people and run to save her own life.

That was an over-simplification, she knew, and at least somewhat unfair. She'd steadfastly refused to leave, resisted all Chronos's efforts to convince her…until uttered a single phrase. "Three hundred billion." The population of the Hegemony, the vast sea of humanity beyond those on Calpharon…all of whom were doomed to servitude and oppression if the battle ended at the capital. And Chronos wouldn't leave, wouldn't pull back the fleet, unless she came as well.

"Yes, Number One. I will see that Ajia and Ragus reach the ship." Cassis was Ajia's governess, but she also watched after Ragus, Akella's older son, the product of her union with Thantor. She'd never liked the Master rated just beneath her, but she'd agreed to the mating anyway. Hegemony law was clear, and while she wasn't expressly required to conceive a child with the Master ranked next below her, it had seemed the most honest interpretation of her duty. She regretted it now, at least on some levels. Thantor had shown his true colors since Ragus's birth, and he'd exposed himself as her rival, if not an outright enemy. But the son they had produced showed all signs of high intelligence and capability, and her premier duty was to give birth to the next generation of Masters.

And she loved her son, despite the fact that she was beginning to hate his father.

"Will you be coming soon, Number One? There is not much time." Cassis sounded genuinely worried which, Akella realized, she was. The governess was of the Arbeiter class, though highly rated in that grouping, but

Akella had become very fond of her. The two had developed a friendly relationship, and Akella had told Cassis a hundred times to use her name and not her title. But amid the fear and tension of the pending withdrawal, the governess had reverted to formality.

"I will be there in time, Cassis. Until I arrive, see to the children. Get to the ship as quickly as possible. There has been no announcement, but too many people know already, and I doubt the secrecy can be contained much longer. There is no way of knowing what will happen in the streets when the word spreads."

Cassis nodded. "Yes, Number One. I will see to it."

"Go now." Akella leaned down and kissed Ajia, and then she did the same to Ragus. "Go," she repeated, and she turned away, pretending to be looking for something on her desk, but mostly trying to hide the pain on her face from the children.

The evacuation had been kept secret for far longer than she'd imagined possible, but as much as that was helpful and useful, it also cut at her insides. She hated herself for what she was doing, and she struggled to pull her mind away from the billons being left behind. She'd begun to privately question the hierarchy of the Hegemony, the rigid rank structure that segregated people onto career paths, placed floors under them, and ceilings above them. But she didn't have to tread so far as revolutionary thought like that to fuel her raging guilt. More than ten million Masters were being left behind as well as the billions of lower-ranked citizens. That was a lot of prime DNA, entire genetic lines that would be lost…in addition to the incalculable human suffering.

She turned and walked toward the door. She had to speak to her closest aides. She was bringing much of her household staff with her. More corruption, men and women who would escape whatever fate awaited

Calpharon, not based on their genetics, but on their closeness to Akella.

She wasn't sure if it was the time she'd spent speaking with Tyler Barron, or the intensity with which the 'inferiors' on the Rim had resisted Hegemony conquest, but she'd begun to see the hypocrisy that had permeated her people's society. Pure dedication to genetics was one thing, harsh in some ways, but perhaps defensible. But the Hegemony's government had as much corruption and dishonesty as the Confederation's. The ships about to leave Calpharon would carry less than one one-hundredth of one percent of the population, and that small number would include servants and sycophants and others rated well below millions who would remain...all in violation of the Hegemony's sacred dedication to genetic elevation.

How many bloodlines will be abandoned so I can take my household, or so some other Council member can stash a flock of mistresses aboard?

She was angry with herself, profoundly disappointed, but she tried to push the thoughts away. Chronos wouldn't withdraw the fleet if she didn't leave, and if the Hegemony and its allies didn't preserve at least some of their military strength, the war truly would be over. It was an excuse, perhaps, but if it got her through the next hours...

She walked out into the antechamber of her house, and she nodded to the two guards standing there. She generally detested the trappings of her office, but if word got out, things could get...dangerous. It would be foolish to go out without the security detail, and she just nodded to the two men, a signal for the veteran Kriegeri to follow her.

Protecting me gets them a ticket out of here too...

She had some final duties. She knew she couldn't really do anything for those who would be left behind, but she had to do what she could.

And she had to leave a message for those who would inherit command in her absence, the Masters left behind to surrender to the Highborn. She dreaded recording that communique.

Then she was going to make sure Chronos's household was evacuated as well, and most crucially, his other children. There was some duty in that, at least. Chronos was Number Eight, and any interpretation of Hegemony law would mandate the evacuation of his offspring.

But that's not why she was doing it. Her real reason was contrary to the law, and in utter defiance of Hegemony culture and tradition.

She was doing it because she loved Chronos…whether or not it was forbidden.

Chapter Thirty-Three

Free Trader Pegasus
Somewhere in the Badlands
Year 323 AC (After the Cataclysm)

"Andi…Andi…"

She could hear a voice, calling her name.

"Andi…I'm sorry to wake you, but…"

And a hand on her shoulder.

Andi awoke with a start. "Vig…" She turned her head as she lifted it from the workstation. The side of her face was numb from being pressed against the hard surface. "I'm sorry…I just closed my eyes for a bit." She tried to push away the grogginess, with limited immediate success. "What is it? Is everything okay?"

"Everything is fine, Andi. And that 'bit' has been eleven hours. I almost tried to get you into your cabin a few times, but you were *out*. I did manage to get Sy to her bunk. She was more or less sleepwalking with my hand on her back, but all I could manage with you was to make sure you were still breathing and tell everybody else to stay the hell out of here. Not that you'd have heard them if they were all in here playing drums."

"Eleven hours…" She felt a flood of awareness as Vig's words set in. She didn't believe it at first, but a quick series of pains in her neck and back as she tried to straighten up told her just how stiff she was. "Why didn't you wake me? We have a lot of work to do before we get to Hegemony space." She wanted to sound annoyed, but she could already tell how much better she felt for the sleep.

"I don't know, Andi…maybe it's because the two of you were at it for something like ninety-six hours without a break of more than a few minutes. I know you think you're indestructible, but you can't just keep going forever…and if that stuff you're working on is as important as it sounds, you need to stay sharp, and make sure you get it right."

Andi wanted to argue, to lament eleven lost hours, but she knew Vig was right. She'd been so determined to find information that might be useful to Tyler and the fleet, and so immersed in the fascinating account of the empire's later days, she'd lost all track of time. And any sense of just how incoherent she'd become.

"Here's a suggestion, and it would be an order, if you weren't the captain and me the long-suffering second in command…go take a nice hot shower, and grab something to eat, a *real* meal, not just a nutrition bar shoved in your head while you're reading. That will take an hour, maybe less…and then you'll be back here, and ready to go for another marathon."

Andi looked up, again ready to argue. But the words just weren't there. She was starting to really wake up, and she realized how much the sleep had done for her state of mind…and how much a shower and some fresh clothes would add to that. Still, it was hard to step away. She felt something like a gravitational pull from the workstation, almost an addiction drawing her back to her work. She'd never been an academic, nothing close to one, but the history that had been unfolding before her had her attention riveted.

"Maybe a shower…and a quick bite. But then I have to get back to this." A pause. "Don't wake Sy up, though. I've got enough translation to do without…"

"I'm awake. Some sleep—and I already had my shower—and I'm ready to go…right after I grab a quick bite. I can't stay away either. Hell, as tired as I was, I think I dreamed of the old empire." A pause, and then Sy's voice turned somber. "Besides, it's all fascinating, what we've uncovered so far, but it's not tactically very useful. We were all wrong on what the Highborn are. There's something reassuring that they're not aliens of some kind…and depressing, too, that we're fighting our own kind yet again. Or something derived from our own kind. But we still need to find some weaknesses, some ways to defeat them. These people played a role in bringing down the empire—how large we don't know yet—and they obviously survived the Cataclysm, and prospered after. We need to know more, as quickly as possible."

Andi nodded. "I agree completely." She twisted around in place, considering for a moment forgoing the shower. But then she stood up. She felt repulsive, and she was growing jealous looking at Sy in her bright and clean clothes.

"I'll be back in fifteen minutes…" She turned and walked toward her cabin, imagining the feel of hot water cascading down over her.

Maybe twenty…

Ruins of the Andros Estate
Planet Samara
Tirion Vega System
Year 11,703 IR (Imperial Reckoning)
Year 31 BC (Before the Cataclysm) by Confederation
Calendar
354 Years Ago

The great shafts of electric blue light rained down from the sky, like manmade bolts of lightning. But the strikes were vastly more powerful than natural electrical discharges. The fire came down from no less than eight imperial battlecruisers positioned in orbit, and they destroyed everything in their path. Structures collapsed, even vaporized and partially transformed into boiling pools of molten metals and stone. Nature's great creations were far from proof against the fury, and they fell before the onslaught. Mountains crumbled, and vast sections of the sea boiled. Huge stretches of forest— swaths of millions of the great Gray Walnut trees, sought after across the empire and the original foundation of House Andros's wealth, were reduced to ash.

Samara had been inhabited by humanity since before the empire's founding, a prosperous, vibrant world, one that had even retained some level of its former energy amid the decline and malaise of the empire. But now it was a graveyard, its cities in ruins, its surface ravaged by beam and blast and fire.

The planet's population, save for Lord Andros and his closest retainers, had no idea what had provoked such dreadful imperial wrath, what had caused the emperor to unleash such unprecedented power and brutality against this once-beautiful world. Indeed, Andros and his inner circle had been taken by surprise themselves, and they'd barely managed to escape, to take refuge in the secret family shelter, dug deep enough into the planet's crust to endure even the vast devastation rained down by the imperial fleet.

Ellerax watched silently, as the tragedy unfolded. He stood on a hill, in an uninhabited area away from the bombardment, next to his small vessel. His presence wasn't, strictly speaking, necessary, but he'd wanted to see what had happened. He had decided it was best that Andros escaped, but the calculation behind that decision had been within a scant few percent of even.

The devastation had been severe, the bombardment's intensity almost beyond reckoning. Andros and his closest insiders would realize, of course, that the imperial authorities had determined, with considerable certainty, that they were deeply involved in a plot to destabilize the empire, even to kill the emperor himself. There was little doubt about that. The empire didn't obliterate populated worlds lightly.

The secret police had been suspicious for some time, but they still had no real evidence. There was little doubt someone had warned the empire. One of those involved in the project had talked, someone with deep and extensive knowledge of Obsidian. Only an inside source could have given the imperial authorities enough to justify so deadly a response.

What Andros didn't know, as he cowered in his secret shelter, what he would never know, was that source had been Ellerax himself. The leader of the Firstborn had gradually taken a larger and more pronounced role in Obsidian, but despite his repeated urgings, Andros had been too cautious to follow all of his suggestions.

That had become intolerable. Ellerax acknowledged Andros's role in his own existence. It wasn't gratitude, exactly, but he wasn't ready to entirely overthrow his patron. And Andros still served a purpose. The nobleman had spent vast portions of his wealth on the program, and he'd just lost more in the bombing of Samara, but he'd proven to be adept at hiding wealth. Ellerax no longer seriously listened to the human's opinion on important matters, but he recognized Andros's utility. More than half a meter taller than even the largest humans, it was difficult for Ellerax and his brethren to interact with subtly or secrecy. Though Andros himself had now been branded a traitor, he still had his own people in key positions. That would be useful going forward.

Yes, Andros still had a place in bringing about the new order of things…but he'd needed to be coaxed, pushed forward into accelerating operations, as Ellerax had long urged. Now, he was exposed, pursued by the secret police, his entire house renegade. There would be no choice except to initiate the final effort without delay.

As long as Andros made it off Samara.

Ellerax was certain his patron would escape. He had ensured it. He had evaluated and analyzed every possibility. First, his leak to the imperial authorities had been wrong in several key areas, including Andros's location. Samara had been obliterated because it was the center of the Andros holdings, a strike against a house that had been exposed as dangerous rebels. But there were no troopships with the armada above, no vast legions of imperial soldiers set to land, to comb the wreckage, looking for high-ranking survivors.

No, the imperials believed Andros and all his key personnel were on Demania. Indeed, Ellerax had provided what seemed like incontrovertible evidence that this was so.

Demania was no doubt being subjected to the same kind of brutal assault as Samara, one that would almost certainly be followed up with the intensive ground search Samara had been spared. One that would find nothing.

The planet was completely uninvolved, with Obsidian, and even with House Andros and its various tentacles. Its population was just over three billion, and there was little doubt at least half of them would perish. To most, that would seem a high price to pay for a diversion, but Ellerax had not even considered it in such terms. It was a useful tool, a way to give Andros the desired escape route, along with the requisite push to accelerate the project. To Ellerax, a billion and a half humans—or ten billion for that matter—was a small price to pay to usher in a new and golden future, one where humanity was led forward by those who now existed expressly for that purpose.

Mankind would have leadership, drive, renewed vigor.

They would have gods to rule over them.

Chapter Thirty-Four

12,000,000 Kilometers from CFS Dauntless
Sigma Nordlin System
Year 323 AC (After the Cataclysm)

The Battle of Calpharon – The Breaking Point

"Hit them now, and hit them hard, by God!" Reg Griffin had already launched her two torpedoes, and she'd hit with both of them. That had been no surprise. It was almost impossible to miss at the absurd ranges from which her people were attacking. It was the perfect tactic, almost overpowering...save for one horrifying aspect. The staggering casualties the closing wings endured closing to such ranges. The fighter corps had always endured some of the highest casualty rates in the service, and sayings like, 'There are no old fighter pilots' had been common. But the hell her people had faced in the battle still raging all around had made the worst of the 'old days' seem like a stroll in a pleasant wood.

She'd lost count of the fighters in the group immediately around her position, probably because she couldn't bear to confirm the empty slots on the order of battle. Too many ships had been destroyed, and others had completed their attack runs and turned about to begin their trips back to the fleet, to their landing platforms.

At least the ones that still had landing platforms. She'd lost count of the battleships destroyed as well, and those that had pulled back with severe damage. The line couldn't hold much longer, and she knew she should follow her squadrons, and set her own course back to *Dauntless* in the hope that Anya Fritz's sweating technicians had somehow kept the bays open.

But she didn't. At first, she'd determined to stay and direct the still-incoming waves, each one smaller than the last, as fewer and fewer battleships managed to get their remaining bombers into space. She'd been looking for Stockton the whole time, intending to ask him what he wanted her to do next.

But she hadn't been able to find him.

At first, she'd suspected that he was just far off on the other end of the formation, but now she'd searched everywhere and found no trace of his ship. Her first thought was, he'd turned about and was on his way back to *Dauntless*. But she didn't believe that.

'Raptor' Stockton did a lot of crazy things, but the idea that he had headed back while his waves were still coming in seemed almost ridiculous to her. If he'd had any chance at all of leading yet another substantial attack wave out, perhaps, but it was clear that wasn't going to happen. By her best estimate, there were fifteen hundred bombers that should have been part of the current wave still stuck inside their motherships, or destroyed in the bays. There was no reason for Stockton to rush back, not when his leadership would do far more good directing the attacks of the ships that made it to their targets.

So, where is he?

Reg was getting edgy, nervous…but it wasn't in her to

imagine that Stockton's ship had been destroyed. She knew the defensive fire was fierce, and even with all the damage the bombers and the battle line had inflicted on the enemy, the Highborn were still getting off intermittent missile volleys. The area of space around the enemy line had become the graveyard for the fleet's squadrons.

There had been hundreds of casualties, but it seemed inconceivable that Stockton could have been one of them. Still, her stomach tightened with each passing minute. Finally, she began comming the wing commanders, asking if any of them knew anything. The first three were as unsure as she was, but number four's response almost made her throat seize up.

"He got hit, Commodore. His ship wasn't destroyed, but he was moving at a high velocity...directly through the enemy fleet. I tried to get a fix on him, but with all the Sigma-9 emissions...I lost him. I've been trying to find him ever since, but he's just...gone." The wing commander was James Dillon, one of the toughest and grittiest pilots in the strike force. And he sounded almost as though he was about to burst into tears. His tone, even more than his words, struck Reg.

She threw her head back in her seat, struggling to gasp for air, to force it down her throat. *No...no, it's not possible. It's not possible...*

"Send me the location data you have, Jim...now!"

An urgency gripped her, a wild, uncontrollable need to go out and find Stockton, to locate his damaged ship. There wasn't much she could do if she found him, and there was no way to get a rescue ship this far through the enemy formation. That made her effort almost futile from the start. But if she didn't look for him, she would have to accept...that he was gone.

She listened to the wing commander's

acknowledgement, and a few seconds later, she plugged the incoming data into her nav computer. She stared at the screen, struggling to hold onto what little hope she still had.

Stockton had been on the far side of the enemy line...and heading farther away from the Confederation fleet...deep into the system, behind the Highborn formations.

Where there was no hope at all of rescuing him.

It was utterly pointless to follow, to take even more risks onto herself. Even if she found him, there was nothing she could do. But she just couldn't leave him out there alone.

Whatever the risk.

"All incoming squadrons, pick the targets doing the worst damage to the battle line...and get in, launch, and blast the hell out as fast as you can."

She flipped off the comm, not wanting to listen to the flood of questions and concerned remarks about her orders. She had something to do, and she didn't want to talk about it.

And she damned sure didn't want anybody else coming with her.

She plugged the coordinates into the nav computer, and she blasted off, farther past the enemy line, in the direction Stockton's ship had gone.

If he was out there, she was going to find him.

If she could stay alive long enough.

*   *   *

"All ships report new course established, Admiral."

Clint Winters just nodded, and as he did, his cold and stony gaze passed over the tactical officer. Winters wasn't angry, at least not openly, but his intensity was raw, and hot like the inside of a reactor core.

His force had turned about, setting a course to reinforce the main fleet. The battle looked grim from where he sat, and he had been far from sure his mostly-light vessels would make enough of a difference. But there had been relief of a sort that he was at least going to stand with his comrades, that they would fight, and if need be, die, together.

Now he was heading back where he came from, his new course away from his friends and allies, and toward the new enemy forces pouring into the system. Winters was a cold realist, and he'd known the challenges the fleet faced. But he'd held out some hope, at least, some thought that if the fleet fought hard enough, savagely enough, they would find a way to prevail.

That was gone now.

The enemy ships were still streaming through the point ahead of his forces, over two hundred so far, and no sign yet of an end. There were none of the larger vessels, the battleships, but that was cold enough comfort considering that the cruiser-sized Highborn ships were more than a match, even for the few larger hulls of his scant battle line.

Winters had led a few of the smaller forces sent out to harry and delay the Highborn fleets, but this would be his true baptism of fire against the mysterious enemy. He had reviewed the data the fleet had collected from the last major battle, and he and Tyler Barron had discussed their plans endlessly. Winters had been almost anxious for the enemy to strike. He was very direct in his approach to things, and if there was a fight coming, he was always the first to say, 'bring it on now.' But he felt the usual force that drove him weakening. Not even the Sledgehammer could look at the Highborn approaching, watch their ships winking in and out of the scanner grid, and not feel some trepidation.

Still, he would go to his grave denying it was fear.

He looked over the display, noting the velocity of the emerging enemy units. His job had been to protect the flank of the main fleet while the battle was fought. But Winters was enough of a realist to know the battle couldn't be won. The fleet would withdraw. Soon…or the war would end there and then, And, that meant his duty was clear. He had to keep the enemy flanking force from blocking the fleet's retreat path through the system's second transit point. If the damaged, fleeing units of the main force were hit on the flank by fresh Highborn ships, a defeat would soon escalate to utter catastrophe.

He watched as more and more ships came through, bringing the enemy total closer to three hundred. That was more than his people could possibly defeat. The next hours would tell if it was more than they could contain.

And if they could hold back the Highborn for long enough, just what price they would pay for that success.

*   *   *

"All batteries, open fire." Sonya Eaton was standing in front of her chair. She wasn't sure what had driven her to rise, the tension of the battle, or the grim determination she felt to lead her ship forward, to savage the enemy any way she could. Or perhaps, it was just an understanding of the vast power she controlled.

She listened to the acknowledgements from the main gunnery officers. The organizational chart for *Colossus* was unlike any she'd seen before for a Confederation ship. There were literally hundreds of weapons on *Colossus*, of varying sizes and degrees of power. The main guns, the primary armament that had served the vessel in its imperial days, were silent, non-functional. Neither

Hegemony nor Confederation science had been up to the task of repairing the titanic guns. But even the vast ship's secondary weaponry dwarfed anything she'd seen on the largest battleships. And even though she knew the ranges of the weapons, and she'd seen them test fire at those distances, it was still hard to believe.

There was no sign on *Colossus*'s bridge that the offensive array had opened fire, no change to the power systems, no flickering of lights, no audible sounds. But the screens across the bridge, and the enormous 3D main display in the center of the voluminous space, lit up brightly as several dozen beams raced forward, moving across nearly half a million kilometers of space. No armament Eaton had ever seen, and certainly no energy weapon, had anything like that kind of range. But the great shafts of energy blasted forth from *Colossus* and ripped across space, taking almost two second to reach their targets.

And to her astonishment, hitting several of them.

She'd opened fire at long range mostly to get the enemy's attention, to distract them from their continued obliteration of the main fleet. To take some of the pressure off of Barron and the others. But she hadn't expected to score any hits so far out.

The greatest challenge to fighting the Highborn was overcoming their mysterious use of Sigma-9 radiation, and effectively targeting their ships. That reality had forced the bomber squadrons, and even the battleships of the line, to close to point blank range to achieve acceptable hit ratios. And the cost for that in shattered vessels and spacers' blood had been immense.

But *Colossus*'s targeting systems had zeroed right onto the enemy vessels, and the strange phasing effect caused by the radiation did not shake the locks. Long range was still long, and two seconds was a considerable time for an evading ship to move enough to shake even the best targeting…but the deadly fire struck no less than three of the Highborn ships.

And it struck them hard.

Colossus's weapons were antimatter-powered, all of them. The energies driven through the massive emitters challenged her comprehension. She understood the concept of superior technology, but it was still difficult to understand forces so far beyond what she'd known and seen that they seemed almost…magic. If a Confederation laser managed to travel half a million kilometers without losing the cohesion of its photons, and spreading into the equivalent of a kilometers-wide flashlight, it would be lucky to retain enough power to light a birthday candle. But the old imperial weapons not only hit at such ranges, they hit hard. The Highborn ships shook under the impact, and their hull plating gave way, the shots penetrating deeply, inflicting internal damage.

She sat, stunned, still for a few seconds. Then she snapped out more orders. Maintain fire at maximum rate…and increase engine thrust." A pause. "We're going in, people…and we're going to show these Highborn just what Hell really looks like."

* * *

"*Colossus* is engaging, Admiral." Atara's words were entirely unnecessary, at least to provide information. But Barron knew his longtime comrade had not intended the words for him. She knew he was watching himself, that if anything, he'd seen the massive vessel open fire before she had. The report was for the others on the bridge, an effort to sustain the morale of the exhausted and scared officers and spacers. *Dauntless*'s people were among the Confederation's best, but they weren't made of stone.

The relentlessness of the Highborn assault, the eerie ability of their ships to seemingly blink in and out of normal space, and the utter devastation wrought by their deadly beams, had worn down their resolve, breaking down courage in an unstoppable drive toward hopelessness.

"Yes…and she is coming in right on their flank. Just as we planned. That will be a surprise to the enemy." Barron's reply was heavier with bullshit than he typically liked, but he, too, understood his people needed all the support they could get. *Colossus* was coming against the enemy flank, and the old imperial vessel's weapons were at least the equals of the Highborn's fearsome guns. But whatever its size, *Colossus* was one ship in one place, and for all the shock and awe of seeing the immense battleship coming into the battle, Barron knew it wasn't going to be enough. Especially not with the enemy coming through point one as well as point three.

Barron watched, and he was startled as the first shots scored several hits. The range was still long, and despite Anya Fritz's best efforts, she had been no more successful than anyone else at repairing the vessels titanic main batteries, or even really understanding how they functioned. But even the great ship's secondaries were monstrously powerful, and its restored imperial scanners and firing routines appeared to be vastly more effective at targeting the Highborn ships.

He was still staring at the screen as another round of fire ripped out from *Colossus*, and another three Highborn ships were struck…and one disappeared utterly from the display.

He felt a burst of hope, but he realized almost immediately, it was misplaced. *Colossus* would hurt the enemy, certainly. But it was only one ship, and the enemy fleet was vast.

And none of them are in range yet. Colossus *is big, but that doesn't mean indestructible…*

The cold dose of reality hit even harder as he realized *Colossus* was the most forward of every vessel in the fleet. The flank attack would be effective in hurting the enemy, no doubt, but Sonya Eaton and her spacers had the longest journey to pull back, to escape from the system.

Barron had left ships behind before. Tactical necessity was often a harsh taskmaster, and while he carried the scars of those instances, he also knew they had been necessary. No commander could lead if he wasn't prepared to send people to their deaths when necessary. But *Colossus* was the one ship in his fleet, *Dauntless* included, that *wasn't* expendable. Any conceivable effort to stop the Highborn would center on that chunk of imperial technology, as a weapon in itself, and as a base for continued research and development.

We've waited too long already…we need to pull out now. Colossus *has to break off…and soon.* He didn't want to test just how much punishment the vast ship could endure, but he wasn't willing to bet if could survive being englobed by Highborn warships.

He stared down at the comm. His last conversation with Chronos had been inconclusive. He believed the Hegemony commander had been close to agreeing on a joint withdrawal—and the attendant emergency evacuation of those who could escape from Calpharon— but there had been nothing since.

Now, he knew he had his own decision to make. If Chronos wouldn't give the order, would he issue his own, pull his fleet and the Alliance forces—and *Colossus*—out, and return to Confederation space to prepare for the Highborn's inevitable arrival?

Could he go and leave his new allies behind to face utter destruction?

He would have to make that decision, and soon…but not without one last effort to keep the combined fleet together.

"Atara…get me Chronos on the comm."

Chapter Thirty-Five

HWS Hegemony's Glory
Venta Traconis System
Year of Renewal 268 (323 AC)

The Battle of Calpharon – The Retreat Begins

"I need another two hours, perhaps three. The evacuation is underway, but even limited to only essential personnel, it is a time-consuming process." Chronos was holding back the uncertainty he still felt, the doubts about whether he should—whether he *could*—truly abandon Calpharon and its billions. He tried to tell himself it was the correct strategic decision—it almost certainly was— and also that the inhabitants would be okay, or at least humanely treated. That was a much wider question, and one even his efforts to delude himself failed to satisfy. Calpharon was an immense prize, a world of massive industry, and some of the very best of the Hegemony's population. But the Highborn had shown little hesitation in obliterating planetary populations when it served their purposes.

Chronos didn't know much about the Highborn, who

they were, or why they had come. But he didn't believe they were xenophobes come to annihilate humanity. They were conquerors, almost certainly, and though they had shown brutal ruthlessness in the destruction of some lesser worlds, they had occupied others. He didn't know what life under enemy occupation would be like. Not particularly pleasant, he guessed. But very possibly survivable...until the fleet managed to return and retake the planet.

If that happens...

He tried to remember that Tyler Barron *had* reclaimed Megara, but that was fairly cold comfort. The situations were different, and he had a grim feeling that his last glimpse of Calpharon before his ship entered the tube would be his final look at his homeworld.

He took a deep breath as the comm unit crackled back to life. He was several light seconds from *Dauntless*, and that was enough to be disruptive to a discussion.

"Chronos, I understand the need to complete your evacuation, but we don't *have* three hours. We probably don't have two either. The enemy is closing, and I've got to order *Colossus*, at least, to break off and start a run for the point now. The battle line might hold for another...hour, maybe? But that's all you've got." There was a hesitation, and then Barron's voice returned, his tone strained. "I'm ordering *Colossus* to pull back at once, to the battle line's position. Before the enemy can bring enough force to bear to cripple even that behemoth. And in one hour, my forces will begin a retreat to transit point two. I urge you to have your forces ready at that time. I do not relish the thought of fighting this war without you...but whatever you do, I have my own duty, to the Confederation, and to my spacers. And staying here, allowing them all to die in a hopeless defense, serves no purpose." A pause. "You can't win, Chronos. Calpharon is going to fall whether or not your fleet is destroyed here."

Chronos stared at the comm unit for a few seconds. He'd come to know Tyler Barron fairly well, and he respected his new comrade's opinions. Perhaps more, he had reaffirmed something he'd known since Barron was his enemy. The Confed admiral was no coward. If Barron thought there was any chance to prevail in the current battle, he would fight to the end.

"Tyler…" Chronos hesitated. He knew Barron was right. He also knew he couldn't leave without Akella and his children. And he was still waiting for confirmation the ships had departed from Calpharon. "…I don't know if an hour will be enough. I have to wait for Akella…and for the Council." In truth, he realized he wouldn't mourn too much if half the Council got left behind. "Ninety minutes," he finally said. It was a guess, but he knew he wasn't going to get more out of Barron than that.

Perhaps more importantly, he knew *he* couldn't wait any longer either. He couldn't leave Akella and the others…but they would all be killed or captured anyway if they didn't escape now. Barron was inarguably right about one thing. Even with all three fleets combined, even with *Colossus* on the attack…they weren't going to stop the Highborn forces. And Admiral Winters wasn't going to manage to hold the flanking force for much longer either. Chronos hoped against hope he wouldn't be forced to make the decision to pull the fleet out of the line and make a run for it before Akella and Ajia and the others he cared about had left.

He didn't know what he would do if it came to that. He wouldn't know until he had to make the call.

"Seventy-five minutes, Chronos. We'll hold for that long. That's not arbitrary, my friend…it's the longest we can wait and still have a reasonable chance to escape." A pause. "You won't save anybody by dying here, by losing your fleet. The only good you can do now is to survive, escape to fight another day."

Chronos knew Barron was right...but she still had no idea what he would do if Akella and the children were still on Calpharon in an hour and fifteen minutes. But he wasn't going to get any more out of Barron, and it wouldn't matter if he did. His own calculations matched Barron's. Seventy-five minutes. It was all they had.

"Agreed. Seventy-five minutes. Stand with me for that long, and I'll pull back with you."

He wasn't sure if he was lying to Barron or not...only time would tell him that.

He turned as he waited for Barron's response, and he shouted out an order across the bridge. "Get me an update on Number One and the evacuation on Calpharon."

*　*　*

Reg stared at the row of screens, becoming more frantic with each passing second. Each second of nothingness, of no contact at all. No hint at what had happened to Jake Stockton.

Raptor...

She'd searched everywhere she could, brought herself deeper behind the enemy line. She *had* to break off, at least try to get back to the fleet. *They're going to pull out soon...they've got to retreat, and if I don't get the hell out of here now, they'll leave without me...*

She knew the realities of the battle, and the brutal certainty that the alternative to breaking off would be total destruction. And she knew full well what they'd pounded in her head since the first day of flight school. The battleships always come first. If saving one of the big vessels meant leaving pilots behind, a battleship's captain would send flowers to the memorial service...but he would get his ship out of there.

It was fleet policy, and it had been as long as there had been a Confederation navy. It was common sense, too. A battleship took years to build, and it carried a thousand or more as crew. No number of fighters could match that.

I can't just leave him...

She knew she could be looking for a dead man, that she probably was. The likeliest reason she couldn't find Stockton's ship was because it didn't exist anymore, at least not as anything but a quickly cooling and dissipating plasma. But she couldn't believe that. It seemed impossible. For all the analysis telling her that was very likely just what had happened, she couldn't make herself accept it. She'd come up in the shadow of Raptor's legend, and every time she'd climbed into her fighter, she had strived to follow in his path. She was painfully aware of the bitter mortality of pilots...but it seemed impossible to reconcile with the idea that Jake Stockton was dead.

Her eyes were moist, the tears moving ahead of her tortured mind, realization coming to her aching guts and shaking hands before her mind could grasp it. She'd been determined to remain where she was until she'd found Stockton. But if she didn't break off soon, she knew she never would.

They're probably comming me right now, trying to order me back...unless they think I'm dead, too.

She was too far from the fleet, too deep past the enemy ships and their strange emissions to pick up any communications from the fleet, or even the forward squadrons. No comm signal could reach her, nor would the fleet receive hers. Unless she went back immediately, her first notice of the fleet's withdrawal would be when she saw the ships pulling back.

And then it would be too late.

Still, she couldn't give up on Stockton, couldn't accept that he was gone. Save for one thing a heavy weight hanging on her soul like a chain.

Duty.

Stockton had left her in command, and he had placed upon her the responsibility to look after the wings. 'Take care of my people,' he had said. She would only be failing him by continuing the futile search. If he'd been able to give her one last order, she knew exactly what it would have been.

And she would obey it as though she heard it from his lips.

The moisture in her eyes pooled up, and tears streamed down her cheeks as she gripped her controls, willing her hand to move, to angle her vector back toward the fleet.

To give up on Stockton. To accept that the greatest legend the fighter corps had ever known, the legendary Raptor, a warrior with hundreds of kills, was dead.

She sat for a moment, frozen…and then she jerked her arm to the side, blasting her thrusters back toward the fleet. Toward escape.

Assuming she could make it back past the enemy line. It would be easier for a single ship coming from behind, but that didn't mean it wasn't going to be a wildly dangerous trip. She wondered if she would make it back.

Then she flipped a coin in her head.

* * *

"I need another hour, Admiral…at least." Stara Sinclair's voice was hoarse, raw, as it echoed in Barron's headset. He couldn't imagine the tension she was feeling, struggling to get the returning fighter wings back onboard the tortured battleships…and also with the growing realization that she might need to leave some of them behind. That would be a nightmare, no less for Barron, and he imagined the tsunami of messages coming in from pilots who knew they were being left behind to die. War was full of soul-killing misery, but few things could top that kind of torment.

But he knew there was something else, even worse perhaps, drilling into her consciousness. There had been no sign of Jake Stockton. Barron hadn't worried about it at first, no more than usual, at least, but now a dark feeling was growing. Stockton was always likely to be one of the last ships to return, but the survivors were mostly accounted for. And there had been no sign of the strike force commander's ship.

For that matter, no sign of Reg Griffin's either. Had he lost both of them? Had the fighter corps he would need to badly in the next fight sacrificed its two top commanders?

And had he lost one of his few true friends?

He shook his head. He didn't have time for any of that. He had a fleet to command, one that would be withdrawing in exactly forty-two minutes, regardless of how much time Stara Sinclair needed.

Regardless of where Jake Stockton was.

"Stara…" His voice was soft, sympathetic…but then he realized, that wasn't what she needed. Not just then. Thousands of lives were depending on her, and he had to take the burden off of her. He had to assume it himself, allow her to simply follow his own, ruthless, orders. "You've got thirty minutes, and not a second more. That will barely give us time to batten down the bays, and prepare to thrust out of here. And we're doing that in forty minutes, no matter what the situation." *No matter who is still out there.* He kept that last part to himself, but there wasn't a doubt in his mind Stara was just as aware there had been no sign of Stockton.

"Yes, Admiral." Her voice was stony, cold...but Barron could hear the pain she was trying so hard to hide. "Get them in, Stara, get them all in. If anybody can do it, it's you." He cut the line. Then he turned and looked at the display.

Colossus. The massive vessel was almost back to the battle line's position, after cutting a bloody swath through the enemy's flank. *Colossus* had proven more than a match for the enemy's vessels, but now it was being pursued by at least three dozen Highborn ships. The great battleship had taken more hits than he could easily count, and it was clearly damaged. But Sonya Eaton was driving her giant battleship hard, a relentless effort to bring it back toward the fleet.

Barron just wasn't sure she was going to make it.

"Atara...second and third divisions, break off from current targets. Divert all fire to the ships pursuing *Colossus.* Let's turn that space on her tail into a fiery version of hell!" Eaton very well might not make it back alone. But she wasn't alone, by God! The fleet was with her.

"Bring us around, too. All remaining batteries lock onto the nearest pursuer." *Dauntless*'s primaries had once again lost the battle against the relentless pounding the ship had endured, and despite Anya Fritz's wizardry that had thrice restored them to action, they were finally blasted almost to scrap. It would take weeks, if not a trip to spacedock at a class one shipyard, to fix them now. But the secondaries packed some punch too, and the ships chasing *Colossus* showed the damage their prey had inflicted during the chase. And Barron knew just what he had to do.

"Gun them down, Atara. Every one of them."

Chapter Thirty-Six

20,000 Kilometers from CFS Dauntless
Sigma Nordlin System
Year 323 AC (After the Cataclysm)

The Battle of Calpharon – The Sledgehammer

"I'm coming in…" Reg stared at the screen in front of her, trying not to notice how wobbly and unstable the image appeared. It looked like the whole system might give up the ghost any second, leaving her blind. That would be the end. She wasn't sure she could land her battered fighter anyway, not with *Dauntless* blasting away at full away from the battle.

She was *sure*, however, there was no chance at all if her scanner suite bit the dust.

"I've got you on my screen, Reg. Sending you a beacon now. Just follow it in."

Stara Sinclair sounded hard, determined. Reg knew about Stockton and Stara, and she could only imagine what the fleet's flight control commander was feeling just then. But it wasn't creeping into her voice, not one bit. Sinclair was a stone-cold professional and a veteran of many battles. And the fact that she was personally directing Reg in on her final approach told the pilot just how bad her situation truly was.

"Picking it up now, Stara." *As long as my comm holds out, at least.* Her audio was staticky and scratchy—more battle damage from her desperate run past the enemy line. Still, she figured her comm was in better shape at least than her scanners.

That was something, wasn't it?

Her ship shook hard, and she moved her hands back and forth, redirecting her main engines and firing small pulses. She would normally use her compressed gas positioning jets for minor adjustments, but the last enemy shot, the one she figured had come about ten centimeters from finishing her then and there, had scraped off all of her starboard side jets.

That wasn't going to make landing any easier either.

Still, she should be glad, she thought, that the beam hadn't ripped open her cockpit. It couldn't have been far from doing just that.

She reached out, punching a series of instructions into the AI interface. The computer system seemed to remain functional, but the voice communication circuit was definitely out. She stared down at a tiny screen, reading the system's responses. The computer would do some of the work involved in the landing, but if she was going to make it into *Dauntless*'s bay in one piece, it was going to be her piloting skill and her intuition that got the job done. Matching velocities with a battleship blasting at full thrust while implementing heavy evasive maneuvers was something on the order of hitting a bullet with another bullet.

But since freezing to death as she watched the fleet race toward the transit point was the only other option, Reg was ready to give it her best.

She tapped the controls again, readjusting her vector. Then she hit the thrust again, pushing it almost up to maximum. *Dauntless* had altered her course, and she had to match it…quickly. There was no room for error.

Jake Stockton pushed his way into her thoughts again, as he had every few minutes for the past three hours. It was almost reflex. For as long as she could remember, whenever she'd been in a tough spot in her cockpit, she'd thought of the fleet's legendary pilot, imagined how he would handle the situation in her shoes, and drawn inspiration from that. But this time, as she was fighting to make it back, Stockton himself had not. She was still trying to understand, to accept that it was all real. The fleet had lost thousands of people in the battle, and it faced a difficult and uncertain future, even if it managed to escape from the system. But no loss matched that of Jake Stockton, and perhaps none could, save only for Admiral Barron himself. She couldn't imagine the darkness that would settle over fighter country in each of the fleet's battered battleships as the word spread.

And if you don't stay focused, you're not going to make it back either. And they will need you to get through this. Jake trusted you to take care of them…

She narrowed her gaze, staring at the display in front of her. She was less than a hundred kilometers out. Her vector was spot on, but her velocity was still a bit too high. She tapped the controls for the port jets, swinging the ship around, and she let out a burst of thrust, decelerating slightly. The AI was feeding her data on the screen, displaying *Dauntless*'s velocity next to her own. It would have been simplicity itself to match up with the battleship…at least if it hadn't been changing its own thrust and vector every few seconds to avoid enemy fire. Reg knew Stara would patch her into the ship's nav system when she got closer, and then her AI would adjust her own maneuvers to compensate for *Dauntless*'s.

Assuming her comm held out.

She slipped under fifty kilometers. She was still moving faster than *Dauntless*. She had to be if she was going to catch up. But she was watchful not to approach too quickly. Her systems were all in rough shape, and she didn't want to rely too much on her ability to decelerate quickly.

"You're under twenty kilometers, Reg. Plugging you into the main nav system."

Stara's voice was still solid, but Reg was edgy anyway. she could feel there was something else. A few seconds later, Stara confirmed that suspicion.

"Reg…we're going to bring you into beta bay. I know you usually fly out of alpha, but beta's in a little better shape." A pause. "It's still pretty battered, so you're going to have to be pinpoint your landing. We've cleared as much space as possible, but we had a couple…rough…landings, and some of the debris is heavy. We have to clear space to get the cranes in, but that's not going to happen before you reach the ship."

"Understood." Reg hardly reacted. She had fought like crazy for almost two straight days, gone without sleep, almost without food and water. She had seen a friend, and a mentor she'd almost worshipped, lost in battle along with thousands of her comrades. If it hadn't been for the deep survival instinct that drove most successful pilots, she might have given up, just blasted straight out into the system to spend her final hours pondering the beauty of deep space.

But it wasn't in her to give up. Besides, she had a job to do, and that meant she had to survive.

"I'll manage it, Stara. Just keep me synced with *Dauntless*'s evasive routines, and I'll handle the rest."

Cockiness, something else common in successful fighter jocks.

She brought her ship around again, readjusting her approach slightly. She was half a kilometer out now, and she could see the big ship directly through the canopy of her cockpit. She tapped up the amplification, and she tried to hold back a gasp.

Dauntless was battered. Badly.

There was a huge gash down the starboard side of the ship, at least a quarter of a kilometer long. She couldn't imagine how many spacers had been killed by that hit, how many had been sucked out into the vacuum. There were at least a dozen clear hull breaches scattered all around, and she could see two that were still spewing out geysers of escaping atmosphere and rapidly freezing spouts of fluid.

The Confederation flagship showed the scars of the fight she was fleeing, the wounds of a desperate, losing battle from which escape alone would now seem almost a victory.

She nudged the controls again, making minor adjustments as the range dropped to less than one hundred meters. She could see the opening to the bay now…and it was a jumbled mass of twisted metal. She moved her hand again, and then once more, trying to angle her ship toward the opening that was at best, half its normal size.

Fifty meters.

She decelerated again, reducing her speed relative to *Dauntless* to less than three meters per second as she glided into the bay, missing a piece of twisted girder by what looked to her like maybe two meters.

She could see the floor of the bay ahead…and even Stara's warning had been inadequate to prepare her for the chunks of burned debris covering her landing area.

No, not landing. You're going to crash. The only question is, can you do it softly enough to survive...

She knocked down her velocity again, bringing her ship almost to a halt relative to the battleship and the bay surrounding her. She felt almost as though her fighter was floating just above the deck. If she took enough time, she could nudge it down gently. But she doubted she had much time. Now that she was in the bay, she didn't have her full thrust available...and one wild evasive maneuver by *Dauntless* could slam her into one of the bay walls.

She had to land. Now.

She tapped her controls gently, bringing her angle down slightly toward the deck. There was an open spot. Well, perhaps open was an exaggeration, but it was big enough for most of her ship to fit. She was going to slam into some debris for sure, but none of it looked particularly deadly. At least no huge steel girders ready to rip into her cockpit and turn her into strawberry jam.

She took one last breath, and she dropped the ship down. It landed, harder than her Academy instructors would have liked. A 'C' at best, but that was a passing grade, if not a great one.

But she didn't care about grades. She had brought her ship down. She'd torn off a section of the starboard stabilizer, and battered a few other sections of the fighter. She figured 50-50 the Lightning was a total loss. But she was there, back in *Dauntless*, and not broken into a hundred pieces or screaming as the flames enveloped her.

She took another breath, even deeper than the last, and she leaned back and closed her eyes for a few seconds. She was home, or what had passed for home for almost as long as she could remember.

She silently promised herself two things. First, she would not let Jake Stockton down. She would do whatever she had to do to lead the squadrons, to help them get through the terrible losses they had suffered. She would guide them past the loss of their leader, and keep them on the path Stockton had placed them on.

And, second, if she ever made it back from this accursed place to the Confederation…she would go home to visit her mother. Three times in ten years was not enough…and she was keenly aware that anytime could easily be the last.

* * *

"*Hallinda*, *Oceania*, and *Vergitra* all report main batteries down, Admiral."

Clint Winters sat in the center of his flagship's bridge, looking very much like a man who rated his nickname. The Sledgehammer had a reputation for having a single answer to most problems, and the current fight appeared to be no exception.

"The task force will move forward. I want every ship's secondaries to be in point blank range." The coldness of his voice almost disguised the gravity of what he was ordering. The main fleet was retreating—making a dead run for it—and his ships were still advancing on the enemy flanking force, moving farther from their own line of withdrawal.

There was no choice, not as far as Winters could see. If he didn't hold the enemy, there would be no retreat at all. The hundreds of enemy ships heading toward his force would simply blast right through and cut off the withdrawing main fleet. The result would be catastrophic, more so even than the battle had been so far.

There was only one way to prevent that…to hurt the enemy badly enough that they were compelled to stop and engage his forces. That just *might* work, for the rest of the fleet at least.

But it guaranteed that his own vessels would face a nightmare when they finally turned to follow their comrades.

A nightmare at best. Utter and complete destruction at the worst. And the worst seemed a far likelier outcome.

"The enemy forward line is accelerating. It looks like they might try to make a run past us."

"To hell with that!" Winter's roar was one of his best, filled with fury and determination. "All fire on the lead ships. Nav station, calculate thrust plan to close with those ships, and then to follow them when they reach us and pass our line. Let's see if these bastards can take that much fire and still ignore us!"

Winters knew what he had to do. He also knew focusing on the enemy forward line would leave his ships undefended against the rest of the approaching Highborn fleet. When his ships turned to follow the lead vessels moving on the main fleet, they would expose their own rear to the rest of the enemy formation. He couldn't even guess at the losses he would suffer.

But none of that mattered. Every ship he had, every spacer onboard—himself included—was completely expendable if that was the cost of ensuring the main fleet's escape.

Ensuring that the fight continued. That the battle to save the Rim didn't end there and then.

If Clint Winters died at Calpharon, at least he would do it knowing one thing with unshakable certainty. Tyler Barron would fight the enemy to the last...until he was throwing rocks, if that's where it all ended.

The Sledgehammer sat in his chair, and a grim smile morphed onto his face.

* * *

Vian Tulus stood next to his chair, his hands tightly gripping the armrest to steady himself. The blood dripping down his face created an annoying, almost ticklish, sensation, but he held his hands firmly in place, doing his best to ignore it. He was the Imperator, the role model for all Palatian warriors, and now was the time to set the example. His people had suffered terribly in the battle, and they were going to leave half their number behind them. At least half. They rated nothing less than watching their leader, standing firm, ignoring his wounds, covered in blood and still undaunted.

The cut on his head hurt, but he knew it wasn't serious. It was bleeding more than he'd expected, but that had its value as well, at least for those watching him on the video commlink, looking up from their stations as their Imperator addressed them, calling on them to dig down and release the great Palatian warriors that lived within them all.

It was the leg that was the real problem, and the severity of the pain told him it was broken, probably in several places. It throbbed as he stood, almost more than he could hide, but in truth, it had hurt nearly as much when he was sitting.

And men and women dying in battle should see their leader on his feet.

Even if he is hanging on the edge of his chair so he doesn't fall down...

He sucked in a deep breath, and steeled himself once again to disguise the pain. "I am proud of you, my warriors, honored to be your Imperator. We are far from home, battling alongside allies against an enemy that threatens us all. The way is the way. It is our creed, and has been since the days we threw off the yoke of the invaders, and brought upon them the nightmares they had visited upon our ancestors. And it shall always be the principal that guides us. But we must also remember, ways change. The universe evolves. We are no longer alone, battling only those who challenge us out on the Far Rim. But we are still Palatians, and the blood of warriors flows in our veins. The way is the way. Remember that, my warriors, remember as we claw our way out of this system, bowed but never defeated, that we shall fight again…and as it was at the birth of our Alliance, so shall it be again. We will have our vengeance, and we will bathe in the blood of our enemies."

Tulus turned toward the comm officer, and he nodded, the signal to cut the line. He wasn't sure how much longer he could keep the pain from his face.

Or the doubts. His people needed a leader who was made of stone, implacable, resolute. It was the Palatian way. But Vian Tulus had seen the enemy ships up close, watched as their deadly beams sliced his vessels to scrap. He would be what he had to be, lead his people to the end. But in his mind, and deep in his warrior's heart, hope was rapidly slipping away. He saw only the ignominy of defeat, both during the current retreat, and as far into the future as he could look. He was the Alliance's Imperator, the latest in a line of great warriors and heroes who had led the Palatian people to victory and glory.

Now, he wondered if he would be the last, and if his legacy would be to lead his people to defeat, even back into slavery. It was the worst nightmare for any Palatian leader, the one rallying cry that all his people would shout, from grizzled soldiers to schoolchildren. Never again. Palatia will never yield. But he also knew words were just words, however much passion was behind their utterances.

His only solace was his certainty he would not survive to see that final pass. Vian Tulus would die in the last fight, there was no doubt in his mind about that. None.

Death before dishonor. Always.

* * *

Barron stood on *Dauntless*'s bridge, staring in abject horror at the spot that had been Atara Travis's workstation. The place that was now charred and twisted beyond recognition.

The last hit. It had been the last hit before *Dauntless* managed to escape from the enemy's firing range. The bridge was buried deep in the ship, the most protected part of *Dauntless,* save only for the reactors. But every part of a warship carried vital equipment, and it wasn't the impact of the Highborn beams that had struck the control center. It was the series of internal explosions a particularly devastating hit had triggered.

Half the bridge was a nightmare of savaged metal and flesh. Four or five fires were still burning, and the air was thick with caustic fumes. And all around the stricken area were bodies. At least a dozen of his bridge crew had been killed or wounded, but as much as Tyler Barron cared for every spacer under his command, his pain was keenly focused at that moment.

Directed like a laser on the unmoving form lying on the bridge floor in front of him.

Atara had fallen the instant the explosion ripped into the bridge, and she'd lain a meter from her chair, surrounded by fire. Barron had run through the flames himself to pull her free, even before the damage control circuits showered the bridge with flame suppressant. His survival suit had mostly protected him, though both legs of his uniform, and he could feel pain from beneath the damaged protective layer below, burns from his time standing in the fire. He didn't know how bad they would be, but his ability to stay on his feet suggested they were nothing he couldn't endure.

Atara was in far worse shape. Her hands and face were burned, and along one arm, even her survival gear had been melted away. Her leg, at least, was clearly broken, a diagnosis made simple by the grotesque angle at which it bent almost exactly in the middle. There was blood everywhere, but at least a dozen lacerations. She was dead, Barron had been sure.

Then he saw her take a breath.

It was soft, barely noticeable. But he was sure. She was still alive.

"Medic!" Barron shouted, his voice almost a guttural growl. "Medic...over here!" A trio of medical technicians had just raced onto the bridge, and even as he bellowed his command, two of them raced over to him.

"Admiral...you're wounded, sir. Let me..."

"Forget about me. I'm fine. Admiral Travis needs your help." For a moment, he felt jealousy toward some of the enemies he'd faced, men like Gaston Villieneuve, who wouldn't have hesitated to make clear to the medics that their own survival was tied to Atara's. The thought of losing her, the comrade who'd been like a sister to him for almost two decades, his shadow in every battle he'd fought, was almost overpowering. He couldn't lose her.

He couldn't watch her die.

But it wasn't in him to threaten to murder a medic who failed to save her.

"She's badly injured, Admiral. Gravely. I don't know if we can..."

"Save her." There was no threat of consequences, no hints of punishment for failure. But the two words were spoken in a tone of utter command, one no spacer on *Dauntless* could ignore when it came from their beloved admiral.

"Yes, sir...we'll do...all we can." The medic turned

and shouted toward the bank of lifts. "Get that medpod over here. Now!"

Barron looked down at Atara for a few more seconds, struggling to hold back the wetness in his eyes. But, as always, he felt the cold hand of duty reaching out, grabbing him, pulling him away…as it had dragged him from everything he cared about. He had thousands of spacers, and hundreds of ships, and they were all counting on him to get them out of the system. To save them from total defeat and destruction. And there was nothing more he could do for Atara.

Except get the ship carrying her out of danger.

He turned and moved back toward his chair, wincing at the pain in his legs. His eyes fixed on the main display, checking the positional data. There was no time the for grief, nor for anger nor cries for vengeance.

But there would be. Once his people were safe, he would cry for those he lost—and even more if Atara was counted among the dead.

And those cries for vengeance would come, too. They would come with a certainty he couldn't deny.

And if he lost Atara, the price he would extract would be more terrible than anything his darkest thoughts could conceive. He would destroy the enemy, somehow, whatever it took. Whatever effort. Whatever sacrifice.

He swore a bloody oath to himself. The Highborn must die. All of them.

Chapter Thirty-Seven

CFS Dauntless
Omega Zed System
Year 323 AC (After the Cataclysm)

The Battle of Calpharon – To Fight Another Day

"Admiral, we've updated the loss reports. The first division had three battleships destroyed, four badly damaged, out of a total strength of ten. The second division suffered three ships destroyed and one crippled and abandoned, with three more heavily damaged. Third…"

Barron held up his hand. "Lieutenant, please…not now." He stood in front of the lift along the edge of *Dauntless*'s emergency bridge. The main control room was mostly non-functional, but it had been the heavy release of toxic fumes into the space that had finally compelled evacuation. The emergency bridge was smaller and less comfortable, but it was fully operational, with everything Barron needed to command the ship and the fleet.

Everything but clarity of mind.

His thoughts were a mad jumble, bouncing back and forth between the war, Andi, the losses his people had suffered…and at that moment, Atara, down in *Dauntless*'s battered sickbay. He'd checked on her half a dozen times, but all he'd gotten from the doctors were evasive answers with no real meaning. Now, he was going to go down there himself. He didn't have the time, not even close to it, but he didn't care. She'd been at his side for two decades. He owed her that much.

Let the doctors lie to my face…

He stepped into one of the lift cars, and he tapped the controls. The primary sickbay wasn't far from the main bridge, but unlike the battleship's control center, it had escaped significant destruction. That, at least, was a small mercy. Barron couldn't imagine how crammed full of casualties the place was, but at least that wasn't exacerbated by battle damage.

He'd avoided reviewing the loss figures as well as the bulk of the damage reports streaming in. There was nothing he could do about any of it, and he knew there was only so much he could take. He had too much to do to risk turning into a quivering wreck. He hadn't even managed to get his mind around the staggering scope of the losses the fleet had suffered. Jake Stockton's death had hit him like a punch to the gut. And he'd had no word from Clint Winters or any ships from his task force. He hadn't written off his second in command, not yet, but things weren't looking very good.

If he lost Atara, too…

He stood silently as the car slowed to a halt and the doors opened. He stepped out into the main sickbay, and into a level of chaos beyond even what he'd imagined. He looked all around, trying to spot the ship's chief surgeon. But his quarry found him first.

"Admiral…I thought I might see you down here." The officer hesitated, looking uncomfortable. Then he extended his arm. "Perhaps we can talk in my office."

"I want to see Atara."

"Commander Travis is in a med pod in partial suspended animation. All you could do is put your hand on the glass, I'm afraid." A pause. "Please, Admiral…you can see her in a minute. First, let's talk."

Barron nodded and followed the doctor, the pit in his stomach telling him he knew all he needed to know from the doctor's demeanor. But a spark of hope refused to die. The two stepped into a small room, and an instant later, the doors closed, cutting off the cacophony outside.

The doctor was about to say something, but Barron spoke first. "I want the truth, Doc. No evasive answers, no overblown responses. Don't 'handle' me. I just want to know, and I want to know now." A pause. "Is she going to make it?"

The doctor looked like he was going to answer, very likely just the kind of longwinded reply Barron had forbidden. But then he remained silent for a few seconds, and he looked down at the floor. Finally, he managed to come close to returning Barron's gaze.

"No Admiral," he said, "I don't think so. She's just too badly injured. We can keep her alive for a short while, but I don't think there is any way to save her."

* * *

"Two minutes to transit, Admiral. All remaining ships are on a straight-line course for the point."

Clint Winters grunted his acknowledgement at the report. The bridge was filled with smoke, and his ship, like the sixty or so others that remained from his four hundred vessel task force, had been savaged. Great breaches had been torn into the hull, and Highborn beams had bored holes deep into the vessel, slicing into vital systems and killing crew.

By any reasonable measure, his task force had been destroyed. At least as an effective fighting unit. But it had stayed in the fight long enough to cover the main retreat. It had completed its mission, done its duty. Now his battered survivors were making a run for it.

He could call it a retreat, perhaps even a withdrawal, but the Sledgehammer had never had much use for bullshit. Every ship he had was in a headlong rush to the point, blasting full at whatever thrust level remained in their tortured engines. There were a few lagging behind, the victims of damaged thrusters and reactors. Those crews were very likely going to die, but for the first time in eight hours, Clint Winters was beginning to believe that *some* of his people were going to make it out. His flagship, even. The vessel had taken a barrage of hits, but through some strange fortune, both its reactors and engines remained at seventy percent or better operational capacity. The enemy was still in pursuit, and any instant the fatal shot could come. But his forward ships were already transiting, and his own vessel would be following in less than two minutes.

"One minute to transit."

One minute…

He breathed deeply, staring at the display. The point filled the center of the screen, a hazy circle, black against the black of space, but somehow different enough to be seen. A blurry countdown of numbers above showed the decreasing range. All around, flashes appeared on the screen and then vanished, the shots from half a dozen Highborn vessels in close pursuit. The ship was within thirty seconds of transit, but Winters knew that was still plenty of time to die.

The enemy wouldn't follow if his ship made it through, at least he didn't think they would. Their forces were spread all across the system in total disorder, and they had no idea where the combined Confederation and Hegemony fleets were deployed in the next system. Going through in small groups was tactical idiocy, and the Highborn had exhibited a strong knowledge of fleet operations.

No, they wouldn't follow, and that meant they had twenty seconds left to kill the Sledgehammer and his flagship.

Most of the other ships had already transited. About fifteen were strung out behind Winter's ship, mostly due to engine damage and the resulting thrust limitations. The admiral didn't like the idea of going through the point while some of his people were still struggling to get there, but he'd given the order for every ship to make its best speed, and he owed his flagship crew the same chance he'd given all the others.

Besides, he could do literally nothing for those whose ships were slowed by damage. Nothing except wish them the best.

Which he did as his ship slipped into the point, and into the relative safety of alternate space…bound for the next system.

And for the next battle. Because if 'Sledgehammer' Winters was sure of anything, it was that there would be another fight.

And he had some scores to settle.

*   *   *

"We're here to bid farewell to one of our own. On a day when we are mourning thousands of comrades, and when others dear to us remain in the sickbays, many clinging desperately to life, it is hard to single out one officer, one spacer for special note. There were so many heroes at Calpharon, so many friends who will be missed. But even among heroes, one man stands tall, and he casts a shadow over all of us."

Reg stood and watched as Admiral Barron spoke, and she could see the strain in his face as he struggled to maintain his composure as he spoke to the entire fleet. He was on a podium that had been hastily set up on what was left of *Dauntless*'s beta landing bay, and he spoke to the crew of a fleet that had been savaged, to spacers who had all lost friends, mentors, leaders. There was some relief at having made an escape from the Sigma Nordlin system, but beyond all the pain and anguish of loss, there was one other inescapable fact looming over the entire fleet like a dark shadow. They'd been beaten by the Highborn, soundly whipped, and if they'd inflicted considerable damage on the enemy as well, that was cold comfort.

And they'd lost Jake Stockton.

Reg still couldn't believe it. She was devastated, of course, but it all felt very unreal, theoretical. Some part of her refused to believe Stockton was really gone, and that pointless determination held back much of the pain. Hearing Barron's words wore that resolve down, just a bit, but it still held. It wasn't based on reason, nor on analysis, but she was content to continue to fool herself. She had much to do, more than seemed possible. There were casualty reports to review, and vast rearrangements of the OB...more holes to plug than she could easily grasp. If a bit of self-delusion helped her get through it all, so be it.

"All we can do for Admiral Stockton—and especially those of you in his beloved fighter corps—is to behave as you always have, to make him proud. And that is what we will do, all of us. Our fight is not over, far from it, and even without Jake, we must go on. Fight on." Barron stared forward for a moment, and Reg could see the pain in his gaze. Stockton had been one of Barron's closest friends. They had fought side by side for twenty years, from one war to the next. But there was something more driving that hurt. Reg knew Atara Travis had been badly wounded. She didn't have any details, but as she looked up at the admiral, the man who remained the last hope for the fleet, she began to feel cold realization, about Stockton, about all of them.

Is there no end? Will the loss, the death never stop?

* * *

"The reactors all appear to be fully functional, Commodore. The outer sections of the ship suffered heavy damage, but most of it appears to be limited to newly installed Hegemony and Confederation systems. Very little of the original imperial hardware seems to be badly damaged."

Sonya Eaton listened as the aide detailed the myriad ways in which *Colossus* had been battered in the fight, but she found it difficult to concentrate. Perhaps it was exhaustion, or numbness at all the death and loss the fleet had suffered. She even tried to see some base satisfaction in the Hegemony capital suffering what Megara had just a few years before…but it didn't work. She didn't like the Heggies, and she still carried a heavy weight of resentment for the former enemy responsible for so many deaths, her sister's included, but she couldn't quite hate them anymore. They had fought bravely alongside the fleet, and now all she could feel for them was sympathy. Worse, her inability to enjoy the misfortune of the Hegemony only made her angrier, and moving toward acceptance of the now-allied Heggies felt like a betrayal of Sara.

"We'll continue this later, Commander. I just received

a message from Admiral Barron. He's sending Anya Fritz over to take command of repairs as soon as she gets *Dauntless*'s crews sorted out. Make sure this is all organized so Commodore Fritz can properly evaluate and prioritize operations." Sonya had been surprised when Barron had told her he was sending Fritz, though she quickly realized she shouldn't have been. The fleet was badly battered, but it wasn't destroyed, and *Colossus* was its single most powerful weapon. The war would go on, and if there wasn't much hope as far as she could see, there was a surprising amount of determination remaining among the crews. She was hesitant to call it 'morale,' as it had a dark, almost morose feel to it. She wasn't sure many of the fleet's spacers were hopeful of victory, but she was damned sure every one of them wanted revenge. She didn't know what would happen when the Confed fleet fought the enemy again, but she was sure of one thing.

It would be a nasty, bare-clawed struggle. She'd never seen more condensed fury than what saw all around her.

And in the fighter squadrons most of all.

For all of *Colossus*'s immense size, the ship only had a few fighter bays that had been hastily installed to house the first Hegemony squadrons. But the pilots on the massive vessel had retreated to their small section of the ship and shut the hatches, and a dark cloud lay over the whole area. She could almost feel the seething rage on the bridge.

Sonya still couldn't believe Jake Stockton was gone. Next to Admiral Barron himself, Stockton had been the fleet's biggest hero, and to the wings, he was almost a deity. He'd survived so many close calls, come back from so many apocalyptic battles, most of his pilots had come to view him as invulnerable. No one had ever survived the amount of combat Stockton had, not in a fighter. Not even close.

His death was like a dagger to the heart for the thousands of pilots who'd so long revered him. Who still did.

She hadn't known Stockton all that well, but she felt his loss as keenly as most in the fleet did. She hadn't even realized how much she had bought into the pilots' view, how she'd always assumed that whatever else happened, the fleet's strike force commander would be there. Stockton's loss would be felt by all, in more than just an emotional way. The wings were crucially important to the war effort...and she couldn't imagine anyone could fill his shoes.

Anger might lead his people into battle, for a time at least. She was almost afraid at the frozen malevolence she could feel drifting up from the pilots' quarters. They would fight with unimaginable fury, she didn't doubt that. But she wasn't sure that would be enough. Anger might replace the morale effect Stockton brought to his wings, but nothing could fill the void where the greatest fighter combat tactician who'd ever lived had been. Stockton's death only portended even greater loss to his squadrons, and Sonya winced as she imagined watching them throw themselves at the enemy in incoherent fury.

She turned and walked back to the huge room behind the bridge, the place she'd commandeered as her office. She had a million things to do, and rest was far, far down on that list. But she needed a few minutes to herself.

She slipped inside and leaned against the wall as the door slid shut. Then she let out a long, deep breath.

"Well, Sara...I did my best, sister. I tried to make you proud."

She looked across the room, and she saw Sara's face, a shadowy image hovering in the forefront of her mind, as a stream of tears began to roll down her face.

* * *

"What is it, Anya?" Tyler Barron had nothing but respect for his longtime engineer, but he was in a dark place, and he'd been snapping at everyone around him. The losses at Calpharon, the state of the war, the death of Jake Stockton…and now, Atara Travis lingering near her own demise…it was all too much. And Anya's cryptic message, her insistence that he meet her outside the landing bay—or what was left of it—and her refusal to tell him what it was about, had rubbed him the wrong way.

Not that there had been any good ways recently.

"There is someone here to see you, Admiral." Fritz was usually deadly serious, but her normally deadpan voice seemed unusually light. He was starved for anything less than morose, but the cheery sound of her voice only pissed him off. "You dragged me down here to meet with someone? In case you forgot, Fritzie, I'm in command here. People come to *me*."

"Not me."

Barron stood, frozen in utter shock. *No, it can't be…*

"At least not always. You come to *me* your share of times, too."

Andi!

He spun around, toward the voice. It *was* her. For an instant, he refused to believe it. It wasn't possible, an apparition. He was hallucinating. It couldn't be her, not so far out.

But it was.

He lurched forward, throwing his arms around her, pulling her close to him. His mind was a vortex of conflicting thoughts. The last place he wanted Andi was in such a terrible place, so soon after the horror of the battle. But she was there, in his arms after so long, and for a few precious moments, the rest of the nightmare receded, and Tyler Barron felt something he could hardly remember.

Happiness.

"What are you doing here, Andi?" He asked the question, but for those few seconds, he didn't really care. All that mattered was she *was* there. "How?"

"*Pegasus*, of course. I put the old crew back together. Honestly, it was the easiest trip through the Badlands I ever had. Nothing like an invasion to clear out the troublesome elements. Not too many frontier toughs wanted to tangle with the Heggies, it seems."

"You came all the way out here?"

"Yes…I had something I had to do. Someone you had to meet."

Barron stared in wonder as another familiar form slipped into view. Lita Mareth had been Tyler Barron's governess more than thirty years before. "Lita…it's been a long…" His words stopped abruptly. Lita was carrying something.

Someone.

Andi turned toward the governess and scooped the young child into her own arms. "I want you to meet Cassiopeia Barron." Andi smiled, and as she saw moistness gathering in Tyler's eyes, her own tears began to stream down her face. She looked up at him and said, simply, "Your daughter."

Chapter Thirty-Eight

Forward Base Striker
Vasa Denaris System
Year 323 AC (After the Cataclysm)

"The Highborn are humans. Or, at least, they were created by humans. From humans…" Andi stood at the head of the table, or at least the long metal sheet propped up on storage crates that passed for one. Base Striker, named for the Confederation's lost admiral, and one of Tyler Barron's mentors, would eventually be the center of resistance to the Highborn invasion, a massive logistical center, armed to the teeth, with facilities to support massive fleets and direct operations across a vast swath of the Rimward Hegemony and the old Badlands.

But just then it was a single shell, barely pressurized, with three decks, almost empty save for the piles of crates strewn all about. The facility didn't even have its own power yet. It drew energy through a series of umbilicals to two battleships stationed alongside. If the enemy attacked anytime soon, they could destroy the Pact's new headquarters with a single shot.

Andi hated the name. Pact seemed…she wasn't sure. Odd? Pretentious? But alliance would have been too confusing with the Palatian Alliance part of the mix, and Pact actually came naturally, from the document formalizing the whole thing. It was an astonishing agreement, one negotiated mostly by Tyler, who'd proven to be a steely dealmaker despite his oft-stated disgust for politicians and their ilk. It wasn't ratified yet, but she didn't think anyone who'd been in the deadly fight at Calpharon gave much of a shit what a bunch of Senators lightyears away thought anyway.

"Humans? So, they are not aliens, after all?" There was surprise in Akella's voice, but even as the Hegemony leader spoke, her eyes moved across the table to Ellia. The Hegemony researcher has suggested hints of exactly what Andi had just declared so definitively, but Akella had found it difficult to believe. She'd known of what had then been called the Others as long as she had conscious memory, and they'd gone from a phantom 'bogeyman' threat in her eyes to a real and terrible danger…but they'd always been *aliens*. At least in her mind's eye.

"They were created in the waning days of the empire. As best we have been able to learn, they were not developed to destroy humanity, nor even to enslave it. The old records we have found—and which we have brought with us—suggest the project that resulted in the Highborn was conceived to *save* the empire, to combat the lethargy that had sapped its strength and brought that vast realm to the verge of collapse."

The words were powerful. A few of those in the room, Tyler of course, and Clint Winters, already knew all Andi was explaining. She'd briefed them all individually. Indeed, she'd even delayed her private reunion with Tyler to tell him what she'd learned. It was *that* important.

Though, maybe someday, we'll be less important, the two of us…and left alone. The three of us…

She hoped that with all her heart, but she didn't really

believe it. She *might* slip into obscurity one day, assuming the Confederation survived the war, but Tyler never could. He'd been born into a role he couldn't escape, and his own list of deeds had only cemented him in that prison cell.

"The effort failed, of course. I'm afraid we haven't managed to extract much of the later data yet, though I believe we will ultimately secure more information. What we know is, the Highborn began to split from those who created them. They seemed to become arrogant, and to think of themselves as gods, and of normal humans as supplicants…lower beings to worship them, even as, in a twisted way, they guided humanity forward and protected human civilization."

Andi hesitated, looking out over the room. Two rows of stunned faces stared back at her, even from those who already knew all she had just said. It was a lot to comprehend, and she herself was still struggling with it. The Cataclysm had always existed for her as a historical event shrouded in mystery. The empire fell…everyone knew that. But no one understood the details or the causes, not with any specificity.

The Highborn had their place in that story, and she understood that to a degree. But the genetically engineered…gods, monsters, people—it depended on one's perspective, she supposed—had not caused the decline. In fact, they had been created in response to the slide already in progress, one that threatened an empire that had endured for a hundred centuries.

Andi had begun to develop an idea of the primary stimuli that brought on the downfall…and she didn't like what she'd begun to piece together. She was hesitant to even mention it, but she'd seen too many references…and anything that had led to the deaths of a trillion or more human beings couldn't be kept hidden.

No matter how unpleasant its implications.

"This is rather more…conjecture…I'm afraid, but I think it is something that needs to be said. The Highborn were a failed solution to the empire's troubles, but they did not create those problems. The empire was already in a parlous state when the Highborn were created. We will have to study more…a great deal more. But I believe what we have uncovered so far strongly suggests an answer to what has always been an unanswerable question. Why did the empire fall?"

She hadn't even talked to Tyler about what she was about to say.

"If there had been an invasion, even a civil war, at least one beyond the violence of the Cataclysm itself, we would long ago have found records of it. A plague, some kind of widespread failure in food production, any major disaster…again, there would have been some historical evidence. Why not for the Cataclysm? Why so much mystery?" She paused. "Because, while the actual final fall of the empire was violent and deadly, the events leading up to it were not. There were no massive wars, no pandemics, nothing of the sort. The empire declined because of its prosperity, because it had united all of humanity. Because it had no enemies on its borders, and no real dissension within. People became apathetic, and less and less productive. They wasted their time in pointless disputes over meaningless issues. For the first time since humanity clawed its way from the deep jungle to build the first civilization, there was no pressure on most people. No war, no famine, no uncontrolled disease. It seems like paradise, but instead it was a road to hell. We lost our spark, our drive…and that condemned us to decline, and perhaps to total destruction."

Andi was surprised at herself. Everything she'd just blurted out was her own read on what she'd seen, and very far from certain. But it all made sense, and despite the continued stunned looks around the table, she got the sense it did to everyone else as well.

They all looked as horrified as she was.

"Our parents and our grandparents—and our great grandparents—faced a stark choice. Struggle to survive or face extinction. The Rim, and the Hegemony, recovered as quickly as they did—and a few centuries is not a long time in this context—because of the way our ancestors approached that choice. The apathy, the decadence, was gone. Those who strived, who fought and struggled, lived…at least some of them did. The rest died. But enough grew strong to preserve humanity, and to begin to rebuild. Whether our reality, our cultures and nations, are indeed an actual recovery, or just a blip on the continuing descent to an eternal dark age, I will leave to others to theorize."

Andi was silent, and she found it difficult to breathe, to suck in the air she needed. She'd phrased her words carefully, but in her own mind, she understood exactly what she had proposed. The war, the death, the horrors she and those close to her had endured…was it possible they were *necessary* to humanity's continued development, to its progress?

To its ultimate survival?

She longed for peace, for a calm and quiet life, and it sickened her to think all the negatives, all the suffering, had been somehow *necessary*, at least in a macro-historical sense.

There was a long silence. Finally, Akella stood up. "You have given us much to consider, Captain Lafarge. Knowledge of our enemy can only help, but I believe now our goal must be to expand that understanding, past who they are and where they came from…to how to defeat them. How to destroy them. Whether we are condemned to endure constant war and strife—or to perish from too much peace and contentment—we must first defeat the Highborn."

They had always seen Akella's even temperament, but now everyone saw a glimpse of the rage she was feeling. It was the first time anyone present had seen her out for blood.

Welcome to the club, Number One...to a universe that has less use for intellect than brute force and merciless brutality.

"Yes," Barron said, rising as Akella had done. "That is next on our agenda. We must scour every imperial record we can find, search for any hint of how the imperials dealt with the Highborn." Barron paused and looked at each of those present in turn. "Because the instability the Highborn caused may have contributed to the inevitable fall of the empire, but it is clear the teetering imperial forces somehow managed to defeat, or at least deflect, their efforts. The Highborn have come back from beyond the old empire, not from within...and if they had succeeded, they would be ruling over us all even now. The imperials did *something* to contain them...and we need to find out *what*.

* * *

"There has been some improvement, Tyler. I wish I had more definitive news, but I believe there is cause for optimism." Akella reached out and put her hand on Barron's arm.

Barron stared back at the Hegemony ruler, and he found his head moving, a subtle nod of acknowledgement. He'd been uncertain when Chronos and Akella had first suggested he transfer Atara to a Hegemony medical facility, but in the end, he had agreed. The Hegemony had a higher general tech level, and there wasn't much argument that their medicine was ahead of the Confederation's as well, if not by an immense margin, very possibly by enough to mark the difference between his friend's survival and her death. His own medical officers had been able to do precious little beyond sustaining her in a medpod, so there hadn't really been any other options.

"Thank you, Akella. Atara is very important to me. We've been together, fought together, for a very long time."

"Of course, Tyler. It was the least we could do." A pause. "I do not wish to give you false hope. There is reason for cautious optimism, but she is still in a very precarious state."

Barron understood Akella was trying to give him an idea of the odds without reducing it to so cold and dire a format. His gut told him 60-40 Atara would survive, which wasn't good by any measure, save only the comparison to the nearly hopeless prognosis his own doctors had offered.

"We will hope for the best...and be thankful your technology is ahead of ours."

"Not for long. I will see that the provisions of the Pact are honored to the letter, including the sharing of all technological and scientific knowledge. In a few years, your people will have all the technology of mine. I hope that proves my sincerity about our people becoming allies for the long term. The past is gone. The scars linger, perhaps, but now we stand side by side as we face our greatest challenge."

Barron nodded. He'd been struggling to get past his own resentments and lingering hostilities toward the Hegemony, and Akella's effort to help save Atara had gone a long way to getting him there. If the Hegemony's Number One was correct, and the technology transfers specified in the Pact were in fact made, he believed for the first time that he could truly move on from all that had happened.

Whether that would amount to anything beyond just dying alongside his new allies remained to be seen.

* * *

"Gary, I'm glad you made the trip. I'm sorry to say, I'm going to have to ask you to go right back. We need to get the Pact ratified by the Senate, and if there is any way to do it short of sending Clint Winters back to secure it at gunpoint, I think we'll be far better off."

Holsten nodded. "I expected this conversation, and of course, I will see it done. I'll do what I have to, but I don't really think it will be that difficult. The casualty reports from Calpharon, and the specifics from Andi's research, are very likely to scare the living shit out of the politicians. That's a technical term, of course, but I think one that accurately describes the fear level I expect to find in the chambers."

"It all scared the hell out of me, so I suspect you are right. But make sure, okay? And get word to me immediately if you have any problems. It's not the tech transfers I'm worried about. That's a no brainer. We come out way ahead on those. It's the use of it all, specifically the construction of an antimatter production facility. Akella told me it took the Hegemony thirty years to build each of theirs. We've got two, maybe three years…or we're going to lose this war because we run out of antimatter. The Senate *has* to make this the entire Confederation's number one project, and they have to supply the resources to get it done, even if it craters the economy. We need a national effort, the likes of which we never seen before. It's a matter of survival, and…"

Barron stopped. He'd always been hesitant to interfere in the political realm, and even more reluctant to threaten politicians. To behave like a military dictator, though he'd had his chances to become just that if he'd been so inclined. But if Gary Holsten's efforts failed, if Barron had to go back to Megara from the front...any Senator he didn't line up along a wall in front of Bryan Rogan's Marines would be one lucky bastard.

And they'd all be even worse off if he sent the Sledgehammer instead.

"I understand, Tyler. I will see it done...whatever I have to do."

There was a long silence. Then, Holsten added, "Do you want me to bring Andi and your daughter back to Megara with me? Right now, that's about as far from the fighting as anyone can get."

Barron looked over at his friend. "No, Gary...not yet. It may be selfish, but I'm not ready to let them go. I think we'll have a respite here, probably a fairly long one. We lost at Calpharon, but we hurt the Highborn too, and they've got the burden of invasion, worlds to occupy, lengthening supply lines, greater distance from home bases. It will be some time, I'm guessing, before they can resume their advance, and we'll get plenty of notice from the pickets we've got posted on all the approaches when they do. I'll want Andi and Cassie out of here before the fighting starts again, of course..." Barron paused. Getting Andi out of harm's way had never been an easy task. He wasn't proud of his intention to use his daughter to guilt her into retreating when the time came, but that didn't mean he wouldn't do it. "...but I'm betting we've got a least a year, and probably more..."

He hesitated again, and he looked down at the floor. "And that might be the only time I ever have with them." He didn't elaborate. He didn't have to. Gary Holsten knew as well as Barron did the odds the fleet faced. Morale required some optimism, and a healthy dose of defiance, but inside, Tyler Barron was fighting off the encroaching hopelessness...and he suspected Holsten had no rosier a take on their situation.

He would fight, they would all fight—fight like hell—but that was all he knew for sure. The rest would have to wait. The future would unfold in its own time.

Chapter Thirty-Nine

Highborn Grand Flagship S'Evelion
Imperial System GH9-27C1
Year of the Firstborn 384 (322 AC)

"The conquest of the Hegemony capital is an achievement, Tesserax. There is little question of that." Ellerax stared intently at his subordinate. The two were alone in Ellerax's sanctuary. The leader of the Highborn rarely allowed anyone save his closest servants into the large, but modestly furnished, space. It was his own retreat, the place he came when he wished to think, when he craved quiet, simplicity. But he'd wanted to speak to Tesserax alone, undisturbed. It was sometimes a difficult thing to discipline subordinates, and no less so to commend them...but it was always a delicate act to combine the two, as he intended to do now.

And even more challenging when the subject was one of the Highborn...indeed, one of the Firstborn.

Tesserax sat quietly in the leather chair next to Ellerax, looking as though he wanted to speak, but holding his tongue. Ellerax appreciated the restraint, the control on display. Arrogance was common among the Highborn, and especially the Firstborn, the five hundred specimens

JAY ALLAN

of the first quickening. Ellerax, who acknowledged he suffered no less from the affliction than his peers, felt it was unavoidable. His people had been created to serve as humanity's gods, and humility in deities, in beings superior in every way to the billions who worshipped them, seemed unattainable.

"The resources you required, however—and the losses suffered in the campaign—have greatly exceeded prior estimates by a large margin. Including your own figures, I might add. I would not be overly concerned, Tesserax, but you know as well as I that we face another, far graver conflict, a war we have fought now for almost two centuries, against an enemy far more dangerous than the humans. Indeed, we fight not only for ourselves but to defend our lowly charges, to protect them from destruction even as they battle against us to resist our ordained rule over them. The points you raised in your arguments for the invasion centered on our need to increase the human populations we control, to bring new and fresh genetic lines into the Thrall stock, and indeed, there is little argument to be made against such a view. It is almost self-evident. We long ago planned the reconquest of the old imperial space, and such an effort was overdue."

He looked over at Tesserax, and his gaze hardened. "But we can no longer supply the level of resources you have utilized here. The primary front is stalemated, and we cannot spare any further strength. Indeed, the outright loss of eighteen battleships, is a hard blow, one that was quite a surprise. The surviving heavy vessels will be withdrawn at once, and the flow of equipment and reserves to this theater will be severely cut."

Tesserax shifted in his seat, and finally, he spoke. "High Lord, the conquest of the Hegemony capital is a major milestone, but significant enemy forces were able to escape. Coupled with the evidence that most or all of the Rim is now allied with the remaining Hegemony forces, it will require…considerable…effort and strength to complete the conquest."

"Yes…that is true. An unfortunate aspect of your failure to trap and eliminate the combined human forces when you had the chance." Ellerax allowed a bit of edge into his tone, though not too much. He wanted to express some disappointment in his subordinate, but not to cut too deeply into Tesserax's pride. The Highborn Ellerax acknowledged him as the first of their race and their leader, but they were arrogant and brittle as well, especially the Firstborn. Maintaining their loyalty and obedience was always somewhat of an effort in balance, one Ellerax had mastered over the past three centuries.

Tesserax's expression hardened, but he didn't respond.

"Perhaps we all underestimated the power the humans have managed to reclaim since the empire's fall. We, too, were forced to rebuild after we were driven into the uncharted depths, and now we are stronger than ever. We must remember that these humans, inferior as they may be, are no longer the dissipated and decadent citizens of the ancient empire. Their societies survived the empire's fall, and no doubt, they have seen much strife and battle. It should not surprise us that they possess some strength. Indeed, that is good news, in its own way. We wanted better Thralls than the depleted descendants of the imperials we brought with us on our exodus…and it appears that is just what we have found. I am inclined to believe you were right, Tesserax, to encourage swifter action than we might have taken." Now, he was building the chastised Highborn back up, offered him praise alongside the chastisement, maintaining his loyalty. "You will remain here and in command, my old friend, and you will continue the conquest of all the humans descended from the old empire. They will become part of our war effort, serve with our fleets, and do their part to defend against the true enemy."

Tesserax looked silently at Ellerax, and despite what appeared to be his best efforts, some confusion showed through. Finally, he said, "I do not see how that is possible, Lord Commander, not with the reduction in the forces committed to the theater. Calpharon was a clear target, one the enemy was almost compelled to defend. Now, they could be anywhere. They may spread out, seek to delay our advances. Position themselves at multiple chokepoints. Pacification will be a slow process, and one requiring considerable resources." A pause, then: "There is little to be gained by leaving me in my post without the ability to achieve ultimate success."

Ellerax nodded. He had been testing Tesserax, at least to an extent, and the commander had passed. He had overcome his arrogance and considered the next phase of the campaign coldly, analytically. And he had admitted an inability to achieve victory.

"I am pleased to see your analyses more focused, more realistic. You have my complete confidence, Tesserax, my friend, even after the miscalculations that have plagued the invasion. There is little choice regarding the deployment of more forces to this sector. The situation at the main front simply will not allow it. However, there is one resource I am able to offer you. Time."

Ellerax paused for a moment, and then he continued. "We are beings of thought, of intellect. The success of the campaign to date, limited as it is, has provided considerable gain. Calpharon and the other worlds where the Hegemony populations were spared provide billions of potential Thralls, as well as considerable, if primitive, industry. With some time, and a moderate flow of certain supplies, we should be able to turn the occupied human worlds into the engine to complete our conquest."

"You are proposing we harness the human factories and shipyards, that we build new ships to fight the war here?" Tesserax looked uncertain, but also intrigued.

"I am proposing exactly that, though perhaps 'propose' is not the correct word. By my command, I hereby designate you the viceroy of the Highborn in all the former sectors of the old empire…a volume of space which will now be called, 'The Colony.' Your mandate is to harness the captured resources under your control, and to build the ships and weapons you require to complete the occupation of all human-inhabited space. You will have inquisitors to aid in the establishment of church facilities to facilitate control over the conquered populations…and even now, a large shipment of collars is en route to provide what you will need until local production can be initiated. The Colony will continue the war to bring the humans under our control, even as the resources of our home space feed the war effort on the primary front. It is thus that we will achieve all of our ends."

The two Highborn were silent for a brief moment. Then, Ellerax bowed his head slightly to his subordinate. "I give you a great responsibility, Viceroy Tesserax. Do not give me reason to regret it."

* * *

"Welcome aboard *Stilliax*. I'm afraid this vessel is the only heavy unit that remains to me after the battle at Calpharon and the subsequent withdrawal of the remaining frontline units. Your people put up a considerably better fight than I'd expected, and perhaps congratulations are in order. I believe I have you to blame for much of the difficulty I was forced to endure. It took no small amount of scanner analysis to identify you, and more to isolate your ship, and bring you here alive. I trust it will be worth the effort, so again, welcome to you...Admiral Stockton."

Jake Stockton was pressed against a large structure, his arms extended and held fast to the black metal, looking almost as though he'd been crucified. He was woozy, but awake. And despite the fatigue, the injuries, the grogginess, he stared back at this captor with undisguised hatred.

Tesserax stepped forward, coming closer, looking up toward where Stockton hung, above even his own greater than two-and-a-half-meter height. "I must apologize for the...discomfort...of the restrictor unit, Admiral, but you are a rather aggressive human specimen, and it seems wise to prevent any foolish displays, don't you agree?"

"What...are...you?" Stockton's speech was slow, mildly slurred. "Look...human...but..."

"Ahh...yes. I must appear both familiar and strange to your eyes, Jake. May I call you Jake? Admiral seems so formal." Tesserax smiled, but he didn't wait for an answer. "I am not human, not as you understand it, at least. My kind are—how can I explain this so that you will understand?—derived from your kind. I have lived since imperial days. Indeed, I witnessed what your people call the Cataclysm. We could discuss complexities and nuances of what I am versus what you are, but in simple terms, you are a man...and I am a god. That is a functional description, simple enough at least for you to understand, if not an entirely accurate one in scientific and theological terms. Suffice to say, that is how you will conduct our relationship in the future. You will obey, even worship my brethren and I."

"Never..." Stockton's voice was like ice.

"Yes, I have noticed considerable defiance in your

people, Jake. I must say, you compare very well to the decadent and jaded humans who infested the late empire. Indeed, there have been many theories that the lack of strife and conflict weakened the imperials more than any other factor. What little I have been able to obtain of your Rim histories suggests significant struggle and warfare. It pleases me to see that your kind have rebounded so well, even without our guidance. Your strong have survived, and to a large extent, your weak have perished. When we rule over you, we will ensure that this trajectory continues."

"Go…to…hell…"

"Excellent. Even in the face of what must appear to be certain death, you retain your drive and stubbornness. I confess, you surprise me. But console yourself, Jake. I did not bring you here to kill you. No…rather, I wish to speak with you at great length, to learn all you know of small craft tactics. Your…fighters, I believe you call them…are quite extraordinary. To my knowledge, there was nothing of the sort employed by the imperial navy, at least not in the later era. But they are quite effective."

"Not…telling…you…anything…"

"Magnificent. More defiance. But misplaced this time, I'm afraid. You see, I have been tasked with repositioning and expanding captured Hegemony industry to continue the conquest of the former imperial space. We will be building fleets and ordnance in great quantities, and we will also be drafting and training the captured populations into service. I had an idea in this regard, one I believe will be extremely helpful…and that is the reason I ordered your capture. I have commanded the construction of small attack craft, based on those used by your people, though of course improved by our technology. When complete, they will be quite a surprise to your people, and likely a major factor in our ultimate conquest. But I will need pilots."

Tesserax looked up at Stockton, and he smiled. "That is where you can help, Jake. It is why you are here. *You* will train the pilots, teach them all of your considerable skills, share with them all you have learned of such combat...and then you will lead them into battle when we resume the offensive."

Stockton looked down, a mix of rage and astonishment on his face. "You...think...I'm going...to help...you? Train your...pilots? To fight...my own...people?" Stockton let out a struggled and caustic laugh. "Never..."

Tesserax held his smile. "No, Jake...rather sooner than that. You may be imagining all forms of sanctions...torture and the like. Even steeling yourself for a futile attempt to resist. But put your mind at rest. We need not rely on no such primitive methods. We need only the collar."

"The collar?"

"Yes, Jake, a rather interesting piece of technology, one designed to control creatures of...shall we say limited...intellect. The collar will ensure your obedience. You are still thinking of resistance, perhaps even considering ways you might get yourself killed. But once you wear the collar, you will follow orders without question. You will worship my kind, and you will do as we command. You *will* train new legions of pilots, and you *will* lead them against your former comrades, no matter how horrifying and unlikely that may seem to you now."

"Never...happen. Never..."

"Defiant to the end. You do not disappoint, Jake Stockton. You will serve well. Now, it is time. Time for you to receive your collar, to join us, to fight for a future where humanity is again united…and guided, led. Where men can look up to gods watching over them and know their place in the universe."

"I…will…kill…you…"

"I'm afraid not. In a few moments, such a thought will not even enter your mind, at least not the part of it that can do anything. You might want to prepare yourself, though. I'm told the spinal implantation process is quite excruciatingly painful."

Tesserax turned and began to walk toward the door as the room behind him was filled with Jake Stockton's piteous scream.

Blood on the Stars Will Continue with
Empire's Ashes
Book 15

Excerpt from "Fighting the Highborn"

A History and Tactical Manual for
Combat Against the Highborn, by Andromeda Lafarge.

The Highborn were created to help mankind, to pull the empire back from the abyss. Instead, they hastened the decline, and brought the Cataclysm into being more quickly than the previous decline would have done.

They were created to be teachers, but they longed to become tyrants. They were conceived as mentors, but they took the role of conquerors. They were brought into being to save humanity, yet they came to see themselves as gods.

The Highborn appear to be human, indeed, save for their size and the lack of any discernible physical imperfections, they look just like men and women. Whether they are, in fact humans whose evolution has been enhanced by artificial means, or they are indeed a new species, is a matter of conjecture and debate among scientists. This volume will not concern itself with such questions, for they are irrelevant to its purpose. The guiding principal of this work, the purpose for which it has been written and updated, is a simple one. The Highborn seek to rule over normal humans, totally and utterly. That makes them the enemy of all men and women who crave freedom and self-determination, all those who would not be slaves crawling before manufactured gods. If you are of this mind, read on, for this book is dedicated to one purpose, and one only.

The complete eradication of the Highborn.

**Blood on the Stars will Continue with
Empire's Ashes
Book 15**

Appendix

Strata of the Hegemony

The Hegemony is an interstellar polity located far closer to the center of what had once been the old empire than Rimward nations such as the Confederation. The Rim nations and the Hegemony were unaware of each other's existence until the White Fleet arrived at Planet Zero and established contact.

Relatively little is known of the Hegemony, save that their technology appears to be significantly more advanced than the Confederation's in most areas, though still behind that of the old empire.

The culture of the Hegemony is based almost exclusively on genetics, with an individual's status being entirely dependent on an established method of evaluating genetic "quality." Generations of selective breeding have produced a caste of "Masters," who occupy an elite position above all others. There are several descending tiers below the Master class, all of which are categorized as "Inferiors."

The Hegemony's culture likely developed as a result of

its location much closer to the center of hostilities during the Cataclysm. Many surviving inhabitants of the inward systems suffered from horrific mutations and damage to genetic materials, placing a premium on any bloodlines lacking such effects.

The Rimward nations find the Hegemony's society to be almost alien in nature, while its rulers consider the inhabitants of the Confederation and other nations to be just another strain of Inferiors, fit only to obey their commands without question.

Masters

The Masters are the descendants of those few humans spared genetic damage from the nuclear, chemical, and biological warfare that destroyed the old empire during the series of events known as the Cataclysm. The Masters sit at the top of the Hegemony's societal structure and, in a sense, are its only true full members or citizens.

The Masters' culture is based almost entirely on what they call "genetic purity and quality," and even their leadership and ranking structure is structured solely on genetic rankings. Every master is assigned a number based on his or her place in a population-wide chromosomal analysis. An individual's designation is thus subject to change once per year, to adjust for masters dying and for new adults being added into the database. The top ten thousand individuals in each year's ratings are referred to as "High Masters," and they are paired for breeding matchups far more frequently than the larger number of lower-rated Masters.

Masters reproduce by natural means, through strict genetic pairings based on an extensive study of ideal matches. The central goal of Master society is to steadily improve the human race by breeding the most perfect specimens available and relegating all others to a subservient status. The Masters consider any genetic manipulation or artificial processes like cloning to be grievously sinful, and all such practices are banned in the Hegemony on pain of death to all involved. This belief structure traces from the experiences of the Cataclysm, and the terrible damage inflicted on the populations of imperial worlds by genetically engineered pathogens and cloned and genetically engineered soldiers.

All humans not designated as Masters are referred to as Inferiors, and they serve the Masters in various capacities. All Masters have the power of life and death over Inferiors. It is not a crime for a Master to kill an Inferior who has injured or offended that Master in any way.

Kriegeri

The Kriegeri are the Hegemony's soldiers. They are drawn from the strongest and most physically capable specimens of the populations of Inferiors on Hegemony worlds. Kriegeri are not genetically modified, though in most cases, Master supervisors enforce specific breeding arrangements in selected population groups to increase the quality of future generations of Kriegeri stock.

The Kriegeri are trained from infancy to serve as the Hegemony's soldiers and spaceship crews, and are divided in two categories, red and gray, named for the colors of their uniforms. The "red" Kriegeri serve aboard the Hegemony's ships, under the command of a small number of Master officers. They are surgically modified to increase their resistance to radiation and zero gravity.

The "gray" Kriegeri are the Hegemony's ground

soldiers. They are selected from large and physically powerful specimens and are subject to extensive surgical enhancements to increase strength, endurance, and dexterity. They also receive significant artificial implants, including many components of their armor, which becomes a permanent partial exoskeleton of sorts. They are trained and conditioned from childhood to obey orders and to fight. The top several percent of Kriegeri surviving twenty years of service are retired to breeding colonies. Their offspring are Krieger-Edel, a pool of elite specimens serving as mid-level officers and filling a command role between the ruling Masters and the rank and file Kriegeri.

Arbeiter

Arbeiter are the workers and laborers of the Hegemony. They are drawn from populations on the Hegemony's many worlds, and typically either exhibit some level of genetic damage inherited from the original survivors or simply lack genetic ratings sufficient for Master status. Arbeiter are from the same general group as the Kriegeri, though the soldier class includes the very best candidates, and the Arbeiter pool consists of the remnants.

Arbeiter are assigned roles in the Hegemony based on rigid assessments of their genetic status and ability. These positions range from supervisory posts in production facilities and similar establishments to pure physical labor, often working in difficult and hazardous conditions.

Defekts

Defekts are individuals—often populations of entire

worlds—exhibiting severe genetic damage. They are typically found on planets that suffered the most extensive bombardments and bacteriological attacks during the Cataclysm.

Defekts have no legal standing in the Hegemony, and they are considered completely expendable. On worlds inhabited by populations of Masters, Kriegeri, and Arbeiters, Defekts are typically assigned to the lowest level, most dangerous labor, and any excess populations are exterminated.

The largest number of Defekts exist on planets on the fringes of Hegemony space, where they are often used for such purposes as mining radioactives and other similarly dangerous operations. Often, the Defekts themselves have no knowledge at all of the Hegemony and regard the Masters as gods or demigods descending from the heavens. On such planets, the Masters often demand ores and other raw materials as offerings, and severely punish any failures or shortfalls. Pliant and obedient populations are provided with rough clothing and low-quality manufactured foodstuffs, enabling them to devote nearly all labor to the gathering of whatever material the Masters demand. Resistant population groups are exterminated, as, frequently, are Defekt populations on worlds without useful resources to exploit.

Hegemony Military Ranks

Commander

Not a permanent rank, but a designation for a high-level officer in command of a large ship or a ground operation.

Decaron

A non-commissioned officer rank, the term defines a trooper commanding ten soldiers, including or not including himself. Decarons are almost always chosen from the best of the base level legionaries, pulled from combat units and put through extensive supplemental training before being returned to take their command positions.

Quinquaron

The lowest rank truly considered an officer. A quinquaron officially commands fifty troopers, though such officers are often assigned as few as twenty and as many as one hundred. Quinquarons can also be posted to executive officer positions, serving as the second-in-command to Hectorons. Such postings are common with officers on the fast track for promotion to Hectoron level themselves.

Hectoron

The commander of approximately one hundred soldiers, or a force equivalence of armored combat vehicles or other assets. As with other ranks, there is considerable latitude in the field, and Hectorons can command larger or smaller forces. The Hectoron is considered, in many ways, the backbone of the Hegemony armed forces.

Quingeneron

An officer commanding a combat force of five hundred soldiers or a comparable-strength force of heavy combat or support assets. In recent decades, the Quingeneron rank has been used more as a stepping stone to Kiloron status. Quingenerons also frequently serve as executive officers under Kilorons.

Kiloron

The commander of one thousand soldiers, or a posting of comparable responsibility. Despite the defined command responsibility, Kilorons often command significant larger forces, with senior officers of the rank sometimes directing combat units as large as twenty to fifty thousand. Kiloron is usually the highest level available to Kriegeri, though a small number have managed to reach Megaron status.

Megaron

The title suggests the command of one million combat soldiers or the equivalent power in tanks and other assets, however, in practice, Megarons exercise overall commands in combat theaters, with force sizes ranging from a few hundred thousand to many millions. Megarons are almost always of the Master class.

Blood on the Stars will Continue with
Empire's Ashes
Book 15